Vignettes

Giacomino Nicolazzo

By the same author

THE CHILDREN'S BOOK SERIES

I discovered early on that being a writer is sort of being like God!
I can create my own worlds and populate them with my own
people...
all by the power of my imagination.

This was at one time the closest I believed I would ever get to being
God-like.
But then I met God one day and we had the longest chat!
That's when I found out how really easy the job is!

I truly loved writing this book!
It was a change of pace for me.
Writing it was an adventure in allowing
the Spirit of God
to break through into my writing.

As the days went by...
As the words flowed from my fingertips,
I found myself listening for the nearly silent messages
that I knew were rising from my heart.
I trusted that something much greater,
something far wiser than I
was in control.

And I am blessed to know that you are now reading it.

Collaborators

THE ULTIMATE TEAM

All drawings and artwork – Diana Monti
All photographs, including cover design – Giacomino Nicolazzo
Layout, Design, Graphics – Giacomino Nicolazzo
Graphic Assistance – Diana Monti
Italian Translations – Diana Monti
Editing and Proofreading – Diana Monti
Moral Support – Diana Monti

Vignettes

ISBN 978-1-720-25289-4
NETTUNO PUBLICATIONS
GIACOMINO NICOLAZZO

Dedication

All too often the dedication of a book is skipped over by the reader...more desirous of getting to the reading matter than enduring the triflings of the writer...especially if the dedication is any longer than two words!

But if you were to do that this time, with this book, you would miss out on my dedication to you! You see, just because many of us have not yet formally met does not mean I cannot do this.

Hundreds of my wonderful readers, fans, followers and friends, in both in my real world and my virtual one, came together on social media and helped us design our book cover. This book is dedicated to all of you! I have written these stories for you. Grazie mille!

Acknowledgements

There are so many people that I would like to thank in one way or another for their contributions in making this book become a reality, but I want to begin with my Diana as I always do. You have been with me every step of the way in this adventure. You keep me focused and each day moving the story and our life together forward...always providing me with your most valued opinions, never refusing to lend an ear or a hand...forever offering me encouragement. You see, there simply would be no books, no stories...had it not been for you...I love you baboo!

To all my friends...here in Italy, around the world and those back home in America...in both my real world and my virtual one...thank you for your love, friendship, readership and support. I can truly say I love each and every one of you.

Thanks to all those special souls who have been a part of my life and this book.

TABLE OF CONTENTS

INTRODUCTION

If you've picked up this book today believing that I am going to be explaining God to you or any of the many secrets that surround the Creator of All Things...I would like to apologize now, in advance. If you had hopes of being told who or what God is...again, I am sorry. You will not find such revelations among these pages. You will not find them, not because I do not know the answers to your questions for indeed I do, but rather because I cannot find words adequate to describe this great God. I try...I really do, but they evaporate before they even leave my fingertips.

For me, one of the most challenging aspects in my life-long quest to know and understand God is the formlessness with which God exists. Honestly...think about it for a moment. I consider myself to be a rather good writer. But how can even the best of writers explain something he cannot see, feel or taste? Or something she cannot hear or smell? In our search for God I am afraid our five senses are useless! Fortunately, I do have an explanation as to why my words and our senses are inadequate.

It is abundantly clear to anyone who will take the time to look, God is all around us, everywhere and in all things. God's signature and fingerprints can be found on each and every miracle found in the natural world. It is easy to describe the many things we see, feel, taste, hear and smell in nature and the universe on a daily basis...but it is impossible to use our senses to describe the Creator of those things. And for good reason. God is an experience...not something that falls subject to description, using any of our five senses.

God is felt. God is experienced. And on levels that relate directly to the condition of our own hearts. And as such, God will always elude an accurate or even adequate description by mortal man. Learning this and accepting this is the first step to knowing and understanding God.

We live with the faith and belief that there is a presence and a power that is far greater than we are...a force that nurtures and supports us in ways we cannot even begin to fathom. Our experience of God tells us that this presence is all-knowing and this power is omnipotent and this force presses on us, prods us and pushes us along through our lives.

And then there is this matter of religion...something in my opinion that always gets in the way. Which one is best? Which one is true? Which one does God prefer? I have no answers to these questions. But I do have an opinion! It is my personal belief that it matters not a whit to God what religion we have been born into or have chosen to follow...or if we follow any religion at all. Adhering to a particular religion is not a prerequisite to experiencing God.

And please trust me. I have studied this subject a lot...for decades as a matter of fact. Joseph Campbell has become a veritable hero of mine. I've learned that all of the world's religions, from the beginning of time until this very moment, are really nothing more than man-made institutions, based in, on and around a particular perception of the reality of a God or diety. Most originate from and still rely heavily on mythology. These myths attempt to explain or justify the unexplainable and unjustifiable mysteries of the universe. One religion draws from another...paganistic rituals become normalized...gods and goddesses simply change names and nationalities. Saviors are born. Prophets come and go...

You see, as a species, it is our innate curiosity that leads us to forever require answers to our questions and closure to our *dilemmata*. Religion has become that elixir. It has served that purpose since man first contemplated the shooting stars over his head and quaking ground beneath his feet.

And although I no longer adhere to or practice a particular faith or religion, I neither begrudge nor demean anyone who does. While I maintain that religion is of no direct consequence to the success or failure of one's journey to find and know God, I will readily admit that the structure, fellowship and guidance than can be found within each religion can be of vital importance to many who desire to live a good and honorable life and can help to move them along on their quest in finding and knowing God.

But please...if I can impart any wisdom in you whatsoever, know this: it will never be a doctrine, a passage from scripture or the dogma of any particular religion or faith that will reveal the face of God to you. No my dear friends...I maintain that what is within your heart and the level of your consciousness will be what eventually connects you to God. This is the very same concept that is the common thread which is woven throughout the fabric of all the world's religions...further proof and evidence, I believe, of the veracity of my position!

The reality of the matter is that there is only one God...the one that has created the universe and all things in it. Religions will try to claim exclusivity and give God their own characteristics, but the one true God is having none of that!

And it does not matter what you call God or what gender you may wish to assign to God...such nonsense makes no difference to God either, I am sure! As you will see, I choose to not assign a pronoun at all unless I am telling a story where it is needed for dialogue. To me, God is simply TRUTH. God is simply LIGHT. And only through my focused consciousness will I ever experience that TRUTH and LIGHT.

And here is another wondrous aspect of this God: You don't even need to be seeking God to experience God. God is always God and God is always everywhere...always was, always is and always will be, whether you believe in God or not! You may go your entire life without acknowledging God or believing in God, but that will never diminish the reality of God.

With all this being said, might I suggest that from time to time you set aside a bit of your day to look for and attempt to know this God that is everywhere? If it is easier or more natural for you to do it in fellowship or in a community of believers, then by all means do so. As long as you know that you will be alone when you finally meet God. Your friends and fellow believers will not be there at that moment.

The more time you spend seeking God, the more you will want to know the truths that govern the universe. The truths will eventually all converge into a singular point and the great secret that is God will be revealed to you. You will discover that you yourself are the divinity you've been seeking! You yourself are divine and you yourself are the sculptor of your own existence and reality. You are the maker of your own personal destiny. This is the ultimate promise of spirituality.

Now you are probably asking yourself, what does all this talk of God and self-determination and divinity have to do with a book of random short stories? Well, let me explain that to you.

First of all, Vignettes is not really a random collection at all. Vignettes is a well organized collection of truths...in random order! Vignettes is the odd marriage of entertaining yet powerful and thought-provoking stories drawn from real life circumstances. Some are somewhat fictional and some are somewhat truthful, but all evidence the indisputable truth that God walks out in the open and among us each and every day, interacting with us, conversing with us, prodding us to act and some might even say directing our footsteps.

You see, I am a storyteller...it is what I do. I distract you from your thinking with my words...I use my imagination to do this. I take you away from your routines and your worries and your fears, for however long you will allow me...and I give you a place to hide. I try my best to instill in you hope and faith and I gently push the belief that there are good and better days to come if you will but let them come!

Writing is something I do alone. I've found it a profession best suited for me as I am somewhat of a private person. I am someone who has this uncontrollable need and desire to share my stories...but in the same breath I am a bit reluctant to make eye contact while doing it.

All my stories have a curious edge to them and even a dangerous power. Though they flow from the deepest recesses of my heart and imagination, they are also manifestations of the great truths...your truths and mine. Truth is all at once the most wonderful, yet terrifying force in this world. At times, it is even too impossible to believe.

Each vignette tells a powerful story. And just as each of us perceive God in our own unique and special ways, I leave it up to you to interpret each story and see where God is walking. I will advise you ahead of time. Some of these stories have some pretty rough language in them...even profanity. But I assure you it is never used gratuitously, but always in the context of the story and for its advancement.

I am a storyteller. I have for some reason been charged with the secrets of this world and beyond. I am the calm in the storm, the quiet in the quake and the stillness in the dark. I am the old man with the canteen of water waiting for you when you are dying of thirst. I am the young child who has suffered just as you have. I am the friend who can relate to your pain and through my writing allow you to relate to mine!

I am a storyteller, not a historian mind you, not a writer of fact. It is my only intention and most sincere ambition to create something compelling...something so 'un-put-downable' and riveting that it consumes you for hours at a time. Much of what I write chimes with the bells that ring out in our real lives but is in fact, flowing from my imagination.

There is an old adage that back in the days when day-to-day life was related through stories, a special place was reserved by the fire for the storyteller. For those of you who will come sit by the fire and listen, I will share with you simple stories of life.

Before we get started, let me tell you one final secret. Old storytellers never die. We simply disappear into our own stories. We no longer remain just the one telling the story, but a character in it ourselves. And it is at that precise moment, when our characters come alive and we disappear, that we are able to take you into that other world. Come along now...we're going to take a wonderful trip together!

Vignette 1 ~ Sand Castles

FOR THE MOST PART, at any given time of the day or night this long stretch of secluded beach in front of my little wooden home is deserted. Very few if any tourists ever venture this far south on the island. At best there will be the occasional beachcomber...metal detector in hand, lost in the search for the elusive gold coins rumored to make their way to the beach after the heavy storms stir up the ocean bottom. They come from the wreck of the old Spanish galleon a mile or so off shore.

Mostly what one sees here are the strands of seaweed that tangle themselves upon the twisted pieces of driftwood and the splintered hull of an old wooden boat that lays half hidden back in the dunes. And I must confess something to you. I like it this way. It is more than alright with me. You see, I no longer despair for companionship in these days...I have my memories of her and they serve me well. I've contemplated rescuing and bringing home a shelter dog in hopes that he or she might in turn rescue me, but something holds me back from taking on yet another commitment. So for now, in my lonelier of times, I've come to call these shore birds my friends.

It was my goal...a New Year's resolution as a matter of fact, to turn this summer into a book. An idea has been rolling around in my head for a few years now. I've been having this nagging feeling that God is trying to get my attention for some reason, but whatever He's trying to tell me has eluded me so far. If only God could learn to be more direct. Sometimes I am just too tired or pre-occupied to pick up on such subtle hints.

Having failed so far at all my other New Year's resolutions, I thought I might redeem myself by getting back to my desk and getting this book out of my head and onto paper. For a time there, it looked as if I may well fall short of this one too!

"There's just too damn much noise going on inside my head these days," I told a friend of mine who'd stopped by with a bottle of nice wine and perhaps the hopes of spending the night. "I find it impossible to think straight at the times when I must. I miss her terribly. I miss _us_ even more. It was not supposed to be this way."

It was perhaps those last few sentences and what I said next that dampened her spirits and made her realize that I was just not ready for love or anything that even closely resembled it...

"I was supposed to be the first to go," I lamented. "I was older...by fifteen years and we were not young when we met. She was to live on after my death...and live on well from the book royalties and the little nest egg we'd put together. But God had a different plan for her...one I hasten to add was not shared with me ahead of time."

The wine was wonderful...the conversation and company divine. But when I went to bed later that night I was again alone.

Sometimes I feel as if I've fallen over this massive cliff and I am free-falling out into nothing...desperately trying to find my wings. Everyone around me just assumes I know how to fly, but I know I am only falling gracefully. I am hoping to miss the ground but that isn't the way gravity works.

In my lonelier nights I lay in bed looking up at the ceiling or out my open window toward the sea and I think of my life in Italy. I think about what it was I gained from all those years with her. Other than this belly and a beard much grayer than I'd like to see, the answer to my question is rather elusive. It is not because I gained nothing...oh goodness no! To the contrary! What I gained is as numerous and varied as the myriad memories I have of five thousand days and nights spent together carving out a beautiful life.

How could I possibly list all the many gifts she's bestowed upon me over those years with her incredible and tireless love? I simply cannot do it. But I can say this...I can tell you the one thing I lost from loving her. I lost the need and desire for ever knowing another woman...ever again. In loving her I held nothing back...I have no reserve with which to love another. And the cruelest irony of all this is, I am a person not meant to be alone! What am I to do?

I hate it when I cannot control my loneliness. I cannot tell you how many mornings I have awakened to look out this very window...out to this deserted stretch of beach and listen for the muted waves that are not crashing to the shore...for the silence of the seagulls that are not calling to one another. I wake knowing I will not hear another human voice other than my own all day. It is in these moments of solitude that I try to convince myself that I am not alone...but if I were, that my aloneness is a gift...a beautiful gift meant to strengthen my spirit and my soul.

I wake on the colder mornings of winter thinking about her. Not so much with desire any longer, but with a sense of what is missing. She will forever dance around me like a fairy sprite in a magical forest. In my memories of her, the air is filled with sparkling fairy dust and the sound of tiny crystal wind chimes. Many are the days now that I ache for what it was that I, for so many years, sought in her company.

I dream of her often. And in those dreams we are walking hand in hand along the edge of the surf...my feet in the foam, hers out. Only the faint light of a trillion distant stars lights our path. We walk into the dark night where I soon find we have no other choice but to stop and part ways.

She lets go of my hand. I try to hold on but my attempts are futile. She walks away from me...out over the gentle waves of the incoming sea. I wonder if what I feel witnessing this is anything of what Christ's apostles felt when he walked on water and quieted the storm. I am both marveling and filled with fear as I watch her walk further and further from me and from the safety of the shore line.

Soon she disappears from my sight. I wait a moment or two to make sure she is gone, then I walk back down the beach alone, looking for the break in the dunes and the sandy path that leads me back home, only to find her waiting for me in my empty bed.

The dream always ends the same way...with me holding her soft, beautiful feet as she lies dying in our bed at home. We lay there holding each other. I look so intensely into her face...into her eyes. I want to memorize every last detail. I am desperate in my need to capture this last, lingering moment...desperate to forget the horrible disease that was taking her from me. I pray to God to never let me forget even one line of her beautiful face.

I watch as she takes her last breath and then drifts away from me. I remember the coolness of her forehead when I kissed her just after.

I become the widower again...every time I have this dream. But I refuse to admit that to myself. I prefer instead to think I am still married, be it now only to my aloneness.

In these days I find there is light and more light. In these nights there is still darkness, but thankfully it is lessening. I have decided this is a facet of my life that will for now defy explanation and definition. I have come to discover that I can still live with her in my heart as I also lived with her in this world.

So when it all becomes too much for me, when I need to feel something that moves me, I come out here onto this quiet beach where the wind caresses me and the sun warms and tans my skin. I am no longer looking for or demanding answers to my questions. I forget about needing someone to blame for my aloneness.

I come here often. I've even moved the old Adirondack chair that was once on my porch out into the sand...positioning it just so to make sure it stays out of reach of even the highest tide, though the sun and rains and wind are taking their toll on it.

I come here to clear my head and gather my thoughts. Of late I've been trying to get started on this infernally elusive book. From time to time, as I have done on this day, I bring with me a tablet, a few pencils, my sunglasses and a small radio on which I've found only one station...a gospel station that fades in and out. Today I have brought along a small cooler filled with ice and a bottle of spiced, dark rum. As I said...on any given day I will not see another human being for hours on end. No one will know if I have a bit of rum too early in the day!

So when the young couple from Barcelona, on holiday I would later learn, came walking up the strand this morning several hours before noon, needless to say I was as curious as I was disturbed. They had with them, two small children in tow, both of which were carrying sand buckets and little plastic shovels.

They saw me sitting in my chair and stopped for a moment or two to chat. This is of course how I know they were from Barcelona and were spending their holiday exploring the east coast of America from Pawley's Island up to Chincoteague.

They introduced themselves to me as Mariquila and Javi...no last names were necessary. The two children are four years old. Twins I was told...brother and sister. Their names...Santi, the boy and Izaro his sister. Both were beautiful dark-skinned children with shocking black hair and dark eyes. Their faces seemed to glow when they smiled. One at a time, they both stepped forward to shake my hand. I was enamoured by them both instantly.

That is no doubt what possessed me to ask them all to sit with me for a while and chat. The thought crossed my mind that perhaps I am lonelier than I care to admit.

"Please," I said. "Stay for short while. Talk. You must tell me what has brought you all this way to the Outer Banks."

Mari, as she'd asked I call her, and Javi spread out a blanket and sat down. The children ran off, making their way down next to the surf and instantly went to work building a sand castle. I tried my best to stay focused on my conversation with Mari and Javi but those two little ones kept grabbing my attention. From what I could see, their castle was going to be an extravagant one!

My invitation to stay and chat also necessitated I return to the house for two more glasses. Looking at the position of the sun in the sky I knew it still was not yet lunch time, but for me I found I did not need a special time to begin drinking my rum. But it would have been rude of me not to at least offer to share it with my new friends.

So I excused myself and ran back to the house to get the glasses. While I was there I remembered to bring back two cans of lemonade for the budding architects too.

Upon my return, I plopped back down in my chair and the three of us exchanged pleasantries while I poured the dark rum over the clear ice cubes. The longer we talked the more my thoughts of getting that book started crossed my mind. At first I will admit, I did not have any great desire to talk or to have them stay around much longer than necessary, but as I said, I was fascinated watching the children. I found myself not wanting them to go.

Santi and Izaro were hard at work...oblivious to me...oblivious to their parents or for that matter, oblivious to the whole world! Nothing outside their little sphere of imagination existed for them. I recognized this and realized I was feeling envy.

Meticulously yet effortlessly, they were building and shaping a most elaborate structure. It had gates made of seashells and a drawbridge fashioned from a small piece of wood. On each end of the castle were towers with tall turrets. Santi was explaining to his sister how the guards, armed with bows and arrows and shields, could defend the castle from any invading army.

Izaro was busy digging the moat they would eventually fill with water no doubt, while Santi, the cleverer of the two I must admit, was carefully reaching inside the castle, scooping out the sand and making narrow passageways with his little cupped hands. One handful after another was excavated and purposefully set to the side.

Dear sweet Izaro! How she looked on in rapt anticipation. Her little hands were now folded together in front of her mouth, her eyes as big around as sand dollars. It looked to me as if she were holding her breath...praying the whole thing would not collapse!

A long-ago and deeply buried memory rose up and flooded over me...one from fifty years ago or more. Those two sweet innocent children that I was watching reminded me so much of my own...so much so that I could not help but break into a huge smile. Though I've not seen either of my children in more than thirty years, I realized right then and right there, certain things are timeless...the ocean, the beach and children building sand castles.

Just as Santi and Izaro were close to finishing their project, a huge wave rushed ashore and knocked them and their little castle over, drenching them and reducing their masterpiece to a shapeless, featureless pile of wet sand. I expected the worst! I expected them to burst into tears, devastated by what had happened to all their hard work. But that is not what happened. What they did actually surprised me. Their reaction opened my eyes and unblocked my troubled mind for the first time in months.

Instead of crying or falling into hopeless despair, they simply stood up and shook the sand from their little hands and bodies. And then laughing with anticipation and excitement, carrying the simple tools of their trade, hand in hand they ran further up the beach…this time a bit further away from the water. They promptly sat down and began to build another sand castle.

The words for the opening pages of my book…the ones I'd been searching for and failing to find all this time, simply appeared and came to me in an instant. I knew what I wanted to say, but because of my self-imposed aloneness and the thoughts of such a grand love lost and the toll it has taken on my heart, I was having a bit of trouble as to how best to begin. Now those two sweet determined and indefatigable children had given me my answers.

"Why don't you stay for lunch?" I asked Mari and Javi. "If you have no particular plans or schedule I would love to make us something wonderful to eat. We can sit up in the shade of my patio. The children will love it."

"We really have no place to be," Javi answered, "and no schedule whatsoever. All we hope for each day is to make it a little further along on our adventure."

"And today our adventure will be with you," Mari added.

"Wonderful," I said. "Would you like to help me get things ready?"

"We would have it no other way," Javi said.

Javi called for Santi and Izaro. Without a fuss or any resistance at all, the children abandoned their second creation of the day, picked up their buckets and shovels and came running back to where we were standing.

"Our new friend has been kind enough to invite us to lunch today," Mari said. "Say thank you."

Obediently and sincerely, both of them thanked me...

"Will you help me shuck the ears of corn?" I asked. "Your hands and fingers are the perfect size!"

It was clear the children did not understand my question the way I asked it in English, so Mari repeated it in Spanish...

"Ayúdalo a desvainer el maiz," she said.

Both of those beautiful children smiled once they understood. They nodded their heads yes enthusiastically and smiled.

"OK!" I said. "Vamos juntos!"

"You can speak Spanish?" Javi asked with a bit of surprise as we were walking back the path to my house.

I shook my head no and shrugged my shoulders...

"Oh my goodness no," I answered with a smile. "Only a few words here and there, now and again. Now if you want to talk in Italian, I can talk your ear off! My wife used to call me a chiacchierone!"

"Then you are just like Javi," Mari said. "He is what we call in Spanish a parlanchín. He never shuts up!"

I'd spent the evening before doing a bit of fishing before the sun went down behind me over the bay. The pompano are running this time of year and I always like to try my hand at surf casting. I was fortunate enough to be on the beach at just the right time.

The huge schools of migrating fish come into the shallower water close to shore because the predators are out there waiting for them in the deeper water and they know it. I hooked four nice sized fish within my first twenty minutes or so. I thought about releasing the last one...three were enough, four were more than I would eat in a whole week. But something told me to keep it and so I did. Isn't it funny how things just seem to work out that way at times?

In a rolling kettle of Old Bay, I boiled a few pounds of shrimp I had in the freezer and a dozen ears of corn. Javi helped me roast the pompano over a wood fire in the pit on the deck while Mari and the children cut up a watermelon I'd just bought the day before. Before we knew, our feast was ready.

Javi's father was a banker in Barcelona and his family owned a marina called Marina Port Vell. He worked at the marina and was an avid sailor. We had much to talk about and before the day would end he'd extended an invitation for me to visit any time I could make it to Spain.

Mari stayed at home and tended to the children. She was a very calm woman and so were Santi and Izaro. Those two ate like there was no tomorrow. Little Izaro was on her fourth piece of watermelon and spitting the seeds at her brother when Mari gave her a look. It was subtle but stern and Izaro definitely got the message.

The family had flown in to Charleston and rented an RV three weeks earlier. They headed north with no particular schedule or itinerary in mind. All Javi knew was that he wanted to be on Chincoteague Island by Labor Day. Their flight back to Barcelona left Washington DC the following weekend.

So they made their way slowly but steadily up the coast, parking the RV for the night in one of the many seaside parks that dot the coast here on the Outer Banks. They would take the next day to walk five or so miles up or down the beach, stopping to explore whatever they would find along the way. I guess I was one of their finds.

The time eventually came for the little family to leave. We said our goodbyes and the children knew enough to thank me for their lemonades earlier in the day and for lunch...I was impressed with that! They packed up their buckets and shovels and ran back out to the beach. Maybe there was time to get one last sand castle in!

Mari said something to me that has stayed with me all this time. It was quite simple but I think I can say it was one of the finer complements I've ever received...

"I bet you are a very good writer," she said to me, making me smile.

"Why would you think this?" I asked.

"Because you are a very good listener," she said.

She gave me a kiss and a hug. Javi shook my hand with his firm grip and they walked back out the sandy path to the beach. They rounded up Santo and Izaro and continued on their way. I would miss them. We were not so much two ships passing in the night, we were more like two ships sailing along together for a brief time, though headed for different ports.

Their sudden absence accentuated the solitude and aloneness that has become my life in this little wooden house on the beach. Once they were gone I could feel it seeping back in. My mind began to drift and I had time to think about her again.

She came to me in my dreams that night, only this time she didn't leave me by walking across the water and disappearing into the darkness. This time she sat beside me as I began typing the first words to my book...

"For the most part, at any given time of the day or night, this long stretch of secluded beach in front of my little wooden home is deserted."

Sometime throughout the night I must have stopped writing but I don't remember exactly when that was. I made my way back to bed and slept until well after sunrise. I awoke in the morning and noticed the sheets and pillows on her side of the bed were moved and jumbled. She'd spent some time with me before leaving. I'd like to think she studied my face...memorizing every last detail and capturing our precious moments together again.

Life is now flowing again for me, as regularly as it once did. It has become as dependable as the tides in these days. Nothing was in synch after her passing. Sadness, not hope was the order of my days and loneliness had invaded my nights. I no longer knew what to think or who to trust.

Now when I become despondent, as I sometimes do, I will head out to the beach and sit down in the sand at the surf's edge. I begin building a sand castle and my worries just seem to drift away.

For the longest time I have lived my life understanding the maxim that when the student is ready the teacher appears. And when the student is truly ready, the teacher disappears.

My teachers appeared to me in the form of two four year old children. We didn't even speak the same language but our communication required no words. This was God's doing. God's fingerprints are all over my lesson. And when I was finally ready to begin facing life again with hope and optimism, my teacher's disappeared just as quickly as they'd arrived.

There is a verse from the Bible that I recall. I think it comes from the Book of Luke. I know I should, but I don't know it by heart. For the most part it says, *"The Truth becomes hidden from our eyes as we get older and the world changes us. God reveals the Truth to the little children."*

And they revealed it to me in the form of sandcastles!

All the things in our lives...all the complicated plans we spend so much time and energy contemplating, they are truly built on sand. In this life, it is only our relationships with the people we love that will endure. Death has a way of humbling us, like the wave that knocked down the children's sand castle. Everything is built on sand. Everything passes. And when it happens, only the person who has someone's hand to hold will be able to laugh and start anew. We rebuild and focus our efforts with hope and faith.

For each of us one thing is guaranteed...sooner or later that wave is going to come along and take away what we've worked so hard to build. And in the end, only knowing we have the capacity to love will save us and give us the strength to start over.

The wind that made the dune grasses wave so gently yesterday will be the gales that blow down the trees tomorrow. The gentle sea that guides the sailors and brings them safely home is the same violent, raging tempest that will crash them onto the rocks.

I love this beach and the sea that rushes ashore. But it doesn't make me less afraid of it. I loved that woman beyond words, but I was not always sure of what she was or how she felt about life. Lately, all I really dream about is her reaching out to me through the veil of clouds that separate our worlds. She takes me by the hand and we walk along the beach again...just for a short time...just a bit further.

Vignette 2 ~ Sum Day

BACK WHEN I WAS A LITTLE GIRL, we lived on the leeward side of the bay, across from a stretch of the barrier islands and just north of the little town of Atlantic in North Carolina. Our house was a little thing and nestled back behind the dunes on the same road as the Morris Marina.

Old man Morris's place was about a half a mile above us. He and my daddy didn't get along for one reason or another. It was at the marina that my brother and I could catch the ferry that would take us over to Portsmouth Island and Horse Island too. There wasn't nothin' over there...just miles and miles of the whitest sand beaches in the Carolinas. And of course the ponies were over there too!

I am the youngest of four children in my family. My father's name was Marion...a strange name for a man don't you think? I called him Daddy. He was a commercial crabber, just like his daddy before him, and he'd worked the shoals all around Pamlico Sound since he was a boy. Daddy and my grandpa Elias used to crab together but one day, long before I was born, they had a fierce fallin' out and they just stopped speakin' to one another. I didn't get to see my grandpa much when I was little...never did!

My name is Marty...a strange name for a little girl, I know. It is not Martina. It's not Martha. Nope, it's just Marty. It was Daddy who gimme that name as well as my nickname...Little One. That's what everyone called me, but I didn't like it much. I couldn't wait until I wasn't so little no more so people would stop calling me that. But they never did.

The oldest of mamma and daddy's four children was my brother. He was eighteen when the big storm come up on Cedar Island and the whole Outer Banks. He'd been named Elias John after my grandfather. Most everyone, includin' me, just called him EJ. But not Daddy. Like I told ya, Daddy didn't get along with his father so when he spoke to his own boy he made it a point to call him Johnny.

EJ worked with daddy from time to time aboard daddy's boat, but he knew plain true and so did daddy that he never wanted to be a crabber. He wanted to get famous writin' books.

My older sister's name was Claire Jean. She was sixteen and very beautiful. Mamma predicted she'd be a fashion model someday and have her face on the covers of magazines like Vogue and Mademoiselle.

Then there was Annie Lee. She was fourteen. She was the gifted one in our family. Music was her passion and I swear there was not a single musical instrument made that she couldn't pick up and be able to play in no time at all. She dreamed of a place called Carnegie Hall.

And then of course there was my mamma. Her name was Susan but I would never call her that. To me she was just mamma. Plain and simple, that woman was my hero. She taught me more things than anyone else in this whole world. I loved her dearly and I miss her to this very day.

The front was comin' ashore and Daddy was sayin' the storm was no more than a few hours behind. By early evening the skies to the north and east of us had darkened and were all but black. The rest of the world, or at least as far as I could see, had turned a neuter gray. The wind was blowing almost constantly and it was getting' stronger with every passin' hour. I do not know what was louder...the roar of the wind or the pounding of the waves against daddy's dock just over the dunes. But I could still hear what daddy was saying to EJ out on the front porch...

"This is going to be one hell of a storm Johnny!" he said. "There ain't no denyin' it. I want you to take the Sum Day around to the back channel over to Raccoon Island. Take her to the middle of the river and set both her bow and stern anchors securely. Everyone's probably got the same idea I do, so make sure you keep it the hell away from the other boats. Ya understand? Then get in your skiff and get your ass back here as fast as you can. I'm gonna need help gettin' this place buttoned up. So go on now...don't let me down."

What was a comin' was bein' predicted to be the fiercest storm that would hit the island in nearly fifty years. I can still remember lookin' out the windows of my bedroom and seeing the wind come rippin' down the coast. It let out the darndest high-pitched screams. I could hear thunder roarin' and see lightnin' just tearin' up the whole sky. I couldn't see the bay from my bedroom window, but EJ said he saw it stirrin' up real violent after he'd anchored the Sum Day and was comin' on home in the skiff.

"Huge black waves, like claws, was comin' at me," he told me. "It nearly capsized me twice. I ain't never seen waves like that on Pamlico Sound before Little One. You just wouldn'ta believed it!"

That bay that had been so kind and so gentle to us just the day before had become downright savage once that storm began to hit land.

It was just a few weeks after my twelfth birthday. The summer had been, for the most part, quiet that year. We didn't have any of the big storms we usually get out here on the Outer Banks. By the end of September we would have normally had three, maybe four...maybe even a hurricane. So you can imagine how surprised we all were when the weathermen on every TV channel and radio station began warnin' those of us who lived along the coast that a monster nor'easter was headed our way. Daddy didn't believe it none until he heard it on the Coast Guard channel. He kept a marine band radio on the desk in the livin' room. That's when he finally took it seriously.

EJ was untyin' the spring lines from the Sum Day and makin' sure there was enough gas in the tank on the skiff to get him back home. I run out and down the dock to daddy's boat. I suppose this is good time to tell ya'll that daddy named his boat the Sum Day because he believed that some day was a comin'! And that some day was a day we should always fight for.

"Some day," he used to say to my mother. "We'll have a little money set aside and we'll be able to get the hell away from here."

"Someday," he said to EJ, "you'll be a famous writer livin' over in Raleigh."

"Someday Annie Lee and Claire Jean will be too famous for this little island," he said. "Ya'll will leave and never look back...not even once."

"And someday Little One," he said to me, "a handsome prince'll come along and marry you up and take you away too."

I guess daddy didn't think the same about my potential as he did my brother and sisters'. But that didn't make no never mind to me. I didn't think much of my own potential back then neither!

But sadly, someday never did come for Daddy. Cancer come for him instead. Captured him and took him quickly. He died tired, broken, bitter and all eaten up inside.

"Where do you think you're goin'?" EJ shouted to me just as I was ready to step over the gunnel and into the boat."

"Well," I said, hesitatin' for a moment or two. "I'm comin' with you. Daddy said I could."

"You're lyin!" he answered. "Daddy ain't said no such thing. Now go on...git back on the dock. I gotta get goin'."

I swear that brother of mine could make me scream at times and want to pull my hair out. I jumped back off the boat onto the dock no sooner than he was puttin' the Sum Day into gear and driftin' away. Once the bow thrusters had him ten feet from the dock, he threw that old single diesel engine into gear and off he went, black smoke pouring out the exhausts and mixin' with the salt water behind him. Pretty soon he was far enough up the Sound that I couldn't hardly see him no more.

I went back to the house, tryin' to hold my tears in. Daddy had been up on a ladder, putting the wooden boards up over the windows. He'd seen the whole thing...what happened out there on the dock. But as usual, he didn't say nothin' about it to me. I walked right past him and went straight to my room. That's when I opened the windows and saw the storm a comin' in good. I must admit, I said a quick prayer for EJ...

"Dear God," I said, "please keep that mean brother of mine safe and bring him back before this storm gets any worse. Amen."

I watched everythin' what was goin' on outside. The wild ponies have been runnin' these shores here for as long as anyone can remember. They were downright scared and runnin' up and down and back and forth across the dunes. Legend has it they are the descendents of horses thrown from a Spanish galleon that had run up on a sand bar a mile or so off the coast...straight out east from Hatteras. The captain ordered the crew to jettison the horses, thinkin' it would lighten the load and maybe get the ship off the bar and afloat again. But if you know the rest of the legend, you'd know that didn't work.

The captain and crew didn't know it yet but a storm was workin' its way up the coast and pretty soon quarterin' waves about 10 foot tall hit the galleon broadside...over and over and over again until she was torn apart. The irony of it all, according to this legend, is that every member of the crew, including the captain, died in that storm but every one of them horses made it safely to shore.

As I watched the ponies that day, they seemed to understand that somethin' bad was comin' but they did not know what. They was all huddled together in the tall grasses just this side of the dunes. There was about twenty, maybe twenty five of 'em in all. They shook their heads back and forth and nervously dug at the sand with their hooves. The storm front was beginnin' to tower over top of 'em and the wind and strong gales was a whippin' through their manes and long tails. It was a sight I will not soon forget.

Huge black and gray clouds were racin' across the sky. Bands of rain were just beginnin' to fall. The oak trees on the north side of our old, wood frame house danced and swayed in the rain-laden wind. Static crackled on daddy's marine band radio. He kept it tuned only to the Coast Guard frequency, but this day the weather was gettin' so bad you could hardly make out anythin' the man was sayin'.

"Little One," daddy shouted to me. "I want you to fill the bathtub with water and fill as many of your mamma's pots and jugs as you can find. Check the kitchen drawer for batt'ries and the closet for flashlights. Make sure you put the candles and the stick matches in every room. Do ya hear me now? Are ya listenin'?"

"Yes daddy," I answered. "I'm a goin'"

Shortly after six o'clock, EJ was back at the dock and my two sisters were just home from town. They'd gone to the grocery market down on Airbase Road to load up on canned goods and other things that didn't need to go in the refrigerator, just in case we'd lose power...which of course was a stronger than not possibility.

Mamma had taken the family car and driven into Cedar Island to the church where she helped make some food for the pastor, his daughters and the dozen or so poor homeless souls who lived in a camp just above the ferry landin'. The homeless would ride out the storm in the church basement. Daddy nervously looked at his watch, worryin' about why mamma wasn't home yet.

"I don't know why you have to travel all the damn way to Cedar Island to go to church damn it," he'd argue with mamma all the time. "There's a Methodist Church right here in Atlantic. What the hell is wrong with the Methodists?"

"I would suppose it is a fine church," mamma would say. "But Marion, I am a Baptist. I was born a Baptist and I will die a Baptist. Now that's all there is to it. We will not have this conversation again!"

But they did! They had it all the time...every Sunday morning that's for sure!

By seven o'clock in the evenin', the first heavy bands of wind and rain had begun peltin' the metal roof and wooden sidin' of our house. The storm had cast a bleak and threatenin' blanket of darkness all over everythin'. My brother, one sister and I were clustered anxiously on the couch in the safety of our livin' room while Claire, my oldest sister, was in the kitchen makin' us beans and weenies. That would be our dinner and all we would get before the power went out.

We jumped nervously at the sound of the back porch screen door slammin', hopin' it was mamma. But it was only daddy comin' in and pullin' it shut behind him. He stamped his wet feet on the porch before he come in but he was still drippin' wet as he stood in the kitchen.

"Your mamma'd kill me!" he said, "if she caught me in her kitchen with these muddy boots and wet clothes!"

He bent over to untie and take off his boots before coming into the livin' room. The cancer was in him already but none of us knew it. He stood up straight and set in to stretchin' his arms from side to side, tryin' to ease the aches and pains he was feelin'. As I look back on it now, I think he knew somethin' was growin' inside of him...somethin' cold and dark.

I have an odd and peculiar memory of exactly the way daddy was dressed that day...rain-soaked khaki pants...old, blue flannel shirt with the sleeves ever so ragged, and his ever-favorite North Carolina Tar Heels baseball cap. He was a strong man but just as tall and skinny as a bean pole. Mamma said the man ate more than two people put together but he never did gain an ounce of weight. His clothes just seemed to hang on him like a scarecrow.

He was a handsome man too. Mamma said she fell in love with him the very first time she seen him...which was at the carnival over on the beach in Emerald Isle. She said his face was tanned and he had the whitest teeth she'd ever seen...but she also said the man only smiled rarely. And in all those years since they met, nothing much has changed about his face. He always seemed to be wearin' an expression of anxiety most times. I sure enough do remember it bein' on his face the night of the storm when mamma wasn't home yet. I could tell he was worried about her, but he'd never did say nothin'. I guess he didn't want to scare us none.

He reached over and finally turned off that dad-blamed radio that had now become nothin' but static. I guess he didn't need to hear the man on the station no longer tellin' him a storm was comin' any more...any fool could see that.

He went from room to room makin' sure all the windows was closed and the doors was locked. I heard him start to swear when he found I'd left my window open...

"Little One," he shouted from inside my room. "I will give you to the count of three to get in here and close your windows. Come on now!"

"I'm sorry daddy," I said. "I was a watchin' the ponies."

"They're mighty scared out there, ain't they?" he asked. "Too bad we can't bring 'em in and keep 'em safe in here!"

Every once in a while my daddy's compassion for livin' things would surprise me. And his kindness to me at times could make me cry. He helped me close up my window and then picked me up in his arms...

"Let's go see if your mamma's home yet," he said to me. I never felt safer than I did at that very moment, in daddy's strong arms.

The howlin' wind outside was such a contrast to the unnatural quiet of our livin' room inside...no one was talkin'...it was pretty much dead quiet. We was all thinkin' the same thing. Not knowing where mamma was seemed to make our tension and our worryin' all the worse. Unable to stand it any longer, I leaned toward daddy on the couch. He could see the streaks of tears on my cheeks as I blurted out the words my older siblings refused to utter...

"Where's mamma?" I cried. "When is she comin' home?"

The branches of the overgrown azalea bushes outside the windows was scratchin' against the unevenly-spaced boards of wood siding. The wind was growin' stronger and the storm was a gittin' angrier with each passin' moment. Annie jumped up from the sofa and rushed right past daddy, runnin' into the kitchen. She was desperate for something to distract her from the fear we all felt.

"Daddy," she said. "I'm a gonna make you some coffee, just like mamma does. Is that okay?"

"Sit back down, Annie," he answered in a strained voice. "All of you, just settle down now. Your mamma's okay. Ya need to stop worryin' and believe she's gonna walk through that door any minute. I talked to her on the telephone just before I went outside to put up the storm shutters... she's probably on her way home right now, just takin' her time in this rain."

Suddenly we all felt better. Suddenly we all started talking again, all jabbering at once...

"It's so bad out there...what if a tree falls on her car daddy?" EJ asked.

"Why didn't she come home earlier?" Annie wanted to know.

"Maybe we should call the church again?" Claire asked anxiously.

"I want mamma!" I said, layin' back on the couch with fresh tears burstin' from my eyes and runnin' down my face. "Make the rain stop, Daddy," I begged. "Make this storm go away."

In the midst of all that confusion, the back door opened up. We all jumped up from the couch, scramblin' to our feet and rushin' to the kitchen, expectin' to see mamma standin' there. But in her place stood Carl Albritton instead. He was daddy's friend and the man who ran the Quality Seafood fish dock just off Route 12...

"It is nastier than all hell out there," he said as all five of us stood starin' at him. "I knew I wasn't gonna make it home in one piece so I hope I can ride out the storm with ya'll. I sent Ginny and the kids to Rocky Mount 'til this nonsense blows on through. They got out just in time too! The storm surge is already comin' ashore. Trees and power wires are down everywhere. We are in for a long night I'm afraid!"

Then he musta noticed mamma wasn't with us...

"Hey," he said, "Where's Susan?"

Daddy just shook his head and let out a nervous sigh...

"She ain't home yet Carl," he said. "She's on her way back from the church over on Cedar Island. Should be here any time!"

Mr. Albritton got the most darned-awful look on his face and looked straight at daddy...

"You kids go on in the livin' room now," he said to us. "I need to have a word with your daddy."

None of us moved. We all knew what ever he was gonna tell daddy wasn't good...

"Ya'll git in the living room now," daddy barked. There was a nervous tone to his voice. "Ain't it obvious Mr. Albritton has somethin' personal to say to me?"

Reluctantly we all left the kitchen and went out into the livin' room. But I hid just on the other side of the arch way so I could listen in on whatever Mr. Albritton felt he needed to tell daddy in private...

"Let's step out onto the back porch for a minute or two," Mr. Albritton suggested to daddy. "These walls have little ears Marion, if ya know what I mean."

He motioned with his head and his eyes toward the arch way. Daddy looked over and could see the toes of my shoes extendin' past the baseboard. I thought I was well hidden but obviously I was not.

What had begun as just some high winds and a smatterin' of rain yesterday had built into the worst storm in fifty years. The wind was not just howlin'...it was screamin'. The rain was not just fallin', it was bein' driven...sideways, hard, merciless, torrential! The trees were not just swayin'...they was a creakin' and bendin' and moanin'. Their limbs was bein' ripped away and their leaves was bein' shredded and scattered like confetti. Mr. Albritton's conversation with daddy took place outside in all of that. Needless to say it was brief...

"Marion," he said to daddy with a look of worry on his face, "Route 12 from just south of Lola Road was damn near flooded as I was comin' here. By now it's under two foot a water no doubt! If Susan didn't leave the church by now, she ain't gonna make it home. They was fixin' to close the bridge at the boat dock in Thorofare as I was comin' through. Maybe you oughta call the church and ask Pastor Keener what's a goin' on. There ain't no way we can go out in this weather to look for her if she's missin'. Have you got the number?"

Daddy and Mr. Albritton stepped back inside. They had no sooner shut the door when daddy was a hollerin' for Claire Jean...

"Claire Jean," he said. "Fetch me the phone number for Pastor Keener over at Pilgrim's Rest."

"Daddy," she said. "Is somethin' wrong with mamma?"

"Do as I tell ya child," daddy answered impatiently. "No...ain't nothin' wrong with mamma. Just bring me the number."

Claire Jean rifled through some paper's on mamma's desk until she found the number for the Pilgrim's Rest Original Freewill Baptist Church out on Lola Road...

"252-225..." she started to say until daddy interrupted her.

"Don't read it off to me Claire Jean," he said. "Bring me the damn paper. And hurry up child!"

By the time she brung it into him in the kitchen where the phone hung on the wall, he was already cursin'...

"The damn phone lines are out!" he said. "What the hell am I supposed to do now?"

The monstrous winds were whippin' against the house. We could actually feel the walls movin'. It was terrifyin' to say the least. Broken twigs from the oak trees and sand from the dunes was flyin' in all directions with an unrelentin' fury. The rain was non-stop by this time...comin' down in torrents and sheets and buckets. We lost power a few minutes before a part of the roof came loose. Before we knew it, the storm was inside with us.

It went on like that all night and well into the next day before the winds began to die down a bit and the rain stopped fallin'. We didn't get no sleep that night at all. You see, once it was over, mamma still wasn't home. Mr. Albritton and daddy got in his truck and went out lookin' for her. The phone lines were still down and the power was out. They drove all the way to Lola Road and the Pilgrim's Rest Original Freewill Baptist Church. Pastor Keener was there and was genuinely saddened to see them and hear the bad news that mamma was missin'.

"I sent her home just as soon as the rain was gettin' bad," he told them. "I tried to call you and let you know she was on her way but the phones went down already and I had no way of gettin' in touch with y'all. I did pray real hard though."

Daddy and Mr. Albritton drove back the whole length of Route 12, right down to where it ends at Route 70. They drove real slow, lookin' everywhere for mamma's light blue Dodge Dart. The water in the drainage ditches beside the road was still all the way up to the painted white line of the berm. That is the only reason we can think of they missed seeing mamma's car down over the bank.

When daddy got back he told EJ to take the skiff back out and bring the Sum Day home. He said it was important for him to stay close to the phone in case mamma called. Then he looked at me and said somethin' that has remained with me for these past forty years. They are the most important words my daddy ever spoke to me…

"Little One," he said. "I want you to go along with your brother. You go with him to help bring back Sum Day…just in case he needs a hand. Will ya do that for me?"

"Yes daddy," I said. Then I turned and ran outside. While I was running toward the dock I was shouting for EJ to wait for me…

"Wait up EJ!" I yelled. "Daddy said I should come along with you."

"You're lying!" he shouted back. "He said no such thing."

"Uh huh!" I insisted. "I swear he did. He said today is my someday. You better wait!"

"I felt the presence of pure love," mamma said, speaking directly to daddy. We was all gathered around her bed at the hospital in Morehead City. Nurses kept coming in and out of the room checkin' on one thing or another, askin' if she had feelin' back in her feet yet. Everyone said it was a miracle she was alive.

"It is so very hard for me to describe it now Marion," she continued. "Words are just not good enough. All I can say is, everythin' makes sense. God makes sense. Love makes sense. God is love. We are love…it all makes sense now Marion. Oh how I wish you coulda seen it darlin'. I was surrounded by pure love."

We'd spent the whole storm and the next two days sick with worry, borderin' on grief, about where our mamma was, only to find out she'd been brought to the hospital by a stranger man when the storm was at its worst. The doctor told daddy she'd been unconscious throughout most of it. The stranger was nowhere to be found no more. No one knew who he was or where he'd gone and mamma had no recollection of it whatsoever.

"At first, I was very cold," she said. "And in considerable pain. My legs was trapped underneath me and the seat belt was dug so far into my chest I could hardly breathe. I just don't remember much after a certain point. I do remember that the water kept comin' in though...and there was nothin' I could do to stop it. I just knew I was gonna drown. I just knew it.

But then I remember feelin' all warm and safe. The whole inside of the car filled up with the brightest light. And that is the last thing I remember until I woke up here in this bed. Bits and pieces are comin' back to me now. Whatever it was that happened to me was a beautiful thing...whatever it was."

The day after the last of the rain bands had cleared out and the sun come back to the Outer Banks, the State Police found mamma's car in the drainage ditch along side Route 12, just our side of the bridge at Thorofare. It was upside down and on its roof in a few feet of water.

Billy Beck sent a truck out to haul it from the ditch and set it upright again. Everyone was as puzzled as they were relieved when they discovered no one was inside. We just have no idea how she got out of that car alive or who this stranger man was that brought her to the hospital. The windows was still up for God's sakes...and all the doors was locked tight. How she got out of there is a plain mystery to me. How she got to the hospital, as we would later find out, only God knows.

Over the years I had the opportunity to talk to mamma about what happened to her that day comin' home from Cedar Island during the storm. I do believe I have a fairly good idea that she come face to face with God in one way or another. And I believe that stranger man who brought her to the hospital and then just disappeared...well, he must have been her guardian angel. I have looked at it every which way I can and I can come up with no other conclusion.

She come to live with me out in Asheville after daddy died and some of the things she told me makes me conclude what I just said. She spent her last two years of her life with me. After she passed of natural causes, I brought her back to the cemetery at Pilgrim's Rest Original Freewill Baptist Church out on Lola Road and buried her right next to daddy.

"I felt an all-encompassin' presence overtake me," she said one night at the dinner table. "It was like nothin' I'd ever experienced before. It was complete, total and unconditional love...in its highest form Little One! I was fixin' to drown, that's all there was to it. That water was rushin' in so fast and swirlin' around. I just closed my eyes and began to pray. I confessed all my sins and I begged for God's mercy, prayin' that a drownin' death was not as bad as I'd always feared it would be.

There is a period of time that I cannot recall right now. But I can remember when a light began to fill up the whole inside of the car. I just knew I was bein' surrounded by God's unconditional protection. I will believe to my dyin' day that it was His love that pushed all the water back out that car."

This was the first I was hearin' about anythin' even remotely close to a divine intervention or miracle happenin' to my mamma. So I listened closely and hung on to every word she said...

"And oh my Lord Little One," she said. "When that man opened the door and sat down beside me...well, I cannot rightly explain to you the joy and bliss I was filled with at that very moment. I felt completely safe...like nothin' bad could happen to me. He had the most lovely smile Little One. I was no longer in pain, and all my worries and fears were bein' left behind with my body in that car.

I knew that he was not an earthly man, but a bein' composed of somethin' I can only call love. And it held within it a force or power, somethin' resemblin' electricity or the like. Love is the only word I have to explain it. But I know that makes no sense to you. It ain't the right word here."

I asked mamma if she could recall what the stranger looked like. But she just pursed her lips and shook her head, whisperin' the word no...

"The entire encounter took place quickly," she said. "It was all about God...the ultimate power of God...God's merciful forgiveness. I come to realize that God is more lovin' and carin' than I could ever imagine. It is the greatest power in the universe Marty. I know now that I am loved unconditionally, despite all my faults and all my fears. In those final moments, I knew that my spirit was gonna survive the death of my physical body."

"Did this stranger say anythin' to you mamma?" I asked

"Yes Marty," she answered. "As a matter of fact he did say one thing. He told me that my wanderin' soul needed to get back into its earthly habitat...that it was not my time to die. And that is the last thing I remember until I woke up in that hospital bed askin' for your father."

Just as daddy had predicted, EJ went on to write a few books that caused him to be famous and made him a good bit a money. But he never did leave the Outer Banks. He had no interest in Raleigh whatsoever and after daddy died he felt obligated to stay close by...for mamma's sake. It took her a good while to recover from her ordeal and bein' the man of the family...well, EJ took that right seriously.

He met a girl from Pawley's Island, down in South Carolina, and sooner or later they was married. Her name was Marie. They bought an old wooden house over near Arapahoe and remodeled it quite nicely. Together they've raised a nice little family in it too. I see him from time to time, now that I've moved back to the old wooden house we grew up in...now that mamma's gone. Nobody wanted the house no more and I just could not allow it to go the way of so many other's along that stretch of the leeward shore.

Claire Jean never did become a famous model. She's working for a big bank over in Charlotte...got herself a good job. She never did marry and I find that right peculiar. But then again, neither did I. Maybe I'm a bit peculiar too.

Annie Lee lives over in Kill Devil Hills. She give up her music and married an older man who sells boats for a livin'. Seems he was married before and brought two young children along to the marriage. Annie and him didn't have no children of their own and somehow she become mamma to his youngin's. But she is satisfied and they have themselves a right nice life together.

From time to time, EJ and Annie Lee will come to visit me. If we're lucky, Claire Jean can steal away from her job too. They spend the night and we get out the family photo albums that I held onto and talk about the old days. Sum Day has finally come for each of us.

Sometimes in life, we need a few bad days...maybe even some really bad storms, in order to keep the good days in perspective. So much can change from one day to the next, but there is one thing that always remains the same...the world keeps turnin'.

I have learned one of the many secrets of the universe. Sometimes pain, like that storm that changed my little family, comes out of nowhere. The clearest summer day can end in a downpour. And when you come out of the storm, you won't be the same person who walked in. That's what storm's are all about.

And while I am preachin' here, let me share one more secret with you. There is always another storm out there and every one of us must eventually face ours. When it comes, pray that it will shake you to your roots and break you wide-open. Being broken open by the storm is your only hope. When you are broken open you get to discover for the first time what is inside you. Some people never get to see what's inside them...they miss out on all the beauty, the strength, the truth and the unconditional love. Pray indeed...pray you will be broken open by the storm. And never run from your pain...run head on into it. Let life's storm shatter you.

Vignette 3 ~ Yana's Story

"**I** DO NOT KNOW HOW TO SWIM," she confessed. "And so the thought of getting onto a boat terrified me. And when I saw the condition of boat we were to get on, I panicked. I tried desperately to run away. But my uncle's grasp on me was too tight and he was much too strong. I had no choice but to follow him into my fate."

It was a few months back now when Sergio Abbate, a journalist with the Italian newspaper L'Unità was having a most interesting yet heartbreaking conversation with a young girl and her uncle in a piazza in a northern Italian City. There was another woman with them, another Arab, but she stayed a few steps back and did not speak to the man until nearly the very end of the conversation.

The three were Syrian refugees, granted asylum in Italy and now living near Milano. The journalist was trying to gather a bit of first hand information for an article he'd scheduled for the following week and he knew that in just about any piazza in Italy he could find it. You see, Italy has become ground zero for the people fleeing the violence and war in the Middle East and East Africa, especially those from Syria.

The story I am about to tell you comes from the article Sergio Abbate wrote for his newspaper...

The young girl's name was Yana Ibrahim and her uncle's name was Odaba Rajiha. They were a bit wary of the journalist at first and he couldn't blame them. Each and every day, people like Yada and her family face derision, insults and worse from the Italian people who do not understand them nor want them in their country, and he was after all, Italian.

And so when Abbate showed a genuine interest in them...in talking to them and wanting to know about their story, they were understandably cautious. He had to prove to them that he meant no harm and that all he wanted was to talk and to be able to make their story known to the world. You see, every refugee has a story...

"There were so many of us," Yana began. "More than one hundred and fifty in all. We were packed into that boat so tightly that my knees were bent to my chest. There were too many people for such a small and dangerous boat. Once everyone was in, the boat sank very low in the water. The water was within just a few centimeters of coming over the top and into the boat. I could tell the captain was very worried too...for his own safety and for ours. Yet he pushed us away from the dock and we headed out into the sea."

Yana's parents had both been killed by Syrian soldiers...shot in the streets outside a market near their home. Yana's father lay dead on a sidewalk with her mother hovering over his body, begging the soldier's who now had their rifle's pointed at her, for mercy. But they showed her none. They had been given authority to kill anyone they chose and they exercised that authority without rhyme or reason. It was killing for the sake of killing...

"The boat struggled under the weight of us all," Yana continued. "We had Nigerians and Ethiopian men on the boat with us as well, but they were made to go down through a tiny hatch, into the bottom of the boat...away from us. The captain put a lock on the door once they were down there. It must have been horribly hot and dark, as well as frightening for them. We could hear them screaming and shouting...demanding to be left out, but the captain ignored them, but we could not."

What Yana was telling the journalist was something that was happening dozens of times every week on boats leaving ports all across North Africa, crossing the Mediterranean Sea and bound for ports in Italy and Greece. The human smugglers, the ones who were masterminding such atrocities, were making a fortune off these poor people. Many of them, once aboard dilapidated boats, never stepped foot again on dry land. Thousands were dying at sea while the world watched, choosing to turn a blind eye.

"At times it felt as if we were barely moving," Yana continued. "Sitting as I was, my legs and back had become numb...then racked with unbearable pain. All day long I listened to the droning of the engine and the moans coming from the black men imprisoned beneath me. We were all baking in the hot sun. We had no shade...no shelter. The spray of the salt water cracked my lips and stung my eyes. There was no fresh water to drink...none to rinse the salt from our skin."

Yana and her younger brother Khalil had fled Syria with their aunt, uncle and their cousin...Odaba's one surviving son whose name was Hatem. Both his other sons had met fates similar to Yana's brother, which I will tell you about soon. Syria had become a place as close to hell on earth as one could imagine...

"It was on our second day at sea that I began to worry for my and my family's lives," Yana said. "Many of us were delirious by this time. More than just a few people had become this way. They simply could take no more and so they jumped from the boat, believing that ending their lives was better than continuing on. Some foolishly believed they could swim back to land, but none of them made it. They all drowned...every one of them."

Yana's younger brother Khalil had been born with a heart problem. As he grew up he'd become a very fragile child. Sadly he would not survive the trip from their village of Deir-ez-Zor to the coastal town of Iskenderun in Turkey where they were to board their ill-fated boat. I will tell you more of that story shortly as well...

"It was on the third day that I became convinced we would never reach Greece," Yana said. "The boat was filling with water and we were travelling slower and slower with each passing hour. The black men beneath us were frenzied and beating wildly on the boards of the boat. We expected them to burst through at any moment."

The plan was to travel by boat to Greece and then be taken by truck into Croatia. From there, they would travel again by boat across the Adriatic Sea to Brindisi, an east coast port in Italy. But their boat would never make it through the Straits of Turkey. It would sink and Yana and her family would eventually end up in an immigrant camp on the island of Cypress...

"It was on the fourth day that I had completely given up," Yana said. "I was beyond any hope. I'd come to believe Allah had abandoned all of us. But then someone called out that there was another boat coming toward us. I remember thanking God out loud, shouting Allahu Akbar for all I was worth.

It was a young boy on the other side of the boat, sitting beside my uncle, who saw it first. Then my uncle made it to his feet and he could see it too. It was an old metal boat, badly rusted and coming toward us quickly...too quickly. On it were a dozen or so black men and they were all carrying guns. Someone shouted out they were pirates and cried they were coming to steal from us...to take what little money and valuables we had left...

"If we refuse, surely they will sink us!"

At this point, Sergio noticed that Yana was becoming nervous telling him her story. It must have been difficult to bring those memories back to life. Her uncle asked if she wanted him to continue telling it for her but she shook her head no. She wanted to be the one to tell their story...

"Our captain took out a gun," she recalled. "It looked like the kind Assad's soldiers used to shoot us with in Syria. He shot it into the air three times and then threatened the men on the boat...swearing to Allah he would kill them all if they did not go away. They left...but they were very angry! I foolishly thought we were safe but soon they returned, coming straight at us at full speed again. This time they did not stop."

The pirates rammed the boat, throwing its human cargo of refugees into the air. Their intention was to sink the small, crowded boat and kill every last person aboard. The impact threw many of them into the water...

"Let the fish strip the flesh from your bones," Yana remembered hearing one of the pirates scream.

"They were all laughing at us as our boat was sinking, taking with it women and young children. All the Nigerians and Ethiopians below the deck never stood a chance. Within minutes the boat capsized and one hundred people were gone. The sea went black."

All around her, Yana could hear people screaming and thrashing at the water, trying to keep from going under and drowning. The boat's engine was still running and the propeller was half-out of the water, spinning like a saw...

"I watched as it pulled in and cut a small child to pieces," she said, visibly shaken by the memory. "Somehow, and I do not know how, I found a round life preserver and I dove beneath the water to come back to the surface inside of it, holding on for dear life. All around me there were dead bodies floating. I was one of just a handful of survivors.

We somehow found each other and formed a circle in the water. And then we all began to pray. I first saw my aunt to my right. Then I saw my uncle close by her. They were searching desperately for Hatem. But he was gone...my cousin was gone."

As the day turned into night Yana said everyone had who had survived were losing hope. Many of the men did not have life preservers and so they hung onto the ones who did. Exhausted from treading water, many of them simply surrendered themselves to the sea...

"There was an old man who floated beside me," Yana continued. "He was holding a young baby in his arms. He was a Palestinian man and the baby was his granddaughter. His wife with whom he'd been traveling, and their daughter who was the baby's mother, were both dead."

Yana placed her cupped hands over her mouth and made the most pitiful sucking sound as she began to weep...

"Her name is Malek," the Palestinan man said to me. "Please…I am so very tired. Please…I beg you. Take the baby." Then he gave up and let the sea take his life."

The baby was crying and so very agitated…thirsty and no doubt very hungry. The poor child had no idea what was happening. So Yana began to tell her stories, trying to calm her…

"I told Malek the same stories that my mother had told me as a little girl," Yana said, a faint trace of a smile coming to her face as if she were recalling the stories again. "But the water was filled with diesel fuel and everyone was screaming. My silly, simple stories made very little difference to this terrified child."

Another day passed…then another. It was on their third day in the water that someone cried out they could see a merchant ship approaching…

"We could see it far out on the horizon," Yana said. "For two hours we screamed and shouted and waved our arms. But soon it became dark and we realized the boat had passed us by without stopping."

But God had not abandoned them. God was not going to let the rest of these innocent people die in that dark, cold water…

"In the dark night, a bright light appeared on the water," Yana said. "It was several hundred meters away from us. They had seen us after all and were coming back to rescue us. Soon the light was flooding our little circle of survivors, filling us with hope and joy again. They threw ropes to us and one by one we were lifted high out of the water and to a dry and safe place."

The journalist was curious to know what had become of the baby…

"Malek, the little baby I had been given to protect," Yana said, "was taken to the clinic on the merchant boat. But she was very weak…too weak to survive. She had swallowed too much sea water and diesel fuel and she died shortly after we were rescued."

Yana began to cry silently. Her body shook and tears streamed down her face, but she made not a sound. It was Yana's uncle who continued telling the story…

"Our boat was very small," Odaba began. "We should not have had more than twenty…maybe thirty people on it. But the smugglers are greedy men and they crammed almost one hundred fifty of us aboard. Mothers and fathers held their children in their arms. We could not move.

The boat was not made to cross the sea and the engine was much, much too small for the heavy load of the people it carried. I had my doubts about this captain too. He seemed nervous to me…frightened.

Just before the pirate boat rammed us, a young boy who was sitting beside me fell across my lap. His hands were covering his eyes and he was screaming out loud. For a moment I did not know or understand what was happening. He had seen the boat coming at us before most of us did and somehow knew we were in terrible danger.

As soon as we were rammed, the boat broke apart into many pieces. It was as if a bomb had exploded. Pieces of wood and metal flew by our heads. It was chaos. There was an old woman sitting to my left who was suddenly thrown overboard…but only her body left the boat. Her feet and her shoes remained on the deck. I could not believe what my eyes were seeing. A piece of the boat had severed both her legs. This is when my mind began to fill up with fear and nothing else."

Yana began to cry openly at this point in her uncle's story. She knew what was coming next…

"Yana! I cried as loud as I could," Odaba said. "Yana! Can you hear me?" But it was no use. Everyone was crying and screaming so loud. We'd been left to die in that water and the waves threw us about like plastic bottles.

We spent two days in the water…clinging to each other and clinging to life. On the second day, more and more of us gave up the struggle and gave our lives to the sea. I was very close to such a decision two, maybe three times. But I knew my family needed me and so I endured.

It was a few hours after that when we saw the merchant ship coming toward us. It seemed to take forever to arrive but when it was close enough, someone saw it was flying a Danish flag. We all began to swim toward it as fast as we could.

At first we floated along side the hull, begging for mercy from the men looking down over the rails at us. But no one was helping. It made no sense to us that the boat would come and fail to save us. But soon a man came to the bow of the boat with a bull horn and began to shout instructions to us in Arabic.

For the next hour…perhaps longer, they hauled us out of the water, lifting us with ropes…one by one, until we were all safely standing on the deck. Being that high above the water, I could look out and see what was left of the boat that we had been on. I could also see bodies floating in the sea.

I saw the little boy who had thrown himself across my lap. He was dead, floating face up in the water. I cried…I could not stop crying for that child."

The merchant ship that rescued them took them to the seaport of Gallipoli in Italy...

"But our nightmare did not end simply because we were standing on dry land," the woman who was with Yana and Odaba said, speaking for the first time. Her name was Zinah and she was Odaba's wife. She'd been quiet up to this point, but it was evident she wanted to be a part of telling their story too. "Our journey and our suffering was far, far from over."

The survivors were met by Italian soldiers wearing masks and carrying rifles. Those refugees who survived were taken to what was called a reception center...

"But I will tell you this," Zinah said. "It looked and felt more like a prison than a place meant to receive tired and war-weary refugees. We were taken inside and locked in a large room with many others who had arrived before us. One of the guards who spoke Arabic told us that men and women from the UN would come the next day to talk with us and to take our fingerprints and that we would be given asylum. I had to laugh when he told us to have all our documents ready to prove who we were."

"We have just escaped death in the sea," Odaba said to the man. "Floating for more than two day. We escaped with only our lives and the clothes we wear on our bodies! What documents could you possibly think we would have on us?"

The journalist sat with Yana and her aunt and uncle for nearly three hours in that piazza. It was well after dark by the time they'd finished. And in that time she told him a story that at once broke his heart and bonded the two together at the same time. Such bravery that young girl had shown. She had seen more violence and more ugliness in her short lifetime than any ten children should ever see in a hundred lifetimes.

When he finally published his article, he began it this way...

"Can you imagine witnessing the murders of your own parents and your brother? Could you imagine living every day with death and violence and bloodshed all over your country? Can you imagine risking your life...traveling hundreds and hundreds of miles, fleeing the evilest of men and throwing yourself onto the mercy of strangers in foreign lands whose languages and customs you do not understand?

Now imagine doing all this as a thirteen year old girl with no parents to support you on your perilous journey. Imagine living for weeks at a time in filthy, dangerous refugee camps where the men who guard you could just as easily be the men who rape you or worse!"

These sad events of which the journalist wrote were all true. They were the events in the life that Yana Ibrahim led as a young girl in Deir ez-Zor Syria. Both her parents and her oldest brother Naser had been killed. She and her younger brother Khalil had gone to live with their aunt and uncle.

She continued telling her story to the journalist...

"Nasar was so beautiful," she began to say. "My parents had three children and he was the first born. I loved him more than my words can ever express. He was sweet and compassionate…a composer of music…a simple musician in a traditional Syrian band. The only true love in this life was his violin."

One late afternoon just before dusk, Nasar was walking home with his friends after they'd been practicing their music in an empty warehouse. They were stopped in the streets by a squad of Syrian soldiers. Nasar and each of the young men he was with were carrying their instruments and notebooks filled with sheet music...none of them had any weapons.

One of the soldiers, the one who appeared to be in charge, demanded to see their identification papers and to inspect their instrument cases...

"Nasar was shot by a soldier who was hiding on a roof top with a rifle like a sniper," Yana said. "My brother was singled out for no reason. They accused him of speaking to the rebels. The man interrogating him turned and nodded to the man on the roof and then took two steps back. Nasar was then shot...killed like a dog in the streets...for no good reason whatsoever."

This was how Yana explained what took place that evening...

"The streets were nearly deserted because it was just before the curfew hour," she began, "the time of day when we were no longer permitted to leave our homes or be out on the streets for any reason. If you were caught on the streets after curfew there were no questions asked...no identification papers requested. You were assumed to be a rebel and were shot.

I can remember hearing a single gunshot break the quiet of the evening. I don't know why, but I had a sickening and strange and terrible feeling that Nasar was in danger somehow. I was terrified of such an intuition, especially when we later learned he'd been killed."

The bullet hit Nasar in the very middle of the back, shattering his spine, piercing his liver and violently knocking him to the ground. The other boys ran frantically in all directions to hide, leaving Nasar bleeding and dying in the street alone.

But one of them, a boy by the name of Somar, ran to Nasar's home to tell his father. The boy took Yana's father back to where Nasar lay in a pool of his own blood...

"Bābā...that is how we say father in Syrian," Yana continued, "picked him up in his arms and ran for more than twenty blocks to a hospital. But Nasar lived only a few more hours. He'd lost too much blood for the doctors to be able to save his life."

As Yana was telling this story to the journalist, he was quite taken by the matter-of-fact and mature way she spoke. He found himself reaching down to hold on to her hand. Tears were streaming down both their faces as she continued...

"We were always worried about the Russian bombs and Assad's soldiers," she told him. "Peace no longer existed for any of us. Death and danger awaited us at every corner. I could no longer continue with my studies...not even the schools were safe anymore. Assad's men would come in to our classrooms and take the young girls away."

For the Syrian people, just leaving their homes each day was like playing a game of Russian Roulette. Dozens of poor and innocent men, women and children were dying every day. Yana's little village had become a bloodied battlefield with children her age and even younger dying. Everyone was accused of something...of helping the rebels or helping the soldiers. Most of those who disappeared from the streets were never seen or heard from again.

"My mother was a very brave and very practical woman," Yana began to say, now having difficulty to keep from crying. "Her name was Nada and one day she needed to go out to the market to buy a bag of rice and a few vegetables. My father would never allow her to go by herself. Usually it was Nasar who would have walked with her. But Nasar was dead now and so on this day my father went with her. He made Kahlil and me promise to stay inside the house with the gates closed and locked. We were given strict orders to let no one in."

While Yana's parents were out at the market, a gun fight broke out at the street corner. Assad's men had been searching for the band of rebels that lived somewhere in the neighborhood and when they found them, they confronted them. The shooting began. Almost immediately, Yana's father, who was simply standing outside the market waiting for his wife, was caught in the crossfire. He was shot and killed...

"My mother's sister...my aunt Kamala, lived in that very neighborhood," Yana said. "She was a widow and the mother of two dead sons...all killed by Assad's men. From behind the wall in front of her home, she watched the whole thing happening.

She saw my father shot and then fall to the street. She saw my mother run out of the market in a panic, not knowing what to do. The guns and explosions were so loud, so deafening, so ferocious that she could not get my mother's attention to get her to run toward her.

When the shooting paused for a few moments, my mother saw my father lying dead in the street...between three other men who were also killed."

She ran away in horror into an abandoned building to hide. But once inside, she found the rooms were filled with dead bodies…many dead bodies, thrown and stacked one on top of the other!

Screaming, she ran back out into the street. The shooting had begun again. She began waving her arms wildly in the air and begging for the soldiers to stop…begging for mercy. But it did not stop. And there was no mercy that day. Yana's mother was killed while Kamala watched it all in horror…

"Kahlil and I began to worry after we'd heard all the shooting," Yana said. "And when our parents did not come home we became terrified. My aunt and her son Ashraf came to our home later that day to tell us the worst news we would ever hear…both our parents were dead now as well.

It was only Kahlil and me now. We were all alone against the whole world. It was too dangerous to return to Kamala's house, so for days afterward my brother and I stayed home alone. We were both so terribly frightened.

When a knock came at the gate one afternoon, we panicked. Kahlil made me hide in the closet in a room in the back of our house. When he knew I was safely hidden, he went to see who it could be at the door. It turned out to be my father's brother…my uncle Obada. He had come to take us with him."

It was at dinner that night that Odaba told Yana and Kahlil that the family would be leaving Syria soon. He knew of men who would, for a price, take them all out of Deir ez-Zor and to safety. Yana did not wish to leave her home but she knew she really had no choice. It was but a matter of time before they too would be swept up and killed if they did not leave immediately.

Yana's story is just like so many other innocent Syrian's. The next night, after night fall had come, Odaba led his family through the dark streets, to a place where they would meet up with a man who drove an old truck.

While they crept through the darkness, feeling their way along the buildings and the metal gates, rockets began to fall into a neighborhood just behind them. The sky lit up with balls of fire and the ground beneath their feet trembled. Everything shook as if it were an earthquake. They could have all been killed had they left just five minutes later than they did.

This is where Odaba took over telling the story again...

"We found the man with the truck," he said. "It was stopped at the far end of a soccer field, the engine idling and the driver waving at us to run toward him. He flashed his headlights once and we ran as quickly as we could, carrying what few possessions we were able to fit into our bags.

We climbed into the back of the truck only to find eight or ten other people who were already inside. When the time was right, we pulled out of the soccer arena and began to drive straight west into the blackness of the night...the headlights were turned out through many miles of wilderness...through Aleppo and beyond, all the way to the border with Turkey.

When we arrived at the first check point it was still for the most part dark outside. I guess you could say it was not yet dawn but here was a red glow in the eastern sky behind us. Morning of our first day of exodus would soon be upon us."

At the check point there were four Turkish soldiers waiting. They threw open the tarp that covered the back of the truck and began counting...how many men...how many women...how many children, especially young girls. One of the soldiers took the driver aside and their voices became very loud...

"I could hear the men and they were arguing about money," Odaba said. "Despite the fact we'd given him all the money he'd asked us for, our driver did not have enough to meet their demands. The soldiers had increased the amount they wanted. When the driver said it was not possible, the soldiers turned their attention to the women and young girls in the truck. They wanted thirty minutes alone with them."

Odaba understood what was happening and he jumped from the back of the truck, intending to confront the soldier who was in charge. He felt he had no choice but to defend the women's honor...

"I will not permit you to touch even the sleeves of their garments," I threatened. "You may have your guns and your knives. But if you do not use your rifle to kill me with the first shot, I will take it from you or I kill you with my bare hands."

"The soldier became incensed!" Yana added. "He raised his rifle and was poised to shoot and kill my uncle. What kept him from pulling the trigger perhaps is only for God to know."

Out of nowhere, an officer appeared and the argument came to an end. Odaba was told to get back into the truck and then the driver was told to drive away. As the truck was backing up to turn around, everyone inside was thinking the same thing...

"We are trapped here now," Yana cried. "We are destined to die like all the others have."

"But the driver was not intimidated," Odaba said. "He was an honorable man who promised to take us out of Syria. He took us to another crossing twenty miles to the north. There we found guards who could be paid off with the little amount of money we had. They allowed us to cross into Turkey. Allahu akbar."

But Odaba and the others were not taken to the refugee camp just inside the border as they'd expected. They were taken instead into the city of Reyhanli. There they were hidden in the basement of the mosque of Ebu Bekir Cami. They stayed there for the next three weeks...

"There were men there who hid us well out of sight," Odaba continued, "but for a price of course. It was always and only about the money. We would have languished and died in the camps. I and the other men were taken to one place and the women and children to another. There was very little food in the hiding place for any of us...almost no water and the men who had hidden us also had an appetite for young girls like Yana.

Being separated from her, I was no longer able to protect her and so the worst possible fate awaited the child. I still cannot speak of what happened to her or any of those young children in those weeks in Reyhanli."

"We were moved every few days," Yana said to the journalist, telling him of the ordeal she endured while in Turkey but not talking about the rapes. "From one mosque to another, closer and closer to the sea...until we came to the seaport of Iskenderun. There, with a hundred others, we boarded two very old, very small, very dangerous-looking boats. Again, money changed hands."

The boats they boarded were to take them to Greece. But instead they took them only a distance of a few miles out into the Straits of Turkey before they became stranded. About half way across, the engine in the boat Yana and her family were on began to smoke and then it stopped working altogether...

"We were terrified that the old wooden boat would catch fire and we would sink to our graves at the bottom of the sea," she said. "The man who was steering the boat, I guess you could call him the captain, tried very hard to get the attention of the people on the other boat, but they were too far out ahead of us....a mere speck on the horizon.

So there we were...stranded and all alone. We drifted for three days. Soon we'd drifted so far the captain could no longer tell where we were. A huge black cloud formed in the sky and it seemed to be following us. At night we could not see the stars because of it.

After the second day, we had no food. We had no water. The sun was very hot and it beat down on us mercilessly. Several times we could hear airplanes that were flying over us...one even came down through the clouds and passed very close to us...trying I guess to see what or who we were. But they did not come back for us and they did not send anyone to help us. We were destined to suffer the fate of so many others before us."

To make matters worse, their boat began to leak and the water began seeping in. Soon they found themselves standing ankle deep in seawater. That is when the captain gathered them together to pray and to beg Allah for his mercy and deliverance...if it be His will.

"He was preparing us for the worst," Yana continued. "Then, suddenly...as if in answer to our prayers, a fishing boat came along, appearing out of nowhere. They came up beside us and tied a rope to the front of our boat. After what seemed like an eternity, they began to pull us to a port on the island of Cypress. This, I was hoping, would be where our luck would change...but as it turned out, things only became worse, terribly, terribly worse."

This is the part of the story where Yana's mood changed. She began talking about her brother Kahlil for the first time. She seemed to be on the verge of tears from the moment his name first came from her lips...

"My brother Kahlil was born with a problem with his heart," she said. "We feared something terrible would happen to him along the way and it did. We who were healthy were suffering beyond our limits. I did not believe my sweet brother would survive our ordeal but I prayed to Allah non-stop for mercy that he would. While we were still on land we did not know what to do...whether to stop and go back or continue on, praying to be able to make it to Italy. It was a very difficult situation for us all."

When they arrived in Cypress, Yana's uncle Odaba and her cousin Hatem, along with most of the other men on the boat were arrested and taken to a jail in a town called Larnaca. Yana pleaded with the soldiers not to take her brother because of his heart condition and it was a miracle that they allowed him to stay with the women.

No one was ever told why the men were being arrested...something about "a suspicion of something suspicious" or something else like that.

"We were taken from the boat and forced to live in the hot and filthy tents in a refugee camp outside of the town," Yana continued. "As we waited for the men to be released, I prayed every moment of the day for Allah to deliver us out of Cypress or at least out of those horrible tents.

It was in the camp that I met a young man who was most kind to me. He was a few years older than my oldest brother would have been had he not been murdered. This young man talked with me and tried to ease my worries. He shared what little food he had with Kahlil and me."

The young man was from Damascus and his name was Faez al Shaara. He had quite a story of own...

"It has been my dream since I was just a little boy." Faez began, "to go to the university in Damascus and to become a doctor. When the civil war broke out, my family and I had no choice but to flee. But before we could escape, my parents and two brothers were captured and executed in the street. I hid behind the corner of a building so as not to be seen. I cried to think I was now an orphan. I knew there was no way to live normally or safely in the capital....or in all of Syria for that matter."

Yana felt strangely safe and comfortable in his presence. She believed that he would somehow protect her and so she would not leave his side as he spoke...

"It was a Tuesday morning," he told Yana in one of their many talks. "I was confronted by a group of Syrian soldiers. They were looking for a man who had been seen carrying a gun. I and the three other boys with me were detained and accused of being rebels.

We were made to stand with our hands in the air while the soldiers pointed their guns at us. I felt death upon me and I accepted it as God's will. I cannot describe in words what I felt but knowing God was with me made me courageous and calm.

Suddenly a woman came running up to the soldiers, begging them to spare us. She claimed one of us was her son and the rest of us her nephew and neighbors. The woman fell to the ground pleading and weeping, making quite a spectacle. I'd never seen the woman before in my entire life and she had no idea who any of us were. But it was her superb acting that saved all our lives. For a reason I will never know, the soldiers allowed me and the other three to leave with her. It was later that night when I had finally stopped shaking and that I resolved to leave Syria at once."

Faez said he sat down and spoke with his young wife and her mother with whom they lived. He told them of his plan. He knew of a man who belonged to an underground group who smuggled Syrians into Jordan or Turkey. But they had only enough room in a private car for Faez and his wife. The mother, they argued, was too old and not of their concern. They reasoned they needed to save room for younger people with a longer life ahead of them. The truth is, they could charge more for a younger person.

But when the time came to leave, Faez's wife refused to go...not without her mother. She begged him to stay or at least understand. And so it was agreed that Faez would go alone for the time being and then send for his wife and mother-in-law later when he was safely out of Syria and settled elsewhere.

He packed his bags with a few pieces of his clothing, photos from his wedding and a few keepsakes that he could not bear to part with. The following morning he walked out the door well before sun-up. He met up with the car, and with his heart breaking, he left behind his wife and his entire life behind.

"He too had come through Turkey," Yana explained to the journalist. "Just as had I. He'd gone hungry for days on end, just as had I. He was first placed in a refugee camp with nearly 20,000 other people. The camp was a horrible place...plagued by rape and violence and corruption. The conditions were filthy and for many intolerable. One night, for reasons never explained to him, he was taken from the camp and thrown out of the gate...banned from ever returning. Why, he was not told."

For the next few weeks Faez was forced to sleep on park benches and if he were to stay alive, he began to steal whatever food he could find. A kind stranger came along one day and offered him a place to stay and a promise of help to find him a job.

In Turkey the life Faez was forced to lead allowed him to barely survive. He ate very little and drank even less. He knew that Turkey could not provide him with any sort of future, so after eight months he decided he must move on. He desperately longed for a better life and perhaps in a place where he would be able to carry on with his studies. That is when he too boarded a boat meant to take him to Greece. But instead, like Yana and her family, his fate was to arrive here in Larnaca nearly a month before. Left with no money and even less hope, he did not see himself ever leaving Cypress alive...

"My uncle and cousin, along with most all the other men, were finally released and returned to us in the tent camp," Yana said. "Our journey from Syria to Cypress had consumed 40 days of my young life by that point. Kahlil and I were tired and very, very frightened, but we trusted and loved our uncle very much and so we continued."

Odaba sat them down and told them he had enough money to be able pay their way by boat through the Greek Islands and then on to the city of Diavata at the top of the Aegean Sea. Once there, he would have more money wired to him from a cousin in Paris who had made it out of Syria safely the year before.

His plans were for all of them to cross that part of Greece, in trucks and cars again, and to get to the island of Kerkyra. From there they would cross the Adriatic Sea in boats and eventually arrive in Italy where they could request asylum.

"If all went according to my plans," Odaba interjected, "we would then go on to France and reunite with my cousin. But as you see, this was not God's will for us...our situation became quite dire quite quickly."

As planned, they crossed from Cypress into Greece at Diavata a mere two days before the border between Greece and the Balkins was closed. Word came that they were going to be returned to Turkey because Greece and the European Union had become overwhelmed with refugees...

"We knew that going back to Turkey would cost us our lives," Odaba said. "And so I spoke with a group of men who were leaving later that night in trucks headed for Kerkyra. I told my family we must leave behind all our possessions and join the others who were leaving. It took some doing, but I even talked Yana's new friend Faez into coming with us."

It was just after sunset when the group of about one hundred set out on foot from Diavata to an abandoned warehouse several kilometers from the camp. There they were herded inside like cattle where they waited for hours for the trucks to arrive...

"Inside the warehouse," Odaba said, "there were no lights nor any windows. It was pitch-black inside and the air was stifling, reeking of diesel fuel. After four hours of silent waiting, the trucks finally arrived...but there were only two of them. To move all of us would require at least four, maybe five trucks."

"I do not know how or why we were chosen," Yana said, "but my aunt and uncle, Kahlil and I ended up on one of the two trucks. I looked around between all the frightened faces to find Faez, but he was not to be found. As we were driving out of the warehouse I caught a glimpse of him, still standing inside, waving good bye to me. I closed my eyes and said a simple prayer for his safety. I never saw him again and I have no idea whatever became of him."

Though it was but a few hours of traveling, the drive across Greece seemed to Yana and her brother as if it would never end. The roads were poor...narrow and rutted in many places. The truck they were in had been used for hauling chickens and was covered over with a thick tarp made of canvas. The exhaust made its way into where they were sitting and it burned their eyes and took away their breath.

"We children were thrown around in the back as if we were rag dolls," Yana said. "It was all I could do to keep from crying. And so I made myself think of nothing but freedom…nothing but safety. My dear Syria seemed so far behind me at this point. I was engulfed in sadness and despair. That, I guess, is why I did not notice that Kahlil was leaning over…slouched against the canvas side of the truck."

It was not until they reached the ferry that would take them out onto the island that Yana noticed her brother was not moving.

"That big heart of his…the one that loved everyone so much, had stopped beating," she said. "For Kahlil, his journey to freedom was over. He passed from this world to the next silently and alone. I can only hope he did not suffer."

It was obvious that the thought of his passing still brings tears to Yana's eyes and pain to her heart…

"We were forced to leave his body behind and get on the boat," Yana said, now weeping again. "There was no time to see to his burial."

The men who owned the truck promised to see that Kahlil would receive a proper Muslim burial. They would bathe his body, wrap him in the white linen kafan, pray the Salat al Janazah over him and lay him in a grave so that his head would be facing Mecca."

"We simply had no other choice but to trust them," Yana said. "But when the time came to board the boat, I could not leave him. I rushed to his limp body and held him tightly against mine. I have never wept so hard in all my life. My uncle had to lift me up and carry me onto that boat…all the while I was crying and screaming out for my brother."

And now they were back to where Yana's story had begun...in Italy awaiting a decision if they would be granted asylum or not. The small family languished in the detention center in Brindisi for several months awaiting their hearings where they would request the right to remain in Italy.

"The sounds of traffic out on the street made its way through an open window of the hearing room," Odaba said. "It was very distracting and only made our anxiety all the worse. We'd waited months and lived through hell to get to this point. Our lives were in the balance."

"In each room there was a video camera and a tape recorder," Yana said. "At the time, we spoke only Arabic and so an interpreter had to explain the asylum system to us. This is where we were told that based on the answers to a few questions, our requests could very well be denied."

"First came the formalities," Odaba said. "At first we were all asked the same questions...Is your name spelled correctly? Is your birth date correct? Can you read and write in your native language? But then we were separated and each taken to different rooms where the questions became much more personal."

"I was asked what my religion was," Zinah said, finally speaking again. "And when I answered that I was a Sunni Muslim, the immigration officer frowned and began making check marks and notes on the paper. I do not know what he expected me to say. I mean, anyone can tell by the way I dress I am not a Christian!

Then he stood and without excusing himself or saying as much as a word to me, he left the room. I was left to stare at the floor and worry for the next twenty minutes if I had said something wrong...something that would take me away from my Odaba."

Another man came in, replacing the first. He asked Zinah the same questions the other had already asked. Her answers remained the same.

"For the next hour we each sat inside a different room of the Territorial Commissions for the Recognition of International Protection in Brindisi. We sat on one side of a table, asking for protection. On the other side was a smartly-dressed man who would decide our fate."

Yana, Odaba and Zinah were all granted asylum and given the proper identification papers and a residency card that could be revoked at any time without reason or a legal hearing. It would need to be renewed in five years...

"For the first year I could not help but think we were better off without the asylum," Zinah added. "Once we were given our documents we needed to fend for ourselves...we had to find our own food and shelter. But we were not permitted to work."

"We found ourselves going back to the detention center at night," Odaba said. "We had no permission to stay there but I'd made friends with one of the men who I'd met when we first arrived. He sneaked us in and allowed us to stay at night, but we were required to leave each morning before the guards changed shifts. He made sure to fill a small bag with a little food and a few bottles of water. Had it not been for his kindness I do not know what we would have done."

"And I believe that we all would be better off had we never been pulled from the sea," Yada said. "We should have given up our lives when God first asked us for them."

The journalist, visibly shaken himself, asked Yana if she was alright. The tone of her voice had changed in this part of the story and he could tell she was struggling terribly. Later he would write...

"It was nearly dark when I finished our interview. I felt as if I had been taking advantage of their openness and generosity. Yana's story both mesmerized me and broke my heart at the same time. I had not been prepared for where it had taken me. A human being can only take so much when their basic rights are being denied to them....or sold to the highest bidder.

I found myself demanding to know how any loving and merciful God could allow such suffering of his innocent people."

He asked Odaba before they parted ways, how he could justify his continued belief in a God who had, by anyone's standards, abandoned him, abandoned his family and an entire country. Odaba's answer was quick and spoken without a moment of hesitation...

"If God decides there is a better place or higher purpose for us somewhere other than where we are, we are to submit to His will and follow where He leads. It is not for me to question. God does not need to explain the reason, for God is perfect in His thinking. It is not for me to question why evil has come to my country. It is only for me to be grateful for being freed from such evil and to believe that in time the reason for the suffering we endured getting here will be revealed to us.

The point of such an encounter with God is to give me an opportunity to be close to Him, to hold on to Him for God wants us to hang on to Him no matter what. And always what we receive will be a blessing. We are blessed when we trust enough to bring our pain and our doubts to God and struggle with them in His presence. I may feel wounded...I may feel abandoned, but in my heart I know I am neither. I will receive a blessing I could not have received any other way."

"God sometimes allows bad things to happen in our lives," Yana added, "to prevent something far worse from making us suffer in far greater ways. This is a powerful and wise God we worship and adore. We have little idea how God is working in our lives but I surely know this...we would be dead had we stayed in Syria."

"The ways of God may seem peculiar to us," Odaba continued. "But His ways are beyond our human understanding. He is who He is. We are who we are. He is beyond error. He is perfect in all His ways.

We are in His mercy and love always as long as we follow in His commands. If His ways confuse or disappoint us, we must be careful to guard against the temptation to re-create Him into a God we like better."

When they said their goodbyes later that evening and as the journalist watched the two women dressed in their abaya following a few footsteps behind Odaba, there was but one word that kept coursing through his mind...abandonment.

It sent shudders down his spine and it troubled his thoughts to the point that he could feel it in his very soul...it sent out ripples of sadness and compassion from his heart to theirs.

For whatever unexplainable and unforgivable reason, God had sentenced these poor, innocent, trusting and battered souls to a nearly indescribable and unthinkable fate. He administered it without warning or a satisfactory reason.

I am not so naïve as to think there are not different kinds of abandonment or at least different degrees of it. But rarely is the most terrifying abandonment experienced by the masses. It can only be understood by the rare few who experience something the likes and depths of what Yana and her family endured.

Sergio Abbate struggled to write this story in a manner that would do these poor people justice. He'd come to understand that compassion, on its own, is a noble yet ever so inadequate emotion. It needs to be translated into actions and deeds, lest it wither and die.

The unanswered questions that face us in this day and age of endless streams of refugees and rampant immigration are what to do with all the feelings that have been aroused within us...the knowledge that has been communicated to us. If we feel that there is nothing we can do, then sadly we are lost.

It is difficult to imagine how dreadful, how terrifying life must have been for Yana in her flight from one hell, through another and to yet one more. We may envision it but even though she told her story in such detail as to shake us to our core, can we honestly say we understand what she's endured?

The Italian journalist wrote in his article that he learned a great deal from that sweet, young child...

"What she'd endured made her wise beyond her years," he wrote. "She shows the world that when we really know someone we can no longer hate them. Or maybe it's just that we can't really know them until we stop hating them. Whatever the case, she showed me quite clearly that there is a close link between love and understanding."

Spending time with someone like Yana will change us forever...it will alter our perspective and test our compassion in ways it has never been tested before. The journalist ended his fine article with a short post script...

"By the time our conversation would come to an end, I fully understood their plight and in some odd way, I had come to love them. Perhaps it was something Odaba said to me that brought me to my conclusion...

"He who loves understands. And he who understands loves."

Vignete 4 ~ The River House

HE WAS GOING HOME TO DIE. He knew it. She knew it too but would never allow herself to say it.

There was no doubt in her mind that bringing him home, back to the lowcountry and his beloved river, was going to be an event nearly as sacred for him as the births of his two children had been so many decades before. He'd often referred to that river as his old friend.

In the last few years, as he'd gotten weaker and weaker, he'd begun to believe he'd never see his river again...never sit along its banks or let it work its magic on him. But once their plane had finally touched down in Raleigh just after eight o'clock that morning, and as they were driving east toward the Pamlico Sound on Highway 70, she could see his strength and his spirit were returning to him. And the closer they got, first driving through Goldsboro and Kinston and then coming in to New Bern, the more he could feel his old friend reaching out to him. They were still an hour away from the river house but his mood was definitely changing.

The drive from Raleigh to the Sound would mean driving almost due east...directly into the harsh late summer sun. His eyes weren't what they used to be and he was much, much slower to react to things than when he was younger. And so he decided it was good thing if she did the driving. She said nothing, letting it be his decision, but she thought it best too. As a matter of fact, had he not suggested it, she most certainly would have.

She, as I have been calling her, was his beloved wife...fifteen years younger. Her name was Daniela but he'd always called her Dani. She was his best friend, his confessor and confidante for more than thirty years. And she was intent on being all those things to him for at least a few more. He sat beside her in the passenger's seat of their rented SUV, his hand resting on her leg while he described the sights and scenery along the way. It seemed he had a memory held dearly in his heart for almost each and every one of them. He spoke of them as if they'd all just happened yesterday.

Glancing over at him as he spoke, she could not help but see that he'd become an old man over these past years. He'd aged the quickest over the last three...ever since his heart attack.

He'd grown tired, weary I guess you could say. Living in Italy and marrying Dani had started out like a dream come true. But of late, more times than he'd ever admit, homesickness had set in and he longed for the place of his birth. Now well into his eighties, he suffered the aches and pains that old men do. But in bringing him home, she had breathed new life into his tired and battered spirit. Suddenly, his old age and poor health meant not an iota to either of them.

Having finally come home, after almost a half-lifetime being away, he was more determined than ever to live out whatever time he had left right there on the river, with the woman he loved more than life itself. He wanted nothing more than to spend his afternoons beneath the warm southern sun, sitting in that comfortable old Adirondack chair out on the end of the dock watching the river flow...perhaps cracking a few pistachio nuts from time to time and drinking a bottle or two of half-warm Crystal Coast lager, just the way he liked it.

Surprisingly, the old wooden house was none the worse for wear and tear. With the help of a local realtor they'd kept it rented most of the time that he was gone...though the realtor had passed and he never did get around to replacing him. And so, for the last eight, maybe nine years, the house had been closed up and empty, save for the old furniture and carpets he'd left behind.

When Swindell Bay came into view, she noticed he sat straight up in the seat. Just short of the marina is where they'd turn onto Weaver Camp Road and follow it as it weaved back and forth for a mile or so. By the time they were turning onto the dirt road that would take them back the house, he'd rolled down his window and with his eyes closed, breathed in all the fresh air he could take in to his lungs. To him, nothing ever smelled as good and as the fresh as the air of the lowcountry and the wind coming off the Sound.

The iron chain he'd had installed...the one that was supposed to block the lane, was lying on the ground. She was by nature a fearful person and began to worry about what they might find once they got back to the house.

But as she pulled into the grassy lawn in front, everything looked fine...at least from the outside. With the exception of how high the grass had grown and how badly the house needed a new coat of paint, not much had changed to his eyes...

"What do you think?" she asked, wanting to gauge his reaction to being back.

"It looks just like it did when I left," he whispered out loud. "God...it's good to be home!"

She parked the car beside the house...beneath the two oak trees that had grown monstrously taller than she remembered them being from his old photographs. After standing to stretch her legs and then helping him get out of the car, she took his key ring and unlocked the house. She went around opening each of the window and the shutters and all the doors to get it aired out. He'd promised to help, but as she'd suspected, he was just too anxious. He had something more important he needed to do. While she worked inside, he ambled down to the dock to say hello to his old friend.

She appeared on the front porch after a few minutes and waved to get his attention. She shouted to him...

"We are not staying here tonight," she declared. "There are so many bugs and too much dirt. I've called Mary Beth over at the Clinton Creek Inn and she is getting a room together for us. I told her we needed one with a private bath." And then she turned around and went back in to continue with her cleaning.

He never argued with her any more. As a matter of fact he rarely ever had. He was shaking his head while she was talking, gesturing that he understood, but chances are, with his hearing as bad as it had gotten, he probably didn't hear much of what she said...and she knew it.

But they did spend their first two nights at the Clinton Creek Inn in Bayboro. He seemed surprised when they pulled into the parking lot. That's when she realized her suspicions were right. He had not heard what she said...

"I was looking forward to sleeping in my old bed tonight," he said.

"It's just too dirty and the electricity isn't turned on yet, she answered. "We'll have no water for our showers in the morning. And besides that, the propane tank is empty. How will we cook our meals? Be reasonable sweetheart. I've already made our reservations. We'll go back in the morning."

Though they spent their days at the river house together, working on things inside and out, there was still too much to be done before she'd agree to spend the night. So she told Mary Beth they'd need to stay longer at the inn.

There was an old raccoon that showed up in a different room from time to time while they were cleaning and until he was convinced that he needed to find another home, she had absolutely no intention of sharing this one with him!

It took a few days to chase away the mice and the spiders and eventually that raccoon left too. She kept the windows open all day, letting the fresh, clean sweet air come through. It helped to get the smell of mildew out of the draperies and the old carpets. She knew it was up to her to call the contractors to have the repairs done and to have the utilities turned on. She did it all gratefully, never complaining, not even once.

Job number one for her was to get rid of those carpets...

"I bet that raccoon has pipi'd in every room in this house," she said. "I am having the trash man come by tomorrow and take them all away. We will buy new ones or we'll have the floors sanded and refinished. Is that OK with you?"

"Whatever you want Dani," he answered. "It's all OK with me."

Over the course of a week she filled the house with fresh air and sunshine. They'd gone for short walks together down along the river where she picked bouquets of the fresh wildflowers that grew everywhere. One day a brown and white cat, obviously a stray, wandered onto the front porch and in through the open front door. He was mewing loudly, trying to get their attention...trying to tell them that he was hungry, thirsty and in need of a little human companionship. Once she'd given him a small bowl of milk and part of her tuna fish sandwich, he decided this would be a good place to stay.

The days passed slowly, turning into weeks, until eventually the season began to change. They'd arrived in the final days of summer, when it was darn hot. And though it was autumn now and the days were shorter and the strong heat was lessening, it was still barely tolerable for her. She just was not used to it. So she had an electrician come out and install a few window air conditioners one day.

She found October to be even more beautiful there in the lowcountry than he'd described in the many stories he'd told her over their years together. She would sit with him out on the dock in the afternoon, basking with the warm sun on her face and the breeze coming in off the Sound blowing her hair back off her neck and shoulders. It was enough to make her forget that she was the one far away from home now...5000 miles away from everything that was normal to her. It gave her a better understanding of the times when he'd seemed so homesick.

By the time November came around, the weather was perfect for both of them. But she could see he'd been slipping. She knew it was but a matter of time now.

He was home...and nothing could possibly bother him. Each day, he'd get up and put on the same clothes...an old, worn-out linen shirt that she'd bought for him in Rome ten years before. It was a favorite of his and he refused to part with it no matter how tattered it had become.

It was the same thing with the cut-off khaki shorts and a worn out pair of leather sandals. These are what he felt most comfortable wearing, so for the most part she never said anything about it. One day, after seeing him dressed the same way for days on end, she said something or another about him looking like a refugee. But he just smiled, unfazed. She didn't think he'd heard her say that either.

And then there was that darned old straw hat...the one that he used to wear when he was out in his barn back in Italy! She'd threatened to throw it away years before but somehow he kept it just out of her reach. And somehow he actually was able to bring it along in his luggage without her knowing.

Whether he looked like a refugee or not did not matter to him. He was comfortable and feeling better and that was all that mattered to her too. The sun glasses he wore had once belonged to his uncle Joe...the same man who built the dock on which he sat.

Though the old Adirondack chair had not always been there, he felt as if that dock always had been. You see, for as far back into his memory as he could reach, that dock had been right there...jutting out into the water.

From it, he'd once fished for channel bass and catfish with his cousins. And if memory served him correctly, it was there that his father had taught him to swim, though there really was not much teaching involved.

As he tells it, he'd shown a fear of the water when he was a young boy, so much so that he would sit alone at the end of the dock and watch his sister and her friends out playing in it. One day his father just picked him up and threw him in. He had two choices...sink or swim. He chose to swim.

He'd taught both his own children to swim there too one summer, though his methods I would guess were a bit more conventional.

His swimming days were long over now though…the natural progression of time and a weakening heart had changed his body and robbed him of his strength. So sometimes for hours and more each day, he was content to just sit at the end of the dock and watch as that old river and what was left of his life flowed by so effortlessly.

Since he'd come home, he'd begun keeping a journal, something he'd stopped doing years before. He was a writer after all, though he'd stopped writing his books a few years before as well. From time to time he'd take the journal down to the dock with him and write a few words in it.

More often than not what he wrote was just short sentences, something from a passing thought or brief scribbled notes of a memory that would rise to the surface. Most of the time what he wrote meant nothing. But one day, as she watched him from the kitchen window as she often did, she saw him writing furiously. It made her wonder what he could possibly be thinking.

In their many years together he'd mused from time to time on how lovely, yet how strange it all was…the river I mean. She remembered him telling her one day years before…

"It was always there, yet the water that flowed in front of me was never the same…it never stood still. It was always changing…always on the move."

And now after all these years, the river, in which the changing water flowed, had now itself changed…

"It seems wider to me in these days," he told her one afternoon when she'd brought a sandwich out to him for his lunch. "A bit shallower than I remember too. Either that or the river grass has grown thicker, I don't know. Either way, I guess I'm not supposed to see it the way I did when I was young."

"Everything changes sweetheart," she said to him reassuringly. "Nothing stays the same for long."

"We have!" he said, patting her on the knee. "We've stayed in love and right at each other's side for more than thirty years. I don't know what I ever did to deserve a love like yours...but God sure has blessed me with you. We've defied the odds you know."

"Eat your sandwich," she said, putting the plate on his lap. "You didn't eat much for breakfast."

"Once was a time I could swim across this stretch of the river without stopping," he said while taking his first bite of the sandwich. "Ya believe that? No need to rest or catch my breath. I was a bull back then sweetheart. Look what the hell has happened to me now."

"Don't talk with your mouth full," she joked. "I need to get dressed and run in to pick up bread, eggs and coffee in Bayboro. I will check back on you before I go. Will you be ok?"

"Yeah," he answered nonchalantly. "I'll be fine. Are there any cold beers in the fridge? Sure would make this sandwich go down easier."

Life for him had turned out very much like that old river. Sometimes it had carried him along, gently and peacefully. Other times it raged and pulled him under...sweeping him into places he was not meant to go. And most times, those torrents came out of nowhere. He never saw many of them coming.

Losing the love and respect of his children when he divorced their mother was one of those torrents. Though it had been more than fifty years, there had not been a single day that went by when he did not think of them or miss them to the point where tears would come.

Over his many years, he'd learned the age-old secrets that all rivers hold. His own river was no different than any other. You see, there is no such thing as time to a river. A river flows everywhere at the same time...at the springs of its headwaters and at the deltas that empty into the ocean. They flow over waterfalls and through rapids. They carry the ferries and freighters and fishermen across themselves. They exist only in the present moment, not in the shadows of the past or in the clouds of the future, like people tend to do.

"Are we like these rivers Dani?" he asked her when she came back to check on him before she left. "Am I like that? Have I changed like my river has changed? Have I become wider...more shallow?"

A simple touch of her hand against his and a kiss on the forehead answered his question...

"Yes, I must agree with that," she said. "You've changed. I've changed. The world has changed. But look at us. We've grown old together. And there is nothing wrong with that."

He thought about it for a moment or two and he had to agree...

"I love you sweetheart," he said, letting go of her hand. "Try not to be too long today, OK?"

He was indeed very much like that river...always flowing but always different. Like the waters in front of him, there were times in his life when he meandered along steadily...peacefully, with hardly any movement to be noticed. Other times he had surged into the rapids...furiously raging...bursting from his own banks when there was too much water, too much life inside of him. And there were many times he feared to become stagnant...or to dry up from lack of rain and become a dry bed. This was what the years had done to him.

On that particular day, shortly after she'd driven off, the warm beer went right to his head and it made him sleepy. It was nothing for him to fall into a nap now that he had officially reached old age...something he could not conceive of doing just ten years earlier. He fell into a deep sleep and then into a dream that would leave him restless and anxious once he woke from it.

He dreamed he was in the water of his river, drifting along in an inner tube. And he wasn't alone. There was a little girl with him, ten…maybe twelve years old. She was in a tube of her own.

He felt as if he knew her somehow, though who she was or from where he knew her he could not recall. He watched her spinning in circles in the slow current…her eyelashes fluttering from the water that dripped from her forehead. Her face was drenched in sunlight. Her feet lazily kicked in the water as she propelled herself along with gentle strokes of her cupped hands.

It was something in her smile that haunted him the most though. He'd seen that smile before, somewhere…some time. He was sure it meant something to him, but he'd be damned if he could bring it back…

As they drifted along down the river together, he felt as though a warm medicine was moving through his veins, flushing his cells with a natural, liquid peace. The sounds of chirping birds and the katydids and frogs along the shoreline filled the air. There was the soft song of moving water everywhere around them.

He found himself wanting only to look at her…to think only of her. To his eyes she was the calmest vision imaginable and it released every other thought and every other worry and even the smallest of fears from his mind. His aches and his pain flew from him like flocks of birds, scattering in every direction and filling the sky.

He and the little girl drifted together, side by side, without speaking. They drifted so long that the dark night sky began to set in. They both lay back in their inner tubes and looked up. They could see the stars just beginning to show themselves, sparkling and twinkling in the sky. That is when he began to remember a few things.

He knew the constellations by heart. In a faint flash of memory he recalled the two of them, him and that little girl, lying on their backs right there on that old dock…looking up and pointing at the sky. It was many, many years ago but it was all coming back to him now. The two of them knew each other somehow.

When the river turned to the south and their tubes came side-by-side again, she pointed up toward Virgo and Centaurus coming into view. The moonless sky was awash with stars that night and the water was calm...as smooth as glass. Each star reflected itself in the water around them...hundreds and hundreds of stars, until it almost felt as if they were no longer floating on the water, but drifting among the stars in the heavens above them.

The two of them giggled, pointing with their fingers and drawing imaginary lines in different directions...creating their own, brand new constellations and giving them names.

He wanted to rise up from the river. He wanted to fly to those stars like he'd done when he was young boy. But he had neither the power nor the magic any more. All he could do was let the river carry him along.

The silence of the night was broken when the little girl spoke to him...

"I love you daddy," she said. "I love you very much. I've missed you."

And then the dream was over…

When Dani came back from the market she could see he was still out at the end of the dock. His head was pressed down, his chin on his chest. That cat was nestled in his lap, belly exposed to the sun, and just as sound asleep as he was. She took a photograph of the two of them...something she would want to remember for a long time.

She thought to go down to wake him...it was time for him to be out of the sun. She would bring him up and let him sit in the shade of the oak trees while she got dinner ready.

Just as she was getting ready to touch his shoulder, she noticed the journal was open. Normally she would have never looked at it, but on that day something told her she should...

> *I was born on the path of the Southern wind,*
> *raised where the river is old.*
> *The springtime waters came rushing down*

and I remember the tales they told.
The whistling ways of my younger days
too quickly have faded on by.
But all of their memories linger on
like the light in my fading sky.
I've been to Italy and back again,
I've been moved by the love that I've earned.
Met many fine people and I've called them friends,
felt the change when the seasons turned
I've heard all the songs that the children sing
and I've listened to love's melodies.
I've felt my own music within me rise
like the wind through these autumn trees.
Someday when the flowers are blooming again,
someday when the grass is again green.
My river's waters will round the bend
and flow to the open sea.
Here's to the woman who's followed me here.
And here's to the friends that I've known.
And here's to the song that's within me now,
I'll sing out loud 'ere I go
River...take me along on your sunshine
sing me a song, ever moving and winding and free.
You rolling old river, you changing old river,
Let's you and me river run down to the sea.

"I was a neighbor," an awkwardly dressed man said to her at the viewing. "When he lived here before...well, before you came along I guess is what I mean to say."

His name was Marty Simmons and Dani could not help but see how uncomfortable he looked in his too-tight gabardine suit as he fumbled for the right words to say. He, like so many others, had come to pay his respects.

His words cut her deeply though she knew he meant nothing by them. She knew her husband had a life before she came along. But Marty Simmons never was known for his tact and his words could be as awkward as he himself was.

"And although he had quite a few years on me," Marty continued, "I'd like to think we were friends...good friends. He looked forward to our Sunday morning excursions in my boat, out into the bay. That man just plain loved fishing."

Dani knew they'd come back just in time...a few months later and everything would have been much different. In her prayers at night, she thanked God for giving him these last months to make amends with the heavier things he'd carried in his heart and on his conscience for so long. The river was the only place it was possible, she was sure of that. Had they stayed away, back in Italy, he would have taken many of these things with him to his grave.

In his last days, it became much more apparent how heavy a toll this struggle he was waging with time and his conscience was taking on him. His breathing had become difficult and he'd all but stopped eating. After she left for the market that one day he'd not taken even one more bite of his sandwich.

He hadn't been out of his bed in more than a week. She lovingly gave him sponge baths and brushed his teeth and combed his hair. She would even shave his face for him from time to time. On that particular morning she was finally able to convince him to get out of his pajamas and into his clothes.

She'd moved his bed out into the sunroom...turning it so he could see the river and his dock. She made sure the many windows were always open and the curtains tied back. He loved the fresh air and the sunshine. She made sure there were always fresh flowers on the table and plenty of pillows in bed. She wanted him to be comfortable.

One morning she'd called a neighbor over to help bring the big, overstuffed chair from the living room and put it beside his bed. In the evenings they'd share a pot of tea and she'd read parts of his own books back to him. It was as if he was hearing them for the first time. She would finish when he would fall asleep...scenes of his Italian life running through his dreams.

She loved him very much and she had always done whatever she could to make him happy. But now she was coming to understand her job was nearly done. Once a man has taken that turn toward the last scene in his final act...well, he had to walk it alone. That's all there was to it.

"When the moment comes when we pass from this world to the next," he'd told her once. "All we can do is turn and wave a sad good bye. Keep an eye out for me sweetheart when I go...I promise I will be waving."

That moment came for him in the middle of the afternoon on a warm December day, two weeks before Christmas. It would have been his first Christmas back in America in a long, long time.

She'd known for some time the end was near. She thinks he did too. Death itself had been waiting impatiently outside his door for the last few nights. She could feel it in the house and it made her immensely uncomfortable. Somehow he'd managed to hide from it though, but on that morning when she was helping him get dressed, she knew he would lose his battle before the day was out.

It was the middle of December and even this far south along the coast, the mornings could be a bit chilly. She bundled him as best she could, making sure he wore a sweater that buttoned around his neck. He'd become so frail…he'd lost so much weight, looking more like a bag of bones than the strong man she remembered meeting three decades before. All the warm clothes in the world could not keep him from feeling the cold arms of death that day.

When the sun was finally up and the morning chill gone from the air, he sat on the front porch waiting for her to bring him his morning coffee with two pieces of rye toast. While he sipped his coffee and looked out across his river, she went back inside and called a few of his closest friends…

"I think today is the day you should plan on saying goodbye to him," she told each one. "I don't think you'll get another chance."

And so one by one they began showing up. By 10:00 that morning the front yard of the river house was filled with cars and old pick-up trucks. They'd all come out to wish him off. He'd fought a good fight and they each wanted to say goodbye in their own way. There was perhaps six…maybe eight of his closest friends gathered there that day.

They walked along in a slow procession from the house, across the front yard and down to a small table with a chair sitting along the banks of that river he loved so much. Marty Simmons, the friend who'd taken him out bay fishing on Sunday mornings years before, held on tightly to his arm, steadying his steps when he faltered. The cane he walked with wasn't of much use anymore. At times Marty was almost carrying him.

A few weeks or so before, he'd brought the Adirondack chair in from the end of the dock to river bank and sat it beneath a tree at the water's edge for his friend. For years there'd just been an old, round concrete table there but nothing to sit on. Now, with his favorite chair, he could relax in the shade and write in his journal or just reflect on his life.

She spent the days of his last weeks with him down there by the river's edge. Many were the times in the late afternoons when they'd be there talking about one thing or another. Sometimes they'd just sit in the evening to watch the sun go down. He'd sit in the chair and she'd sit on the grass beside him on a blanket. In these last days they were inseparable.

That chair and the concrete table were there waiting for him when he and his group of friends reached the water on his very last morning. Dani carried a blanket with her to wrap around his tired and frail body…something to keep him warm against what was left of the early morning chill.

"I held on to him as I lowered him to that big chair," Marty said as he recalled that morning. "I wanted him to be comfortable. I gently let go of him and he sank down into it…exhausted. He was having a hard time catching his breath."

Everyone stood around and behind him, giving him time to compose himself. Once his panic had passed and he'd caught his breath again, he began what would be his last conversation with anyone on this earth…

"I used to come down here late at night," he recalled, biting at the air, trying to get more of it into his lungs. "I would wait for those nights when the moon would come out so that I could find my way across the front yard. I have always feared the dark you know…ever since I was a little boy."

Turning to his wife, he smiled and pointed his long and boney finger at her. His hand trembled and shook for he could no longer control it…

"You were already sound asleep Dani," he said. "But sleep wasn't coming for me anymore. Instead I would come out here and think about all those impossible things you tried to convince me of…the things we talked about so late at night."

So many of their conversations over those thirty years seemed to come around one way or another to this merciful God of hers...the one she believed in so strongly with all her heart. But he was convinced her God had abandoned him years before and turned a cold shoulder to him. The things she said to him though, always fell short of changing his mind.

She would get frustrated when he'd refer to God as her God...

"He is your God too!" she would insist when they'd argue in the past. "If you'd just stop being so darn stubborn and forgive Him like He's forgiven you, maybe you'd understand a bit more than you do."

He began to cough and he could not stop. She held his wrists and stretched his arms above his head until it passed. As he began to speak again, she noticed the spattering of blood on his lips and on his chin...even on the blanket. But of course she said nothing...

"I would come out here where you could not hear me and I would scream out loud," he continued, tears now coming to his eyes and quiver to his voice. "You told me so many times that I could do that...do you remember? You told me this God of yours expected me to bring my true self to him. Well...my true self was angry. I was resentful. I would scream as loud as I could. You never heard me."

But the truth of the matter was she'd always heard him. Never once did he leave the house without her knowing. But she knew he needed his space and so she'd watch or listen from the window to make sure he was ok.

She smiled at him, nodding her head. Of course she remembered telling him this...

"I remember every one of our conversations sweetheart" she said. "You argued with me constantly!"

She could tell he was waiting for her to finish so he could speak again. She gestured with her hand for him to continue with what he felt he needed to say...

"I would sit here…right here in this chair," he said. Now he was really fighting back the tears and his voice kept faltering. "And when I had screamed it all out, I would become quiet. I would sit right here. I'd fold my arms across my chest and I'd wait. I waited and I waited and I waited…just as you told me I must. I wanted so badly to hear a voice speaking to me…someone telling me I was a good man. That was all I needed to hear. I wasn't asking for forgiveness. I did not seek absolution…but only to know that my life had been worth something."

She was going to interrupt him…to tell him he was indeed a good man and that his life was worth more than he could ever know. But he charged right ahead with more of what he needed to say…

"I waited…night after night," he continued. "I waited until there was no more moon…until I thought I could wait no more…until I was even more positive that this God of yours wanted nothing to do with me. I had all but given up. Then one night…one night I heard it. I swear I did! It was not like any voice I had ever heard before. It whispered my name."

He raised his arm and pointed across the river…

"It was there…right there Dani," he said. "It was hanging on the wind. Just as you said it would be."

Then he became quiet. He chose to tell none of them what the voice said to him. Instead he turned to his friends and he smiled…

"My time among you has come to an end now gentleman…and lady," he said. "I want you to promise me something. Promise you'll bury me right here…right beneath this tree on the banks of this river."

No one said a thing. But they all knew why he'd made such a request. They all knew that he was home now…that their dear friend wanted to spend his eternity exactly in the place where he had finally found her God and discovered it has been his all this time too…just as she said He was..

His head slowly bent toward his chest and he closed his eyes. Unbeknownst to any of them, his spirit rose from his body and one by one he caressed each of his friends. It was time for him to go. But he lingered, looking at her with his eyes filled with tears. He found it impossible to leave her. No matter how he begged his newly found God, there was no going back. All he could do was sadly wave goodbye and realize that she could no longer see him.

She had his body cremated and although she did not bury him on that river bank as he'd asked, from time to time she'd take his urn out and place it atop that concrete table. She'd sit in his Adirondack chair with his cat in her lap and the three of them would watch as time and that river flowed by...just as he'd done so many times before.

There was a service for him. Afterwards those same friends who'd seen him off at the river's edge, gathered around the big table at Maggie's Place...taking the time to remember him, each in their own way.

He and Maggie had become friends many years before. She owned the local diner down on the waterfront just off Spencer Street. He'd found it a few months after he'd first moved to the river house and became a regular.

Maggie was younger than he was and struggling as a single mother to make ends meet. He'd been very kind to her and her children. He'd done something for them that she was never be able to forget...never!

Just as he had been before he moved away thirty years ago, when he came back he'd become the talk of the little riverfront town again. When he was younger he was known as the Yankee who'd come to Bayboro and won the hearts and minds of the locals. Years later he'd come back as a famous writer and a world traveler. But those who knew him best knew he'd not changed at all. As they sat around that big table, they each told stories of their own recollections and memories of him.

After the funeral, Dani needed to decide what she was going to do with the river house. She stayed for the rest of the winter, returning to Italy in the early spring of the following year. From time to time his friends would drop in to check on her...making sure she was OK and asking if she needed anything. She would always say no...

She celebrated Christmas alone that year...just her and that cat. He'd never named it so she decided she would. Ladro she called it...the Italian word for thief! Anytime anything of hers was missing, she knew where to look. That cat would be playing with it somewhere! Find the cat...find what was missing!

Maggie had put together a dinner of roasted turkey and all the rest of the things American's eat for Christmas. She brought it by in the afternoon and stayed for a while to talk. Maggie told Dani a few things about her husband that she'd never heard before...

"Did he tell you what he did for me and my children?" she asked.

"No, he didn't," Dani answered. "There were parts of his life that he kept private from me...parts before I came along. Were you and he a couple?"

The question took Maggie by surprise...

"Oh goodness no!" she answered. "Please don't think that Dani. May I call you that? Would you prefer I call you Daniela?"

"Dani is fine," she answered. "It's all I've heard for 30 years. I wouldn't know what else to answer to."

"Then Dani it is!" Maggie said as she continued with her story. "But it wasn't because of me that we weren't a couple. He was a good man Dani. Any woman would have been damn lucky to have him. I hope you know that. I hope you know how fortunate you were that he chose you."

And she did. She did know there neither would nor ever could be another man like him...

"I was struggling with life," Maggie said. "I couldn't make my mortgage payments on my house because everything I made was going back in to the restaurant. My refrigerator went out one week and the next my deep fryer. We had a storm a few years after he arrived and everything was flooded for weeks. I had already made the decision that I wasn't going to reopen...I had no insurance and I just couldn't afford to fix the diner. I couldn't afford to lose my house either. I had two children who depended on me. Their daddy left and it was just the three of us against the world."

"What did you do?" Dani asked.

"One morning I got the strangest phone call," Maggie said. "It was from a contractor over in Rocky Mount. He said he'd be at my diner the following Monday morning with a crew of men to get started on the repairs. I had no idea what he was talking about. You must have the wrong number I said...I didn't hire you. I have no money."

"It's all been taken care of," the man answered. "I'm supposed to send my bills to an attorney in Beaufort. I guess you have a secret admirer or something. Whoever it is, set up an account through the lawyer's office. I can't tell you who hired me. It's part of my agreement that he remains secret, but you'll need to meet me and my foreman at the diner at nine o'clock next Monday morning. Is that OK?"

"You need to know it was your husband who did this for me," Maggie said to Dani. "I wouldn't find out for years to come who my secret admirer was. Your husband set up that account with Attorney Davis in Beaufort and just like the man from Rocky Mount said, everything was taken care of. Maggie's Place was as good as new in a few months. You need to know that your husband did this for me for no other reason than kindness."

The two women talked for a bit more before Maggie stood up and hugged her new friend...

"Merry Christmas Dani," Maggie said. "If you decide to stay here, I'd like to be your friend."

"We already are friends," Dani said. "Merry Christmas to you too. You're welcome to stay if you'd like. There's more food on that tray you brought than I'll ever eat."

But Maggie politely said no...

"I'd like to stay," Maggie said. "I really would. But I've got a van filled with more Christmas dinners to deliver today."

"So I am not your only charity case today?" Dani joked.

"It's something I've been doing for quite a few years now," Maggie said. "I guess you could say your husband is the reason for that too."

"Is that a fact?" Dani said. "How is that? If I might ask?"

"After I'd found out what he'd done for me," Maggie said, "I insisted I be able to pay him back. He was equally as insistent that I not! He told me if I wanted to pay him back I could do it by doing good things for other people. So that's what I've been doing ever since.

Every Christmas. Every Easter and every Thanksgiving my daughters come home, no matter where they're at, and we make dinners for twenty, thirty, sometimes as many as forty people. It's the least I can do to pay your husband back."

After Maggie left, Dani did her best to eat the food, though she just picked at it throughout the day. As a matter of fact, she left most of everything for the cat. Ladro's best decision ever was coming to stay at the river house!

It was time to think about going home. She struggled with her decision, wanting to stay, but in the end she knew going back to Italy is what he would have wanted her to do.

"It has been six months now you're gone," her letter to him began. She was back in Italy and picking up the pieces of her life. She was lost. She'd not realized how much she'd come to depend on him for just about everything...

"All our friends here know you are gone," she continued. "The house is filled with flowers. Every room looks like a greenhouse.

This house seems so big now. It is so quiet without you. It is just me and my memories of the past 30 years to keep me company."

She'd gathered up all the flowers one day and took them to hospitals and a few homes for the elderly...

"I sit at your desk at night and I make believe you are here," she wrote. "Everywhere I go...everything I see...everyone I talk to is a memory of you...painful reminders of how much we loved each other. I don't know what to say to them sometimes. So I just stare out the window."

She'd begun to go through his things. Every thing she touched had a memory and a story attached to it, each more vivid and painful than the last. The one thing she made sure to bring home with her was that old straw hat she'd hated so much when he was alive. It had become her most treasured possession now.

"I found your wedding ring today," she wrote while saying the words out loud. "You'd lost so much weight when you became sick. You couldn't keep it on your finger any more. It was in the drawer with your watch and your mother's rosary beads. I know you'd want me to be strong but I could not help but break down when I read what's inscribed in it. *"I will love you forever"*. I wear your ring on my middle finger now. I want you to know I will never break my promise to you."

On her flight home she'd almost convinced herself that this God of hers had betrayed her...

"We didn't get to finish our love story," she continued to write, "not the way you'd written it. We promised each other forever. Why did God need to take you back? What is so important in heaven that he had to have you now? Why couldn't he let me enjoy you for a bit longer?"

But as the months passed and she was getting accustomed to being alone, she'd come to change her mind. She no longer felt betrayed. He'd always told her that everything was just as it should be...

"If I am gone and you're alone, well that must be how God wants it."

She would still believe every word he said...

She remembers their love story with every photograph she picks up and each friend that comes by to make sure she's ok...

"We knew each for more than thirty years sweetheart," she finished. "I think we fit in a hundred years of love. It will be enough to get me through my days now. Rest well my dear husband. I will hold you in my heart forever and I will see you again someday soon."

We are each created, fashioned and designed in such a way as to leave something special behind in this world...something that did not exist before we were born! We leave a legacy behind. We leave our footprints wherever we've stepped and our fingerprints on every heart we've ever touched.

People who make the greatest impact on us are the ones we will remember most. At least that is how it was for Dani. He'd left behind an empty seat...an empty space that could never be filled again...ever.

With each new day, she found a new reason to think anew. She came up with new strength to start over...no matter how difficult the day before had been. She finally understood and appreciated the real gift of life, knowing she had yet another chance to prove her existence worthy.

"We must always choose positive thinking over negative thoughts," she told a small group of girls at the church of Santa Cecilia where she taught a class after Mass. The girls, none older than sixteen, were each getting over the recent loss of a parent and Dani was trying to help them through their grieving...

"We must find the real reason to rejoice," Dani told them. "To breathe a sigh of purpose and be poised to leave something unique behind.

My husband told me many times that everything is just as it should be. As it is, it is perfect. As it was, it was perfect. As it will be...it will always be perfect. If God wants it differently, God will make it differently. Everything has been perfect...it has led to this exact time and this exact place for you, for this very reason.

When we worry about our future we are creating the experience of fear, now. When we regret the things in our past, we create sadness, depression...even anger, now. Resisting what we cannot change is what causes us to lose our peace. The person you lost cannot come back. It may make no sense to you now, but trust that everything is just as it should be. Trust that God will reveal the reason for your pain and your tears when the time is right."

Vignette 5 ~ Connally Avenue

"IT ALL STARTED WHEN I WAS 'ROUND SEVEN YEARS OLD," she said, speaking in her Louisiana drawl, without the slightest inflection of emotion in her voice. She was speaking into a tape recorder that was sitting on the table in front of her. "It all went on way too long."

Her wrists were bound in handcuffs and the handcuffs were locked to a steel ring that was bolted to the table. Her ankles were bound together with leg irons. It was obvious they didn't want her going anywhere.

The shackles dug into her skin, enough so that she could feel the drops of blood trickling over the arch of her left foot. But despite the discomfort, she said not a word. The truth is, she was happy to be out of that house.

"Where did you get the gun you used?" the detective sitting across the table from her asked.

His partner was a woman and she was standing in the corner, in the dim light and shadows about four or five feet from the table. She was there no doubt out of protocol, needing a policewoman in the room when they interrogated a woman. She tried to make the girl feel a bit more at ease and get her to tell them what they wanted to hear...

"We ran a ballistics test on it," she said. "Do you know what that means?"

The young girl, wringing her hands together and shrugging her shoulders, nodded her head. Yes...she understood.

"We think it was used in a shootin' over in Vicksburg about two years ago," the detective added. "A convenience store hold-up went bad and the clerk was killed. It sure would help if you could tell us where you got that gun."

"It was his," she said, looking right into the woman's eyes, ignoring the man who'd asked the question. "He kep' it out in the tool shed.

My boyfriend and I found it one afternoon when we was out there messin' 'round."

"I don't think she evva intended to kill him," another detective said, this one on the other side of the two-way mirror. He was talking to his partner. "And I kin guarantee God-damn-tee ya she nevva meant to kill her little sista. This a shame...that's what it is. Nothin' but a God-damn shame."

"I kin remember hidin' in the bathroom with the door locked when my mother wasn't home," she continued. "That's when he'd come a lookin' for me. I'd hide in the bathtub...pull the shower curtain closed. My sister was still too young back then so I wasn't scared for her. He always favored me anyways."

The fluorescent light on the ceiling was humming and flickering. It distracted her from time to time...

"He'd touch me in places he shouldn'ta," she said. "I knew it was wrong but he always told me he did the things he did 'cause he loved me...like he loved my mother."

"All we're interested in right now is the shootin'," the male detective said. "We got a dead man and a dead little girl. You killed 'em...you've already told us that. We just got a few more questions to ask ya for our report."

They didn't care about the abuse or the rapes. They didn't have any interest in her story. It was 11:00 at night and they just wanted to finish with their questions and get the report written so they could go home. Someone else might want to listen to her story later, but for now they weren't interested in any of that.

Her name was Melissa Talbott. She was nineteen years old and she'd been arrested for the murders of her step-father and fourteen year old sister...

The detective in the adjoining room had listened to and watched the entire interrogation. All he could do was shake his head...

"I'd say the son-of-a-bitch got what was comin' to him," he said. "But ain't nobody in Tallulah Loosiana gonna listen to her or give a damn about any white trash girl who done shot her own little sista. It's a shame I tell ya...nothin' but a God-damn shame."

Standing in a bus depot in Memphis Tennessee twenty two years later, Melissa was on her way back to that small Louisiana town where she was born. She had a bit of unfinished business she needed to take care of.

"All Aboooord! Jackson, Vicksburg and Natchez Mississippi!"

With a long and drawn out Southern drawl, the short, fat man, sweating profusely and dressed in a much too tight blue shirt and black vest, was shouting over the loud speaker from behind the ticket window. Too loudly! She could hardly make out what he was saying...

"Jesus Christ man!" she thought to herself while shaking her head, "it's a God-damn loud speaka. You don't need to yell into it!"

"Bus 210 is boardin' now. Last call for Jackson, Vicksburg and Natchez."

She was traveling alone and with only one piece of luggage...an old worn out tapestry covered bag that used to belong to her mother. The strap, having long ago disappeared, had been replaced with a piece of rope.

As she waited impatiently, or maybe it was nervously, for her turn to board the bus, she fumbled with the rope as she listened through her headphones to an Allman Brothers song...Sweet Melissa.

Mindlessly and out loud, she was singing along with the words...

Crossroads,

will you ever let him go? Lord, Lord.
Or will you hide the dead man's ghost?
Or will he lie, beneath the clay?
Or will his spirit float away?
But, I know that he won't stay
without Melissa.
Yes, I know that he won't stay
without Melissa...

As she stood in line with these odd looking, most unfriendly people...who for whatever reason were going the same direction she was, she remembered all too well how much she hated it in the South and why she left.

"God-damn inbred, redneck hicks," she thought to herself. "Nothin' ever changes down here!"

She liked to believe that she had nothing in common with these people. That's what she told herself. More than a few times it got her to thinking how she should just give up on this crazy idea of going back and take the next bus back to Akron. But she put those thoughts away and boarded the bus anyway. What she needed to do was far more important than suffering through these people.

She was headed back to Tallulah Louisiana, the little town west of Vicksburg Mississippi where she knew she wasn't wanted. The reason she was going back is something I will tell you about as the story goes on.

She found a seat by a window, as far from the others as she could and she threw her bag on the seat beside hers so no one could take it. She plopped down and turned up the music...so loud that the man across the aisle could hear it coming from her head phones. He tried to get her attention, to tell her to turn down the music, but she ignored him.

The bus pulled out of the William Hudson Transit Center and headed south to pick up the interstate toward Jackson. After a few miles she took the earplugs out and finally acknowledged the man across the aisle, who by the way, had not stopped glaring at her the whole time.

She mouthed the words, "Eat me!" to him and then turned to stare out the window. By the time she could see the Memphis-Arkansas Bridge and the Mississippi River she was already lost deep in her thoughts.

She was as nervous and scared about going back as she was hopeful that she could put that piece of her past to rest. It had been a long, long time since she'd been back to Tallulah and that old house at 213 Connally Avenue. That was where her life stopped. She was going back to even a score.

"Once he raped me, it never stopped after that."

Melissa was talking to the prison psychologist at the Louisiana Correctional Institute for Women in St. Gabriel. The charges against her had been reduced to manslaughter and she accepted a plea bargain. She'd been sentenced to fifteen years. With a little luck and a lot of good behavior, the psychologist told her she could be a free woman in ten.

"He was a God-damn drunk!" Melissa said. "It was hard for me to walk home from school with my friends. I was scared to see him drunk, standin' on the street corner outside Dempsey's, screaming at the top of lungs like a God-damn lunatic! God that man had a lotta anger inside him! I hated him. I hated havin' to live in that same house with him."

"What was it that your mother saw in him?" the doctor asked. "He had to have some redeeming qualities for her to put up with all that."

"Not a single, damn one," Melissa answered. "She was scareda him too. When he was drunk our house was like the God-damn sheriff's station. The cops were always showin' up for one reason or another. The people who lived next door complained about all the bickerin' and fightin' that went on at our house all the time.

When the sheriff would show up, my mother would tell me and my sista to go hide under the bed. She said that if they saw us they'd take us away and send us somewhere like where Little Orphan Annie lived. The truth of the damn matter was she didn't want me or my sister tellin' the cops on him for beatin' us like he did."

"So he was violent with you and your sister?" the doctor asked.

"Are ya listenin' to what the hell I'm tellin' ya?" Melissa asked, losing her patience with the doctor who just didn't seem to be getting what Melissa was getting at...

"One time, that fat, bald-headed bastard come at my mother with a huntin' knife," she said. "Threatenin' ta cut us all wide open like a deer! That's when the three of us started sleepin' in the damn bathroom. My mother would put blankets down in the tub and a few pillows. We'd all sleep there. In the mornin' he'd still be passed out so we could at least get up and get somethin' to eat."

"Was there ever any peaceful times in your house?" the doctor asked. "Do you have any good memories of your childhood?"

"Nope!" she answered quickly. "Not a single, God-damn one. Unless of course the day I shot the bastard in the back of the head counts."

"I don't think talk like that is productive Melissa," the doctor said. "You don't want me putting that in your file. Let's get past this, OK?"

"Sure," Melissa said. "Sorry 'bout that. Here's a story that ain't so damn harsh. I can remember him comin' home drunk when I was in the fourth or fifth grade. He broke up all the TV's in the house and tore the phone off the wall in the kitchen. He made sure we couldn't call the sheriff no more."

"Did your mother know how what was happening to you?" the doctor asked.

"Look," Melissa said, fully exasperated by this point. "My mother and step-father had some serious God-damned problems. And they didn't want to deal with 'em, that's for damn sure. My step-father rapin' me was the least of my mother's problems. God, he used to beat her senseless."

"She never had him arrested?" the doctor asked.

"Hell no," Melissa answered. "They yelled at each other all the time. He'd call her a fat cow and a whore. She'd cry, but then come back at him, callin' him a fat, bald-headed bastard. I guess they didn't have much of a sex life either 'cause she'd make fun of him not bein' able to get it up. That's when he'd get really mad. He broke her nose one night and had to take her to the hospital.

When they asked what happened, she lied and said she fell down the stairs. The nurse didn't believe her and asked Carl...that was the bastard's name, Carl, if he'd step out of the room. He didn't want to but the nurse threatened to call the deputy who was just down the hall. He left, but he damn sure was scared she'd say somethin' 'bout what really happened."

"I take it your mother didn't say anything?" the doctor asked.

"I reckon not," Melissa answered. 'Cause when she come home later that night with her face all bandaged up, he was with her. That was as close as he got to getting' caught. He was like a cat...he had nine lives. She was takin' some kinda pain killa that knocked her out that night. He come for me agin."

"I must ask you this again," the doctor said. "You've avoided answering my question twice now. Did your mother know what was going on? Did she know how often he was molesting you?"

"You mean raping me?" Melissa shot back. "You mean fuckin' me? Hell yes she did. She knew about it every God damn time."

As the bus pushed further south, about thirty miles outside of Jackson, Melissa's eyes got heavy and she fell asleep. The worn and tattered old diary she'd been reading sat in her lap, open to a page where she'd written as a little girl about how the camellias used to bloom right outside her bedroom window and fill her room with the most beautiful smell.

From that bedroom window she could also see the fig tree in the side yard and the driveway. The driveway was covered with tiny white seashells. It led out to the street where the broken mailbox stood. It had been broken for as long as she could remember and she wondered why no one ever fixed it.

There were other things she could remember as well, but thinking of them was too painful. So instead she put the earphones back in her ears and listened to the last few minutes of Whipping Post. All those memories seemed like they came from a hundred years ago.

When the bus stopped in Jackson for thirty minutes she woke up, getting off long enough to go to the bathroom and buy a can of Mountain Dew and a bag of chips. She got back on and watched as the bus filled up with more of those people she'd come to hate so much.

The bus pulled out and headed due west on Interstate 20. In another hour she would be pulling in to the Vicksburg bus station on Frontage Road. From there she'd have to take a few local buses through Vicksburg and then cross over the Mississippi and into the little town of Delta Louisiana.

And from there, finally she'd pick up yet another bus that would take her across Highway 80 West, straight into Tallulah. It would drop her at City Hall on the corner of Green Street. Connally Avenue was about ten blocks to the north, just out of town. She'd walk the rest of the way with the rope of her bag digging into her shoulder.

"Things got really difficult for me when I hit fourteen," Melissa continued in another conversation with the psychologist. By this time she'd done five of her fifteen years. She never did believe they'd let her out after ten. She was certain she'd spend all fifteen locked up...

"I'd stopped sleepin' in the bathtub by that time," she said. "Carl started to get a little better. He'd stopped beatin' me so much. He wasn't drinkin' so much neither. He wasn't a stupid man. He knew how I would avoid him and stay out late with my boyfriend. Whenever my mother wasn't home, I'd make sure to stay away."

"Did that make you feel safer?" the doctor asked. "Did you think the abuse was over?"

Nope!" Melissa answered. "I told you he wasn't stupid. Pretty soon he started to just touch me again...like he did at first. But he kept touchin' me a lot and putting his hands down my pants. He put his fingers anywhere he wanted and I didn't like it. He started making me do things to him. He made me use my hand at first but pretty soon he made me use my mouth. It was terrible...disgusting! He smelled so bad and Jesus Christ...what a terrible taste it left in my mouth!"

"When was this happening?" the doctor asked. "Where was your mother? You said you wouldn't stay home when she was gone."

"She was right there!" Melissa answered. "She'd pretend not to know what was goin' on but she did. Carl was playin' her like a God-damn fiddle too...threatenin' to leave her and take all the money and the car. She was trapped just like Maddie and me was."

This was the first time Melissa had used her sister's name. Up to this point she hadn't mentioned her sister even once. The doctor saw it as progress...

"Maddie would just break down and cry for no reason," Melissa said. "That's how I knew he was doin' her too. She'd just break down and cry for no reason at all...in school, even in church. He was really messin' with her head."

"Did you tell your mother what he was doing?" the doctor asked.

"Why?" Melissa answered. "Why would I say anything? She wasn't gonna stop it. She just turned her head so she wouldn't have to admit her husband was rapin' both her little girls."

"What were you thinking about when Carl was doing this to your sister?" the doctor asked. "Did you feel any jealousy?"

"Jealousy?" Melissa barked. "What kind of a stupid God-damn question is that? Was I jealous? Hell no I wasn't jealous. I felt only hatred inside...hatred and rage. This is when I knew I was gonna have to do somethin' to get rid of this bastard."

"Is this when you started to think about killing him?" the doctor asked.

"You sure do ask a lotta stupid questions for a psychologist," Melissa answered. "What do you think? Do you think I was gonna buy him a God-damn bus ticket and ask him pretty-please to leave?"

"I am just trying to figure out what you were thinking," the doctor answered. "It's why we're here. If I can figure out what made you shoot your step father and your sister...and if I can feel comfortable with believing it, I can recommend you get out of here. I can recommend you be given a chance to go live the life Carl stole from you."

"When Carl wasn't drunk he'd become a different person," Melissa said. "I guess time was changin' him. He'd take me and Maddie places...like State Parks and other places. But I felt funny bein' around him. He would buy me anythin' I wanted. But I knew what he was doin'. He was tryin' to buy me off so he could have Maddie. He'd grown tired of me just like he'd grown tired of my mother. The things he bought me didn't make me feel any different about him though. I knew I was gonna kill him...I just didn't know how I was gonna do it yet...or when."

Something had been telling Melissa that she needed to go back to that house one more time. She tried to convince herself she just wanted to see if the camellias were in bloom. But I think what she really wanted to do was to confront her mother.

After she'd been arrested for killing Carl Benson and Maddox Talbott, she was sentenced to spend fifteen years behind bars at the Louisiana Correctional Institute for Women. The charges of first degree murder were changed to manslaughter and the jury found her guilty after forty seven minutes of deliberation.

The prosecuting attorney believed he could have won the case for first degree, but his boss, the District Attorney, was up for re-election and didn't want to take the chance of losing such a case just two months before election day.

I can tell you now that Melissa was paroled after ten years, just like the psychologist had promised she would. That time in prison had been difficult for her and it changed who she was. And I need to tell you that in all the time she was in that prison, her mother never once...ever, came to visit her. That was even more painful for Melissa...it left a deep and lasting wound in her heart. She made up her mind that she would never forgive her mother for it either.

After she was released, Melissa moved to Akron Ohio. An aunt lived there...her biological father's sister. They'd written back and forth to each other quite a few times while Melissa was in prison. Her name was Merle and she'd promised to help Melissa get on her feet once she was released...all she had to do was get to Akron.

Melissa had worked in the prison laundry for the last six of her ten years...making about 30¢ an hour. She'd managed to save a little of that money, no easy feat after buying cigarettes and gambling most of it away. But the day she walked out of that prison, through the same doors she'd walked in ten years earlier, she left with enough money in her pocket for a bus ticket.

She left LCI just after her thirtieth birthday. Ten years earlier when she showed up in the sally port of the jail, she got off the County Prison bus with that tapestry covered bag that her mother had given her...the one with the rope for a strap. In it were a few writing tablets, her grandmother's Holy Bible, a few pair of underwear and socks and a doll that had belonged to Maddie. She wasn't allowed to have any of things on the inside but on the day she was released they gave it all back to her...with everything inside it just like it had been when she'd arrived.

It was exactly 8:15 in the morning once she was finally outside the gate and out of that prison forever. She'd been given a pair of sneakers, a pair of white socks, underwear and a denim shirt with blue jeans. Dressed so conspicuously, she had to walk the two miles west on Highway 74 to the intersection with Highway 30.

Though she kept her thumb in the air the whole time, hoping for a ride, there wasn't much traffic on that stretch of road and anyone who was traveling there could see how she was dressed and would have known instantly she was a new release from the prison.

From the blinking light at that intersection she walked another half mile out Highway 30 to the Highway 30 Truck Plaza where she would buy her bus ticket and wait. It was 8:40 in the morning. The bus that would take her first to Baton Rouge and then north through Mississippi, Tennessee, Kentucky and into Ohio wouldn't arrive until 12:30. It departed at 12:55 PM.

Thirty one hours and nineteen stops later, she arrived in Akron at the Akron Bus Depot on South Broadway. Her Aunt Merle was there waiting for her, just as she'd promised she'd be. It was the first time they'd ever met. Merle had brought along an old photo album covered in lace that had a few photos of Melissa's father...back when he was a boy, when he'd joined the service and was heading off for Vietnam and on his wedding day when he married her mother.

"You look just like your daddy!" Merle said. "I swear. The resemblance is remarkable."

Melissa's father died a month or so after her sister Maddie was born. It was never discussed except to say he'd died of some kind of cancer. But Merle decided it was time for Melissa to know the true story...

"Your daddy was murdered," she said bluntly. "He owed some men from Vicksburg a lotta money, for what I do not know. But what I do know is they got tired of waitin' for it. Your daddy was a house painter and he got himself a big commercial job over in Monroe. It was the biggest job he ever had. He woulda made enough money to nearly pay those men what he owed 'em.

He'd spend the whole week over there in Monroe, livin' in a dirty motel room to save money. It was cheapa than drivin' back and forth from Tallulah every day. He'd come home on weekends to see you and Maddie.

Every week when he got paid his check, he'd pay his men first and then the salesman who sold him his paint. He didn't have no credit and to be able to keep workin' from one week to the next he had to pay cash money at the paint store.

He'd take a few dollars for himself to pay his motel room, buy a little food and a carton of cigarettes each week. He'd give the rest to your momma to hold. He didn't know it at the time, but she was already havin' an affair with that Carl Benson from over in Rayville. They were spendin' your father's money as quick as he earned it. When the job finished up he made arrangements to pay those men from Vicksburg.

He asked your momma for the money...close to $5200 as near he could figure. All your momma did was laugh at him and say she done spent it. He thought she was jokin' but of course he didn't find it funny at all. When he demanded the money and she told him it was gone...for real...well, your daddy got very mad. He hit your mother and nearly knocked her unconscious. He give her a big old black eye and she had him arrested.

You wouldn't remember any of this 'cause you was only a few years old. But your daddy had to spend thirty days in the jailhouse there in Tallulah and when he come out, them boys from Vicksburg was waitin' for him.

When he told 'em he didn't have their money...that his wife went and spent it all while he was workin' in Monroe...well, they dragged him into an alley and beat him to death with ax handles...split is skull wide open. Wasn't more than a month later that Carl Benson was sleepin' with your mother in your daddy's bed."

It came as quite a surprise to Merle when Melissa filled in the parts of the story that no one knew. Nobody had ever even imagined that Carl Benson was molesting those two children. When she'd gotten the news her niece was in prison for shooting him she just had to ask why...

"It made sense to me," Merle said. "I mean...I could understand why a bastard like Carl Benson would end up with a bullet in the back of his head. But it sure surprised me and a lotta other people that it was you that done it. Little Maddie though...I never could understand how you coulda taken that little child's life. Now it all makes sense. You never did mean to kill your sister, did you?"

Melissa just shook her head...

"Nope!" she said, almost in a whisper. "Never did mean to harm a hair on Maddie's head."

After Melissa had been arrested, her mother came to the Tallulah Jail to talk with her. She was in a frenzy and angrier that a hornet...

"I told my mother what he was doin' to Maddie," Melissa said. "Hell, he was still on top of her when the Parish Coroner came to the house to take the bodies. Any fool could see what he was doin to that little girl. Hell...he was still inside her belly."

"What did your mother say when you told her?" Merle asked. "She musta known something was goin' on."

"I'd tried to tell her many times what he was doin' to me," Melissa said. "All she said back to me was that Carl was a good man...that he loved me and Maddie like we was his own. He didn't mean us no harm.

That really hurt me Aunt Merle. It made me believe that deep down inside she knew I was tellin' the truth. But she'd already made up her mind. She wasn't gonna do a God-damn thing about it."

"Now Melissa," Merle interrupted. "Let's get somethin' straight right away. I won't have you talkin' like that and takin' the Lord's name in vain. I won't stand for it in my house. Do you understand?"

Melissa apologized for the language she used. She had absolutely no intention of changing the way she spoke or what she said, but she never let that on to her aunt. She just nodded her head as if she'd agreed. Then she went on with her story...

"When my mother refused to help me or to put a stop to the rapes," Melissa said, "I decided to break the family silence and tell somebody. I asked Miss Lutz, my gym teacher, if I might talk with her after school one day. She said she would listen to me...and she did. I told her how long Carl Benson had been raping me and how he he'd begun touchin' Maddie in places he shouldn'ta. I told her that was how it began for me. She told me straight up she believed me and that she'd make sure Carl Benson never touched us girls again."

The gym teacher took the story straight to Sheriff Boulais. The Sheriff took two deputies to the house at 213 Connally Avenue to get the bottom of whatever was going on. Of course Carl Benson denied everything. But what broke Melissa's heart was to hear her mother tell the Sheriff that her little girl was prone to lying and 'stretching her imagination.'

"But the Sheriff didn't believe either one of 'em," Melissa said. "They had me and Maddie fill up a suit case with clothes and a few things for a few days. They took us both right out of that house then and there. We was both placed with Ms. Carlene who owned the boardin' house on Chatham Street in Delhi...across from the Presbyterian church. Even though I was outta that house and away from that bastard..."

Melissa stopped to apologize for her language...

"Think nothing of it Melissa," Merle said. "In this instance I would tend to agree with you. If ever there was a bastard it was that Carl Benson."

"Even though I was outta that house and away from that bastard," Melissa continued, "I was still really torn up inside. My mother would call me every day to tell me to take back what I said about Carl rapin' me. I knew why she was askin' me to do this. Carl was the one supportin' her with money."

"It musta been terrible for you," Merle said.

"I had just turned my step-father in for rapin' me and molestin' my sister," Melissa said. "I needed to feel loved...I needed my mother's love and support and instead she made me feel even dirtier than I already felt!"

Merle listened to Melissa's whole story, in the car driving home and then again during dinner that first night. She worked in the food service department at the University of Akron and had a small house just a few blocks from the campus...on Franklin Street. She gave Melissa a few weeks to get accustomed to being a free woman and then told her that she'd been able to get her a job at the University too...working with her cafeteria kitchen. The extra money would come in handy for the household bills so she was expected to contribute.

Melissa stayed with her aunt for the next four years. She wanted to think she was ok...or at least getting better. But the truth of the matter was Melissa Talbott had an anger growing inside her again. The last time she'd felt this way she was capable of murder. What she was thinking and the emotions that were consuming her scared the hell out of her...there is no denying that now.

As I said, Melissa was going back to Tallulah Louisiana to take care of some unfinished business...to settle a score. And now she was back. I wonder if you've guessed what it was she'd come back to do?

As she stood at the end of the driveway at 213 Connally Avenue, she noticed two things right away...the driveway was no longer filled with tiny white seashells...like it was when she was a little girl. But yes, the camellias were in full bloom.

There she stood, bag in hand and a look of resolve on her face. In the bag she still carried her sister's little doll. But there was something else she carried in her bag now...something would settle things once and for all.

She stared at that old plank-board covered house where she'd grown up. It had been built up on cinder blocks because the little stream behind the garage would flood every year with the spring rains…leaving the ground wet and soggy for weeks.

The honeysuckle that climbed the front porch posts was in bloom too and for just a few moments she was able to see beauty in it. But the beauty turned to dread when she remembered the pain it had once caused. Whenever she or Maddie were bad girls, they had to cut a switch from the vines and take it to Carl. A honeysuckle switch doesn't cut the skin but it raises a welt and the juice from the flowers stings and burns like acid…

The house had not been painted in a long time and she could see bare wood where the old paint had blistered and peeled. Her father had painted it the year he died. It was doubtful if anyone else had taken a brush to it in thirty years. She was three years old back then...closer to four when he died. Her mother, not one able to be alone for long, bounced back shortly after she buried her husband. She said that was when she met Carl and they fell in love. But Melissa knew differently now. She knew the truth about Carl Benson and her mother...

"All was right in the world in my mother's eyes," Melissa remembered telling the psychologist in one of their many sessions. "She had a man in her life again. It was almost like my father never lived or never died."

But as I said, now she knew Carl Benson had been in the picture for a long time. And when she thought about how her mother had lied to her about her father's cancer and now knew the way he really died...well, it only served to fuel her hatred of her mother all the more.

Stepping onto the front porch, Melissa pushed the front door open, surprised to find it wasn't locked. She stepped inside. It was filthy...cobwebs hung in the corners of the windows...stains ran down the wallpapered plaster walls from where the roof had leaked. The air inside held a foul smell...as foul as the memories she had carried with her all these years. And one by one those memories began to play out in her mind, kind of like a silent, black and white movie the way she explained it...

Back in the day, all the front rooms had been kept closed off...nobody was allowed in them. But she didn't care. She didn't leave her bedroom all that much. In the living room there was a couch that was kept only for company...it was covered in plastic. No one was ever allowed to sit on it.

Her mother kept other precious things in there as well...ceramic figurines, a snow globe that once wound up played the song Waltzing Matilda. And of course the family Bible used to be in there as well. There was an old piano that nobody played. On the coffee table were books about being saved, dropped off by the Jehovah Witnesses that came through the neighborhood every Saturday morning like clock work. She wasn't allowed to touch any of those things either. The doors to the room were always kept closed and locked.

But the irony of it all was that no one ever came to visit them any way. Carl was a drinker and a violent man. No one in town liked him. Everyone steered clear of him and Melissa's mother.

Looking into the living room, she immediately remembered an old lamp on the breakfront cabinet that she loved so much...

"There was a sea shore scene painted on the shade," she recalled to the prison psychologist. "And it would revolve in circles when the bulb was switched on. It looked like the waves were rolling softly, gently on to the shore. I could sit for hours and watch it go 'round in circles."

But the seashore lamp was no longer there...either was the Bible or the Watch Tower Tract pamphlets. She thought to herself it was only logical. Even God had abandoned the house on Connally Avenue.

She walked down the hallway and came to the room that she shared with Maddie. Her body began to shake and the acid in her stomach began to rise. It was all she could do to push open the door and look inside. Expecting to find something else, she was surprised to see it was empty...just the four walls with sagging, drooping wall paper. Even the carpet had been torn out.

Flashes of memory began to come back to her...slowly and indistinctly at first. But soon each piece of furniture began to fill the room of her memory...the dresser...the rocking chair...the little desk in front of the window.

Then the bed appeared. On top of it was a little girl. She couldn't have been much more than twelve…maybe thirteen years old. She was crying. But there was no sound to be heard. Her little wrists were tied to the headboard and a man…a naked man, was on top of her.

It became too much to watch. She could feel a hot, foul liquid rising up from her belly and burning her throat. She fought it back. In her hand she held a gun…a pistol. It was big and it was heavy and she had no idea how to use it. But with both hands she held it out in front of her…shaking…crying…screaming inside.

When it went off, it was so loud it deafened her for a few moments. The naked man on top of the little girl was shaking and his left foot was kicking. Then it stopped. Everything stopped. Time stopped. The world stopped…everything came to a halt.

With the gun still held out in front of her she walked closer to the bed. At the base of the naked man's head, just in the middle of his neck, there was a round, red hole that was becoming white all around it. She continued to move around to the side of the bed. What she saw made her scream in agony. It wasn't the dead man that made her cry out…it was Maddie beneath him.

The bullet had entered the bottom of the man's brain and came out of his head just about his nose. The coroner had testified that the bullet continued into Maddie chest. That was how she died. Melissa made a fist out of her right hand and held it up to cover her mouth, trying to stop the vomit that was now exploding and flying everywhere.

"I dropped the pistol and it spun beneath the bed," she told the detectives when she'd been arrested for the murders. "I remembered hidin' beneath that bed to escape the rage of the man I just shot…the dead man who was now sprawled atop my sista."

In her vision she was looking at the man again, then at the little girl beneath him. She saw the man's naked back...his hips and buttocks moving up and down...up and down...up and down. Faster and faster. Her head began to throb and she could hear her sista whimpering and crying. She could hear the man grunting and panting...out of breath. All those noises swirled around in her head and became so loud inside that she couldn't stand it any longer. She had to run. She had to get out of that room.

She spun around violently, nearly losing her balance. Just before she ran from the room she caught a glimpse of those camellias outside the window.

Coming back was the wrong thing to do. It made nothing better and everything worse. The ghosts that hung in the wind and blew through her life were destined to follow her wherever she went. She would never be free from the chains that bound her soul...her wrists would forever be tied to that headboard.

She backed away from the bed, bumping into the dresser, then into the rocking chair. She spun and ran from the room. Scrambling down the hall, she tripped and sprawled head first into the archway of the dining room.

That is where she came face to face with the devil. It was Judgment Day.

Two years before she'd told anyone about being raped by her step-father, Melissa wrote in red paint on the wall in the tool shed that she was going to kill the man who'd done that to her. "I will kill you," was scrawled across the wall. When Carl saw it, he became furious. Violently he grabbed Melissa by her wrist and dragged her and her little sister out to the shed, demanding their mother come too.

"I demand to know who wrote this," he screamed. His face was twisted and distorted with rage. He demanded their mother talk to her children and force a confession...

"Whoever the hell wrote this will have to deal with me!" he threatened. "Now I want answers!"

Both Maddie and Melissa denied it. They swore they didn't know. But Carl was not satisfied. He made both the children go out and cut a switch from the honeysuckle vines...

"I want your sorry little asses back here in two minutes," he demanded. "And with two switches." He handed Melissa his pocket knife. "And bring 'em back here to me. Understand? We're gonna get to the bottom of this little mystery...I guarantee!"

Right there in the yard he had both the girls strip down to their underwear. Then he went about whipping them both until one of them confessed. It was Melissa, wanting to save Maddie all that pain, that broke down first.

"Why would you write such a thing?" her mother demanded to know. "This is a good man! He supports us now that your daddy is dead. You will apologize to him this instant. Then you will clean those filthy words off that wall!"

But Melissa said nothing. She didn't move...she didn't even blink her eyes. She wanted to tell her mother everything right then and there but in the back of her mind she'd remembered what Carl warned her of as he climbed off of her after the first time he'd penetrated her...

"If you breathe as much as a single word about this to anyone," he warned, "your little sista will get it even worse. This is our little secret Melissa. Do you understand me? Don't make the mistake of thinking I won't do it neither. This stays just atween the two of us. I love you baby girl. Do you know that? Do you believe I love you?"

All she could do was nod her head. She was shaking so badly she couldn't speak...

"Good baby girl," he said again. "I knew you'd see things my way. Trust me, you may even get to like what we are doing...you'll see. You'll love me just like I love you."

Melissa pulled herself to her feet by holding on to the archway at the dining room. One of the two tall wing back chairs that used to sit in each corner of the room was turned toward the window, facing out into the side yard. She could see someone sitting in it. She knew who it was...she knew it was her mother...

"I come back to kill you too!" Melissa said. "It's judgment day mother. You need to pay for what you done to me and Maddie."

"I died fifteen years ago," the woman sitting in the chair said without turning around or showing her face. "You're too God damned late! I died when my baby girl died and they took you away for killin' her. I knew what I done was wrong. My heart broke that day and my soul is black and cold now."

"Turn around and look at me mother," Melissa demanded. "I want you to see who does this to you."

When her mother stood from the chair and turned around, it took Melissa's breath away. She'd become old and ugly and broken...

"How did that make you feel mother?" Melissa demanded to know. "How could you live with yourself knowin' you betrayed your youngin's?"

"It made me feel real, real bad," her mother said. "It made me feel terrible...deep down inside of my heart. I knew what was goin' on all the time. I knew what he was doin' to ya and I did nothing to stop it. I tried though."

"You did nothing!" Melissa screamed. "You turned your eyes away from our sufferin'."

"That isn't true young lady," her mother answered. "That just isn't the truth. I tried to get you away from this house as much as I could. Don't you remember how I signed you up for swimmin' lessons at the YWCA. And for Girl Scouts. I even wanted you to play softball so you would be gone on Saturday mornings when I wasn't here. But you didn't really like those things all that much. What was I supposed to do?"

"Do you have any idea how pathetic you sound?" Melissa demanded. "You turn my stomach mother!"

"I loved you baby girl," she answered. "But that man had a power over me. I always stood up for you."

"Don't you evva call me baby girl again!" Melissa demanded.

"You just don't remember," her mother added.

"You turned on me mother," Melissa screamed again. "I did everything you asked of me. I joined those teams because it took my mind off being raped. It kept me away from this house, just like you'd wanted. Then why did you turn on me? You were so cruel to me...so mean. All those horrible names you called me. All those insults. Do you have any idea how much it hurt? Why mother? Why me?"

"Because I was jealous of you!" her mother hissed. "He didn't want me no more...he wanted you."

"You were of no help to me," Melissa screamed. "Or to Maddie. You abandoned us. You chose him...you let him rape me then you turned your back on Maddie. You were always putting us down...calling us names.

All the time I was wondering, "Why me? Why am I going through all this pain?"

"I swear baby girl," her mother said, now weeping uncontrollably. "If only I could turn back the hands of time, I would not have let anythin' happen to you or Maddie. But I didn't say nothin' because it was like he controlled my mind or somethin'! He kept tellin' me how much he loved you children. I knew he didn't love me no more. I didn't do anythin' because I knew he'd leave...he'd go away. How would we have survived baby girl? Tell me...what would we have done?"

For the first year or so in prison, Melissa suffered from terrible night mares and flashbacks of killing her step father and little sister...

"I couldn't eat...I couldn't sleep...I couldn't get any of it out of my head," Melissa said. "I got to the point where I didn't wanna live no more. I tried to hang myself with a bed sheet and all they did was throw me in a room with a big window so they could watch me...the lights were on twenty four hours a day. I had to piss and crap in front of them people mother! Do you have any idea how humiliatin' all that was?"

Melissa was eventually admitted to the prison hospital where she was finally able to talk with someone who wanted to hear her story...

"Somebody finally knew what I'd been going through," Melissa said. "Finally...I found someone who cared. She made me kneel with her and pray that I could become strong enough to put all that behind me. She'd come by every Sunday mornin' to take me to church with her at the prison chapel.

I was beginnin' to feel better about myself when I was goin' to church. The only thing that was helpin' me was knowin' God understood what I went through. But then one day I figured out God always knew what I went through. And He never did nothin' to stop it either! What kinda God would allow a little girl to be raped like that? Why kinda mother would do nothing to stop it?"

"You need to do what ya come here to do baby girl," her mother said. "I've been prayin' you'd come back. 'Course I didn't think it would be like this. But it makes sense...don't it? Go ahead...let's get this over with. I'm tired. I wanna go home to Jesus now."

From where Melissa was standing she could see where she'd dropped her bag when she came in the front door. Slowly she walked over to it and reached inside, fumbling to find the pistol.

She walked back to the archway and pulled the hammer back until a bullet rotated into line with the firing pin.

When it went off, it was so loud it deafened her for a few moments....just like the first time. Her mother fell to the floor, collapsing like a blanket onto herself.

Then everything stopped. It all stopped. Time stopped. The world stopped...everything came to a halt.

She looked at her mother laying face down in a heap on the floor. A small stream of blood was snaking across the wooden boards, coming slowly toward her. It just kept coming...it didn't stop. She couldn't take her eyes off of it.

When it finally touched the tip of her shoe, she heard a second explosion and then felt the bullet passing through her head behind her eyes. The pistol fell to the floor, spinning beneath the dining room table.

Melissa's Aunt Merle had learned about Melissa's suicide and the murder of her mother a few days after it happened. The police, during their investigation, went through Melissa's bag and found a stack of letters...letters written by Merle Stuempfle of 610 Franklin Street in Akron Ohio, addressed to Melissa Talbott c/o The Louisiana Correctional Institute for Women in St. Gabriel, Louisiana. In a matter of minutes they had Merle's telephone number and gave her the bad news.

It became Merle's mission to bury Melissa beside her father and sister Maddie. She refused to identify her ex-sister-in-law's body or accept responsibility for burial. Having no other living relatives, Madelyn Talbott was buried in a pauper's grave in Monroe Louisiana.

There was a short service at the graveside for Melissa. Dr. Etheridge, the prison psychologist, drove up from St. Gabriel. A handful of Melissa's friends from high school were there too. Willie Ray Shaw, the young boy Melissa was 'messin' around with' in the tool shed the day they found Carl Benson's pistol even came.

But perhaps more telling of Melissa's impact on her little town was when Sheriff Boulais, the two deputies who had investigated the molestation claims and the four detectives who had originally interrogated her when she committed her first murders, all pulled into the cemetery single file in their police cars.

Merle had prepared a short eulogy to be given just before Melissa's body was to be lowered into the ground...

"I grew up here in Tallulah," she said. "Melissa's daddy was my brother. He died tragically. And while she was still too young to understand, Melissa came to see her father as the first person in a long line of people who would either abandon her or betray her.

I attended the Shiloh Baptist Church over on Highway 71. I know the Bible very well. I know the Bible is God's Word and that Jesus is the son of God and that we've been given the Holy Spirit who will dwell inside those of us who will but believe.

I also know that Melissa believed God had abandoned her. Like Saul, she was empty. Life seemed cruel and pointless. She walked around like a corpse. She had no joy. She found no peace. In this world she encountered people who showed her no kindness nor had any patience with her.

She had no Fruit of the Spirit! How could she? How could she when she believed with all her heart that God is a cruel God...a punishing God...a God who could turn his back on her?

Melissa became sick about a month ago. It was not a sickness of the body however...she suffered a disease of the spirit. A terminal disease. Her heart had become hard and her thinking was that of a reprobate. She began having the sickest thoughts...blasphemous thoughts. I tried to set her straight with words of Scripture but the enemy had won and she'd surrendered.

But today, I know that the Spirit of God is with Melissa. And I believe she knows it always has been. It was her fate...her lot...her destiny in this life to suffer as she did, to be able to find God in the way He had determined she must.

I don't know why it had to be this way for her. I have prayed countless hours, asking God to tell me why such a life was required for such a sweet child. But it is not my job to question God. It's only my job to worship, obey and adore. I know who God is and I will continue to let people know who He is and how true and ever present he remains even though they may believe He has abandoned them.

Everywhere you go. Every place you look. No matter who you are. God is with you."

Vignette 6 ~ Emilio & Teresa

I WAS PRETTY YOUNG BACK THEN…maybe eight years old…nine at best, but I can still remember the sad story. News of it swept through our little neighborhood like a grass fire. Everyone was talking about it…over back yard fences or at their dinner tables. I remember seeing my mother break down and cry when they told her that her dear friend Teresa had suffered a stroke and died at the kitchen table earlier that morning, eating breakfast with her husband Emilio.

This is a story about love and devotion…

For as long as I could remember, Emilio and Teresa Bevacqua lived three doors up the street from us when I was growing up. I also remember that everybody in the neighborhood liked them. They were close friends with my parents and came to our house often to play a card game on any given Saturday night or to have dinner.

They came for Christmas and New Year's parties as well and throughout the summer they were always invited to barbeques in our back yard. Emilio and Teresa had no children but they were always very nice to my sister and me. As a matter of fact, they were nice to all the kids in the neighborhood.

An ambulance had been parked outside the Bevacqua's house since just a little bit after seven o'clock that morning. We'd all heard the siren come into our quiet little neighborhood and when it stopped up the street, everyone came out of their houses and gathered on the sidewalk.

Though she was a few years older than my mother, she and Teresa had become wonderful friends. So when my mother saw the ambulance parked in front of Teresa's house, its lights flashing and the back door wide open…well, my mother panicked and ran out of our house.

She was thinking something happened to Emilio. The thought never crossed her mind that something might have happened to Teresa. She got up to the front door and was met by a somber looking man wearing all white clothes…

"I'm sorry," is all he said.

My mother rushed past that man and toward the kitchen where she could hear Emilio's voice. He was talking to the other man from the ambulance who was also dressed all in white. There, lying on the floor on her side in front of the table was my mother's dearest friend. Her eyes still wide open as if she had been surprised by something or seen something she hadn't expected.

I don't think I will ever forget the look on my mother's face as she was walking back down the sidewalk to our house. She was sobbing and weeping. When she came in, her eyes were filled with tears and she had the most excruciating look of pain on her face. We were standing in the living room waiting for her...my sister, my father and me. She walked straight past all of us...straight to her bedroom. She closed the door behind her and stayed in there for an hour. My sister and I stood in the hallway outside her door and could hear her crying. We didn't know what to say or what to do.

Later in the morning of the same day, Emilio came to our house and knocked at the front door. My father answered it, but when the two men were face to face my father didn't know what to say. His eyes expressed sympathy and he felt great sadness in his heart for Emilio, but my father wasn't very good at expressing his emotions. Speaking compassionately or empathetically did not come easy for him...he just wasn't built that way. His own father was the same way...and, well there you go. The apple doesn't fall from the tree sometimes does it? And so the two men just kind of stared at each other for a few moments.

My mother had been in the kitchen making her meatballs when she heard the knock at the front door. That was how she dealt with bad news...she cooked. And since she'd learned of Teresa's passing earlier that morning, she'd been in the kitchen cooking and crying and asking God why.

She looked out and saw my father standing in the doorway talking to someone, but ever so quietly. Not being able to see who it was or hear what was being said, made her curious. Curious enough, to wipe her hands on her apron and go see.

She went to the door and looked around my father's shoulder to see her dearest friend's husband standing there, his face streaked from tears and the look of utter grief in his eyes.

"May I speak with you for a few minutes Mary?" he asked my mother quietly. Then glancing at my father he added, "Privately...if it's ok? Maybe you can come up to the house in a bit. I will need some help with my Teresa."

As odd a question as that was to ask my mother, she didn't even think twice before answering...

"Now Emi?" she asked. That's what she called him...Emi, short for Emilio I guess. When she said it, it sounded like she was saying Emmy. "Do you need me to come right now?"

"Yes," is all he could say. "Yes I do Mary. Please."

And so my mother untied her apron and asked for a moment to freshen herself and get her purse. It took but a minute or two for her to be ready...

"Is there anything I should bring with me?" she asked.

"No Mary," Emilio answered. "Nothing...nothing at all."

Slowly they walked down through our front yard and turned onto the sidewalk, heading toward Emilio's house. He was unsteady on his feet and had walked with a cane since being diagnosed with rheumatoid arthritis the year before. The pain in his hips and knees made it nearly impossible for him to walk some days. And so they took their time.

I was kneeling on my sister's bed, looking out her bedroom window, and watching the two of them slowly make their way up our street. I remember distinctly what it looked like...two friends, one grief. Even for as young as I was, I don't think I will ever forget it.

There was a long black hearse parked out front of Emilio's house. Two men in dark suits were standing beside it. They were from the funeral home and they'd come to take Teresa back with them. Emilio's brother Carlo had called the undertaker earlier that morning, after the police and ambulance left.

Emilio stopped walking when he got close to the hearse. He began to tremble, his cane dropping out of his hand and falling to the ground. He just stood there staring at it, unable to bend down to pick it up. The tears began to flow from his eyes. The poor man was lost...defeated. Grieving.

The two men from the funeral home, seeing that they were making Emilio nervous, left the side of the hearse and were now standing on the small stoop at his front door, waiting respectfully for him and my mother. Before Emilio could start walking again, he had to gather all his strength and resolve to say something important to my mother.

"I need you to show me how to put make my Tre beautiful today," he whispered, holding his breath and trying not to break down.

He had never called her Teresa...always Tre, since he first met her down along the river twenty five years earlier...

"Those men have come to take her away," he continued, pointing to the men on his front stoop. "I want her to look her best. We have been married for more than twenty years now. I always told her she was the most beautiful woman in the whole world...no matter what. I need you to help me make her beautiful again...one last time Mary."

"We will make her look like the belle of the ball Emi," my mother said. "I'll take care of everything. And you will help me. Are you ready now?"

He nodded his head and gestured to her that she might pick up his cane for him. He managed a bit of a smile when she put it back in his hand. Then they started walking again.

When they reached the small front porch, Emilio ignored the two men from the funeral home, turning his back to them before opening the door to his house. He gestured for my mother to go in first. She politely nodded to the two men, saying hello, but Emilio still refused to acknowledge them.

It is important that you know he was not being rude, I assure you. But in his mind, if he acknowledged them he would have to admit that his dear Teresa was dead. He wasn't ready to do that yet. It would come...in time, but that was not that time.

"We tried to explain to Mr. Bevacqua's brother that we will take care of these things for Teresa after the director prepares her body," one of the men said to my mother. "But we understand Mr. Bevacqua wishes to do this himself. And so of course, we can wait. It's not a problem for us whatsoever."

Emilio could not help but look at the men after what they'd just said. He struggled a smile at them. He led my mother by the hand down the short hallway to a bedroom where Teresa's lifeless body lay on one side of the bed, her hands folded over chest. The men from the ambulance had been thoughtful enough to close her eyes.

She was still dressed in her nightgown and robe from the morning. Beside her, Emilio had laid out her favorite dress and all the other things he thought a woman would need to wear beneath her clothes on the day of her funeral.

On the other pillow, the one on his side of the bed, lay a pair of silver earrings, each holding a perfect white pearl. There was her silver watch as well and a necklace that he had bought for her in Venice when they visited Italy a few years before...

"Oh Mary...how she loved that necklace!" he said, slowly shaking his head and grimacing. "She said it would remind her always of the gondolas and the canals, the food and the music of Venice. She loved Saint Marks Square the most. We were going back next year...did she tell you?"

But he didn't wait for my mother to answer...

"I've already washed her face," he said. "I want you to show me how to put on her make up now...and how to brush her hair the way she wore it."

To say that my mother was nervous would be an understatement. It was very difficult for her to see Teresa this way. She knew her dear friend's spirit had already left her body but Emilio needed her at that moment and well, she would do anything for her dear friend, even in death.

"We'll put her stockings on first," she said. "Do you know if she has a new pair Emi? As I remember, she kept them in her top drawer of her dresser. Please...check to see if there is an unopened package in there."

And there was. She'd bought two pair when she'd found them on sale just two weeks before at Sterns Department Store. They were the ones she always wore...her favorites...the ones that were real silk and had the tiny, opaque black triangles around the top.

"I need you to lift her leg up off the bed for me," my mother said to Emilio. "Can you do that?"

Ever so gently he put both hands beneath her calf and lifted her leg. My mother began to pull the stocking over the tips of Teresa's toes but she hesitated for a split second. Teresa's feet were cold and getting stiff. My mother pulled her hands back for just a moment, not being able to do what Emilio needed her to do.

She told me many years later what had happened...

"I just froze for those few moments," she said, "in a panic. The reality of what I was doing swept over me and I nearly became ill. My dearest friend in this whole world lay dead in front of me and I was putting stockings on her legs for goodness sake! The whole scene was so surreal."

Emilio could not help but notice my mother's momentary hesitation. I guess it was obvious what she was feeling. He grimaced and shook his head when he saw the look of pain and anguish on her face. All he could do was close his eyes and keep praying beneath his breath.

My mother recovered soon enough though. She had to tell herself that what she was doing, while so very, very strange, was what her friend would have wanted her to do. With the next move, she pulled the stocking over Teresa's foot and her ankle. With one more gentle pull, she stretched it up over Teresa's smooth, cool calf, past her knee and up her thigh.

Knowing he'd seen her hesitate, she now worried about how Emilio was dealing with this strangely intimate process of dressing his dead wife. His hands had been shaking since they'd begun and now he was praying the Hail Mary out loud, in whispers, over and over again...

"Holy Mary...full of grace, the Lord is with thee."

"You're doing good Emi," she said, trying to reassure him. "Let's do the other leg now, ok?"

The two of them worked together to finish Teresa's stockings and then my mother gently and delicately got Teresa into a bra and her slip. Emilio had chosen the dress Teresa had always joked she wanted to be buried in...the one with the black empire collar and the white buttons.

It was easy to get the dress over her head and shoulders but because Teresa was getting colder and more stiff as the minutes went by, my mother struggled to get her fingers through the sleeves and to pull Teresa's arms through. That's when she began talking to her friend, just as if it was any other day...

"Can you help me here a little Teresa?" she asked. "Just give me your fingertips honey. Let me pull your arms through, OK? Then we can take a little rest."

Once the dress was finally on, my mother smoothed it over Teresa's shoulders and down the front...pulling it gently over her stomach and hips and spreading it just so across her knees.

"Ok, Emi," she said. "Let's make her beautiful now!"

Teresa was an Irish girl and had the greenest eyes and the most beautiful auburn hair. Her skin was as smooth and white as porcelain. My mother picked out just the right eye shadow and coral lipstick from the dressing table Teresa kept in the corner of the room. As she was getting ready to begin the make up, Emilio stopped her…

"Please Mary…I want to do it," he said. "Please. Will you show me how? I want to be the one who makes her beautiful today. Would you mind?"

"Not at all Emi," she answered. "Not at all."

In a matter of twenty minutes or so he had finished and done a darn good job. My mother rubbed a bit of rouge into Teresa's cheeks and lightly powdered her nose. Tears filled Emilio's eyes but he said not a single word…

"I'll tell the men in the living room that we're ready, ok?" my mother asked. "Why don't you get her black hat from the closet?"

"She's was so beautiful," he said, finally bursting into tears…tears that would not stop.

"Yes," my mother answered. "She still is. She will always be beautiful Emi. Why don't you stay with her for a few more minutes…I will get the men."

Emilio sat down on the edge of the bed and began to talk with his Teresa…

"This has all happened too quick Tre," he began. "I wasn't ready. I never got the chance to say goodbye to you or to kiss you one last time. Those thoughts to do something like that never crossed my mind. I believed with all my heart we would live forever, and if by some strange twist of fate one of us was going to leave, it would be me first."

They'd been sitting at the breakfast table in their little kitchen when Teresa must have felt the first signs of pressure building in her neck. She dropped her fork and with both hands, clutched at her face and neck. She fell back in her chair first, her jaw dropping down and the scrambled eggs in her mouth falling onto her chest.

Her body tensed when she felt the pressure rising from her neck and settling behind her eyes. She made an attempt to reach toward her husband but instead fell forward onto the table and then onto the floor.

Emilio dropped the cup of coffee he was holding, trying to stop her from falling. But it was too late. She landed on her left side and for a moment looked as if she was going to say something to him. Then her body tensed again, her eyes widened and she was gone.

"It looked as if she couldn't see me," Emilio told my mother as they'd been dressing her. "She reached out for me and I knew something was wrong...she was in trouble Mary and I didn't know what to do. I failed her. I'd promised her on the day I proposed to her, that I would be her knight in shining armor...that I would always protect her. But I failed her today, didn't I?"

"No Emi," my mother said, brushing the tears from his cheeks with both her thumbs. "Don't say such a thing. You were her knight in shining armor. She told me that all the time. I don't know why this happened...I've asked God a hundred times since this morning. I guess there are questions we are just not meant to have answers to."

Teresa's viewing was three days later and the funeral was the following day. We went to both as a family. I had to wear my Sunday suit and my sister wore a dress with white silk gloves and a little hat. There were a lot of people who showed up to pay their last respects to Teresa and to try their best to console Emilio. I was much too young to appreciate what was going on, though I'd been to the funerals of both my grandparents. There was so much crying and everyone seemed so stiff and hesitant.

My father wasn't very comfortable with death...he never had been, and so he didn't spend much time inside at the viewing, just long enough to kneel in front of Mrs. Bevacqua's casket, say a prayer and then bless himself as he stood. Instead of staying inside with my mother and Emilio, he went out with the other men who were smoking cigarettes and talking about baseball scores.

My mother stayed inside with Emilio though, right at his side throughout the whole viewing and the funeral the next day. She was a great comfort to him and he held on to her arm when he felt a few times as is if he was going to faint.

It was a strange thing to choose back in those days, but Teresa did not want to be buried. She had this fear about being beneath the ground ever since she was a little girl. I'd heard in the years after her funeral, that she'd fallen into an abandoned well on a farm her grandfather owned over in Eagles Mere and it took twelve men and nearly a whole day to pull her out. I have no idea if that is true or not but if it is, it would give credence to why she wanted to be cremated instead of buried.

At first the Catholic priest tried his best to talk Emilio out of it but to no avail. Emilio was determined to give his wife exactly what she wanted.

"I must protest Teresa's decision," the Monsignor demanded. "To cremate the body is a sin. The human soul cannot be treated in such a manner!"

"The way I look at it Father," Emilio said. "It's her soul and her eternity. It is what she asked me to do and I plan to keep my promise to her."

"Then knowing this," the Monsignor said, "You must know you are sentencing her to Purgatory! She will leave this world with venial sin darkening her heart. God, in his divine love and mercy, surely knows that Theresa has accepted Jesus as her Lord and Savior, but she will none the less need to purify her soul. Then and only then will your dear Teresa's spirit have the holiness and purity to share in the beatific vision in heaven."

"Father," Emilio said, "with all due respect, you are wasting your time if you are going to stand in front of me and tell me that Teresa McMahon-Bevacqua is not at this very moment in heaven. There has never been a better woman to walk on the face of this earth...and you know this!"

"Emilio," the Monsignor said, "I ask you to reconsider. Each of us stands in judgment before the Lord and we must render an account of our lives. You will have to answer for this decision. Are you prepared to stand before God knowing you defied his laws?"

"I will tell God that I was true to my vows," Emilio said. "I will continue to love, cherish, honor and obey my wife."

"But only until death parts you," the Monsignor insisted.

"Father," Emilio said abruptly, "this conversation is over."

After the Mass for the Dead, the casket is usually taken to the cemetery where a small ceremony takes place at the gravesite and the priest recites the Eternal Rest Prayer...

> *Eternal rest grant unto her, O Lord,*
> *and let perpetual light shine upon her.*
> *May her soul and the souls of all the faithful departed*
> *through the mercy of God, rest in peace.*

Emilio asked the Monsignor to say this prayer while Teresa's body lay at the altar, before she was cremated...but he refused.

It was a weeks later when I was playing in my yard with a friend from across the street when we saw a black car from the funeral home drive up and stop in front of the Bevacqua's house. We stopped what we were doing to watch the man get out of the car carrying a small box.

"I wonder why they always dress in black," Rocky asked me.

"Haven't got a clue!" I answered. "But it's creepy don't ya think?"

The tall, thin man dressed in a black suit knocked on the door and when Emilio answered, we watched as the man handed the box to him, nodding without speaking and then turning and walking back to his car. Emilio acted a bit surprised...holding it in both hands and slowly moving it up and down. It was heavier than he expected it to be.

I started out telling you that this was a story of love and devotion. At the time, I was ten years old and I had no concept whatsoever of what those two things meant. But six decades later now, I know very well what they mean. I understand completely how much Emilio and Teresa loved each other...

"We met in high school," Teresa told my mother at one of their Saturday lunches, "at a party a few of our friends were having down along the river in Sylvan Dell. It was 1942. We'd all just graduated high school and everyone was celebrating. When my girlfriend introduced me to him I found it odd that we had gone through school together, especially in a little town like this, and neither of us had really noticed or met each other before. But we sure did at that party!"

The two met in the summer before Emilio went off to war, like most of the other boys in town. They were together every day until he left for Fort Dix in New Jersey on the 16th of October 1942, exactly one week after he turned eighteen.

In those five months, Emilio and Teresa fell in love. They tried their very best to cram as much fun and serious talk into such a short period of time. She feared he wouldn't come back but knew enough not to say anything. You see, he feared the same thing.

He served as a medic in France and saw death and brutality and other things too horrible to describe. No young man should ever see such things. He came home in 1944 after being wounded in Saint-Lô on the 18th of July. He was on a battlefield tending to the wounded when Allied bombers began to drop their bombs on the American troops. Before the radio operators could communicate with their field headquarters to get the bombing to stop, Emilio and thirty four other GI's were wounded and sixteen others were killed.

When he came back to town, the first thing he did was go right to the McMahon house and ask for Teresa. He was standing in the doorway in his dress uniform, looking no longer like the young boy who'd left two years before, but as a proud man now.

"He was different when he came home," Teresa told my mother. "Different in good ways and in bad. He didn't joke or talk as much as he did before, he was very serious. But he communicated the deepest emotions to me through his eyes and the way his hands touched mine. I knew right then and there I was going to marry Emilio Bevacqua and he hadn't even asked yet!"

Emilio took Teresa down to that place along the river where they had met at the party and he got down on one knee. She said she could hardly breathe when he took the ring box out of his uniform pocket and opened it up.

"Every minute of every hour that I was away from you," he said, "I thought of this very moment when I would ask you to be my wife. I promise to love you and cherish you and obey you all the days of my life. Will you marry me Teresa McMahon?"

And of course she said yes. Six months later they were husband and wife.

Now, it was twenty years down the road and he was taking her back to that place one last time. Standing on the banks of the river, he held her in a way he'd never held her before. He tightened both his fists around handfuls of her ashes and tiny pieces of bone...no bigger than pebbles. It was time for him to say good-bye to her. There was a soft breeze blowing that day. He opened his hands and released her into it...

"You were always the most beautiful woman in all the world Teresa," he said out loud as the ashes drifted across the breeze and settled on the water. "I need you to wait for me again my dear...like you did once before. I won't be much longer. I beg you to wait for me."

Emilio Bevacqua died exactly seven months to the day after he released his wife's ashes to the wind. Weeks before he'd asked my mother to take all Teresa's things and if he himself should die, to give his to the Salvation Army across the river. He must have known his time was near...

"Maybe someone can make use of all my old things," he said. "I don't have much use for them any more."

My father and five other men from the neighborhood acted as Emilio's pallbearers. His brother Carlo delivered the eulogy. He talked about Emilio, the beloved brother. Emilio, the dedicated husband. Emilio, the war hero who repeatedly put himself in harm's way to save the lives of his brothers in arms.

"I don't need to tell anybody in this room," Carlo began, "why my brother was one of the most amazing people you will ever meet. You could have met Emilio for thirty seconds and known that this man...this man was someone special. I look around today and I see how many people he has touched, not in fleeting ways, but in a deeply profound, life altering ways."

Carlo nodded to a young man sitting in the front row, and then to the young woman sitting beside him...

Each of us has our own story of my brother. Each of us has a moment we cling to for something that was most characteristically Emilio. And the beautiful part about it is, they're all different. They're all different because Emilio was so many things to so many people. Whether it was his compassion toward anyone who needed it, or his incredible strength and relentless faith in God. For some it was his patience...for others, his obstinacy.

But there's one thing that he had in common with all of us. Whether it was his best friend of fifty years or the homeless woman he'd met on the street yesterday...Emilio loved us all. And with his whole heart for exactly who we were at exactly the moment he knew us.

My brother took us flaws and imperfections and all. All he wanted was for us to be happy. He believed that each of us has a journey we're in the middle of, each of our lives are in various stages and all Emilio wanted for any of us was to be happy."

Carlo talked for nearly thirty minutes that day...never pausing, never reading from a piece of paper. Carlo spoke straight from his heart.

"It was Emilio's wish to be cremated as well," he said, looking now at my mother. "And he asked you Mary to see that his ashes are cast into the same breeze on which Teresa has crossed over."

It was again a lot to ask of my mother, but he had depended on her for so many things since Teresa's passing. She knew what it meant to him, so of course she said yes.

It was my father who took her down the old Dell Road to the place Emi had described where he released Teresa to the wind. Just a bit west of Giordano's vineyard there was a clearing in the trees that ran along the river. Over the bank was a small spit of land that extended out into the water a few feet. Just across from there was the small island. That island was where Emilio, Teresa and their schoolmates all celebrated their graduation back in 1942. It was where he had proposed to her when he came home from the war. It was now 1964 and with exception of the trees getting bigger and the high water from a few floods washing things away, not much of the old river had changed.

My father pulled his car off the road and went back to the trunk. She hadn't noticed but after Emilio's funeral he'd taken a few roses from an arrangement near the casket. He'd taken them and kept them in the car for just this very day.

He waited for my mother to get out and when she did, she was holding Emilio's urn filled with his ashes...

"Let me carry that for you Mary," my father said. "Are you sure you want to do this?"

"I told him I would and I mean to keep my promise," she answered. "If you want to wait here I'll only be a few minutes. I will understand."

"No," my father answered. "I'd like to be with you if it's ok? It's important to me. I don't know how to explain myself very well Mary...but you've made me very proud of you in these last weeks. You are an angel Mary. I have no doubt about that. You are too good for this world. You are too good for a selfish bastard like me.

I've taken you for granted too much and for too long. I want you to know that it stops here...right now. I want to be a better man. I want to be a better husband. I want you to feel about me the way Teresa felt about Emilio because I feel about you the way Emilio felt about her. I've just been too proud and too damn stupid to show you. It changes today sweetheart...I swear."

What my father said that day made my mother burst into tears. She wasn't ready for it. She wasn't ready because she'd never heard him speak like that before.

He helped her over the guard rail and then went down over the slippery bank first, reaching back to help her down. Together they stood along the water's edge. My father took the lid off and placed Emilio's urn and his ashes down on a flat rock along the river bank. My mother took a handful of them in each of her small hands and began to say a prayer for her friend. Emilio loved the 23rd Psalm...

"The Lord is my shepherd. I shall not want. He maketh me to lie down in green pastures, he leadeth me beside the still waters. He restoreth my soul. He leadeth me in the paths of righteousness for his name's sake. Yea, though I walk through the valley of the shadow of death, I will fear no evil for thou art with me. Thy rod and staff they comfort me. Thou preparest a table before me in the presence of mine enemies. Thou anointed my head with oil, my cup runneth over. Surely goodness and mercy shall follow me all the days of my life and I will dwell in the house of the Lord for ever."

As she prayed this Psalm, the wind picked up a bit. It made her smile for she knew it was Emilio. He was telling her he was ready to go and so very impatient to see his Teresa again. So when she finished her prayer, she stretched both her arms high out in front of her, opening her fingers and letting the dust float out into the breeze over the slowly moving water.

All this time, as my mother was saying her prayer, my father had been pulling the petals off the red and white roses...one by one until he had a handful. And then with one sweeping gesture, he tossed the rose petals out onto the surface of the water. He took hold of my mother's hand and together they stood watching them float away in gentle orbits.

After they'd both had their moments of silence and personal thoughts of Emilio, he gestured for her to start back up the bank. Again, he went first and reached back to help her up. Holding on to her arm to steady her, he helped her over the guard rails and out onto the quiet, empty country road.

They drove home in silence. It's hard to know what my father was thinking. As I said, he wasn't very good with his emotions and what little he'd bared down at the water's edge with my mother was pretty much an anomaly for him.

But my mother was satisfied. She reveled with what had happened over the last weeks and months. She'd lost her dearest friend and then a man she respected as much as her own father. She would miss them both terribly for a long time to come. But she wore a smile for the whole ride back, knowing that she'd been a good friend to both of them.

But honestly, I think that what she was most thankful for and pleased about was the experience she had with her husband down by the water that day. He'd shown a side of himself that she never knew existed but always prayed she'd see one day. She was certain that God had something to do with it...sure that He'd entered my father's heart and opened his eyes.

Emilio and Teresa Bevacqua loved each other genuinely, deeply and dearly. They honored the vows they'd made to each other on their wedding day and they lived lives of honesty and integrity. Emilio was a brave and honorable man. Teresa was a loving and generous woman. Together they made quite the couple.

I was always curious as to why they never had any children. My mother explained it to me one day, without explaining it really. She told me that the wounds Emilio had suffered in the war kept him from being able to have children of his own...

"That's why they loved all you kids in the neighborhood as much as they did," she said to me. "To them, all of you were their children."

What I did not tell you in this story was how incredibly generous and kind Emilio and Teresa were to the children in the neighborhood. We couldn't wait to go trick or treating at their house. At Easter they had Easter Egg hunts in their yards and they always seemed to do special things for us at Christmas. Amazingly, they remembered each and every one of our birthdays...each year we would get a birthday card with a dollar bill in it.

But there is one special story that I need to tell you...of Danny and Patty Jacobson, the two children that they took in and raised for five years. It happened before my family had moved on to the block in 1955. They were the young man and young woman sitting in the front row as Carlo eulogized his brother.

Danny and Patty's father, John Jacobson, had been killed in the Korean War. He was older than most of the men he fought with and even had a family back home in the States which few of them did. His wife Dorothy had begun to suffer from depression in his absence and he had made a special request to be discharged to take care of her. Sadly and ironically, his family emergency discharge papers were approved the same day he was killed.

On August 31st 1951, at what became known as the Battle of Bloody Ridge, John Jacobson was one of the thousands of men, young and old, who were slaughtered in the incredibly violent and fierce fighting along a string of desolate and muddy mountain tops just north of the 38th parallel in North Korea. He died in the rain.

Danny was fourteen at the time and his sister was eleven, going on twelve. They lived in a house with their mother down on Fleming Street, a few blocks away from our neighborhood. When the men from the War Department pulled up in front of their house to deliver the news no soldier's wife ever wants to hear, it was more than Dorothy could take.

Within a week of receiving news of her husband's death, Dorothy sunk into a depression so deep that she committed suicide by hanging herself from a rafter in the garage behind the house. It was Danny who found her when he came home from school that day and took her body down. Danny and Patty had become orphans.

They had no other immediate family and it was not long before the County social workers were making plans to put them into foster care. This is where Emilio and Teresa came into their lives.

They volunteered to become Danny and Patty's guardians. They requested the children come live with them so their schooling and church and life itself was not more disrupted than it had already become. A court hearing was held and the judge signed the guardianship papers the same day.

I am going to make this brief because all the details aren't really necessary...only the outcome is what matters.

Emilio and Teresa raised those two children as if they were their own. When he turned eighteen, Danny applied to Villa Nova college near Philadelphia and was accepted. He wanted to become an engineer. The Bevacqua's paid for everything.

Patty had met a young boy her senior year in high school. Their teenage romance led them to marriage after graduation. Emilio gave her away at the altar on her wedding day and a grand reception was held at the hotel across the river.

Following the deaths of their parents, Danny and Patty felt lost to the world. Danny did his best to remain strong for Patty's sake, but he would break down in tears out in Emilio's workshop in the back yard when no one was listening. But God was listening. In time his pain and suffering eased.

One of the lessons Danny learned from the tragedy that had destroyed his family was quite simple. Every time we think we've lost love and are all alone, God breaks through the dark clouds of our despair and pain and lets us know that He is love and He is never lost to us...and that there's always enough of Him to go around in the form of angels on earth like Emilio and Teresa.

Those two incredible people, Emilio and Teresa, taught many of us children in the neighborhood a great lesson, though I admit I did not know any of the story of Danny and Patty until just a few years ago when I was talking with my father on the telephone. He filled me in on the whole thing and all I could do was to sit quietly and think back on that sweet old man and his wife and how kind they were to me. The lesson I learned was just as simple as the one that Danny learned.

This relationship we have...between us and God, is one of the greatest mysteries in this Universe. It reveals itself in many ways, but in the instance of Emilio and Teresa, it was revealed in the simplest and most beautiful way possible...kindness and compassion to children in need.

Teresa was sitting with Patty one afternoon a few months after she and her brother had come to live with her and Emilio. She took after her mother...temperamental...prone to bouts of sadness and despair that could last for days. And although she was very grateful to Teresa, and expressed it often, she resisted loving her. She feared that should she allow Teresa into her heart, she would somehow be diminishing the memory of her mother. Teresa sensed the rejection and it hurt. But never once did she turn away from that young girl.

In the months after her mother's funeral, Patty was becoming angry and short-tempered. Her fight was with God...she was furious at Him...furious that He'd taken both her parents. But a quarrel with God can be terribly one-sided and so she lashed out at anyone who was in the way. Teresa made it her mission to stay in the way...to take the anger, to take the blows.

"Do you know that even before you were born, God knew you and loved you," she said. "God's love for us is unconditional. He loves us even when we don't believe in him."

It was a difficult concept for Patty to understand or accept. She wasn't ready...

"I know you don't believe this now," Teresa continued. "But in time you will. I want you to think of it this way. Emilio and I never had any children of our own. We couldn't. But in our hearts we had love for children we'd not yet met. You could say we loved you and your brother before we knew you. It is the same with God.

And when you are married, you will be thinking of starting a family of your own. You will find that love grows in your heart for these little souls you've not yet met. And you will love your children...for life. Just as you do this, so does God. God loves you for eternity. So open your heart today Patty. Forgive Him and begin to love Him back."

This is the lesson we all should learn just as quickly as we can. We must allow ourselves to be loved by the people who really love us, the people who really matter. We spend far too much time chasing after people who don't love us or don't matter and demanding or hoping or praying they will.

We are all just looking for someone to listen to us...someone willing to give us their time and their concern...to listen to our dramas and our difficulties. It is all so very important.

Vignette 7 ~ William T. Scarboro

"MY GREAT-GRANDDADDY'S NAME WAS WILLIAM T. SCARBORO."

My wife and I were having our lunch in a small diner in downtown Manteo on the Outer Banks in North Carolina several months ago and I could not help but overhear the old man's conversation over my shoulder. He was sitting in a booth behind us and telling quite a story to another man, much younger than he and looking rather out of place.

"Ya evva heeya a Scarboro Creek, down island from heeya?" the old man asked. "Well, it's named afta my family. We have lived righ' cheer in Dare County for nigh on two hunnerd and twenty yeeahs even though when my great-granddaddy's people come heeya it warn't known as Dare County. If my mem'ry serves me, I do believe where great-granddaddy's house was built was Currituck County at the time."

The old man telling the story was William Thaddeus Scarboro IV. And he was speaking in that dear and familiar coastal North Carolina drawl that my wife and I'd come to love so much since moving here the year before. My wife, being European, could barely understand what the man was saying but I could clearly make out every word and I must say, he commanded my attention for more than an hour.

That morning we'd decided to get up very early and take our small trawler from our home down in Arapahoe, and head northeast across the Pamlico Sound and up to Roanoke Island. I'd named our boat the *Amore Mio* and the night before I'd fueled her up and stocked her for the day. We were ready to go bright and early.

Well actually, we left well before the sun was up. I will no doubt be in trouble for revealing this, but my wife loves her sleep more than just about anything. So I need not tell you she was not the most enthusiastic first mate I'd ever had on board!

It's a good seven, sometimes eight hour run across all that open water, depending on the weather and the direction of the winds.

And I must say, it is best attempted before the morning sea breezes start to kick up the chop out there on the Sound.

My first mate fell back asleep almost as soon as we were under way and she didn't wake again until we were well north of Stumpy Point. That is where I came to a northeasterly heading in order to cross the bay on a steep angle and come into Roanoke Sound between Duck and Hog Islands. But I hadn't minded the morning solitude. The smooth water and the sun coming up off my starboard rail gave me plenty of opportunity to think a bit about the day and what I'd hoped to accomplish.

Now if you'd have asked my wife, she'd have told you the purpose of our little jaunt was really to just get away together for the day...to get out on the water and enjoy the glorious environment that is coastal North Carolina. But I must confess, I had a bit different aim in mind. While we were on Roanoke Island, I thought I might do a little research for a new book I'm writing.

I am always looking for a new story and I'd read about the wreck of Blackbeard's pirate ship just off the Carolina coast, southwest of Hatteras at the Beaufort Inlet. A friend of mind, a fellow writer who lives out near Asheville, told me about the Outer Banks History Center up on Festival Island in Manteo...

"It is just a short ride across the causeway," he told me in a phone call one evening. "It's east of Manteo and could well be a treasure trove of information for you. I found it by accident one weekend when Kate and I were hiking on the barrier islands over there. We spent a good three hours inside. You should seriously considering going there for your research."

So that was my reason for this long run across open water. But I must admit, crossing it with my wife and being able to spend the day with her is worth its weight in gold to me. If I accomplished nothing else, it would still have been a perfect day.

We came in to the Manteo Marina through Shallowbag Bay. It was just before one o'clock by the time we tied off. I looked at my watch and calculated our time on the water to be just under eight hours. I paid two of the dockhands to hose the salt water off *Amore Mio* and top off the fuel tank while we were gone. While my wife looked after a few details aboard, I went in to the marina office to rent two bicycles for our excursion. The dockmaster, whose name was Tim Matthews, suggested he'd just add the rental cost to our dockage bill. And so I thanked him and we were off, headed into town...

"Where are we going?" my wife insisted to know.

"I want to spend a bit of the morning at the Manteo Town Hall on Budleigh Street," I answered. "I have some research I've wanted to do for a few weeks now. We won't be long, I promise. Then I'd like to ride across the Festival Park Causeway to the history center over there. After that...we'll do anything you want."

I'd expected a bit of an argument from her or at a minimum a disheartened groan, but when she readily agreed to do whatever it was I wanted and told me it was perfectly well for her to just spend time with me, well, I knew it was going to be a good day!

Town Hall was a nice place but did not give me much of the kind of information I was hoping for. So we got on our bikes and rode across the causeway to the history center.

By about three o'clock I'd gotten enough information and reference materials to get a good start on the story that I'd planned to title simply, "Queen Anne's Revenge"...which was the name of Blackbeard's pirate ship. I was fascinated to find out what I did about the ship. I hope you will forgive me if I share a little of it with you now before I get on with my story. My bet is you will find it interesting too!

Long before it had fallen under his command, Blackbeard's ship was owned by a wealthy Frenchman who had made a small fortune in the slave business for a decade and more. It was known as *La Concorde* and was piloted by a Captain whose name was Pierre Dosset.

On March 24th 1717, the 200-ton *La Concorde* left the port of Nantes in France, sailing west out of the Loire River to enter the Atlantic Ocean at St. Nazaire, ultimately bound for the Caribbean and the island of Martinique. She was armed with sixteen cannons and a crew of seventy five men, a mix of enslaved Africans and the rest were Frenchmen.

Traveling southerly along the western coast of Africa, *La Concorde* stopped in Benin in early July of 1717, taking on board five hundred sixteen captive Africans. Captain Dosset and his officers also received twenty pounds of gold dust from the African traders.

La Concorde finally set sail from Africa for Martinique on October 2nd 1717. It would take about eight weeks to cross the Atlantic and they followed a route known as the Middle Passage. By the time she had neared the end of its voyage, sixty one of the slaves and sixteen members of the crew had died from scurvy or dysentery, with another thirty six becoming seriously ill from the same.

By November 28th she was just off the coast of St. Vincent and less than one hundred miles from their final destination of Martinique. That's when she encountered two heavily armed sloops, one with one hundred twenty men and twelve cannons aboard and the other with thirty one men and eight cannons. The larger, more heavily armed of the sloops was commanded by an Englishman by the name of Edward Thatch. With Dosset's crew so weakened and thinned by disease, he was powerless to defend his boat or his own honor. Captain Dosset surrendered without resistance.

Edward Thatch and the pirate Blackbeard were in fact one in the same. The pirates immediately seized *La Concorde* and after running up their flag, set sail along with other two sloops for the island of Bequia in the Grenadines. Once there, Blackbeard ordered the French crew and remaining slaves put ashore. After removing the armaments from the smaller of the two sloops, he handed it over to Captain Dosset and his crew to be able to continue on their journey, defenseless as they were.

The French lost little time in giving their new and much smaller vessel the appropriate name of *Mauvaise Rencontre*, which in French means Bad Encounter. It took them two trips on their smaller ship, but they eventually succeeded in getting the remaining African slaves from Bequia to Martinique.

While anchored in Admiralty Bay off Bequia, Blackbeard began to outfit *La Concorde* to suit his chosen profession. She was ultimately fitted with no less than forty guns, assembled from a variety of captured ships. While searching the ship, the pirates discovered a young cabin boy hiding in a locker. His name was Louis Arot. It did not take long for the young boy, under threat of torture and his ultimate death, to inform Blackbeard's men of the twenty pounds of gold dust that was aboard.

Louis Arot and three of his fellow Frenchmen voluntarily joined the pirates, but ten others were taken by force including a pilot, three surgeons, two carpenters, two sailors and of course...the cook.

Blackbeard kept *La Concorde* as his flagship and rechristened it *Queen Anne's Revenge*. He sailed from Bequia in late November of that year, marauding through the Caribbean, taking prizes and adding to his fleet. He sailed north along the Lesser Antilles plundering ships near St. Vincent, St. Lucia, Nevis and Antigua. By early December he'd arrived off the eastern coast of Puerto Rico.

By April of 1718, Blackbeard's fleet and his growing band of pirates were of the Turneffe Islands in the Bay of Honduras. This was where Blackbeard captured the sloop *Adventure*, forcing the sloop's captain, David Herriot, to join his company or be killed. Of course the good captain acquiesced!

After that confrontation, Blackbeard's fleet began sailing east once again, passing near the Cayman Islands and capturing another sloop off the coast of Cuba, adding yet one more ship to his flotilla.

Turning north, they sailed through the Bahamas and were following the North American coast northward. The month of May found the *Queen Anne's Revenge* and three smaller sloops in Charleston Bay. In what is considered the most brazen act of his career as a pirate, Blackbeard and his ships set up a blockade of the port of Charleston for nearly a week. During the blockade, they seized several ships attempting to enter or leave the port. They detained one particular ship, the Crowley, and took its crew and passengers as prisoners.

As ransom for his hostages, Blackbeard demanded a chest filled with medicine and medical supplies. Once it was delivered, he was true to his word and released his prisoners unharmed. Soon after, he sailed out of Charleston Bay and continued on a northerly course along the east coast of what was known as The New World.

Soon after leaving Charleston, Blackbeard and his fleet came to the barrier islands along the North Carolina coast. They attempted to navigate the Old Topsail Inlet, now known as the Beaufort Inlet. But being unaware of the sand bars that show themselves only at low tide, both the *Queen Anne's Revenge* and the *Adventure* grounded themselves. The crews had little other choice but to abandon ship when even the high tides proved incapable of setting them free.

The following passage, from a deposition given by David Herriot, the former captain of the Adventure, explained what he'd witnessed take place...

"The Thatch's ship Queen Anne's Revenge run a-ground off of the Bar of Topsail Inlet. The Adventure run a-ground likewise about Gun-shot from the said Thatch."

There is another written account of the groundings, this one by Captain Ellis Brand of the HMS Lyme. In his letter to the Lords of Admiralty dated 12 July 1718, he wrote the following...

"On the 10th of June or thereabouts a large pyrate Ship of forty Guns with three Sloops in her company came upon the coast of North Carolina ware they endeavour'd To goe in to a harbour, call'd Topsail Inlet, the Ship Stuck upon the barr att the entrance of the harbour and is lost; as is one of the sloops."

In his deposition, Herriot further claimed that for some reason unexplainable, Blackbeard intentionally ran the *Queen Anne's Revenge* aground. He surmised it was an attempt to break up the company, which by this time had grown to more than three hundred pirates.

Herriot's assertion may have some merit as it is also written that Blackbeard, after looting all the plunder aboard both grounded ships, left behind many of the pirates, handpicking a special crew to sail out of the inlet on the third sloop which had not run aground

History tells us that Blackbeard's career came to an end at the Ocracoke Inlet further up the Carolina coast, six months after the grounding of the *Queen Anne's Revenge*. Having all he could stomach of the pirates in his colony, Virginia Governor Alexander Spotswood assembled an armed contingent of ships and men led by Royal Navy Lieutenant Robert Maynard.

They confronted Blackbeard and his crew just after sun up and in a desperate battle aboard Maynard's sloop, Blackbeard and several of his crew were killed. Maynard returned to Virginia with the survivors of Blackbeard's crew in chains as well as one grim trophy...the severed head of Blackbeard himself hanging over the sloop's bowsprit.

It was in November of 1996 that a wreck was discovered in Beaufort Inlet. After several years of intense research and examination, the wreck has been identified with considerable confidence as that of *Queen Anne's Revenge*, still with its forty guns aboard.

In all my novels, I prefer to have a narrator tell the story...a disinterested third person who talks to my readers as a friend. This narrator is joined quite often by my characters and the dialogue can get quite interesting. When I began to consider writing a book about Blackbeard and the wreck of the *Queen Anne's Revenge*, I of course knew I would have to come up with a narrator.

It was my dear wife, in a stroke of genius one evening as we were having dinner out on the patio, who suggested the story be told by the young Louis Arot...from the perspective of someone of the young boy who had survived the wreck on the sand bar and went on to witness the battle with Lieutenant Maynard. Arot would have escaped that confrontation as well and would be telling the story from a rocking chair on the front porch of a small home, within view of where the ship went down on the waterfront, in Beaufort where he'd settled after giving up the life of a pirate.

And so when the time comes that I start putting my story together, you all will get to meet Louis Arot and get to see a pirate's life from his young eyes.

As we were getting ready to leave the history center, my wife suddenly announced that she was hungry. Being married for as long as we've been, I've learned not to ignore such an announcement! And I knew exactly what she wanted. She wanted a good bowl of the Hatteras chowder that Manteo is famous for!

So I inquired to the woman behind the main desk as to where we might find our chowder and a pair of crab cakes to go with it. Along with such a scrumptious lunch, nothing but a cold bottle or two of Mill Whistle lager, a local beer, would do. The mere mention of the Mill Whistle Lager turned a few heads in the history center and brought four or five other people into the conversation. Almost unanimously, the Butter Bean Cafe down Highway 64...on the corner with Bowsertown Road, was recommended as our best prospect.

Now here's the story I began telling you before I became sidetracked with all that talk of the pirates!

From what I could hear, the younger man, the one who as I said looked so out of place in the diner, was sitting across the table from William T. Scarboro's great grandson, William Thaddeus Scarboro IV and asking questions. The man was a newspaper reporter for the News & Observer newspaper over in Raleigh. He'd learned that the last living descendant of any Civil War veteran from Roanoke Island was still living in Manteo and he'd driven all the way across the State to interview him. And it was my good fortune, as I will explain later, that the interview was taking place right there in the Butter Bean Café.

And if I might clarify something that I said previously. While it was true the reporter was asking Mr. Scarboro questions, in all honesty he only asked one or two that struck at the heart of the story he'd come to gather. Mr. Scarboro did all the talking and with the exception of a short break or two, he talked non-stop for the next two hours!

"Great-granddaddy was born righ'chere on January 12th in the year 1845. He come inta this world in an old wooden shack up where the airport is now. 'Acourse it's been torn down and bulldozed under for longer'n I've been alive," the old man continued. "There's a damn runway runnin' right over where mosta my family was buried. The County moved the graves when they wanted to put that airport there. Nevva did unnerstand how they got away with disturbin' a soul's eternal restin' place. Don't seem very Christian ta me."

He paused for a few moments before adding, "And believe it or not, William T. Scarboro died on the twelfth day of January in the year 1960."

"That would have made him one hundred fifteen years old when he died," the reporter said, after scribbling the two dates down on a napkin and doing a little math. "Are you sure about that?"

"Am I sure about it?" the old man snapped back. "What kinda damn stoo-pid question is that? You don't think I kin cipher as good as you? You don't think I know how old my great-granddaddy was when he died? Hell...I don't s'pose there's much good reason to be talkin'to you today."

The reporter apologized and tried to get back on track...

"What can you tell me about him," he asked. "What kind of man was he? I know he died before you were born, but what kind of stories did your family pass down? Any that you can share with me?"

"Sure," the old man answered. "I figured that's a why we're heah. I know a great deal about him. Ya see, when he come back home after the war...after Antietam and Gettysburg, then Camp Hoffman...well, he wasn't the same no more. He took to doin' a bit of drinkin' and carousin' I guess ya could say. But he eventually settled down...what with havin' just one leg and all. Mostly what he done after he got his anga outta his system, was to hole up in that wooden shack he was born in an' he wrote a few books. I got one of 'em righ'chere with me today. I figured you'd be askin' me about 'em. Want me to read a little of what he wrote?"

The reporter jumped at the chance and while the old man read I could not help but eaves drop...

I remembered from my history books a little bit about the Battle of Antietam. It took place in September of 1862, during what Shelby Foote, a famous war historian, called some of the most brutal days of the Civil War...

"The Union Army had been badly beaten at Manassas," Shelby writes, "and was in the midst of turmoil as President Lincoln fired one ineffective general after another. At this point, it still looked as though the Confederacy might actually win the war and secede from the Union for good.

Less than three weeks after the Confederate victory at Second Manassas, some 86,000 Union troops under 35-year-old Major General George McClellan clashed with 40,000 Confederates led by 55-year-old General Robert E. Lee at the Battle of Antietam in west-central Maryland. The 23,000 killed, wounded or missing by nightfall made September 17, 1862, the single bloodiest day in American history."

Now from what I know and remember, the battlefield itself is located on the far western edge of the State of Maryland...just outside the small town of Sharpsburg. My father took our family there one summer on a vacation through Gettysburg and Washington DC.

The battlefield has been preserved and is one of the most amazing historical undertakings I have ever seen. It quite literally looks every bit as it did at the time of the battle itself.

On a clear day, when the crisp wind is blowing across the tall grasses, you can almost imagine yourself in another time. You feel that if you looked up, you might actually catch a glimpse of a wave of weary soldiers, trudging on toward either death or victory. Of course, some people can claim to have done more than just imagined what went on...some people, like William T. Scarboro, had actually lived to tell and write about it.

The battle opened at dawn on the 17th day of September when General Joseph Hooker of the Union Army had his artillery begin firing on General Stonewall Jackson's men, who were bivouacked in a cornfield north of town. This is where William T. Scarboro IV began reading from his great grandfather's book...

"After a hurried march of more than two miles," the old man began, "we reached the field of battle & went immediately into action, slippin' through a piece of woods and straight into the face of a terrific fire of artillery and musketry. Several of the men who stood beside me were killed instantly. Other's retreated to the woods with very bad wounds. Many men hesitated and took shelter behind trees. Our Captain could not force them forward.

But the rest of us passed through the woods and crossed over a fence. We crawled on our bellies under a most gallin' fire of grape & canister from the artillery & musketry. More of our men froze and could not be rallied beyond the fence. An officer amongst us drew his pistol and threatened to shoot anyone who would not move. I mounted the fence & moved forward, completely exposed to the terrible barrage of fire which swept away everythin' before it.

I found shelter behind the trunk of a pine tree that had been splintered and exploded by a union cannonball a mere few seconds before I reached it. It exploded right before my eyes. I turned around to look back and I witnessed my entire regiment breakin' and retreatin' to the woods behind the brow of a hill...overwhelmed by confusion & disorder. I tried to get back to them, feelin' exposed even as I hid behind what was left of that tree. But my legs would not function. My brain would not allow me to stand. And my heart would not permit me to run."

As I listened to the old man read from his great-grandfather's book, I scribbled down as much of what he was saying as I could, trying not to look obvious. This would be the story I would take back from Manteo. This is why we'd come today! I cursed myself for leaving my tape recorder on the boat...

"The men who had retreated were soon joined by a Major and a Lieutenant, whose names I cannot recall for the life of me now," he continued to read. "They were ordered to form a left flank and were very soon into the engagement again. From where I hid, I commenced ta loadin' and shootin' with all my might. But damn if my gun did not get chocked after the fourth or fifth round. I picked up the gun of one of my comrades who had fallen by my side and I continued to fire.

I could barely see the second line of the enemy, but when their men would fall, the rest would close in and fill their places. Their first line was lyin' by a fence and I could see the old Stars and Stripes wavin' high over them. I fired as near as I could at the men around the flag. I do not know whether I killed any one or not durin' this time.

The left flank of my regiment was severely attacked and nearly destroyed. That Major ordered them to retreat until the reinforcements we were waiting for could join us. They were comin'…or so we were told. I was nearly tired to death."

It was at this point when the reporter realized he'd forgotten to turn on his own tape recorder. He interrupted the old man and asked if they might start over again…

"Nope!" was all the old man said. Then he went back to reading…

"Tired, scared as hell and discouraged, we still marched on. As we came in proximity of the main battleground, scores of wounded men passed before us, headin' to the rear. They were a reminder to each of us of the bloody work that lay ahead. A little further on, to the left of the pike, we stopped & were given the order to "load at will."

No sooner had we done that then the Yank's batteries give us shot & shell in an abundance so great as to cause muscular contractions in the spines of the entire line. But all the dodgin' in the world could not save us. Occasionally a shell, better aimed than the rest, would come a-crashin' through our line makin' for even more corpses & mutilated trunks.

The Major, seeing the replacements were nowhere to be found and concludin' they were not comin', took notice that we were in point blank range of the batteries. He ordered the left wing forward under the hill, makin' sure the Regimental Colors continued to advance along with us. In shoutin' at his Lieutenant, the Major was quite animated in his speech and mannerisms…

"We can take that unholy battery," he said, arms and hands wavin' wildly in the air. I was surprised he did not draw enemy fire. He ordered us all forward! "We can take it!" he exclaimed. "We can send these Yankee bastards straight to hell!"

We passed through a field strewn with dead and dyin' men. We moved from side to side to avoid the volleys of shot being laid down on us. We had almost reached the battery when the Major was struck in the cheek by a rifle ball, fired by an infantry soldier standing tall in rear of the Union ranks.

Still he pressed us forward to come within twenty yards of the battery. Just at this moment the guns opened upon us again and swept down the remnants of gallant men who had blindly and loyally followed the Major. The Major himself fell at the first discharge, being struck about the ear by a grape shot.

We were finally ordered to lie down in the field & let the stray shot and shell whiz over our heads and burst all around us. This went on for what felt like an eternity but the truth is, it lasted no more than ten or fifteen minutes. When the firin' seemed to dissipate and the guns were quieted considerably, we were then ordered to get back on our feet and march to the left, into the woods again.

Lyin' just in front of our lines was a great number of dead and wounded. One poor fellow lay just before me with one leg shot off; the other shattered and otherwise badly wounded. He was fairly shriekin' with pain."

The waitress stopped by to refill the coffee cups on their table. Mr. Scarboro took this as an opportunity to take a break from reading and excused himself to use the rest room. While he was gone, the reporter had a near catastrophe. As he was haphazardly shuffling his papers he dropped his pen on the floor. Reaching for it, he bumped the table with his shoulder and knocked over his glass of water. The water drenched his note pad and then his pant leg when it ran off the table. I found him to be a most disorganized person and wondered how he could possibly be a reporter. When I whispered that to my wife, her response amused me...

"Maybe he is like that American detective," she said. "What is his name...Colombo?"

I smiled and shook my head at her answer...

"Maybe he is indeed!" I said.

I sat quietly in our booth, going over everything I had heard and managed to capture in the conversation behind me. My wife had eaten her bowl of chowder and her crab cake and was picking at mine. Even my bottle of lager had become warm.

I could not have found such a wealth of information for my writing had I read every book in the history center and gone through every single record in the Manteo town hall. I had truly hit the jack pot.

Mr. Scarboro returned to the table, taking notice the puddle of water on the floor and the reporter's wet pant leg. I honestly wondered if he thought the poor man urinated in his pants.

I also found it a bit amusing that he returned carrying a single piece of pecan pie for himself, none for the reporter. Before he started to read again, he cleaned the entire plate and finished his cup of coffee. He picked up right where he left off...

"There was no halt ordered for us," the old man continued, after finding where he'd left off. "Not until we reached the northern boundary of Miller's corn field. That was where we first came face to face with our enemy. They had set up another battery on top of the hill and they were firin' over us. After an hour of the most ungodly fightin' I had yet to see in the war, our line silenced those guns. We silenced them but we could not capture them.

A period of quiet for a few minutes followed, but then another infantry line appeared on the crest of that hill and engaged our line almost immediately. It gave the Yanks time to re-man their guns.

The flag of my regiment had been shot down at least a half-dozen times before it disappeared for good. Each time, another Johnny Reb soldier had picked it up and carried it a bit further into what came to be known that day as Bloody Lane.

Our line did not advance any further. Instead we kept our same position. The next move the Yanks made was in our immediate front. They were tryin' to get another big gun in position to bear on us. They came up in a gallop of horses but we were able to kill or wound nearly all of 'em. The artillerymen were left defenseless and they soon disappeared as well…all in a failed effort.

How aptly that road was named. It had truly become a bloody lane as we advanced into yet another cornfield. The fences were down on both sides of the road and the dead and wounded were literally piled there in heaps. As we passed by them while crossin' the road to get in amongst the corn stalks, a wounded Yankee boy made a thrust at me with his bayonet. I was able to avoid it by turnin' my head and fallin' backward. When I stood again I got a good look at him, I could see that he was badly hurt. I pondered his fate but for a brief moment and then continued on.

As we pushed forward into the cornfield beyond the road, a private by the name of Zebulon Spencer, a young red-headed boy in a regiment from South Carolina, was in the front rank just before me. That poor boy went down with an awful cry. I had no choice but to continue movin' on. Stoopin' over him as I passed, I saw that he had fallen forward, lyin' on his face. He was motionless and I had no doubt that he had passed on to the next world.

Just as I was about to render a short prayer for God's mercy on his soul, a strand of canister went flyin' over our heads. That was my dread. I could endure rifle bullets, but when the big iron went swishin' through the air with a sound as though there were bushels of them, it made me wish I was anywhere but there.

I had just gotten myself pretty comfortable too when another canister burst over me and completely deafened me for what seemed to be minutes. I felt a blow on my right shoulder and my jacket became covered with an odd, unrecognizable white jelly.

I instantly reacted and felt whether I still had my arm or not. I will remember until the day I die how grateful to God I was that it was still whole. At the same time I felt somethin' wet and warm on my face. With the sleeve of my jacket I wiped it off.

I looked at my sleeve and realized what I was lookin' at was blood. It was then I looked to my left to see that the man next to me, Ernest Kessler, was missin' the upper part of his head and almost all his brains had gone into the face of the man next to him. If I recall correctly that man was George Wallace Merkel. Kessler's brains were so thick on Merkel's face it was so that he could scarcely see."

This time it was the reporter who asked to take a break to use the rest room. I could no longer continue to eavesdrop and knew I had to get involved somehow in this conversation.

Knowing what I did about the Battle at Antietam, I was filled with such excitement that without thinking, I turned to the old man and asked a question of my own...

"Does your great grandfather write anything in his book about Colonel Tew?" I asked, the words barely out of my mouth before I'd realized my transgression. I was set to apologize, but the old man was nodding his head at me and smiling. I had obviously asked the right question at the right time.

When the reporter returned, Mr. Scarboro continued reading...

"Just then, a Yankee horseman waved his hat at us. It was our own Colonel Tew that returned the compliment. It was the last I saw of him as a grapeshot round came out of nowhere and swept him off his horse and into the realm of the dead.

Our skirmishers returned fire, killin' the assassin. Then what was left of our bloodied regiment, if you can call thirty men a regiment, began to fire on their advancin' line. Slowly they were approachin' us, comin' up the hill, firin' as they come. Slowly and efficiently they were retirin' our skirmishers before we could retire theirs.

That nameless Lieutenant had returned to our ranks, replacing the Major, and he was now orderin' our skirmishers to rejoin and to come into the line. Just as they were comin' into place another wave of Yank's appeared right before us, as if out of thin air. They were a scarce fifty yards off, but as if with one mind, our whole line poured a deadly volley into their ranks. I saw them drop, reel and stagger. We drove the rest of them back beyond the crest of the hill.

We reloaded, and we waited for them to again approach. This time their first column joined with their second. They rallied and moved forward again. But we met them with the same reception, and back again they fell only to be joined by their third line.

"Here they all come agin," I heard someone to my right begin to yell. "Here they come agin!"

I could see their mounted riders cheering them on, and with a sickly "huzza!" they all again approached us at a charge. But another volley of ours sent their whole line reelin' back to where they come from."

Mr. Scarboro continued reading for another ten minutes or so. We'd finished our lunch and drank the last few swigs of the Mill Whistle though it was warm. I stood and picked up our check, intending to pay the cashier and just go. But something made me turn around and walk back to that other booth and introduce myself.

I handed Mr. Scarboro my business card...

"I beg your forgiveness," I said, "but my wife and I could not help but overhear your great grandfather's most incredible story. I am a writer and your story has intrigued the hell out of me. I would love to be able to sit with you some day in the near future and ask you a few more questions...from a different perspective than what the good reporter here today has asked."

The truth of the matter was that the reporter didn't ask a single good question, other than to ask to start over when he took notice his tape recorder wasn't running. For the entire conversation he did nothing but half listen and take scribbled notes.

"What kinda questions you figurin' on asking me?" Mr. Scarboro inquired.

"Well," I answered, "the book you read from tells us everything your great grandfather endured during the Battle of Antietam. And knowing what I do about the Civil War I would assume he fought bravely in another campaign or two before he was discharged and sent home. I would like to hear the story about what your great grandfather's life was like in the years after the war. Do you know anything about that period of time?"

"I sure 'nough do," he answered in that delightful drawl. "I never knowed the man but I knowed his offspring. My grand-daddy, William T. Scarboro II used to tell us his daddy's stories...not so much about the war itself but the years after...how he met my great grandmother and how she and my own daddy, William T. Scarboro III, nearly died in childbirth.

Truth be told, my great granddaddy become a righteously religious man once he stopped all that drinkin' and carryin' on."

We invited Mr. Scarboro to come down to Arapahoe to our home for lunch some day of his choosing. I asked only the opportunity to ask him questions about his great-granddaddy that the reporter just had no earthly idea to ask.

"Arapahoe's a fur piece from heeya," Mr. Scarboro said. "How would you propose I get there? The State of North Carolina saw fit to take my drivers license from me a few years back...said I was blinder than a bat!"

"Do you like boats?" I asked.

"Sure do!" he answered.

"You name the day and date and time," I answered. "My wife and I will come up to pick you up and take you back aboard our trawler. You can spend a weekend relaxing with us in Arapahoe if you'd like. Deal?"

"Deal!" he answered, reaching out to shake my hand.

As my wife and I were leaving the diner, Mr. Scarboro motioned to get my attention.

"We lost some of the noblest men in the South in that damn war, ya know," he said as I was turning to face him. "The wounds are still felt here. I would ask you write a bit about that if you will."

We left the Butter Bean and rode our bicycles back to the marina. It was after six o'clock by the time we were stepping back aboard *Amore Mio*. We'd already planned to spend the night in Manteo and take our time going back to Arapahoe the next day, so we showered aboard and relaxed a bit. We also discussed what we might do for dinner...

"Do you feel to cook tonight?" my wife asked me.

"Not really," I answered, looking at my watch. "It's almost eight o'clock. Should I see if we need reservations at the 1587?"

"No," she answered. "I don't feel to eat anything big or fancy tonight. Do you mind?"

"Not at all," I said. "You relax and I will make us something in the galley."

I quickly put together BLT's and cut up some fresh fruit that I'd brought along from home. We sat out on the fan tail enjoying the light dinner and a bottle of wine. It was a beautiful September evening.

"What did you think of Mr. Scarboro today?" I asked. "Did you understand what he was saying?"

"Not very much," she admitted. "But I could see how excited you were. It will make a very good story when you put your touches to it. Do you think he will call you? And will you really come all the way back here on *Amore Mio*? It is an all day trip. You could drive it in half the time you know."

"I know," I answered. "But I promised and I thought he and you and I could sit up on the bridge and talk on the way home."

"Whatever you wish," she said. "You know I will do anything you need me to do."

We finished our light dinner just a bit after ten o'clock. I could see that she was exhausted so I suggested she get ready for bed while

I'd clean up, do the dishes and put things away. By the time I got to the stateroom she was sound asleep.

Mornings on the water happen quickly. There are no mountains or trees to block the sun, so when it shows its face in the east, the day comes on strong and fast. And so it was the next morning.

I fooled around in the engine room for a while and then did a few things up on the bridge. She sat on the aft deck in her pajamas and robe and read a bit more of a Pat Conroy book she'd been reading...Beach Music.

By ten o'clock we were untied and making our way back out through Shallowbag, south under the Highway 64 Causeway bridge and past Cedar Island. We made Hog Island in just a little under thirty minutes.

It was a grand and glorious day as we crossed the vast expanse of the Pamlico Sound. The water was almost smooth and the winds were light, blowing from the Northeast. It was a perfect day to be out there.

Stumpy Point was behind us in another hour. By six o'clock we had entered the Neuse River and I could see the causeway bridge in Oriental off our starboard rail. After a short stop at the fuel dock in the Harbor Marina to top off the fuel tank, we were underway again and beginning the last and most familiar leg of our trip. By seven thirty we were tying up at our dock...home, safe and sound.

The story about William T. Scarboro never did get published in the Raleigh News & Observer. The reporter's editor canned it, calling it 'old news'...'too violent'...and 'no doubt embellished'. They ran instead an article that was very negative on the current US President. I was disappointed to see that but even more disappointed to not be able to read what the reporter gathered from his afternoon with Mr. Scarboro. If his writing was half as sloppy and disjointed as his attention span was short, it was bound to be an interesting if not amusing read.

And after waiting to hear from William T. Scarboro IV for nearly a month, my disappointment grew. I'd resigned myself to the fact that I just wasn't meant to get the rest of the story. I looked at what I had and although it was deep and plentiful, something inside me told me it was not the story I was meant to write.

But then one Sunday afternoon the phone rang in my writing room. I had a premonition as to who it was and I was not disappointed once I answered it. I recognized the voice immediately...

"I will be at the Manteo Marina this Tuesday mornin' 'round nine o'clock," Mr. Scarboro said matter-of-factly. "Tim is a good friend of my family's and he done told me I could wait for you out on the end of Dock C. But I'd rather sit inside and drink the man's coffee. So that'll be wheya I am. I trust you're a man of your word as well and you'll be here to meet me as you promised."

I knew Tuesday afternoon was already scheduled for a phone conference with my editor but I immediately agreed to Mr. Scarboro's arrangements and said I'd be there. It would take a little doing but I'd get out of my commitments...

"Ya'll promise you'll be heeya?" he asked again. "I'd like to bring along my oldest daughta iff'n you don't mind. I reckon you'd like to talk with her too. She is the family historian now that my daddy has passed. She'll prob'ly know things I've long forgotten or have never been told. Is it alright iff'n she comes along?"

"Come hell or high water I'll be there Mr. Scarboro," I said. "And yes...your daughter is more than welcome too."

"Well, in that case we got us a bit of a small problem," he continued. "Sarah is deathly afraid of the water. I don't think we'll git her out on your boat iff'n ya leave the dock. Is there any chance we could have our chat righ' cheer in Manteo? Maybe back at the Butta Bean?"

There was nothing I wanted more than to sit and talk with that old man again and truth be known, if he wanted to talk on Mars I'd have found a way to get us there...

"I have a better idea," I said. "If Sarah doesn't mind just sitting on *Amore Mio* in the marina, we'll talk on the aft deck and I can make us a lunch a bit later. How does that sound?"

"What the hell is amohrey meeoh?" he asked.

"It's the name of my boat Mr. Scarboro," I answered. "It is pronounced ah moor ay mee oh. It's Italian. Like my wife."

"Why doncha start callin' me Bill, like ev'rybody else does?" he asked. "Mr. Scarboro was my daddy!"

"OK," I said. "Bill it is. I will see you on Tuesday morning at nine o'clock at the marina."

"Make it ten," he said, obviously changing his mind but choosing not to say why. "That'll gimme more time to get somethin' else done that's been houndin' me."

Having a most congenial and agreeable editor, I was able to beg out of my phone conference for that Tuesday and spent the evening before we left, stocking the *Amore Mio* again and checking the marine forecast for our trip back up to Roanoke Island. The fuel and water tanks were topped off. The refrigerator and dry storage were full. Everything was a go.

I knew she wasn't ready for another long trip but my wife didn't complain whatsoever. Tuesday morning just before three o'clock, I brought the *Amore Mio* to life and slowly we were making our way down to the Neuse River. It was my hope to be in the open water of Pamlico Sound by sunrise...and we were right on time.

We were also right on time docking at the Manteo Marina transient dock...fourteen minutes early as a matter of fact because of a most fortunate trailing wind that pushed us all the way from Oriental. Mr. Scarboro and his oldest daughter Sarah Gwaltney were standing outside the dockmaster's office waiting. I let go with one quick burst of *Amore Mio's* air horn to announce our arrival.

"It's a might nice boat ya'll got ma'am," Mr. Scarboro said to my wife as we were tying off and shutting down the engine. "I reckon it cost a pretty penny too!"

"It's a big hole in the water that I throw my money into," I answered from the bridge, a bit of sarcasm in my words that went unnoticed.

We said our hellos and proper introductions. Small talk ensued for ten minutes of so. Soon we were all sitting around the table on the fantail and getting settled in for our conversation. I placed my tape recorder in the middle of the table after asking if either of them minded being on tape.

"Where do ya'll want me to start?" Mr. Scarboro asked. "I think the last of what ya heard was the Battle of Antietam. Ain't that right?"

"Yes," I answered. "Your great grandfather and what was left of his regiment were pinned down in a cornfield with a mounted Union Brigade scattering them to the four winds."

"Ya'll got a good memory," Mr. Scarboro said. "And a right nice way with words."

"My father told me that you wanted to know what became of his great grandfather after the war," Sarah said. "After he came home. Is that right?"

I noticed that Sarah did not speak in the same coastal drawl as her father. I was a bit disappointed and hope I did not let on with an expression on my face. It was also apparent that Sarah was going to be doing most of the talking. She appeared very intelligent.

"Let's start on his return to Curritick County," I said. "Is that good for you?"

"No, it isn't," Sarah answered quickly. "Let me rephrase that...it is not good for you. Your story, should you decide to write it, would be woefully lacking if you had not heard the most defining part of William T. Scarboro's story. Did my daddy tell you that while he survived the Battle of Antietam, he was taken prisoner in June of 1863 during the Battle at Gettysburg?"

"No, he did not," I answered. "But in your father's defense, my wife and I left while he was still talking with the reporter. He may very well have told that part of it, but we were no longer in the Butter Bean."

"I have brought along great-great granddaddy's last book," Sarah said, sliding a thick folder stuffed with yellowing pages across the table to my wife. "He wrote it in 1913, fifty years after his capture by Union forces at the Battle of Gettysburg. But for reasons that he disclosed to no one, it never did get published. These hand-written pages are the only record we have of that part of his story."

"I am ready when you are," I said, turning on the tape recorder. "This is voice activated and each side of the tape lasts ninety minutes. When you stop or pause talking, the recorder stops or pauses at the same time. Are you OK with that?"

"I most certainly am," she answered. "I have the very same tape recorder for my job in Virginia Beach."

Sarah pulled the folder back in front of her and opened it to a specific page...

"These are the exact words written by William T. Scarboro," she began. "They are in his own handwriting and uncensored to the best of my knowledge."

She pulled the tape recorder a little closer to her and began...

"I have often thought long and hard that before I draw my last breath and rise from this earth to join the Silent Host that fell before the roaring cannon and rattling musket, that I would give my experiences as a Confederate soldier and as a prisoner of war at Camp Hoffman, Point Lookout in Maryland.

I have been often asked by my children and grandchildren for my experiences and a brief history of my war record. Now, after fifty years have passed, I have consented to do this, though they were harrowin' times for a young Southern man...especially my prison experience. What I am about to say may indeed seem incredible, except to those who were there and experienced the same, terrible suffering. I can only from a clouded memory give a brief outline, for to do otherwise would make for an unbearably large volume.

Chapter I

When I was seventeen years old, I left my home and loved ones behind in Currituck County, North Carolina on the second day of

June in 1861. Myself and three other companions, eager to commit to the fight against the Northern invaders and no longer able to wait for a company to be formed in Currituck, took to walkin' west and went to Greenville where we were to join up with Zebulon Baird Vance who commanded the 26th North Carolina Regiment. I was quite afraid that the Yankees would be whipped before we could get there.

We were immediately enjoined into the service of the Confederate Army and assigned to Company B...one of ten companies composing the 26th Regiment. I was small for my age, not weighin' much over a hundred pounds, and tender looking too, with not a sign of beard on my face.

R.S. Weir, Captain of Company B, looked at me as though he doubted the propriety of receivin' me. He doubtless would have rejected me had it not been for my companions who were beside me and older than I. They testified that my parents was willin' for me to join the army, though in reality they were not. I'd run off in the dead of night.

It was not long before Captain Weir's gamble on me paid off however and he found that I was made of good stock. I was often detailed to perform some peculiar or difficult task because I did not give out as some did who were much stouter than I.

I suppose we remained at Greenville for two or three months drillin' every day. Finally, to our great joy, we received orders to go to New Bern where the Yanks, led by General Ambrose Burnside, were attemptin' to establish a fort there on the Neuse River.

The Union men and the Southern sympathizers in New Bern were havin' a hot time. The Southern sympathizers were in the minority and were bein' terribly persecuted by the Union men. We soon restored order and gave all who wanted to join the Confederate Army a chance to do so.

We were next ordered to Malvern Hill and into the jaws of the Union Army led by General George Brinton McClellan in what would come to be known as The Seven Days Battle. We charged within 25 yards of the Federal positions, further encouragin' the good General to withdraw from the York-James Peninsula.

Upon on our return to Eastern North Carolina, we engaged in multiple skirmishes with Union forces. Our most important responsibility however, was to protect the back door to Richmond, our glorious Confederate Capital, and assure a steady and uninterrupted flow of vital supplies comin' in from Wilmington."

Sarah paused at this point, shuffling through the stack of papers...

"You've already heard about how things went at the Battle of Antietam," she said. "I will skip over this and go right to March of 1863 if that is OK with you."

"I am holding on to your every word Sarah," I answered. "This is your story to tell."

Sarah continued without looking up from the table...

"The 26th was placed into service in Virginia and attached to General Robert E. Lee's Army of North Virginia. We were told we were movin' north into Pennsylvania. It should come as no surprise we ended up in Gettysburg. The 26th would forever etch its name in the history books with what would become of us in fightin' with Pettigrew's Brigade.

On the 1st day of July, 1863, our regiment was called upon to assault Federal troops of the Iron Brigade posted in Herbst's woods on McPherson's Ridge. The battle opened with shootin' all along the line on both sides. After brutal fightin', which saw the regiment break through three separate lines of resistance, we were able to force the Union troops to withdraw from the position of strength which they had held. Though we'd achieved our goal, it was at a tremendous cost.

The regimental colors were shot down fourteen times. The regimental commander, Colonel Henry King Burgwyn, Jr., was killed. His second-in-command, Lieutenant Colonel John R. Lane, was seriously wounded. Out of eight hundred muskets taken into the fight by the 26th on that bloody day, five hundred eighty eight men were killed, wounded, or missin'.

The first day's battle closed with no perceptible gain by either side. The day came to an end with our two armies lookin' each other in the face. The cannon din and sharp shootin' ended when night fall covered us.

Under cover of darkness however, the Yanks had brought up a battery of cannons and at day break on the second day they fired about one hundred and fifty shots into our ranks, claimin' a great number of casualties and causing considerable death.

Along the fortifications we kept up a continual firin' all day, killin' and woundin' a great many more on their side. The dead and wounded were left on the battle field. Some of the wounded scratched around to save their lives but most remained there to perish in the bloody grass and hot July sun.

Day break on the third day brought with it an unexpected charge from the infantry assigned to protect and defend that Union cannon battery. Though they attacked our lines at every point, we were successful in repellin' them, despite endurin' heavy loss. However, while we were rejoicin' our temporary victory, the Yanks were greatly reinforcin' their line.

Having taken us by surprise, with less than eighty men effective in our company, we found ourselves dwindlin' in number quickly. The Yanks had been receivin' reinforcements all day, until now they numbered over ten to one of our worn-out, battle-weary boys. During a lull in the fightin' a council of war was held. The same was communicated to Union officers, who proposed we surrender.

Captain Weir was in the council and refused to surrender. He contended a way must be made open for us to march out with our dignity. This was the first intimation we had that we were now prisoners of war. We were corralled into a horse pasture and guarded by two dozen Yank soldiers until it could be determined where we would be taken.

All our cookin' utensils, camp kettles, skillets, coffee pots, tin pans, tin cups, plates...everything, our bedrolls and personal effects were taken from us and scavenged by our Federal captors. We had nothin' to do but stand around our fires at night fall and talk of our experiences and narrow escapes durin' the three days of carnage."

It was at this point that Sarah asked we take a short break. From talking so much her mouth and throat had become dry and she asked for a bottle of water or better yet, a sweet tea. We stood and stretched while my wife went below to the galley to bring back a jug of sweetened iced tea she'd made the day before and a tray of finger sandwiches, predicting just such a request.

After a few minutes of small talk, Sarah began reading again, this time from Chapter Two...

"The next mornin' after our surrender we were marched for two straight days to an abandoned knittin' mill in a town called Harney, just across the Pennsylvania border into Maryland. As we were the first batch of prisoners to be held in Harney, we were quite a show for the townsfolk.

The people had to see us, so we were marched out from street to street and made to stand in the town square with hundreds of people runnin' over each other to get a glimpse of us. Some would curse us and call us poor, ignorant devils. Some would curse Jeff Davis for getting' us 'poor ignorant creatures' into such a scrap. I suppose the children had been told that we had horns and tails, for they crowded near us and kept sayin', "where are their horns and where are their tails, I don't see them."

From that day on, it seemed that they never tired of lookin' at us. They visited the knittin' mill everyday in great crowds until an order was issued prohibitin' it. Then some enterprisin' Yankee built an observatory just outside the prison wall and charged admission for people to climb it and gawk at us. It was crowded from morning until night.

We were held in Harney, inside that knittin' mill for nearly a month. It was in the middle of the night toward the end of August I believe, our days and nights had begun to run together, that we were awakened and ordered to collect our blankets and whatever meager possessions we were left with.

At daybreak, when we could be more properly guarded, we were then marched due west for several miles to a train station along side a river. We were crowded into cattle cars like so many head of livestock and after a twelve hour ride through the flat countryside of Maryland, past Baltimore and Annapolis, we eventually arrived in St. Mary's County. Taken from the cattle cars, we were marched for three miles to our new home...Camp Hoffman in Point Lookout Maryland.

The camp was originally built to hold political prisoners...Southern sympathizers accused of assistin' the Confederacy. But as the war dragged on, it was expanded upon and used to hold Confederate prisoners of war. We were not the first to arrive and experienced terrible, filthy, over-crowded conditions.

By September of 1863, we Confederate prisoners totaled more than 4,000 men. By Christmas of that year our ranks had swollen to more than 9,000. At its peak, Camp Hoffman held more than 20,000 Confederate soldiers, which was double what the camp could legitimately hold. We came to believe the entire Confederate Army had been captured and sent to Point Lookout.

The overcrowdin', poor sanitation, exposure to the elements and drinkin' water that had been fouled by our own excrement was takin' its toll. Every week, more than a dozen prisoners succumbed to various illnesses as a result. Even more died as a result of torture, treachery and malicious intent.

The prison had a wall around it nigh onta sixteen feet tall. There was another wall that that run right down the middle and divided the prison into two large areas. One was known as prison number 1 and the other was prison number 2. Each prison contained about four or five acres of land and each held 4,000 prisoners.

The gates to the two prisons stood side by side and opened into each prison. When we arrived from the Harney knittin' mill, we were told that if we would take the oath of allegiance to the United States we would be put inta prison number 2 where there would be bountiful rations, plenty of blankets and fires to keep us warm.

But if we chose not to pledge our allegiance to the United States, then we would suffer the discomforts and indignities notorious of prison number 1. They would not tell us what such discomforts and indignities were however and would make no promises as to our survival.

As a matter of regret many of us went into prison number 1 rather be seen as disloyal to the Confederacy, myself included. The guards were placed on the wall with loaded guns. Each had instructions to shoot to kill with the least infringement of prison rules.

The barracks was anythin' but comfortable, no matter which prison we'd chosen. There was eight rows with twelve narrow bunks, stacked three high...one above another. By spoonin' two could lie in one bunk. We slept on the naked planks, straw being allowed but mattresses forbidden. Some poor bony fellow's hipbones was through their skin from sleepin' on them naked planks.

We was not allowed fires in our stove after night fall. In our emaciated and rundown condition, with little or nothing to wear but our light southern clothin' and many of us in rags, you can imagine how terrible our condition become when the weather turned cold.

We had no chairs nor benches upon which to sit, and so when we sat, we sat on the floor. We was guarded by a heartless set of wretches. They were men who had never been to the front and as such were not baptized in the fire of battle. Therefore they were cruel and mean in the extreme, often shootin' unsuspectin' prisoners without the least bit of provocation. After taps, as they called it, no lights were allowed and after that all was quiet as death until mornin'.

As for our rations, there was just enough to keep us ravenously hungry all the time. One half loaf of baker's bread, eight inches long, divided between eight men. That is one inch to the man twice a day. Along with that we was given one tablespoonful of navy beans with a piece of pickled beef or salt pork about the size of a person's forefinger.

We had a kitchen sergeant who had the cookin' done for our barracks. When ready, it was handed to us in a tin cup through a window, along with whatever liquor it was cooked in. The guards would throw down apple cores and peelin's, just to enjoy seein' our poor starvin' boys scuffle for them.

The hospital was just outside the prison wall in a private house. There was a ditch four feet wide and three feet deep around it. It was planked up side and bottom and from the hospital it passed through our prison, and in it all the filth of the prison was deposited, includin' food scraps from the hospital, such as pieces of meat, baker's bread, onions and beef bones.

At the head of the ditch was a large tank. It was pumped full of water every day by a detail of prisoners. We all knew when the flood gates would be raised and the water turned loose. It would come sweepin' down, bringin' the garbage with other filth deposited in it during the day. Our boys would be strung along the sides of the ditch and as it come floatin' by, we'd grab it and eat it like hungry dogs.

Beef bones was a choice morsel. We would take them and pound them up and place them in tin cups and boil them until the marrow was boiled out. When it become cold, there would be a thin cake of tallow on top. We would spread it on our bread like butter. Had Lazarus himself been laid out at our gate, he would not have gotten a crumb. A little snowbird would have starved to death at our feet.

I now, after fifty years, recall some of the fitful scenes of the starved, emaciated young men with whom I served. Those once proud Southerners who had been victorious in many a battle, were now kicked and cuffed, starvin' and sick at heart, deep in despair with no hope...sittin', waitin' for the scraps from the hospital to be washed to their feet with the garbage and excrement all clumped in the same ditch together.

There are no words adequate to depict the outrageous cruelties and barbarities perpetrated upon helpless prisoners by some of those in charge. The small pox was ragin' all the time but we cared nothin' for that. We did not have vitality enough to produce a scab.

I used the blanket of one of my comrades who had been carried to the pest house for delousin' and I was glad to get it. The scurvy was also terrible, eatin' our gums away and our teeth fallin' out, leavin' us a perfect wreck, all for the want of proper food.

There was another species of sufferin' that befell the tobacco users. It was a pitiful sight to see them followin' those who were lucky enough to have a little money to buy tobacco, waitin' and watchin' until they spit it out of their mouths only to pick it up off the ground and put it in their own mouths or take it back to their quarters and dry it to smoke it.

Being heavily guarded and surrounded by water on three sides, any ideas we might have entertained concernin' an escape were quickly dashed when the ones who did attempt it were recaptured, brought back to the camp and hung by the neck until dead. Their bodies were left to hang until the smell become so bad the guards had no other choice but to order them taken down.

Sometimes our boys, for some trivial offense, would be punished by bein' thrown inta the white oak, as we called it. It was a guard house made of white oak logs, twelve or fourteen inches in diameter, notched down close with one small window in the end.

Inside was a dungeon...eight or ten feet deep. It was entered through a trap door in the floor, down a set of steep steps that led into this dark, foul hole. It was pitch-black in there. One could not see his own hand before him when the door was closed. One who had not been in such a place cannot have the least conception of it.

I was thrown in this place for the trivial offense of attemptin' to get a bucket of water at an officer's well while our hydrant was out of fix. I spent four of the most wretched days of my life in that terrible place. I was taken out by the same guard who put me in there, and the cursin' he give me when he let me out would be a sin for me to repeat today. I opened not my mouth; I knew better.

I received one more genteel cursin' while wounded in the prisoner's hospital, of which I will speak on later.

There were some of our poor boys, for small infraction of the prison rules, forced to ride every day what the guards called Morgan's mule. The monstrosity of a saw horse was built after the pattern of those used by carpenters.

It was about fifteen feet high and the legs were nailed to the scantlin' so one of the sharp edges was turned up. This made it very painful and uncomfortable for the poor fellow who would be forced to ride it bareback. Many a time heavy weights were fastened to his feet and sometimes he was made to hold a large beef bone in each hand, simply for humiliation and the biting flies it would attract.

This performance was carried on under the eyes of a guard with a loaded gun. Each day for several days in a row, the offendin' prisoner, stripped of his clothin' and boots, would be brought out to Morgan's mule and forced to ride it for at least ten hours, unless of course he fainted or fell off from pain or exhaustion. Very few were able to walk after this hellish Yankee torture. We had to fetch them and support them back to their barracks."

The church bells at the Mount Olivet United Methodist Church over on Ananias Dare Street began chiming, letting us know it was noon time. It was a good place to stop for the morning. Exactly eighty nine minutes and twelve seconds of tape had been used to record Sarah's story so far.

And though it was wildly interesting and so well written, I still did not feel we had gotten to the gist of William T. Scarboro's story...at least not the one I wanted to write.

We had a leisurely and relaxing lunch on the fantail of *Amore Mio*. We talked about quite a few things. Sarah told me she worked in the City Attorney's office in Virginia Beach. But noticeably not much was said about the story we'd been discussing. It had been quite intense up to this point and we all sensed a break was needed.

Mr. Scarboro did finally voice his opinion on the reporter from the News & Observer and his thoughts about having his story declined...

"I didn't much expect to see my great-granddaddy's story get printed," he said. "Least not in that rag from Raleigh. Nobody much cares about the Civil War no more in these days. It has become politically incorrect to even bring it up.

The northerners still come down here and plunder our heritage though...this time takin' down our statues and tellin' us we can't fly the Dixie flag no more...on accounta it bein' racist or some nonsense like that. Mosta them folks don't know they ass from a hole in the ground when it comes to that flag. That flag was a battle banner of the General Lee's Army of the Potomac and had not a damn thing to do with slavery or State's rights. But nobody wantsta heeya that either."

Sarah quickly changed the subject, knowing her father would go on at length talking about that flag if she didn't stop him...

"I am absolutely fascinated with your wife," she said to me. "Her beauty and that Italian accent! Since I was a little girl I have dreamed about visiting Italy. My mother too! Right up until she died four years ago, we used to sit up late at night and watch the Turner Classic Movies together, especially whenever there was one with Sophia Loren or Gina Lollobrigida in it."

The two women discussed all things Italian until I suggested it was time to get back to the story. As Sarah was turning the pages of the old, yellow and dog-eared paper, I was really hoping this seemingly endless dissertation on William T. Scarboro's war experience was going to amount to something that I could write about...

"I am going to jump to the next chapter now," Sarah said. "I know you didn't come all this way to hear about Morgan's mule or a dark dungeon in the ground. But to understand what I am about to tell you of my great-great grandfather, you needed to hear these things first."

I had already flipped the tape cartridge in the recorder before lunch. My wife reached out and turned it on before Sarah began reading...

"I'd received a short but devastatin' letter from my sister Rebecca in the winter of 1864," she began. "Sometime in mid-December as I recall. Her words cut to my heart and made me terrible homesick, more so than I'd been since leavin' home...

"My dearest brother," the letter began. "I almost feel ashamed to begin this letter with wishes that it finds you well. How could such a thing be possible I ask myself, considerin' your plight. It is with great regret and sadness that I must inform you that our mother has fallen deathly ill. I do not expect her to survive the next weeks let alone be here when you return when this horrible war comes to an end. At times, she is nearly delirious and speaks to you in her delirium as if you are right here present at her side.

I have struggled in prayer as to my decision to let this news be known to you for I know it will serve no other purpose but to weigh heavy on your heart. But Ophelia and I both believe you should know this before receivin' another letter from one of us that would simply inform you of her passin'.

Please dear brother, if you can, find it in your heart to pray that God has mercy on our mother's soul and that she is dispatched straight to heaven upon taking her last breath.

All my love,

Rebecca"

After readin' the letter several times, each time becomin' increasingly more angry at my pathetic situation, I came to the same conclusions. My mind turned only to thoughts of escape. Trustin' no one in confinement with me other than another soldier from the 26th by the name of Randall Tibbs, with whom I had become friendly, I showed the letter to no one. Eventually however I did bring Mr. Tibbs into my confidence.

Together we discussed and began to formulate a plan that would aid in our escape and insure avoidance of our recapture. The best I could figure, if I were to travel over land, I was more than five hundred miles from Roanoke Island and my mother. However, if was able to get aboard a boat headin' out of the Chesapeake and followin' the eastern coast of Virginia, I was less than one hundred and twenty five miles from home. The very thought of my proximity to all things safe and normal and my inability to reach them, made me nearly suicidal.

But before we could do any considerable reckonin', our plot was uncovered by a Yankee guard who'd taken notice to the letter I carried with me nearly constantly...

"Mr. Scarboro," he said, addressin' me with a bit of unexpected respect. "You carry that letter with you as if it were an original copy of the Declaration of Independence signed by William Hooper himself. What could possibly be so important in that letter that would make you hold on to it for dear life as you do?"

Before I could come up with a reasonable answer or a believable excuse, that guard snatched the letter from my hands and set to readin' it himself...

"I believe I must show this to Captain Stanford at once," he said. He turned and walked out of our barracks with my letter in his hand and I was powerless to demand its return.

I was certain that punishment would be dealt out to me harshly, as I had drawn a sketch of the configuration of the south wall on the back of the page. Along with a few notes and arrows, it was abundantly clear that I was contemplatin' an escape. When two Yankee guards returned to our barracks to escort me to the Captain's quarters, I had already resigned myself to the unbearable experience of the white log again.

Standing before Captain Stanford, I began to feel my stomach turnin' and my bowels loosenin'...

"How long have you been here at Camp Hoffman," the Captain asked me.

"Since August of '63," I answered. "More than a year now sir."

Until the day I die I will never understand what compelled Captain Stanford to do what he did next...

"The date on this letter is 13 August 1864," the Captain said. "In reading the sad news contained in it, where your sister believes your mother's time was short, I am inclined to think that your mother may have already passed Mr. Scarboro. You have my deepest sympathies."

"Thank you sir," I answered, returning the respect and decency he was showin' ta me. "These were my own thoughts as well."

"Would you like to go home and see your mamma?" he asked.

I did not understand what the man was sayin' ta me and truly believed that my hearin' had deceived me. It made no sense ta me at all and I musta wore a look of confusion on my face for I did not nor could not answer him.

"We have a supply boat leavin' in two days," Captain Stanford continued without waitin' for my answer. "It is headed for Fort Hatteras to retrieve fresh replacements for this camp. I will instruct the ship's Captain to put you and a detail of two soldiers ashore as Nags Head at which time you will be ferried across to Roanoke Island."

I was left speechless by the Captain's offer. I musta appeared deaf and dumb to the man as I stood in front of him completely silent...

"I will need your answer immediately," he added. "And I will advise you ahead of time Mr. Scarboro, should you attempt to escape or cause me any aggravation whatsoever, you will be recaptured and shot. Your family members will be arrested for aidin' and abettin' and every single one of your barracks mates will receive the full measure of my vengeance. These things must rest upon your conscience as you make your decision."

This Yankee Captain was givin' me permission to go home to see my ailin' mother who I had not seen since I joined the Army. He told me I would be marked present at roll calls until my return such as to not alert the Regional Prison Inspector to such highly irregular leniency.

I was placed in leg irons and wrist shackles and taken from the camp two days later under cover of darkness. Upon boardin' the supply ship, I was taken below decks and locked inside a small storage compartment not bigger than a closet. There were no windows nor any type of light in my quarters and I made the entire journey to Nags Head in utter blackness, save for being brought my meals and water and the emptyin' of the bucket meant for me to relieve myself...a task provin' to be nearly impossible with the listing ship and in total darkness.

It was either on the second or third day of sailin' that I felt the boat beginnin' to slow and eventually come to a stop. I had the sensation of risin' as the boat came to rest atop the water rather cuttin' through it. Soon I could hear men's voices outside my door. The door was opened and I was taken up a ladder to an exposed deck near the back of the boat. The intense sunlight burned at my eyes and I found it unbearable to not hold my hands over them.

I was required to climb down ova the side of the boat on a ladder made of heavy rope, one that moved and swayed with my every step. Slowly I climbed downward to an awaitin' row boat that bobbed in the waves surroundin' the larger ship. Being shackled hands and ankles, made for a most precarious descent.

One of my guards was already in the smaller boat and once I was safely aboard as well, the second guard come down the ladder to join us. We pushed off the hull of the supply ship and once out of its shadow began rowin' toward shore. In ten minutes we were being received by a detail of five Union soldiers who I found less than congenial.

Without a wasted moment, I and my guard companions was placed in the back of a wagon drawn by two horses and taken across the barrier island to a ferry landin' operated and guarded by the Union Army. I was to learn that all of the barrier islands, from Topsail in the south to Portsmouth in the north were under Federal control. The Sounds of Albamarle and Pamlico were likewise controlled.

We come ashore again at the dock at Fort Raleigh at the northern tip of Roanoke Island. For as far as I could see, all I could see was black faces. My island home appeared to have been overrun by the Negro. But how could this be, I pondered. One of my guards, somehow versed in the recent history of Roanoke Island, explained it to me...

"The Union Army has controlled this island since the late summer of 1862," he said. "When Fort Raleigh fell. By the end of summer the port cities of Plymouth, Elizabeth City, New Bern, Hertford and as far north as Norfolk had also fallen to Union forces as well. Much of eastern North Carolina will no doubt remain under the Federal command until this horrid war is resolved."

Many a slave had been freed by the Union Army's invasion of North Carolina. Major General John G. Foster, not knowing was to do with the burgeoning ranks of the coloreds, declared them to be contraband, thus making them illegal to own, possess or sell.

"A settlement has been established here," my guard continued. "It's known as Freedmen's Colony. Each of the male colored's has been given a plot of land and is paid by the Union Army for his labor. Even schools have been established to teach the colored children readin', writin' and cipherin'."

If that wasn't the damndest thing I ever heard I thought to myself. Now me personally, I did not agree with the ownership of slaves and did not have a dog in that fight. My reason for joinin' up with the Army was an act of honor for me...my homeland was bein' invaded and I felt a moral obligation to defend it. My daddy taught his children that it ought'n be thought of as right, decent or moral that one man should own another, regardless the color of his skin. But I was perplexed as to where the land was bein' obtained to give to these freed coloreds.

"Most of it was taken from the Southern sympathizers," the soldier told me. "They were given a choice...either cede their property voluntarily and leave the island, or face its seizure and be jailed. Most folks just give up their land and homestead and moved into the interior."

From Fort Raleigh, my family's homestead lay a bit more than six miles away ta the southwest. I am sure I ran at least for the last two thirds the distance with my two guard companions ridin' atop Union horses behind me. When I entered the lane back to the cabin, I was relieved to see nothing had changed much in two years.

Ophelia, my youngest sista, musta seen the two horsemen and a stranger on foot coming toward the house and stepped out onta the front porch armed with a shotgun, pointed directly at the three of us...

"Ophelia!" I shouted. "Don't shoot! It's me...Billy...your brother!" But she did not put the gun down, takin' notice no doubt to the blue uniforms on the men accompanyin' me.

"You ain't Billy Scarboro!" she shouted back at me. "Now go on...ya'll get back outta heeya the way ya'll come in."

"No, Ophelia," I shouted back. "It is me. It is your brother Billy. I come back to see mamma. These men mean no harm. They are only here to assure my return to Camp Hoffman."

"Mamma is dead," my sister said. And that stopped me right in my tracks.

The guards released me from my shackles and gave me my privacy with my sisters. They entrusted me to my word that I would be right there, waitin' for their return in three days. Shortly, Rebecca come outta the house as well and the three of us embraced and cried like children.

I would learn that my daddy had been arrested by the Union army, charged as a sympathizer and taken to a prisoner camp in the south near Wilmington. My brother John was killed at the battle of Deep Gully near Fort Anderson on 14 March, 1863. My oldest brother Robert was likewise killed in the beginnin' of May 1863 at the Battle of Chancellorsville in Virginia. My sisters were left alone to take care of the homestead and my ailin' mother, who had succumbed to the debilitatin' fevers caused by typhus...a disease brought to the island by the coloreds.

For the next two days my sistas would speak of horror stories suffered by the good folks of Roanoke Island at the hands of the Yankee invaders. With each story, an anger within me was brewin' and would soon become a tempest that would nearly cause me to renege on my promise to return to Camp Hoffman. I was fully intended to leave the island and do my best to join up with a Confederate outfit, the first I would find. It was my most earnest intention and strongest desire to go back to killin' Yankees.

However, it was my uncle Carl, my daddy's brother, who talked sense into me, remindin' me of the fate my broken promise would deliver to my barracks mates back at the camp. Late in the second day of my freedom on Roanoke Island, Uncle Carl put me atop a horse and with a Negro on a mule, delivered me back to Fort Raleigh.

In another three days I was bein' marched back through the gate of Camp Hoffman. I had returned to find things is total disarray. There had been an uprisin' and many of the men I'd returned to spare torture were now dead.

The next mornin' I was detailed to help bury the dead. I am sure I do not exaggerate when I say in places the dead were piled upon each other three and four deep. Sometimes we would find a poor wounded comrade pinned down by several dead comrades lyin' atop him. Our brave Commander who had seen to our dignified march out of Gettysburg had been killed...felled by eight mini balls. There was truly not much left of that poor man's torso.

We dug trenches two and one half feet deep and wide enough for two bodies to lay side by side. We spread a piece of oil cloth or blanket over their faces and then went to the gruesome work of coverin' 'em up. Every one of the dead who could be identified had a small piece of plank placed on their head with their names on it. Thus we left them until the Resurrection Morn.

The uprisin' inside camp Hoffman was the worst slaughter I'd seen in any of the battles I'd been involved in. We lost nearly seven hundred in less than the three hours the shootin' lasted. Nearly two thirds of those killed were North Carolinians.

My inner anger had now reached a boilin' point and I was more determined than ever to escape that camp and join up with the first Confederate unit I could find. It was on the 16th in the evening that I was desperately wounded in an attempt to scale the wooden fence at the south end of the camp. A Yankee soldier, not bein' more than twenty steps from me, shot me in the back of the right thigh when I was within a mere foot of the top. I fell outside the fence and ran a short distance before collapsin'.

While lyin' on my back on the ground unable to help myself, I took notice to two other prisoners hidin' themselves in a thicket of pine saplin's, both wounded themselves as was I. I was approached by four Yanks who dragged me to my feet. They musta seen me lookin' into the thicket and soon those two poor souls were dragged out as well. Three of the soldiers were in the act of runnin' their bayonets through me and those two other men and had it not been for an officer who came along and stopped them, we would have joined the departed in those trench graves. The officer came closer and revealed himself. It was Captain Stanford.

Just about this time an ambulance showed up, seemingly outta nowhere. We were loaded inta it and carried to a private house that was bein' used as a hospital for the Union soldiers who'd been wounded in the uprisin'. We was the only confederates in the hospital and were moved to another building in St. Marys City that had been prepared for the other nearly two hundred wounded prisoners.

Many of our boys, the ones wounded so badly and havin' little chance of recovery, were left outside on cots. Many died for want of attention as well. I was taken inside but no medical care was given to me. It was about the ninth day when my wound commenced to painin' me terribly. One of the doctors examined me and declared I had a bad case of gangrene. I was carried to the gangrene ward and placed on an amputation table. Chloroform was administered and they done their cuttin' without me knowin' anythin' about it.

When I come to again, I was snugly wrapped up in my bunk, cryin' like a baby. In a few days the gangrene returned. I was again placed on an amputation table and chloroform was again administered. There were two things that stuck closer to me than a brother from those surgeries. One was that infernal itch one gets all over the body, not just at the wound. And the other were the greyback body lice. We all got 'em from the filthy amputation tables we was forced to lay on.

I had a really bad case of the itch. While in the gangrene ward it became very bad...so much so that my hands were swollen and my fingers stood apart. Sores and yellow blisters came between them and they oozed a corruption that smelled to high heaven. I could scarcely touch anythin', my hands was so sore. The doctor prepared sulfur and grease for me to rub my hands with. A glass container of it was placed on a small table at the head of my bed. Someone passing by musta knocked it off and it broke inta a hundred pieces on the floor. It made for a right terrible smell.

The nurse, a young man who was a most disagreeable sort, asked if I done it. I told him "No!" He said, "You are a damned liar" and then he stood over me and cursed me for the next five minutes. I ain't never heard such vile oaths fall from the lips of no man. I was in his hands and helpless and said nothin'. However, I got over the itch and the cursin' and in a few weeks I was able to travel. That is when I was sent back to Camp Hoffman, walkin' best I could on my single crutch."

Sarah placed a book mark at the page she'd just finished reading and announced she needed to take another break. It wasn't negotiable! She was exhausted from all the reading and becoming a bit emotional as well.

I looked at my watch and it was nearly fick. The afternoon had flown by and I had become completely immersed in William T. Scarboro's story. I knew Sarah was right at the precipice of his story and that whatever it was I sensed about the man when I'd first heard mention of his name was about to be revealed.

When Sarah resumed reading, she jumped to the last chapter in the book...Chapter V.

"In makin' this statement of my war experiences and prison life, I have endeavored to state the facts as they occurred to my mind after a lapse of more than fifty years. I have only given a sketch, especially of the lives and hardships of the Confederate soldier on the march...of short rations and often none...of the forced marches by day and by night, through rain, snow and ice, cold mud; thinly clad, oft times barefooted with bleedin' feet, all for a cause so dearly loved.

About the 10th of April, 1865, we were told General Lee had surrendered to General Grant. We received the news with great sorrow for we wanted to be exchanged so we could have a chance to even up with the Yanks for their cruelty to us. We were told we would be released on takin' the oath of allegiance to the United States Government.

In squads of two to three hundred, we were released every day until the camp was empty. There were a good many of us who said we would not take the oath but we were plainly informed that it was the only way we would be released.

On the 13th day of June, 1865, the oath of allegiance was administered to us and we, through the providence of God, walked out of the prison gates free men, with free transportation papers in our pockets, takin' us back to our homes.

My comrade in arms, Randall Tibbs, and I rode on a buckboard wagon from the camp to St. Marys City where we stopped over for several hours, awaitin' the train that would take us further north toward Washington DC and off the peninsula. Eventually we would begin travelin' south through Richmond Virginia and eventually into glorious North Carolina.

While we waited in St. Marys City, we were conducted to the 5th Street Market. It was there that the Ladies Aid Society met us with canned goods and second hand clothin'; all of which we greatly needed. Some of us were in rags. My left pants leg was worn off almost to my knee and my other pant leg was pinned to my waist.

I had not a coat and but one old ragged shirt, which I had worn since the day I was captured. A good merchant took pity on me, or perhaps he was ashamed to see me walk the streets of his city in my destitute garb, and took me into his store. He give me a good pair of pants, a shirt and a pair of boots of which I needed only the left one.

From there we took the railroad further north to Alexandria where we waited several hours to change trains and begin our arduous but eagerly anticipated journey south. We traveled through Richmond, east toward Williamsburg, south again through Hampton where the end of the line came for us. We walked for nine miles to the ferry crossin' and eventually landed in Portsmouth. We were on our own from there."

This is where Sarah stopped reading again. She got a most serious and worrisome look on her face, as if troubled by what she was about to say.

"My great-great grandfather's ordeal was not even close to being over yet," she said. "Having spent two years starved and tortured in a prison camp, and having only one leg requiring him to walk on crutches, the prospect of traveling from Portsmouth to Roanoke Island was the most daunting task he had faced so far. Had it not been for God's intervention along the way, we would not be sitting here today reading his words."

Sarah told me of the events leading up to that intervention and the moment she'd finished I knew that my long wait for a story had been worth it...this was a story about redemption.

"My great-great grandfather and Randall Tibbs were walking on the foot path along side the Dismal Swamp Canal, an hour north of Elizabeth City. They were trying to reach Forbes Bay where they were to catch the ferry that would take them across the Albamarle Sound. Walking was painfully slow with one of them on crutches.

Suddenly and without warning they were surprised by three Union soldiers, deserters. They'd been hiding in the woods attempting to stay out of sight of the Confederate gangs that rode through these parts hunting for and executing Yanks that had been separated from their units. When the three men leaped from the cover of the thickets, they easily overpowered my great-great grandfather, knocking him off balance and onto his back into the dirt.

But Randall Tibbs was a monstrously large man and even the two long years in confinement and near starvation somehow did not diminish his strength. He swung at one of the men, catching him squarely at the chin. His fist continued into the man's throat, crushing his windpipe and knocking him to the ground where he gasped for breath in utter futility. In less than a mere minute the man was dead.

As the first man lay dying, Randall Tibbs turned his attention to the second attacker. But before he could assail the man, the man pulled a revolver from his waistband, shooting Tibbs in the belly just below the rib cage. It would end up being a fatal wound as the bullet struck an artery. Randall Tibbs lay on the path as his blood flowed into the dirt and life flowed out of his body.

The last of Yanks was poised directly over my great-great grandfather, ready to thrust a bayonet into his chest. At that very moment, two gun shots rang out, in such close succession as to sound like one shot and its echo. A mini ball struck the one attacker in the face, just below his left eye, instantly killing him. He dropped his rifle and bayonet and crumpled to the ground.

A fraction of a second later, the second mini ball hit the attacker who had killed Randall Tibbs, striking him squarely in the chest and shattering his breast bone. He likewise fell dead into a heap beside his comrade.

Two men on horseback, both in the uniforms of Union officers, galloped up to where my great-great grandfather lay on the ground. As one of the men alit from his horse, the most amazing of coincidental reunions took place.

The officer was none other than Captain Jerome Weatherby Stanford, the Commander of Camp Hoffman, the very same man who had shown William T. Scarboro such extraordinary leniency and compassion and later saved his life while he was attempting to escape. Stanford and a contingent of men were tracking down Union deserters and returning them for court marshals.

The two men recognized each other instantly. It was not merely coincidence that their paths crossed again...

"You have saved my life yet again sir," my great-great grandfather said to the Captain who was pulling him up to stand with his crutches. "I do not rightly know how to thank you."

"Where are you headed Mr. Scarboro?" the Captain asked. "My Lieutenant and I will see to it that your travel remains safe from this point on. We can get you to the ferry in Elizabeth City."

"That was indeed our desired destination, sir," he answered. "It is precisely where we was headed before being assailed by these dreadful and despicable men."

"They are deserters Mr. Scarboro," the Captain answered. "We've been tracking them for days."

Captain Stanford shouted back to his detail of soldiers who remained out of sight and hidden in a patch of woods, ordering a horse be brought forward for Mr. Scarboro. Once positioned and secured into the saddle, together the three men rode, trailed by the contingent of Yankee soldiers, also on horseback.

They made their way through the narrows of the Pasquotank River and into Elizabeth City. Below the city was Forbes Bay. Here they made sure my great-great grandfather had a proper place on the ferry that would take him to Fort Raleigh on the northern tip of Roanoke Island.

"You have been like a guardian angel to me," my great-great grandfather said. "This is twice now."

"We all a have purpose in this life, Mr. Scarboro," the Captain said. "We are all angels just as we are all demons. We are just human after all."

"Many times over the short course of my life," my great-great grandfather answered, "I have been offered proof of God's existence. You are one such experience Captain Stanford. I shall never forget you and will be forever in your debt sir. If God sees fit to make our paths cross yet again, I pray I will be in a position to repay you for your Christian kindness."

"Forgive the people who have harmed you Mr. Scarboro," the Captain said before leavin' him at the dock." That is all I ask of you. You have every reason to hate. But I pray you can forgive them their transgressions. War distorts the human heart and blinds a man's eyes with violence and hatred that is not normally within him. The only ones who can forgive us are the dead."

Before we ended our conversation that evening, Sarah said she wanted to read a short post script that her great-great grandfather added to his never-published book.

"I think the words he writes sum up the person that war made of him. It would be nice if you could include them in anything you choose to write about my family."

"I saw and talked to two men a few weeks back," the post script begins, "one from New Bern and the other from Wilmington. I asked them about our dead at each of those two places. The man from New Bern said the cemetery there was enclosed with a stone wall five feet high and at the entrance, a beautiful arch stood with the word "AMERICANS" spannin' it. The graves are decorated every year, as are the union soldiers.

"The flesh and blood and bones of the Confederate soldier will be consumed by the same worms that eat the flesh and blood and bones of the Yankee," he said to me. "In death, it don't make no nevva mind what you thought in this life...only what ya done to yer fella man."

While it is true that it has been over fifty years since the war has ended for us, there are things many of us who fought in it and had the grave misfortune of becomin' prisoners of war, cannot forget. It is difficult for us to forgive the diabolical deeds perpetrated by devils who called themselves God fearin' men. Difficult, but we must not allow it to become impossible.

In our meditations, our minds run back upon that field in Antietam or another in Gettysburg where thousands upon thousands of young lives ended...simple men far from home with no fond and lovin' mother to speak a lovin' word in their dyin' hours or to close their eyes in death.

They now rest in their rude pine coffins with their old Confederate blankets as their shroudin'. When we think of our deceased comrades, we can but wonder was it the grape shot and canister that took 'em from us or neglect, disease and starvation. The all wise and all powerful God is the only one who knows for sure.

I want to say in conclusion that I have taken and enforced Captain Stanford's admonitions to me and have long since forgiven those who had us in their power and treated us with such ungodly cruelty. I have not the least spark of bitterness in my breast against them any longer. I pray they have repented and have been forgiven by their Maker and that we will all meet once again on the shores of sweet deliverance."

Vignette 8 ~ Bird Key

"**S**OMETIMES," SHE SAID. "Sometimes there are things that just need to be confessed, Mitch…they can't be kept in any longer…no matter if the people who don't want their secrets told will get hurt by it. The truth has to come out sooner or later."

It was a few minutes after eleven o'clock on a hot, sticky moonless night in July. The water was lit only by the stars and from what I was told, the mosquitoes were out in force. A young man and his younger sister were standing at the end of an old wooden dock on Bagley Cove, a back wash off Kings Bay. The young man, in his late twenties was wearing cut-off cargo shorts, a well-worn Ron Jon Surf Shop T-shirt, flip-flops and a Citrus County Sheriff's Office baseball cap. He seemed nervous…aggravated might be a better word for it.

Though he was trying to quit, because his wife hounded him constantly about it, he was smoking another cigarette. Mostly to keep the mosquitoes away or so he said. But he flipped it out into the water before kneeling down to re-tie one of the ropes from his boat to a cleat on the dock. The stern line had worked its way loose somehow and the back of his little center console Grady-White kept drifting in and out, bumping against the rub rail in the slow moving current.

The young woman was his younger sister…younger by about eight years. I guess I'd have to say she was the more agitated of the two though. And for good reason! She was telling him that she was about to bring both their worlds crashing down at their feet.

Though this really has nothing to do with the story, I am compelled to mention it to you anyway. Her four year old son had been diagnosed with ADHD a few years before and the doctor had prescribed a medication to keep him calm…a dextroamphetamine. From time to time, she would steal some of it. She'd taken three pills that night. She thought about taking the whole bottle once but she just wasn't that brave.

Her brother could tell she was high. And if the truth were known, he knew she used quite a few other prescription drugs as well, none of which were in her name. He'd been trained to know such things.

After she'd said what she'd said a few minutes before, the only sounds to be heard on the dock that night were the lapping of the water against the pilings and the crickets along the edges of the cove. Every so often you could hear a gator grunt and from time to time a night bird would cry out. Other than that, it was dead quiet.

This scene I am describing took place on the dock at the young man's home just outside the small town of Crystal River along Florida's Gulf coast, three years ago. It's a part of the coastline that's come to be known as the Nature Coast.

What I am about to tell you is only as true as the people who told it to me. I only knew the young girl in passing, but the young man I am talking about is a friend of mine...well, he used to be. He told me the whole story one of the last times I went to visit him.

His name is Mitchell Pope and he'd become a deputy with the Citrus County Sheriff's office three years after he got out of the service back in 2009. He'd joined the Army straight out of high school, the same year his mother died. By the time he was 21, he was on his second tour in Afghanistan. He was discharged early when his father had become so sick, diagnosed with Stage 4 lung cancer. Before he died the following year, he'd gotten Mitch to think about taking the test to join the Sheriff's Office. But Mitch came home aimless and angry, content to drink with high school friends at the local bars and tell his versions of his war stories. Trust me...I heard them all.

His sister's name was Stella...Stella Pope. She had just turned 21 years old the night she was arguing with her brother on the dock and at the time she had a son she'd named Clint. He was four years old at the time and a real handful for her. Let's just say Stella was not doing too well as a single parent. Clint needed a lot of attention...more than she was able to give him. And he needed a good amount of discipline too. A father figure would have worked wonders for that boy, but Stella never did say who Clint's father was. On the child's birth certificate the line for father reads 'unknown'.

Mitchell and his sister were about to have a most disturbing conversation...one that would end in a very loud argument with temper's flaring. They were not seeing eye-to-eye on a very serious matter...one that could destroy Mitchell's life if it ever got out.

And oh...by the way, it's called the Nature Coast because, for the most part, it is wild and primitive and undeveloped...in some places it looks just like Florida did a century ago and more. The coastline is mostly salt flats...beds of sea grass in shallow, brackish water, affected by the rise and fall of the tides. There are quite a few small islands in the salt flats too...keys I guess would better describe them. The uppermost island of the three Bird Keys was one of those places where time seemed to have stood still. It was also the perfect place to hide Mitchell and Stella's secret for the last five years.

The words she'd just uttered, about confessing something or another, faded out into the dark night and disappeared...as if they had been spoken and unspoken all at once. As if they were of the utmost importance and totally useless at the same time...

"I-can't-go-back-in-time," Mitchell said, accentuating each word emphatically. "Not now Stella. Not with my job. You know this, right? I can't retrace our steps and undo what we did. It's not like writing a book for God's sakes...I can't just rewrite the ending to make it happier or to end the way you want it to end. You need to think about this before you bare your conscience and ruin our lives."

"Do you think I am happy about doing this?" she asked, getting angrier and more animated...pacing the length of the dock and protesting loudly now.

"Keep your damn voice down Stella," he whispered. He knew how she could get when the medication would take a stronger hold on her. "Voices carry across this stretch of water. You never know who's out there listening."

"It's been eating me alive ever since we did it, Mitch," she said. "I knew it was wrong back then. I know it's still wrong now. I knew this day would come sooner or later. But this dream I keep having...it freaks me out Mitch! I swear it was the devil talking right to me!"

"But why now?" he demanded to know. "It's been five God-damned years Stella! It's the past. Why dredge it up now? What good will any of this do?"

"It will clear my conscience," she answered. "These voices in my head are too much for me!"

"Fuck your conscience Stella," he shouted, catching himself and toning down his voice. "There's more at risk here that your God-damned conscience. Think about your girlfriends. Think about my wife and my kids. Just keep your mouth shut Stella...and stop taking your son's medication! That's a big part of your problem...it ain't your conscience!"

"You're my older brother," she said. "You know what happened to me. You can't just trivialize it like this...like nothing happened. There were a lot of stories from that night...from that whole summer if you remember. And now they've all become one...one big ugly mess all balled up together. Besides that, some of them are true and some aren't. But what we did Mitch...what we did is the Gospel truth and you know it."

"You know what a lie is, just like I do," he said. "You've told enough of them. Your whole God damn life's been a lie! We don't have to know the truth about your past to be able to see what's coming at us in the future Stella. We have been on a collision course with this thing for five years...now it is coming back to roost because of your conscience? If you do this...well, whatever is going to happen is going to happen. It's inevitable and I can't stop it this time. I can't protect you."

"Just don't you forget one thing, Mitchell Pope," she said, her voice loud enough again to be heard across the water. "I'm not in this alone. You have as much to lose as I do."

"That's why I'm telling you to keep your God-damned mouth shut Stella!" Mitchell said.

He walked away from her, leaving her out on the dock in the dark...

"Go home Stella," he shouted without looking back. "Go home and take care of your kid. Forget about this conscience bullshit of yours. I'm telling ya...you don't want to make me angry!"

Maybe it's time I give you a little history...

Stella Pope's innocence came to an end one night five years earlier...just like the summer did that year. She was sixteen years old when she'd met a boy at a party out at the Fort Island Beach on the end of Fort Island Trail. Most of the coastline in Citrus County as I said is pretty wild. But the County built a nice little beach out at the end of the road where an old Spanish fort once stood...it's long gone in these days though.

The beach is like a State Park almost...it's got restrooms and covered picnic tables and bar-b-que grills. There's even a roped-off area in the Gulf that's used for swimming.

It was one of the few places where high school kids could go to sneak a little beer on the weekend or maybe smoke pot from time to time. There were two Sheriff's patrol cars that would come by every hour on the hour after it got dark. Like clock work, right at the top of the hour, a spotlight would scan the beach and two deputies would get out of their cars and walk out of the darkness of the parking lot to see what the kids were doing.

About five minutes before they'd show up, the kids would hide the beer coolers and disguise the pot smoke that hung in the air with cigarette smoke. Any of them who were too drunk or too wasted, hid in the mangroves...out of site until the deputies left.

Truth be told, the deputies knew what was going on out there. Most of them had grown up in Citrus County...Crystal River or Homosassa, and they used to do the same thing when they were in high school. As long as nobody got out of hand the deputies for the most part looked the other way.

Luke Bishop was a young boy from Tampa. He was in Crystal River on summer vacation with his family and was staying at the Plantation Inn just off Highway 17. They'd come up a few days before and planned to stay for two and a half weeks. He was just 18 and had graduated from Hillsborough High School earlier that year. He had plans to attend the University of Florida at Gainesville on a football scholarship in the fall. Because he could catch a football better than most, his next four years were pretty much assured to be easy and quite an adventure for him.

His father was a Colonel in the Air Force and worked out at the base at MacDill...some kind of a systems analyst or something, at least that's what Luke told Stella later that night after they'd met. Luke's mother didn't work. He used to joke about his family...

"My father works a high security clearance job with the government," he'd say. "My mother just gets high! She drinks like a fish and eats anti-depressants like they're tic tacs."

While they were staying at the Plantation Inn, Luke had made friends with a busboy in the restaurant who told him about a party later that night out at the beach...

"Ya wanna go?" the busboy asked. "It's a pretty good party. Lotsa people. You can get righteously wasted for five bucks!"

"Are there any girls come to it?" Luke asked. "What's the chances I can get lucky if I go tonight?"

"Anything's possible dude," the busboy answered. "Sometimes the girls get pretty tore up on beer and Xanax...that is if anybody's scored any. They usually end up skinny dippin'. You can have your pick then."

"What time?" Luke asked.

"I get off work at nine o'clock," he answered. "Meet me over by the boat office at the marina, OK? I got a green Chevy S-10."

Stella and two of her friends had planned all week long to go to this party. But if her brother found out where she was going, he never would have let her leave the house. As I said, Stella and Mitchell's mother died in 2006 and their father died in early 2010. Mitchell had been taking care of the house and her ever since.

He would have said she was too young to be going to a party with boys and beer, having just turned 16 in April. So she lied to him and told him she was going into Inverness to the movies...at the mall. She was happy he didn't ask what was showing because she'd forgotten to check.

She and her two girlfriends showed up at the party a little after nine o'clock. Luke was already there, sitting on one of the picnic tables and drinking from a bottle of Corona when she came walking across the sand from the parking lot in her tight cut off shorts and a halter top. She was a good looking girl and he set his sights on her right off the bat...she never had a chance.

He said to his friend, "Gonna get me some that!"

"She's jail bait man," his friend said. "You're crazy. I'd stay a hundred miles away from that shit!"

Luke Bishop could be very smooth and very convincing when he needed to be. He was a good looking kid too...blue eyes, long blond hair, good build. He made sure she noticed him but didn't go to her. He knew sooner or later if she was interested she'd come to him. That's how it always worked. You see, he'd done this quite a few times before. To him it was a game of conquest...nothing more.

And sure enough, she ended up going over to where he was sitting. She was the one who started everything that happened that night and in the coming week. Had she only known how dangerous that boy was...

"I haven't seen you around Crystal River before," she said. "Are you new here?"

"Brand new!" he joked, suggestively glancing down at his crotch. "And in an easy to open container too."

She had no idea what he was talking about. But not wanting to appear naïve or let on she didn't understand, she laughed at his joke.

They talked for another half hour and he told her all about himself...the records he'd set for the varsity football team, his 4.0 GPA and his scholarship to UF in the fall. For an 18 year old kid he had some pretty impressive credentials. Stella liked him...she liked him a lot. He was funny and good looking and most importantly, he paid attention to her...making her feel important, like she mattered. To her, that meant everything. To him, it was just part of his game. She was none the wiser.

Someone said it was time to hide the beer...that the Sheriff's patrol would be there in about ten more minutes. So they moved all the coolers into the bushes and the two boys who had already had too much to drink were taken into the mangroves and told to stay there, quiet and out of sight until the deputies left.

"I have to hide too," she said. "My brother knows all these guys on the force and if he finds out I'm here my ass is grass. I'll be back though. Please don't run away."

"I got a better idea," he said. "Let's hide together."

She tried not to let it show, but she was very happy about his suggestion. She really liked this boy...

"Gimme just a minute," she said, intentionally making eye contact with him. "I'll be right back."

She went to tell her girlfriends to make sure they waited for her at the end of the night...

"Oh my God!" she said. "I met this beautiful boy tonight. Did you see him? He's a really cool guy." With as seductive a look as a 16 year old girl could muster, she added, "Maybe I'll just give it up tonight!"

As her girlfriends were giggling and cheering her on, she ran back to Luke at the picnic table. He was waiting for her with four more bottles of Corona. He'd already drank three or four and was feeling pretty confident. He'd also given her one as soon as she showed up.

She was not much of drinker and after her second beer she was having a bit of a hard time talking with out slurring. But she was having the time of her young life and had plans for Luke Bishop. She grabbed him by the hand, pulling him from the picnic table. Together they ran across the beach into the dunes.

While she was drinking her beer he was pulling a joint out of his shirt pocket and lighting it...

"Oh my God!" she said. "What if somebody smell this? I'll be in so much trouble."

"Relax Stella," he told her. "The wind is blowing out into the Gulf. Nobody's gonna smell nothin'."

She'd already had too much to drink and after she'd smoked his pot any inhibitions or reservations she might have had went up in smoke. One thing led to another. He kissed her and she kissed him back. They fumbled with each other's clothes. Things got out of control. She wanted to stop but then again she didn't...so she didn't. It all happened so fast...too fast to think about anything other than what was happening...and then it was over.

She gave him her virginity that night. He said all the right things at all the right times. He was smooth and very convincing. Everything went just as he planned. Like I said, she never stood a chance.

They stood up. He was pulling on his shorts while she was nervously fumbling with her bra. He wasn't talking any more and the whole thing got very awkward quickly. They walked out of the dunes, going back to the party. More than a half hour had passed and her girlfriends were frantic when they saw her again...they wanted to leave. Stella thought about staying...she really did not want to go. Not yet at least. She just wanted to cling to this beautiful boy.

It wasn't supposed to be this way...it wasn't what she'd envisioned it would be like the first time. But if she didn't go with her girlfriends, she'd have no way back home and then she'd have explaining to do to her brother. She wanted to kiss him again but was too embarrassed. A million things were running through her head, none of which she understood or made her feel any better.

Her belly hurt. Her bottom hurt. Her lips hurt. Everything hurt. But it was the most wonderful hurt she'd ever felt. Summoning all her courage, she leaned into him, closed her eyes and tried to kiss him goodbye. But at the last moment he turned his face away. She opened her eyes in shock. All that good hurt turned to bad...just like that!

The whole ride home with her girlfriends she stayed quiet and sullen.

Now he was leaving in another week or so. She tried calling him at The Plantation but he was never there. He didn't return any of her messages. She was too mortified to go there in person. She knew the bus boy...the kid who'd brought Luke to the party, but she didn't know him well...only his first name and that he worked in the restaurant at the Plantation. So she called him there one afternoon, desperately begging him to get a message to Luke.

His name was Chris Carlyle. He was a few years ahead of her in school and had already graduated. He was from Lecanto. No matter what he said, he wasn't going to help her. He promised to get a message to Luke, if he saw him, but couldn't promise anything. The truth of the matter is he did see Luke and he did give him Stella's message, but Luke never called her again.

She tried to convince herself that what had happened just happened and it shouldn't be something that hurt so badly. I mean, it was only sex! All the girls she knew had already given up their virginity. To them it was no big deal.

It wasn't his fault and it wasn't hers. So why was she feeling like she did something wrong...so dirty? Why could she not stop crying? Why couldn't she get out of bed?

What happened to Stella was clearly nothing more than deceit...nothing less than betrayal. Luke Bishop had robbed her of something he had no right to take...no different than had he stolen her purse. He took from her the most valuable things she possessed...her innocence and her trust...things that could never be replaced.

And so now, all she was left with was embarrassment and regret. She was the owner of a hard lesson well learned. She'd expected it to be love. She'd expected...well, who knows what she expected. But it sure as hell wasn't what she ended up with. Never again would she think to call the feelings of intimacy and oneness that she'd experienced with that boy, love. It was anything but. She knew she could never get back what it was he'd stolen.

It had all been one big, terrible mistake, she simply had to admit it. When she talked with her girlfriends afterwards, they all said that she should know what it felt like to be a woman now. But it was not true. She was still very much a little girl. She was just a sixteen year old kid...one who still believed she could fly with Peter Pan...breathe underwater and walk without touching the ground.

She had been fooled by Luke Bishop, plain and simple. She honestly believed he loved her. He said he did...and not just once! Many times that night. Why did he lie? Why did he have to say all those things to her if he didn't mean them?

Five days had passed and she was frantic by this time. She needed to talk with someone but she had no one other than her brother. And most of the time lately he'd been drunk or stoned. He was supposed to be taking care of her but the war did some bad things to him and he was having trouble taking care of himself.

But what other choice did she have? She had to take the chance that he'd understand. He was the older brother. He was her hero...

Stella told him what had happened...the whole thing. She confessed how she lied to him about where she was going that night. She told him how good looking he was...about drinking the beer and smoking the pot...

"And when the deputies were coming to check on what everybody was doing," she said. "He took me into the palmetto scrubs so no one would see me and be able to tell you."

"Are you telling me that he raped you?" Mitch asked. "I'll kill the son of a bitch!"

"Oh my God no!" she said. "But he won't call me back. He ignores my messages. Why is he doing this Mitch?"

"Did you say no?" her brother asked. "Did you tell anybody about this? If he raped you, you should have come to me right away."

"Well not exactly," she said.

"Not exactly what Stella?" Mitch asked sternly. "He didn't exactly rape you? You didn't exactly say no? What exactly are you saying?"

"I wanted it at first," she said. "I really did. But then I got really scared and asked him to stop. But he wouldn't. He wouldn't stop until he...well...you know!"

"I don't know what you want me to do," Mitch told her. "Boys are just like that. I wish I could give you the answer you want Stell, but I can't. It's just the way things are. You'll get over it."

But she wasn't going to get over it. She'd counted on him and he let her down. All she could do was cry. For days afterwards that's all she did. Reality always has a way of ruining our dreams, doesn't it?

The boy had gotten what he'd wanted...what he'd set out to do. Stella was nothing more than a victim...his victim. And now he had his sights set on another girl...on another conquest for the summer. For him, all this was nothing more than a game.

She made one last attempt to find him. If she could just see him one more time, maybe he'd change his mind. It took every ounce of courage she had, but she went back to Fort Island Beach the following Friday night, hoping he'd be there. And he was. But it was too late.

She acted brave when she saw him walking with the other girl, down at the water's edge along the beach...her beach. They had their pant legs rolled up, walking in the surf...her surf. The girl's hand was in his hand. She pretended she was ok. She tried to be strong but she wasn't.

In her mind, that was supposed to be her. Now her heart had been broken into a thousand jagged pieces...so sharp that even the most casual graze of the slightest memory from that night would catch on one...tearing her wound even bigger.

She begged her friends to take her home and they did. She went into the house alone. Mitchell was out with his friends. She walked into the bathroom and started running the water in the bathtub. As it filled, she went out into the kitchen and took a steak knife from the drawer. She held it in her hand wondering if this was going to hurt. She just stared at it and began shaking. Then she threw the knife across the room and ran to her bedroom, throwing herself across the bed. She cried like she'd never cried before. It wasn't until she heard the water running over the top of the tub and splashing onto the floor that she stopped.

Now you're probably a bit confused with my story at this point...so let me tell you what happened five years earlier...

As you already know, the young girl's name is Stella. Her older brother's name is Mitchell...but everyone called him Mitch. He lived in a small but respectable waterfront community that backed up to Bagley Cove. It was on the Crystal River in Florida, closer to Kings Bay than to Crystal Bay. He'd inherited the home when his father died. He'd just joined the Army and was headed for Afghanistan when his mother died three years before that.

He'd been a deputy with the Sheriff's office for almost three years. When he'd come home from Afghanistan he suffered from bouts of PTSD and ended up doing a lot of drinking. His father urged him to go to the VA but Gainesville to the north and Tampa to the south were just too far away...at least that was his reasoning. So instead, to get rid of the nightmares and the anxiety, he drank.

But eventually Mitchell got his life straightened out. This secret he holds with his sister nagged at him constantly and was what made him make the decision to change. He'd started to attend the Baptist Church in Ozello for a while but eventually stopped. God and church were not things he was raised with and after a short while he tired of it.

But he did run into an old high school sweetheart at church one Sunday morning. I'll tell you more about her later but for now what you should know now is that they ended up getting married and she gave him two children...a boy and a girl. He ended up going to work for the Citrus County Sheriff's Office and they lived a comfortable life, nothing fancy though.

Stella's life was much different than her brother's. She collected assistance and food stamps. She'd worked as a waitress for a while, then a clerk at a convenience store. She'd even tried working in one of those kiosks you find in the mall, selling some kind of facial cream made from salt and sand and crushed seashells from the Dead Sea. Nothing lasted. She went from one job to the next. Thank God for welfare.

She lived in a small 2 bedroom Section 8 apartment in the town of Crystal River, two blocks from the High School. The government paid her rent, bought her food, gave her health care...even gave her a cell phone. She had a 4 year old son she'd named Clint. Although she'd been a promising student in high school, she dropped out when she'd become pregnant with her son.

Since both her parents had died, all she had in the world was her boy and her older brother, whom she relied on for so much.

I have been telling you of a secret Stella and her brother had been keeping for a long time. I guess it's time to let you in on that now too...

Just before sun up on a summer day toward the middle of August five years earlier, Mitchell Pope had walked the length of that same dock on which he had been arguing with his sister. He stepped down into his skiff. Sitting in the stern, he pulled the choke on the outboard engine all the way out and then yanked hard on the rope to start it. The little 25 horsepower Evinrude coughed and sputtered for the first few pulls. He adjusted the choke again and on the fourth pull it started. A thin tie-die swirl of oil and gasoline formed on top of the water behind him.

He stood to untie the ropes that held the boat to the dock and with his right foot he pushed himself away. A turn of the throttle handle made the motor slip into gear. It nearly stalled once but he adjusted the choke one final time and the motor evened out.

The water was glass-like calm that morning. He turned west toward Crystal Bay and followed the river shore for a little more than a mile...to where the river splits at the Twin Rivers Marina. He continued to hug the north shoreline for another three miles. Soon he was at what was called the Little South Pass...Crystal Bay and the open water of the Gulf of Mexico lay out before him.

But before he got out into the channel, he steered his skiff to the southwest, passing three small islets on his right known as Rocky Island, Needle Grass Island and Snake Island. Taking a wide swing, he stayed to the outside of Big Grass Island, making sure anyone on the beach at Fort Island wouldn't take notice to him.

The tide was going out and the water was getting shallower as he passed Mullet Key. Once he came to an open stretch of water, he turned the throttle as far as it would go. The bow of his skiff picked up as he skipped across the water. He was headed for three small islands...the ones the locals called the Bird Keys.

Pelicans flocked to the Bird Keys by the hundreds during mating season. On the furthest island north there was a sheltered lagoon with a naturally sandy beach. I guess you could say that was where this secret really begins.

With the island in sight, he headed straight to the small cove on the eastern side where the Army Corps of Engineers had cut down the mangroves about ten years before. What was left of one of the trees lay on the beach, embedded in the sand...half in the water and half out at high tide.

He and his friends would go there after a night of partying back when he was in high school. They'd sit on that same tree trunk, drinking beer, talking about their futures. Mitch had made the decision to join the Army when he graduated, sitting on that very tree trunk. Some would stay to watch the sun come up in the morning. Then they'd all get into their little boats and go home.

But the tide was running out when he got there that morning and he only had so much time to do what he'd come to do. This whole scene I am about to describe unfolded quickly...

In the water of the lagoon there was a body. It lay in one of the shallow pools left behind when the tide was out. The water in the pool wasn't much deeper than four or six inches. The body was right there where his sister said it would be, in the mangrove roots.

It was a boy...*the* boy...the one she'd met at the party two weeks before. His stiff body was floating...rocking back in forth with the weak movement the low tide was making. Somehow a bubble of air had become trapped under his white shirt and it looked as if a balloon were beneath it.

He lay face down in the water and his long blonde hair floated out in all directions. His arms extended out from his sides and they too lay atop the water. The toes of his boots were dug into the mucky sand...anchoring him right there and keeping him from being drawn out with the receding tide. It was time to do what Mitch had come to do.

He jumped from his skiff with a length of nylon cord in his hands, sinking up to his shins in the muck and sand. At first he didn't want to touch the body. He stood there in the water and just looked at it. A million different things ran through his head...things that were bound to happen if he went through with this terrible plan.

But in the end he did go through with it. The one thing that he could not do is see his little sister suffer for what she'd done. If this boy had raped her like she said he did, then he deserved what he got. Mitch had come to do a job and by God he wasn't going to leave until it was finished...once and for all.

Reaching beneath the boy's chest, he strung the cord under his armpits. He tied it into a bowline knot and pulled it tight. He walked the rope back to his boat, tying off the other end to one of the oarlocks. Then he climbed in and started the motor again.

With another quick pull of the starter rope, the little motor came back to life. Putting it in reverse, he backed away slowly, watching as the cord tightened and then suddenly snapped up tight by the weight of the body, throwing a hundred tiny drops of water into the air. Reluctantly...begrudgingly, the body began to move.

Once the body was floating, he pulled it close to the left side of his skiff and tied it off. Turning the skiff around, he now headed out toward the open water of the bay. Along the way, his knot had become untied and the rope that was attached to the body stretched out behind him by about ten feet. He didn't take the time to stop to pull it back closer.

Not more than four hundred yards offshore there was a sand bar. Just on the other side of it is where he put the motor into neutral and drifted for a few more yards...out to that point where he knew the bottom dropped off quickly and the water deepened to about 40 or 50 feet. At the bottom of that drop off, the current was much stronger and the water got much colder. That is exactly where he wanted to be...exactly where he needed to stop.

The night before he'd loaded four concrete blocks into the front of the skiff...two of them tied together to the other two by a few feet of rope. Once he was at that point where the bottom dropped off, he brought the boat to a stop.

Pulling on the rope now with all his strength, he brought the body up to the rail again, tying it off short this time so it couldn't sink or move. He took the rope that was tied to the first two concrete blocks and looped it twice around the boy's neck. Then he looped the rope from the second pair around his knees. Throwing all four of the blocks overboard, they instantly began pulling hard against the rail of his little boat...beginning to tip the skiff.

Quickly, he took his diving knife and cut the rope from beneath the boy's shoulders. That was all there was to it. The body began to drift backward, sinking into the murky darkness of the bay. In a few seconds it was gone...out of sight.

He wasted no more time out there. It was going to be a long and difficult run back home. Already his conscience was on fire. He did what he had to do in Afghanistan because...well, because it was war and he had to. But this was different. This was just an innocent kid and killing him just wasn't right. It made what he'd just done all the worse.

He headed straight back and tied up the skiff. He walked the length of the dock again toward the house, this time with his head down...lower than his spirits.

Stella had been waiting for him on the front porch. All they did was look at each other, nothing was said. Not another word was ever spoken about what happened that morning. Not until Stella's conscience became too heavy five years later that is.

Now you are probably wondering how that boy's body got out there on Bird Key in the first place. You probably want to know more of the details...am I right? Well, I've brought you this far...I suppose I owe you the whole story. But let me warn you, this is where things start to really get strange.

Luke Bishop's rejection of Stella Pope, after he'd taken her innocence and then ignored her as he did, was more than she could bear. Throughout the week following the party, thoughts about that night in the dunes and all the beer and the pot weighed so heavily on her mind. It became worse and worse for her. She'd confided in her brother as I told you, hoping he would do something to Luke...maybe have him arrested or something. After all, she was only 16. She didn't know what the legal term was but that didn't matter...she knew what he did to her was wrong...

"He raped me Mitch!" she screamed at him, kicking her feet and hitting him in the chest with her fists. "I kept saying no...no! Stop...please don't do this. But he didn't stop. He just kept doing it."

"This isn't what you told me earlier in the week Stella," he said. "You're changing your story. And are you telling me nobody at that party heard you screaming for help?"

"You weren't listening when I told you what he did to me," she shouted. "As usual you were drunk. You're not taking care of me like you promised daddy you would!"

"Stella," Mitch said, making her stop her tantrum. "You should have come to me right away...that night. I'd have taken you to Seven Rivers Hospital and they would have examined you...taken samples and things like that. Then I could have done something about this. But not now!

We could have gone to the Sheriff and told him what happened. They'd have picked him up for questioning. But now a week's gone by. You've showered...all the evidence is gone. I don't know what you want me to do. It will be your word against his. There aren't any witnesses. This is just how things are."

Having no one else she could talk to, Stella turned to her girlfriends for comfort. The three of them came up with a most bizarre scheme to punish Luke Bishop for what he did. It was a juvenile idea, not very well thought out and destined for failure before it even began. Whatever made him agree to it is anybody's guess. Maybe he wasn't as smart as everybody thought he was.

Jeanne Randall and Zoe West were Stella's two best friends. They'd known each other since elementary school and did everything together as a trio. But no one would have ever guessed they were capable of doing what they did.

According to their plan, Zoe was going to get word to Chris Carlyle, the bus boy at the Plantation, that Jeanne wanted to hook up with him...before he went back to Tampa. The story was going to be something about her being at the boat ramp, just above Fort Island Beach that Saturday night, waiting for him. If he was interested, he should show up at about 10:00, after it was dark...and not to tell anyone and come alone.

And he did. Luke had ridden a bicycle all the way out from the Plantation...more than seven miles. They talked at the boat ramp for a few minutes. What was said I don't really know, no one but Jeanne does now. She pointed to the sandy path through the palmetto scrubs that led down to a narrow strip of sand at the water's edge...

"It's private," she said. "Nobody ever goes down there. That's where I want to do this, OK?"

Luke shrugged his shoulders and agreed...

"Good with me!" he said. "Let's get this on!"

He was none the wiser what waited for him down there. He thought he knew what was going to happen but he really had no idea. That's when she took him by the hand and led him down the dark path...

"Did you bring a condom?" she asked.

"Always carry them," Luke answered quickly. "Never leave home without them."

They reached that narrow strip of sandy beach. Jeanne was standing in front of the water and he was facing her...his back turned to the palmetto scrubs. It was pretty dark that night. There was a moon but the clouds obscured most of it. Their passing provided for short openings when the moonlight could get through.

Stella and Zoe were hiding back in the palmetto scrubs, out of sight and staying quiet...

"Well, what did you bring me out here for?" Luke asked, beginning to unbuckle his belt. "Stella must have liked what happened...enough to get your interest. I'm ready when you..."

The baseball bat struck him in the side of the head right at his temple before he could finish what he was saying. It stunned him at first. He reacted by putting his hand up to his head and turning to see what just happened to him...he had no idea another one was coming. Zoe swung her bat with all her might and it struck him in the face...right at the bridge of his nose. That one made him drop to his knees.

Horrified by what they'd just done, Stella screamed out his name...

"Luke!" she cried. "Luke! Oh my God Luke. I'm sorry...I'm so sorry."

But Luke didn't answer. He just fell forward onto his face in the sand. He didn't move. Stella dropped to her knees beside him...

"He's not breathing!" she screamed. "He's not breathing. Oh my God. Call 911...call 911!"

"We can't call 911 Stella!" Jeanne screamed. "Jesus Christ! What's the matter with you? You killed him...you fucking killed him! You said we were just gonna mess him up. Oh my God! Oh my God! Oh my God!"

Zoe had become hysterical, screaming and crying and shaking her head...

"No! No! No! No!" she cried. "It wasn't supposed to be like this! Oh my God! What are we gonna do now?"

Jeanne put her open hands out in front of her chest, gesturing for Zoe to stop carrying on...

"OK!" she said, taking a deep breath. "We gotta think about this for a minute. Are we sure he's dead? Are you sure he's not breathing Stella."

"I don't know...I don't know...I don't know!" she cried, wildly shaking her hands and fingers at her side with her elbows bent. "I can't check. I can't do it!"

"Zoe," Jeanne shouted. "You do it. You hit him. You do it."

Zoe nervously knelt in the sand beside Luke's body. She tried to roll him over but he was literally dead weight and she wasn't strong enough.

"Help me roll him over," she said.

"No way!" Jeanne said. "I'm not touching him!"

"Put your ear on his back," Stella said. "Can you hear if he's breathing? Can you hear a heartbeat?"

Zoe did what she was told. She laid her head in the middle of his back and listened. There was nothing. No breathing. No heart beat.

"Oh my God!" she said. "I think he peed himself. I can smell pee everywhere."

"Is he breathing?" Jeanne demanded to know. "Who gives a shit if he peed himself? Is he dead?"

"That's what it means," Stella said. "When we die everything lets loose. We pee ourselves. Sometimes there's even poop!"

"Oh how gross!" Zoe said. "He's dead. He's dead and he pissed all over himself. Oh my God!"

Luke Bishop was indeed dead. One or the other of the two girls killed him...or maybe both. But none of that would matter to the police or a judge. In reality they all killed him. Now they all had a problem on their hands.

"We need to get rid of his body," Jeanne said. "We need to do it tonight."

"Are you fucking crazy?" Stella screamed. "What we need to do is call the cops. We can say we found him like this. Or we can just go home...act like nothing happened. Like we weren't even here."

"But Chris Carlyle knows we were here!" Zoe said. "Remember? You made me tell him this whole story about Jeanne wanting to hook up with him. When Luke doesn't go home tonight, Chris will tell the police what he knows about us meeting him here tonight."

"This is all the more reason we need to get rid of this body," Jeanne added. "We can just say he never showed up. That's our story, OK? He never showed up."

Jeanne's father kept his boat at the dock of a family friend not more than a mile or so back out Fort Island Trail from the boat ramp. It was a smaller boat, about sixteen feet with a 50 horsepower outboard motor. He used it for river fishing.

She knew where he kept the key hidden and he'd taught her how to start the motor and drive it. There would be no one around that time of night so the girls could take the boat, do what they needed to do and have it back before anyone ever knew it was gone...

"We'll go get my father's boat and come back here," she said. "The three of us are strong enough to pull him into the water. We can tie him to the back and then pull him out into the Gulf. We'll just let go of his body out there. Maybe the sharks will eat him or something."

"I can't do this," Stella said. "Jeanne, this is wrong. Please...let's just go home and say he never showed up."

"Then here," she said, tossing Stella her cell phone. "Why don't you just call your brother...or the cops, and tell them what you and innocent little Zoe here did...how you just killed the boy who screwed you!"

Luke's bicycle was still leaning up against Jeanne's car when they got back to the parking lot...

"What are we gonna do with that?" Zoe asked.

"We'll take it with us in the boat," Jeanne answered. "We'll dump it out there too. Put it over in the palmettos for right now."

The three girls got into Jeanne's Mini Cooper and drove out of the parking lot, heading back out Fort Island Trail with the headlights off. As they were reaching the turn off that would take them back a short dirt road to where the boat was kept, they could see headlights coming at them from up ahead, about 500 yards off. Jeanne turned and sped down the lane, turning the car off and sitting in the dark when they reached the dock. She worried whether they'd been seen or not.

It was the Sheriff patrol, making their routine stop out at the beach. Jeanne looked at her watch. It was ten minutes of eleven. She began to worry if they'd hidden the bicycle well enough, in case the deputies went down to the boat ramp too. But she couldn't worry about those things now.

There was a waterproof electrical box on one of the pilings of the dock. Jeanne's father kept the key to the boat under the lid. She opened it up and hesitated at first...not wanting to just stick her hand in there in the dark. There could be spiders or fire ants any other thing that bit. So she waited for another few moments before braving it...

"Thank God," she said, pulling the key out and holding on to it tightly. It was attached to a small red and white foam rubber float that looked like a little buoy. In case someone dropped the key in the water it would float...not sink to the bottom.

Getting the key into the ignition and getting the boat started in the dark took a bit of doing, but soon enough the motor was idling. Jeanne told Zoe and Stella, who were still standing on the dock, to untie the ropes and then jump in.

"Untie the ropes and throw them to me," she said. "We're gonna need them both."

As they slowly made their way down the river, they talked about exactly what they were going to do when they got back to where Luke's body was laying...

"I'll drop you off at the boat ramp first," Jeanne said to Zoe, clearly taking charge of what they needed to do. "You bring the bicycle down the path to where we are. Stella and I will get as close to the beach as we can with the boat. Zoe, are you listening? You need to hurry because we'll need you to help tie him up and pull him off the sand."

Zoe was already crying. All she kept saying over and over again was, "Oh my God! Oh my God! Oh my God!"

"Get a grip Zoe," Jeanne barked. "We don't have time for this. Just do what I tell you and this will be over."

The three girls struggled to roll him over and get the rope stretched under his back beneath his armpits. Jeanne tied it into a knot and then tied the other end to an eyebolt on the back of the boat. None of them knew how to tie a strong knot and when they first tried to pull away to drag his body off the beach, the one around his chest came untied. Jeanne jumped out of the boat into water that was about waist deep.

She tied another knot, this one hopefully better and tighter than the last. She climbed back into the boat and put the motor into gear again. Slowly the rope tightened and the body began to slide off the beach into the water. The knot held.

"Oh my God!" Stella said. "What about the bike?"

"Shit!" Jeanne said. "Zoe, come with me. I'll need your help."

She hadn't said anything yet, but Zoe was terrified to be in the water at night. She had visions of alligators and snakes coming at her from all directions...

"I can't," she said quietly. "I'm afraid. Please...you help her Stella."

"I don't care who helps me but it's got to be right now," Jeanne said, going over the side of the boat again. "Stella...God damn it...Now!"

Stella was shaking and crying. Mindlessly she obeyed Jeanne and jumped into the water. They struggled to get the bike lifted into the front of the boat and then get back in themselves.

To get out into the Gulf, they had to go around Fort Island Point which took them right behind the beach. Anyone who was still at the party would hear them going by and maybe even recognize them...

"We need to turn off the motor now," Jeanne whispered.

"Oh my God why?" Zoe asked. "Let's just keep on going. I want to go home!"

"If anybody's still on the beach," Jeanne said, "they might see us. And if they recognize us, we're screwed. The tide is going out and we need to float with it. Do NOT say a word...do you understand...not a peep!"

They made it around the point without being seen but the current was taking them straight for Big Grass Island. Somehow Jeanne needed to steer the boat to the north side of the island and stay between it and the sand bars. She cursed out loud when she realized she'd left the oars back at the dock...

"I'm getting out," she announced. "Stella, I need you in the water with me again. Zoe, pull that bar on the motor all the way toward you and hold it tight. Stella and I will swim and pull the boat this way. You need to keep the rudder in one place. Do you understand?"

"No!" Zoe said. "What's a rudder? I don't understand any of this. I want to go home."

"Just do what she says," Stella answered. "Please! This will all be over soon and we can all go home."

When Stella turned her head and realized she was in the water with the boy she'd just killed, within just a few feet of him as a matter of fact, she reacted by vomiting. She started to cry again. Jeanne put her hand over Stella's mouth...

"God damn it Stella," she said. "So help me, I'll kill you too if you get us caught. Now just shut up and kick your feet under water. Help me pull the boat this way."

There were still about ten kids left on the beach drinking beer and talking. It is a small miracle that no one saw the three girls in a boat with a bicycle in the front and a dead body following closely behind.

When they got past Big Grass Island they'd reached that point of the bay just in front of the break...that place where the waves start to cap and break. Jeanne climbed back up into the boat and reached out to help Stella get in. Stella was drenched to the bone and shaking like a leaf.

When she thought they were far enough away from the beach to not be seen or at least recognized, Jeanne turned on the motor again and took the boat through the small, breaking waves. When they'd gone another hundred yards she felt something bump the bottom of the boat. Just once at first, but then again and again. Suddenly the boat stopped.

She'd run up on another sand bar, straight west of Big Grass Island. She put the motor in reverse but there was too much weight in the boat to budge...

"You two get out for a minute," she said. "We're stuck. We are too heavy."

Zoe began to cry again...

"I can't Jeanne," she pleaded. "I can't get in the water. Please don't make me."

"I'll get out and push," Stella said. "Maybe that will work. Zoe, you stay right where you are, OK?"

Stella jumped out of the front of the boat, staying as far away from the boy's body as she could. She sunk past her ankles in the mucky sand. When she tried to pull her feet free, the muck pulled her sneakers off. They disappeared. She pushed with her shoulder, rocking the front of the boat up and down until it came off the sand and drifted free...

"Get in!" Jeanne said. "We need to find where this sand bar ends."

The clouds had all been blown inland and the moon was out and shining bright. Jeanne ran south along the sand bar but it didn't seem like it was ever go to end. It was getting late...well after midnight. She knew her parents were going to be madder than hell and she'd have to explain where she'd been and why her clothes were wet.

Before they knew it, the water was getting deeper and Mullet Key and the Bird Keys came into view. She'd fished out here with her father one summer...for snook when they were running. It was at that moment that her plans changed...

"We're gonna take him over to the lagoon on the backside of one of these islands over there," she said, pointing off the bow. "I fished with my father out here last year. It's a very isolated place. Nobody goes out there. We'll untie him and hide him in the mangroves. Zoe, I want you and Stella to push the bicycle overboard now."

"I thought we were going to take him out into the Gulf," Stella said. "Why do you get to change the plan?"

"Because I'm the only one who didn't kill him!" she shot back. "And besides that, we don't have anything to weight his body down with. He won't sink and there's a chance the tides will take him back to shore. All this would have been for nothing. This is a better plan. Trust me."

And they did trust her. In the moonlight Jeanne found the entrance to the lagoon and steered the little boat in through the inlet back to where the re-growing mangroves were the thickest. They untied his body and with their feet hanging over the side of the boat, pushed him into the web of exposed roots of the trees.

"Now let's go home," she said. "We have to come up with a story for where we've been tonight and why we're so late. If we all tell the same story we can't get caught in any lies,"

"It was a mistake," Stella cried to her brother when she got home. It was after three in the morning. He'd been drinking for most of the night with his friends but he'd been waiting up for her. The whole story she and Jeanne and Zoe came up with unraveled as soon as she saw her brother's face...

"We didn't really mean to do what we did," she said. "I swear it was an accident Mitch. I meant to hit him in the shoulder. No one was supposed to die. We just wanted to teach him a lesson. You believe me, don't you? You can't just turn away from me now Mitch. You're my older brother. I have no one else to turn to."

"God damn it Stella!" Mitchell shouted, putting his fingertips to his temples and thumbs to his cheeks. He grimaced and said, "Are you fucking kidding me? Are you serious? You killed this kid? What do you expect me to do now? I can't make this right."

"Make it go away Mitch," Stella cried. "I didn't mean to do this. I swear!"

"Where is this kid's body?" he asked.

Stella told him the whole story about Jeanne's father's boat and getting stuck on the sand bar...

"We took to him an island out there somewhere," she said. "I think Jeanne said it was Bird Island or something like that. He's in the mangroves in a little lagoon."

"Bird Key?" Mitch asked. "Are you sure it wasn't Bird Key she said?"

"Yes!" she said. "That's what she said. Bird Key. I'm positive. Do you know where it's at?"

"Do I know where it's at?" he shouted. "Everybody knows where the hell it's at Stella! They'll find that kid's body in no time...if they haven't already. Everybody fishes out there!"

"Mitch," she begged. "Ya gotta do something. I don't want to go to jail. I want this to go away!"

Stella literally had a break down right in front of him, collapsing to the floor. She was crying and screaming...utterly inconsolable...

"OK! OK! OK!" Mitchell said. "I'll think of something. Jesus Christ. I can't believe you were this stupid!"

When Luke Bishop did not return to the Plantation Inn that night or the next day, his parents were frantic that something bad had happened to him. He told them he was just going out for a bike ride that night before. Nobody but Chris Carlyle really knew where he was going. Chris Carlyle and the three girls who made up the whole damn story that is.

Luke's parents called the Sheriff's Office to report that he hadn't come home and that he wasn't answering his cell phone either. They sent a deputy out to investigate but the deputy was a rookie and really didn't seem to be taking the situation very seriously. He asked around a few places but never knew to interview Chris Carlyle. It was Chris who had to go to the Sheriff's Office the next day to tell them what he knew.

Luke became an official missing person after he'd been gone for 72 hours. After Chris had told his story to the Sheriff's detective, Jeanne Randall, Zoe West and Stella Pope became persons of interest. They were each picked up at their homes and taken to the Sheriff's Office in Inverness. Since they were minors, a parent or guardian was supposed to be with each of them. But Mitch could not be found so Stella was held in a room on her own until he could be located.

A different detective interviewed each one of them. The story they'd come up with was Jeanne, Zoe and Stella had gone to the mall shopping and then decided to head into Belleview near Ocala for another party. Stella didn't feel like going so they took her home about nine o'clock. The party was out in the Pine Forest beyond Marion Oaks and quite a ways from town. Along the way, Jeanne said her car got a flat tire and they were stranded for hours while she and Zoe tried their best to change it. They were sure to say no other cars came along that night.

To make their story more credible, Jeanne actually punctured her front right tire with her father's boning knife when they took the boat back to the dock. She was still driving with the mini-spare on the day she was picked up. Zoe corroborated everything Jeanne said.

As for Stella, Mitch eventually got word that she was at the Sheriff's Office in Inverness. Though he'd been drinking, he drove straight there and demanded to see his sister. He'd given her a different alibi to use, other than being with the other two girls. He'd come up with when Stella first told him about Jeanne's idea and made sure he told Jeanne and Zoe too...

"The three of you girls telling the same story isn't gonna work," Mitch said. "One or the other of you might get tripped up. So this is what you'll say. If anyone asks, Stella was home with me all night after nine o'clock. I will vouch for that."

Stella's alibi was the strongest by far. No one doubted Mitchell Pope when he said something. He never lied. Stella was allowed to go home with Mitch, in his recognizance. But the detectives were having a hard time believing Jeanne and Zoe. Something just wasn't adding up.

You see, when Jeanne was asked about the supposed arrangements to meet Luke at the boat ramp, she told the detective that she'd changed her mind and didn't go...that Luke gave her the creeps and she decided to stand him up.

But when Zoe was asked about the hook up, her answer was completely different. She said that they waited at the boat ramp but Luke never showed up that night and so they decided to go to the party in Belleview instead. It was that contradiction...that discrepancy that made the detectives decide to keep the case against those two girls open and active.

Luke's parent stayed in Citrus County for another week and became part of the search parties looking for the missing teenager. News crews from as far away as Tallahassee came to cover the story. But there was quite literally not a single trace of him to be found anywhere. They found no clues at the boat ramp and they never found the bicycle either. His disappearance was complete and eventually Luke's family went back to Tampa. They would not return until the arrests were made years later.

Mitchell's part in all of this is what made him sober up and get straight. It took some doing but he was able to put what he did behind him. As I said, he took the Sheriff's Office Entrance Examination and passed with flying colors. A year later he was wearing the uniform.

I promised earlier to tell you about his high school girlfriend. Back in high school he'd dated a girl by the name of Sharon Breeze. He met her again out at the Ozello Baptist Church one Sunday morning and they started to talk. He called her one night, out of the blue, and asked if she'd like to go to dinner with him. But she'd heard a lot of stories about Mitch since he'd come home from Afghanistan...how much he drank and his fits of rage and anger. He'd developed the reputation as someone a good girl would want to stay away from. So she turned down his invitation to dinner.

But Mitchell Pope was nothing if not persistent. He called again several more times, each time telling her how much he'd changed and what a good guy he was. She eventually relented and they had dinner together at Norma's...a small Italian restaurant in a shopping plaza in Crystal River.

Mitch drank sparkling water all evening and was the perfect gentleman. They saw each other a few more times and the romance they'd had in high school rekindled. To make a long story short, they married the following year and by the time Mitch had made his third year with the Sheriff's Office, they had two beautiful children...a boy they named Henry Phillip after Sharon's father. He was two and a half years old. And a daughter they named Beatrice after Mitchell's mother. She was just thirteen months old.

Stella and Clint remained living with Sharon and Mitch for a few months after the wedding but eventually Sharon tired of her being around and demanded she get her own place. It created a huge argument and Mitch had little other choice but to back his wife.

So he helped Stella find the Section 8 apartment near the high school and wanted Clint to spend his days with Sharon and the children while Stella worked at the mall. He had everything to live for at this point and even more to lose if it ever got out that he had anything to do with Luke Bishop's disappearance.

What brought about Stella's confession though...and yes, she did actually confess and a lot of people were dragged in to it, was brought about by a dream of all things, believe it or not. The ghost of Luke Bishop had haunted her every day since that summer evening of her sixteenth year. She saw that boy's face every where she turned. And for good reason.

You see, the month after she and her girlfriends killed Luke Bishop and took his body out to the mangroves on Bird Key, she missed her period. She missed the one the following month as well. She was pregnant.

She was pregnant and she'd killed the father of her baby. The guilt drove her nearly insane. When Clint was born, there was absolutely no denying whose son he was or who his father was. He had the same blue eyes...the same blond hair...the same dimple in his chin that Luke had. Stella had to struggle with her guilt every day after her son was born.

She started back to school that August, but by October she was showing and everyone knew she was pregnant. The kids in school were exceptionally cruel to her and she eventually dropped out. At first, she was a good mother, spending all her time with Clint...reading books to him, taking him for walks. But as he got older...when he was about two, he became rambunctious and disobedient. He couldn't concentrate on things very well and jumped from one interest to another. He just about drove Stella crazy. She was not equipped to be the mother of a child with special needs.

This went on for a year and a half. Stella hated her life. Between the guilt of what she'd done and the incredible burden having a child was causing her, she started taking drugs and partying more and more. More than once, while she went out with her girlfriends for a beer or to get high, she left Clint at home alone rather than take him to Mitchell's house. When Mitch found out what she was doing, he threatened to take Clint away from her.

Jeanne, Zoe and Stella's friendship dissolved after the murder and they eventually stopped seeing each other altogether. This did not go unnoticed by the Sheriff's office. You see, they'd never stopped investigating Luke's disappearance and the detective, a man by the name of Mike Schultz, was positive that one or all of the girls knew what had happened.

Stella's growing guilt made her turn to God and religion, trying to ease her conscience. But if you don't mind me saying, she went about it all wrong. She thought she could bargain with God...to negotiate forgiveness. But she was not yet willing or capable of paying the price forgiveness and a clean conscience would cost.

One of her neighbors was a Jehovah's Witness and invited her to come to one of their services at the Kingdom Hall in Dunnellon. But after she'd been accepted into The Society it did not take long for her to tire of the morose and strict practices she found were being forced upon her. To be honest, those people only made her all the more anxious and nervous. She came to believe that God was nowhere to be found among them.

The last straw came when she spent a week in the hospital after needing surgery to stop internal bleeding after having a cervical cyst removed. She began bleeding while in the recovery room and needed a blood transfusion given through an IV. But before she was admitted to the hospital she was required to provide a document stating she was a Witness and if rendered unconscious or unable to speak for herself, would refuse certain procedures. Such a thing as a blood transfusion of any kind is not allowed for the Witnesses.

Her condition was made all the worse as a result and as I said, I believe that was the final straw for her. When she'd determined she was not going to find God or forgiveness with the Witnesses, she left the church and never went back. They hounded her for months afterwards, requesting first then demanding, that she return. They tried to convince her that she would be corrupted by the outside world.

"The world corrupted me a long time ago!" she said to an elder who had come by one night to convince her to return. "Now please leave my home and don't ever come back!"

Several months before she would end up confessing, she began having a strange and recurring dream where she found herself dressed in a white wedding gown, standing at the back of a church. Her husband to be was standing at the altar with his back to her. Just who he was exactly remained a mystery in her dream.

The church was filled with white flowers and white linens on the altar. Everything was fresh and pure in the dream. Even her husband was dressed in white.

The organ music would begin and she would start down the aisle toward her husband and the altar. But before she could reach him the floor opened up and swallowed her. She would drop into a deep, deep pit filled flames and screaming voices. Each time she had this dream she woke in a start, panicked and sweating.

But one night the dreamed changed. It began the same way...the organ music, everything draped in white. She was holding her bouquet and started walking toward the altar and her husband who was all dressed in white. This time the floor did not open up. This time just as she was reaching the altar, her husband turned around to reveal himself to her.

When he turned around she screamed and dropped her bouquet. It was Luke and his eyes and nose had been eaten away by the crabs and the fish where he laid at the bottom of the bay. The front of his white tuxedo was drenched in the blood of his son who he was holding in his arms. The blood ran from wounds all over Clint's body and puddled on the floor at Luke's feet, staining everything in the dream red.

The dream was more than she could take. It broke her. Her conscience exploded. During the day s would cry and could not stop...this went on for days. She began recalling each and every moment of the night she killed Luke. The anxiety of that dream haunted her for days afterwards. She was now finally ready to pay the price forgiveness would cost.

The next morning she dropped Clint off at her brother's home and drove straight to the Sheriff's office in Inverness. She asked for Detective Schultz and over the next two hours, revealed every grisly detail of what had happened that night, why they did it and how they got rid of the body.

At first she said nothing about her brother's involvement...saying instead that she and Jeanne and Zoe took the body out past the sand bar and after tying weights to it, let it sink to the bottom.

Jeanne Randall and Zoe West were brought in for questioning and though Jeanne remained steadfast that she never touched Luke or his body, Zoe confessed to everything and implicated her. They were arrested and charged with first degree murder and two other very serious charges.

In the questioning of Stella Pope it eventually came out what Mitchell had done. When the County Sheriff showed up knocking on Mitch's door later that evening, with a photograph of Luke Bishop in one hand and the sworn statements of the three girls in the other…well, as I said when I began telling you this story, the truth was finally going to come out!

This story has become much longer and more detailed than I had intended. I am so sorry for keeping you so long. So let me bring it to a close…

Jeanne Randall was convicted of manslaughter, not murder. Her lawyer successfully argued that she never struck Luke Bishop as the other girls did. She received a ten year sentence for that crime. For the crime of disposing of a body, she received an additional five year sentence to run concurrent with the manslaughter charge. Since she was found guilty of manslaughter and not murder, the charge of conspiracy to commit murder was dropped. Jeanne is currently serving her sentence at the Lowell Women's Prison in Marion County.

Zoe West was convicted of second degree murder, conspiracy to commit murder and disposing of a body. She is serving a forty five year sentence, also at Lowell but has no contact with Jeanne.

Stella Pope entered into a plea bargain in exchange for testimony against Jeanne and Zoe, but mostly for testifying against her brother. The State did not have enough evidence to bring charges against him without her testimony. Stella could not bear the thought of going to jail forever and losing custody of Clint, so she betrayed the only person who had ever really helped her.

In exchange for her testimony, Stella was sentenced to five years at the Women's Reception Center in Ocala where she would receive in-patient mental health and drug rehabilitation counseling. Depending on her progress, she was told she could be released by August of 2018.

She temporarily gave up custody of her son. He was placed in foster care. He would be brought to visit her twice a month and on his birthday. She would have thirty minutes of supervised visitation with him on Saturday mornings.

Upon her release, she would have to agree to submit to ten more years of supervised probation and could regain custody of Clint after two consecutive clean years. Clint would be nearly twelve years old by then.

The one who suffered the most in this messy ordeal was Mitchell Pope. For his part in disposing of Luke Bishop's body, he was sentenced to five years at the Moore Haven Correctional Facility in Glades County. Naturally he was fired from the Sheriff's Office and Sharon divorced him. In a very bitter court action, she forced Mitchell to terminate his parental rights to his children. He signed a quit claim deed and Susan sold the house on Bagley Cove, taking all the money and both children to Indianapolis where she could be close to her parents.

At his sentencing, Stella tried to apologize to her brother...begging him once again to understand her, rather than the other way around...

"I never should have done what I did for you six years ago," he told Stella in the Citrus County Courthouse. "In one way or another I have been protecting you all your life. I knew you were depending on me when that boy took advantage of you. I didn't do the right thing by you. You were right...I promised daddy I would look after you. Had I been a man of my word none of this would have happened...none of it!"

In the end, all Stella Pope did was exchange one guilty conscience for another. She could no more live with the knowledge she'd betrayed her own flesh and blood as she did, than she could live with the guilt of knowing she'd killed another human being...the father of her own child at that.

She was released from the Reception Center after serving two years. She went first to a woman's shelter until a place was found where she could live permanently...another Section 8 apartment where the government would resume taking care of her again.

She did not do well on her own. When I tell you she was all alone in this world, you can take that quite literally. Other than her son that she was allowed to see for an hour on Saturday afternoons and her probation officer that visited once each week, she spoke to and saw almost no one.

That horrible dream of Luke returned...the one where he was waiting for her at the altar. I guess it was only natural that her thoughts would turn to suicide.

The last time I went to visit Mitch was just last month. Stella Pope killed herself in her apartment over in Hernando. Her landlord found her in the bathroom after the neighbors began complaining about the smell coming from her apartment. He found her in the bathtub with her wrists slashed. This time she didn't turn on the water for some reason.

He called the Sheriff's Office and I was the deputy that was sent out to investigate. I was the one who found her suicide note folded on the kitchen table. And although I had to enter it into evidence, I made a copy of it and took it to Mitch...

It is so very hard to talk with anyone when all you want to do is kill yourself. I am writing this but not to anyone in particular. I have no one. I don't even know if anyone will ever read this.

But in these last moments before my departure, I feel more clarity than I have ever felt in my life. I know this is the right thing to do. This is the honorable thing to do. It is what God has told me I must do.

In one minute, I will be free from these voices, from this pain and from these dreams. I have decided to kill my conscience before it kills me.

Maybe someone can tell my son that I love him. And Mitch, if you ever read this, please know how very sorry I am for what I've done to your life. Maybe ending my own will settle my debt with you.

Stella

Vignette 9 ~ Ermanno

"IN THE END, THE WAYS OF THIS WORLD ALWAYS WIN OUT JIMMY," she said. "That is just the way it is."

This is a true story I am about to tell you. It is sad, I will make no excuses. But it is also a story about something that is sorely missing in our world these days...forgiveness. It is as if we have forgotten how to forgive. And unless we learn to do it again, and soon, we may also lose our ability to forget and then we shall be doomed!

The men began coming into Ermanno and Anna's tiny little tabaccheria on via Pontebuco about nine months ago. A tabaccheria is pretty much what it sounds like...a tobacco shop. But you can buy other things there as well. The men I speak about came to buy cigarettes or to charge more time on their cell phones. Some, strangely enough, even bought lottery tickets.

They always seemed to have a few euro in their pockets and so Ermanno was happy to wait on them. Anna was not so happy though. She didn't trust them...almost immediately. She could sense they were not good men. But her husband was different...he trusted everyone. He welcomed them...

"They are poor immigrants Anna," he said to his wife. "In a strange country. They know no one other than their own. Certainly they are worthy of our compassion!"

The day that Anna and I spoke, we'd gone to the coffee shop just down the block from her shop. As we waited for our order, she explained to me that this was just her husband's nature...to trust people rather than to doubt them. He'd always been that way and she'd lost hope that he would ever change.

"But people should be doubted!" Anna insisted. "Especially people in these days. I tried to tell him that doubting people is part of getting to know them. It is the only way we will know if you we trust them or not. But he would not listen to me. And now look where that foolish old man is."

"Tell me what happened Anna," I asked. "Can you talk about it without crying?"

"Oh Jimmy," she said looking into my eyes and sighing. "I will do my best. But it is very difficult for me."

The waiter brought us our coffee and each a small glasses of sparkling water. I asked if he might bring a small place of biscotti too. She took a sip of the strong coffee and began to talk...

"There were only a few of them at first," she said. "They pretended to not speak Italian and so they communicated with my husband with hand gestures and by pointing to things on the shelves here or there that they wanted. When they talked to each other though, they spoke that gibberish that was their own language, whatever it was.

At night they would gather outside on the street corner, in front of our shop or sit on the steps of the other small shops around ours. No one really knew who they were or where they came from. One day they were just there. You could see they were aimless...they had nothing to do and nowhere to go.

Their complexions were so very dark. They stood out among the local people here. We are very fair-skinned here in the north...for Italians you know! Everyone noticed them. It may not be a good thing, but we have always been suspicious of strangers, regardless of the color of their skin or the language they speak. I think it is only normal...only human nature, don't you? So sadly, or perhaps not, no one trusted these dark men. No one but my foolish husband that is."

"You're right," I said. "That is just the way things are most places nowadays. Strangers can seem so suspicious...even dangerous. I found that out for myself. It took quite a long time for me to be accepted here in this little village. You don't know the stories but I almost did not stay here after I bought my farm."

"My husband found out these men came from the north of Africa," she continued. "Morocco I think he said. They came across the sea in boats, many of them at the same time...in the same boats. They come to Lampadusa. It has been all over the news lately and in the papers. Surely you must have read about them by now. They were mostly young men...only a few women and maybe a child or two from time to time."

"Yes I've seen the newspapers and the TV news," I answered. "It's becoming quite a problem here and you just don't know who to believe anymore."

These "dark men" that Anna was talking about were refugees. From what or who they were fleeing was never really clear to any of us here in Italy and how they ended up here in our little village, so very far away from Lampadusa, is an even greater mystery. The government here does things without the citizens knowing. It is not really a democracy...not really a republic. Politicians and leaders do what they want to do regardless of what the people want.

"It wasn't long before we noticed there were more of them out on the street corner at night and on the steps," Anna continued. "Many more of them! They would come into the shop in the morning just as we opened. Sometimes there would be as many as ten or twelve of them in this little space of ours all at one time. They could not even turn around. It made me very nervous. I begged Ermanno not to let them in all at once but he would not listen to me."

Before I go on, I want to tell you a little about my friends Anna and Ermanno Pavese.

Ermanno and Anna have two children...two sons. Agostino and Carlo. From time to time Agostino would help them around the shop, mostly at night after he worked his regular job. I call him the good son because that's what he is. His parents are old and he considers it his duty to take care of them.

"I will be 75 years old in another month or so," Anna said. "And Ermanno...he is a year or two older than me. We wanted to sell the shop and retire years ago, but things are not so good here in Italy as you know. We have another son...Carlo. He fell on hard times and lost his job two years ago. He asked to borrow money from us...a lot of money. He is our son...how could we say no?

He has gone away to Spain now and we don't hear from him anymore. He took most of our savings and our trust along with him. But he has not paid us back. So we have little other choice now but to continue to work. Our pension is tiny...it is not nearly enough to live on."

It was at this point in our chat that Anna paused for a moment or two, to gather herself together a bit before she could tell me the rest of the story...

"Agostino came in to the shop one day and noticed there were many things missing from the shelves," she continued. "He said something to his father, but Ermanno would not listen to him either."

"Papà," he asked. "Have you forgotten to reorder these things? Has Filippo not come in to check on you lately?"

Filippo Gardi was their supplier for many of the things Anna and Ermanno sold. He was a very good and conscientious man and Agostino could not believe he'd been avoiding his parents...

"No," Ermanno answered. "I have not forgotten to order anything. And Filippo is here every week now."

"It is because these black men are stealing from us!" Anna said to her son. "They are robbing us in broad daylight and your father will do nothing about it!"

"Is this true papa?" Agostino asked.

"I do not want to make any trouble with these men," Ermanno said. "They tell me they will pay for what they've taken and I must believe they will."

Ermanno would not admit this to anyone, least of all not to Anna or his son, but he was afraid of these men...

"I know my husband," Anna said. "I could see fear in his eyes. We tried to watch things better during the day but with so many of them in our shop at once...in and out...coming and going. It was impossible."

This is when she started to cry so I suggested we stop talking for a while or change the subject. She became quiet almost immediately.

There were more and new refugees that came into Anna and Ermanno's shop in the next weeks and months...all young men, no women. And these new refugees had no money...at least this is what they claimed. They said they were waiting for their benefits to come from the Italian government. Ermanno believed them again and so he would charge their cell phones or give them cigarettes and other things from the shelves.

In a book behind the counter, he would write down their names and how much they owed. They promised to pay him back when the benefits came...but of course they never did. They had no intention to pay. They gave him fake names and wrong addresses. As time went on and the shelves became more bare, it got to the point where Ermanno simply had no other choice but to say no to them. And that is when the trouble began.

"I had to begin taking money from what was left of our savings to pay our suppliers and our bills," Anna began to say again. "And then these men turned on him. He had tried his best to be kind and compassionate...to make them feel like human beings, but when his generosity ran out, they turned on him like animals."

They waited until one of the nights when Agostino did not come in to help close up. Three of them went into the shop...one stood at the door to make sure no one else came in. Another pushed Ermanno behind the counter with a knife pointed at his chest. The man made him open the cash register.

"They took all the money we had," Anna said. "Even the few coins. Before they left, the man with the knife held it to my husband's neck. He put a finger over Ermanno's lips and warned him to tell no one. Then he laughed in my husband's face. They all walked out talking in that gibberish language of theirs."

Ermanno had become so frightened that he soiled his pants. He was too embarrassed to call the police, so he just closed the shop. He pulled down and locked the steel shutter behind him, got in his car and then he drove home.

"He was shaking like a leaf when he came through our front door," Anna recalled. "I could tell something was terribly wrong. But he was too nervous to tell me anything right away. So I called Agostino and, good boy that he is, he came immediately."

Ermanno told his son what had happened and Agostino immediately called the police. They agreed to meet Ermanno and Agostino at the shop. But when Ermanno could not provide a good description of the men, sadly, they said there was little they could do.

That is just the way things are here in Italy. The police mean well...they really do. But they are mostly impotent...useless, especially when immigrants or gypsies are involved. That is because our laws here are written to protect the criminals and to leave the Italian citizens, usually the victims, defenseless.

Agostino took his father home and they discussed what to do next...

"Before something even worse happens to you papà," Augustino said, "I want you to think about selling the shop. I can move back home and help with the bills. I will give up my apartment. And in the meantime, promise me you will not allow these people to come back in."

"What am I supposed to do?" Ermanno argued. "Just say excuse me...but you are no longer welcome in my shop? Do you have any idea the kind of trouble such a thing will start? No Agostino...I cannot do what you ask. And I would never ask you to give up your apartment and your life. So speak no more of this foolishness."

Agostino knew his father was right. To say no to these people would only bring more trouble. So from that point on, it was decided that Agostino would work behind the counter at night...promising his mother that he would not miss a single evening.

For weeks this is how it was but one night Agostino had an appointment that he could not cancel. He argued with his father to close the shop at 3:00 as usual and not open at again at 6:00 that night like other nights. It took some doing but eventually he convinced him.

But by 6:00 that night, Ermanno must have changed his mind or something. He drove to the shop and opened for business as usual. There was a light rain falling. At first, it was an uneventful night...only a few customers here and there, no doubt because of the weather. But then, just before he was ready to close at 10:00 the worst thing in the world was about to happen...

According to the newspaper account, two of the Moroccan men entered Ermanno's shop just before closing time. There was only one customer in the shop at the time. One of the Moroccan men, the same who had robbed him before, now carried a pistol instead of a knife. The other man was holding a baseball bat.

The man with the pistol placed the barrel firmly against Ermanno's forehead. Without speaking, he motioned with his head for him to open the cash register. Ermanno, frightened beyond words, was looking down at the floor. But when he looked up and their eyes met, Ermanno recognized the man immediately.

"So you recognize my face?" the Moroccan man said. "This is very unfortunate for you. If you are a smart man...if you value your life and that of your wife, you will forget you saw me here tonight, yes?"

Ermanno, now shaking uncontrollably, did exactly as he was told, even as his urine was running down his leg. With the barrel of the pistol still pressed against his forehead, he typed in the code to open the register without ringing up a sale.

When the register drawer opened, the man reached in and took out all the money. He even knew where Ermanno kept the larger bills from earlier in the day...the fifties and the hundreds...under the register drawer.

With what he came for stuffed into his pockets, the man turned to leave, gesturing for his accomplice to follow. But before the man with the bat was out the door, he turned around and for no good reason at all other than senseless violence, swung it at the customer in the shop, violently hitting him in the ribs and knocking him to the floor. Then both the Moroccan men fled into the dark night.

When Ermanno had not come home by 11:00 or had not called Anna, she knew something was wrong. She should have called Agostino but all she could think about was getting to her husband.

She drove an old Lancia...about 15 years old. It gave her problems starting from time to time. So as she sat behind the steering wheel that night, she said a quick prayer before turning the key. God must have heard her prayer because the car started. She drove straight to the shop, about four kilometers away.

When she pulled into the parking lot, she could see that all the lights were on inside the shop and the front door was wide open. Without thinking of her own safety she ran inside. It was Aldo Morini, the customer who had been with her husband, whom she saw first. He was lying face down on the floor, conscious but moaning and in very great pain. Three of his ribs had been broken, one puncturing his lung. He was struggling to breathe.

Looking to her right, that is when she saw Ermanno's feet extending from behind the counter. That is when her nightmare began...

"I must have screamed like an insane woman," she told me. "The owner of the bakery two doors down came running. He saw Aldo on the floor and then saw me kneeling over my husband's body. I think he was the one who called the police and the ambulance."

Ermanno was lying on the floor behind the counter. He was not conscious. Having the pistol held to his forehead must have been too much for the old man. He too was having trouble breathing and his heart was barely beating. When the ambulance arrived the paramedics could not bring him back to consciousness.

They rushed him to Ospedale Bellaria, a hospital that was conveniently just down the street, less than a kilometer. He had sunken into a coma and was not responsive. The trauma of being robbed at gunpoint and seeing his friend Aldo beaten nearly to death was more than his conscious mind could stand and so he shut down. A priest was called to his bedside to administer Last Rites. Someone had called Agostino and he arrived just after midnight. Together he and his mother stayed with Ermanno all that night.

As Anna and I were talking, we got quite a surprise when Agostino showed up and sat down with us to talk...

"My mother said she was meeting you here today," he said to me. "I wanted to stop by and tell you how grateful we are for your friendship. I want you to know that my father loved you very much...like a son."

I did not know what to say to such a kind compliment. All I could do was hug him and ask him to sit with us for a while...

"Would you like a caffè?" I asked him. "Or something stronger to drink?"

"No thank you," he answered. "I am fine. But I will sit and chat with you for a while if you don't mind."

For nearly a month, Ermanno remained in the hospital, unconscious and on a breathing machine. His condition was worsening daily. The doctors had spoken with Agostino and Anna about removing his feeding tube and taking him off life support...

"It is doubtful that your father will ever awaken," the doctor said to Agostino. "Each day we are seeing signs of his organs shutting down. It is just a matter of time now. You may not be able to see it because of his paralysis from the trauma and the disguise of the coma, but the break down of his organs can be excruciatingly painful for your father. I have had many patients go through this very thing. But since they cannot tell us, we do not know."

But Agostino was adamant that no one was going to take his father off life support. He held out hope that God would work a miracle somehow...

"Agostino," the doctor said. "You are a smart man. I have known your family for as long as you have been alive. I knew you as a little boy. I knew your brother as well. I watched the two of you grow up. You were your father's pride and joy Agostino. He always worried about Carlo, but he knew you were strong.

But you must know something now...and I must be the one to tell you. I would never question a man's faith or doubt what he believes...but God does not work the way you are thinking in this matter. Your father, for all intents and purposes, is already gone. What you see in this bed before you is just an empty body...a body that is failing and quickly. You must give this careful thought Agostino. And think about what is best for your mother too. Look at her. This is so very hard on her as well. I am watching her suffer terribly."

As time passed it became more and more apparent that there was little other choice for Ermanno but to remove him from life support and set him free...

"My husband's condition worsened and it took us all by surprise," Anna said. "I understood what he'd gone through. I understood the medical facts too. But I just never thought it was going to end his life."

"Had he ever spoken to you about these end of life decisions," I asked. "Sooner or later they must be made."

"No Jimmy," she answered. "He has no will or anything of the like. Everything fell on my shoulders to do. I had to make the appointments with the attorney. But every time I would set an appointment he would find some reason to break it. This kind of talk terrified Ermanno. Now...what am I to do?"

Ermanno began having stomach and digestive problems in the second month of his coma. It took the doctors much too long to determine what was wrong and render a diagnosis. But once it was finally made, it left Agostino with very little time to discuss with his mother what to do.

"I could see what the doctor had been telling me," Agostino said. "My father's condition was causing him great pain. He had lost an incredible amount of weight. He could not breathe or eat on his own. There was a catheter for his urine and he was forced to wear a diaper like an infant."

One morning Ermanno's intestines ruptured of gangrene from a fully blocked artery. He was rushed into surgery for a bypass and the placement of a stent. They removed more than a meter of intestine. He survived the surgery, but the doctors were not optimistic that he would heal.

"He couldn't heal," Agostino said. "Within 24 hours, his organs began to fail one by one. I spoke to the doctors on every shift of rounds. I asked every question I could think of. What about this? Have you tried that? Will this work?

I asked the advice of friends and even the priest in San Lazzaro. No one had the courage to tell me what I already knew in my own heart that I must do. I was only looking for validation. I finally sat down with the surgeon and I asked him to be brutally honest with me."

"His condition is not compatible with life," I was told. "His organs will shut down one by one, and he will only remain alive through artificial means."

"My husband was a fiercely independent man Jimmy," Anna said. "If the only way to live longer would involve a machine, he wouldn't want that. The doctor suggested if I wanted to let him pass naturally and with some level of dignity, that we keep him on fluids and pain medications, but nothing else. He would also write an order that I could ask for an increase in his morphine and a sedative if I noticed him going through any discomfort."

"My father was past the point of waking up and having a conversation with any of us," Agostino said. "So whatever we were going to do, I needed to do it without his approval. I called Carlo in Spain and talked with him. I told him what had happened and gave him some time to understand that our father would not get better, only worse, and that if he wanted to say goodbye, he would need to come home immediately."

So Anna and Agostino went along with the doctor's plan. They stayed with him around the clock. If he would as much as wince, they'd ask the nurse to increase the morphine.

"I had made the decision to let my father die peacefully," Agostino told me, "rather than postponing the inevitable. I always thought I was a pragmatic man and could justify doing such a thing, but perhaps to the family pet or an animal in suffering. But to this very day I have doubts that run through my head over and over again. Did I do the right thing for my father?

I went home one evening questioning myself. What were people going to think...that I killed my father? I thought about my reasons for doing what I was doing. I was trying to spare the man I loved so very much, pain and a loss of his dignity. I found myself in a position that made me feel quite uncomfortable. I could stop the pain and let him pass in peace, but would God have mercy on my soul on Judgment Day?"

Ermanno looked more peaceful as he began his death. Somehow, in a way she could not explain, it even made it a bit easier on Anna too.

But one night, in the middle of the night, Ermanno began to moan. He seemed restless. Up until that time he had not made any sounds at all. Anna was with him at the time and immediately rang for the nurse.

"I asked to have the pain medication increased," Anna told me, "but the nurse became angry and scolded me."

"You are going to kill him," she said to me. "You know that right? You know that doing this is wrong? You are not God. You do not decide when he dies...only God has such authority!"

"I was so shocked at first," Anna said. "But then I remembered what Agostino had told me about his father's dignity. I then told the nurse it was not her business. It was between me and my husband and God. I told her I was not seeking her opinion or her approval. But I must tell you Jimmy...what she said to me, pierced me to my heart."

It was in the morning when another nurse came in to change out Ermanno's IV that God decided to make a liar out of the doctor. A miracle was about to take place...

"Ermanno opened his eyes," Anna said. "The nurse had come in to change an IV and she was the one who noticed."

"Well hello Mr. Pavese!" she said to Ermanno. "How nice of you to grace us with your presence this morning."

The nurse looked at Anna and excitedly motioned for her to come to the bedside...

"You talk with your husband," the nurse said to me. "I must go get the doctor."

"I cannot put into words what I felt when I could look into my husband's eyes again," Anna said, "and know he was looking back at me. I could see he wanted to say something to me but he was so very weak. I put my mouth down very close to his ear and I whispered to him how much I loved him and how happy I was to see him again. He closed his eyes again, but only for a moment. He nearly smiled and I knew he'd heard me. He motioned for me to come closer. This time I put my ear close to his mouth."

"Azhar," he whispered to me. "Azhar."

"What does this mean tesoro," I asked. "What does Azhar mean?"

"Azhar did this to me," he whispered again. "Azhar."

Ermanno stayed awake for an hour that day before lapsing back into his coma. They transferred him from Ospedala Bellaria to Monte Catone, a very special hospital in the quiet hills near Imola, further east from San Lazzaro. It is a place for patients who have suffered severe mental or emotional trauma. When they sent him there, it is doubtful if he would ever go home again.

"What will you do Anna?" I asked. "What will become of you if Ermanno does not get better?"

"What can I do Jimmy?" she answered. "He is all I have. He was my whole world for most of my life."

"And the man who did this?" I asked. "This Azhar...has he been punished?"

"No," is all she said. "No one has been held to blame. As I said, in the end, the ways of this world always win out. That is just the way it is."

There is a 'For Sale' sign on the shutter of the tabaccheria but no one seems to be interested in it these days. The dark-skinned men still congregate on the street corner and the steps. There are many of them now.

Several weeks ago I ran into Anna and Agostino at the supermarket in Centronova. He was helping her shop for a few things. I asked how Ermanno was doing and was dismayed by the news they gave me...

"My father died in February," Agostino said. "He got a bit better for a while and we were filled with hope. He spoke to us again. This time so much more coherently. But it was only for a short time. He was able to say good bye to us. He is buried in the cemetery here in San Lazzaro if you ever have the time to stop there and say a prayer for him."

"I am so dreadfully sorry," I said as I hugged Anna. "He was one of the best men I've ever known."

"Do you know what that old man said to me before he died Jimmy?" Anna asked me.

I had the strangest feeling Ermanno said something about forgiveness. I was right.

"He said he forgave the man who did this to him," Anna said. "He said he began to feel sensation in his feet. It moved up his legs and then up his entire body...

"When I felt it leave me" he said to me, "I instantly knew that all the anger and hatred and animosity I held in my heart for this man was over. I have forgiven him."

"How can anyone forgive someone for such a thing?" Anna asked me. "I will never forgive this man who did this...who took my husband from me. I will take my hatred of him to my grave."

Agostino gave the eulogy at his father's service...

"My father passed away this week," he began. "There was no drama. It was as if he fell asleep and moved on. He was able to find a very special place in his heart to forgive the man who did this to him. My father was an exceptional human being.

I was trying to find the right words to speak today...to try to understand how he was able to forgive. I came across an old newspaper clipping in my father's safe at the tabaccheria. He must have cut it out years ago and held on to it for some reason or another. It was dated 29 December 1983.

It was a story of Pope John Paul II and the man who tried to kill him. John Paul met with him in his prison cell. He brought him a gift in a small white box...a silver rosary with mother of pearl beads. They spoke for a mere twenty one minutes and when it was all done, John Paul had forgiven him.

When I read John Paul's words, I was able to get a glimpse into my own father's powerful soul and the mercy he held in his heart...

"Forgiveness happens inside the person doing the forgiving. It heals our pain and our resentment before it does anything for the person we are

forgiving. They might never know about it. Forgiving from the heart can sometimes be heroic. Thanks to the healing power of love, even the most wounded heart can experience the liberating encounter with forgiveness.

Asking and granting forgiveness is something profoundly worthy of every one of us. If we really want peace, we must make the first step. We must forget offenses and offer the bread of love and charity."

Every year on the anniversary of Ermanno Pavese's death, a bouquet of white lilies is left as his grave. Anna has never been able to determine who leaves them but they are always there.

She spoke to the man who tends to the grounds in the cemetery, asking if he might know...

"I have no idea who he is," the old man said. "He looks to be a foreigner...very dark skin."

Vignette 10 ~ The Cigar Box

IF THERE IS ONE THING YOU WILL LEARN FROM LIVIN'
IN THE SOUTH or spendin' any significant time here, it's that
history awaits you around every turn. And more often than not, it
rises up when you least expect it. Sooner or later you will come face
to face with the ghosts that haunt these little towns.

I myself have been out hikin' through these mountains and by
chance I have stumbled upon old Indian burial mounds. Most of
them are benign but there are those that hold the most brutal stories
of days gone by. The horrors and atrocities that my ancestors
perpetrated upon the simple, peaceful and quiet people who lived
in these mountains long before the white man come along...well,
they are enough to make you hang your head in shame.

And speakin' of man's inhumanity ta man, let me assure you that if
you stand long enough outside the ruins of some long-ago
abandoned plantation house, sooner or later you are gonna hear
it...be it ever so faint. You will hear the old Niggras singing their
spiritual songs. Songs 'bout Jesus and 'bout goin' home to a
paradise somewhere over yonder...one that's been made and waitin'
just for them.

Walk down the streets of even the smallest towns here anywhere in
the South and you'll discover heaved up sidewalks...slabs of old,
cracked concrete that have been pushed aside by centuries-old,
gargantuan pecan trees...monstrous towers of timber and leaves
that hold centuries-old stories of the many lovers who have sat
beneath 'em and sinners who have conspired around 'em...even the
strange fruit than hung from 'em in our darker days.

But perhaps no place else tells the stories of the grim Southern past
like the homestead graveyards one finds down here. Small,
forgotten patches of ground, on lonely hillsides, surrounded by
rustin' steel fences and broken gates that no longer open. They've
been over-run by the weeds and withered grasses, victims of
decades of neglect. But if you take the time to read the headstones,
pronounce the names carved upon 'em and take into your heart the

words written about the deceased who lay beneath your feet...well, you may very well leave a changed person.

You see, here in the South, everythin' is eventually captured. Everythin' is reclaimed in time. History clings to you like a wet shirt.

I woke up this mornin' with a poundin' head and the most god-awful taste in my mouth. I am not quite sure how I got home or even inta my bed last night. That may be a damn good reason for this head ache. When I woke, I sat at the end of my bed, wipin' the crust of sleep from my eyes and tryin' to focus on the clock to see what time it was. Twenty six minutes after ten! Damn...I am just too old for this nonsense!

From a heap of clothes I found on the floor aside my bed, I pulled on a pair of faded old blue jeans. On top of another heap, I found that old plain, grey, baggy T-shirt...the one with the big hole under the armpit. I have been meanin' to wash it for the last two weeks or so but I just don't seem to be able to get around to it. I am fairly sure, or at least immensely hopeful, that this stain is bar-b-que sauce or tobacco juice on the front...and not blood. If it is blood, then I musta been drunker than I thought last night!

I have yet to take a shower or even comb my hair for the last few days. But I damn sure will brush my teeth today just as soon as I can find my way to the bathroom! My momma used ta have a sayin'...

"When your breath smells as bad or worse than your butt son...ya'll got trouble!"

Her words are ringin' quite true today. I got trouble!

Now I've made a conscious decision to hide from the world today. I just want to get in that little car of mine and drive...just disappear into these mountains. I have plans to do exactly that. I will grab that worn out black jacket that someone forgot or left behind here one night about a month ago or so and wrap it around my body. No one has asked about it or come back to claim it, so I guess its mine...loser's weepers, finder's keepers has always been my philosophy.

And yes...I know it is July. I know it is warm outside. I know. I know. I know! And I know that wearing that jacket is not necessary in the least, but for some strange and inexplicable reason I have the strongest desire and most urgent need to cover myself up today. It may well have somethin' to do with the significance of this date in my own personal history. For the longest time I've been pretty much able to ignore it. But this year it come a'crashin' back inta my world like a ragin' wild boar.

I haven't always lived here in Collins County. As a matter of fact I was born and raised fifty miles from here, over in Drydon County...near Burkette, the county seat. But that was quite a few years ago now. I had my own reasons for leavin', the biggest of which was my father. You see, my old man and I just did not get along.

We had a come-to-Jesus meeting one day and well, the newspapers and local TV stations had quite a field day with it. After the dust settled and the judicial proceedin's was over, Sheriff Colton stopped by to pay me a visit. He thought it best if I move on and I must admit I did not find the man to be very negotiable in the matter whatsoever.

So I left. I left Tennessee altogether, for a few years actually, which I will tell you about in a minute or two. But the draw of home was so strong I could not help but want to return. So I come over here to the next county to see if maybe I might be able to put down some roots and maybe make a new start. I figured I wasn't leavin' much if anythin' behind...so how damn difficult could it be to start over? But you know, no matter where you go, you turn around and there you are. Every time...sure as hell! And do you remember those ghosts I told about when we first started talkin'? Well them sons-a-bitches, they follow you too.

I have made a few good friends here though ova the years, one of which owns the garage in town. That is fortunate for me 'cause the car I drive can be rather contrary from time to time. His name is

Charlie Price, the mechanic, not the car! Everybody calls him Buck...on account the way his front teeth always seem to jut out through his lips. He can't help it none and it seems downright mean to call him Buck to his face, but he don't mind no more. He become used to it I guess.

Well, the reason I mention Buck...or Charlie I guess I should call him, is on accounta how he's helped me out these last few days to get the old MG up and runnin'. First there was a starter problem. He found one in a junk yard over in Santee. I told him I'd drive over and bring it back if I could use his old truck. I could save myself some money and Charlie a little time. The damn starter cost me a hunnerd dollars. One would have to wonder how much a new one cost, ya know?

Then the fuel pump crapped out on my way over to Henryville. I barely drifted that car off the road before one of them big old loggin' trucks flew by me at the speed of light...bastards that they are anyway. I walked about two miles up the road to a pay phone. It was outside a closed-down convenience store and as I remember they made the best damn fried chicken in the county. I wonder what made 'em go outta business? Anyways...I give ol' Buck a call from that pay phone and he come out with the tow truck and hauled me back.

He was able to rebuild the fuel pump but still, that cost me another fifty bucks. He didn't charge me no towin' bill though. I guess we need to count our blessin's when we can. How far the rebuilt pump is gonna take me today before it takes a shit again I don't know. Buck told me he had ta use a few Buick parts and rig the damn thing to keep it pumpin'. But it's alright with me. Everythin' is just fine. It don't pay no more to get worked up 'bout things. All I know is that I need to get the hell away from here for a while.

Now my momma also had another sayin'. She would say a picture paints a thousand words. But ya know, I must say I have found that is just not always the case. Many times it's just the opposite that's true. I have found that a few words can paint a thousand pictures. Take for instance what lies out ahead of me today on my escape route from reality.

The names of the little windin' roads and minuscule mountain communities around here that I will drive through never fail to inspire my imagination. I'm a gonna pass by signs announcin' I am either enterin' or leavin' places called Hardtack, Little Log, Upper, Middle and Lower Corncrib, Chicken Scratch, Cooterville, Dust Rag, Dough Bag, Big Bottom, Hooter Holler, Quickskillet, Buck Wallow, Possum Strut...yep, they truly can paint a thousand pictures if you let 'em.

Last night before I had that one, 'one-too-many drinks', I remember going through an old photo album I've had on a bookshelf for quite a few years now. My momma used to keep it up when I was a youngin'. But after she left daddy back in '66, hell, I don't rightly think there's been another photo stuck in it since.

What made me want get it down and go through it last night, I don't rightly know. Somethin' had me wantin' to stir the turd I guess. And maybe the fact I come across a few pictures of my old man and me is what got me to drinkin' again last night. God damn! Did we used ta argue a lot or what!

Ever since I was knee-high to a grasshopper, I couldn't do a damn thing right in that man's eyes. If I contemplated that old bastard's demise once, I must have planned it out in my mind a hundred times. The night that got me escorted to the county jail however, was the proverbial straw that broke the camel's back.

You're prob'ly wondrin' what the hell I'm goin' on about...so I suppose I should give you a few details. The best place to start this story is somewhere 'round the middle I guess...

It was back in 1968. I was seventeen years old at the time. I am sixty seven now, just ta put a few things in perspective for ya. A friend of mine by the name of John Carpenter got a letter in the mail one day and the next thing he knew he was on his way to Viet Nam. He tried just about everything he could ta get outta goin...shorta claimin' ta be a homosexual like Bruce Springsteen done of course. He even contemplated goin' ta Canada. But in the end there was no escapin' his fate. And I feel compelled to tell you that he did make it home again...unfortunately it was in a big aluminum Conex container with the American flag draped ova it.

John had a Honda 350 Scrambler…fastest bike I evva rode. When he got that letter from his Uncle Sam, invitin' him to spend a year in a tropical paradise in South East Asia…all expenses paid, well one of the first things he did for some reason was put that bike out in his parent's front yard with a big For Sale sign across the handlebars. He was askin' $300 for it. I was plannin' on offerin' $275. He'd a took it too. I betcha any money he'd a took it. He'd a even thrown in that helmet too…the one with the flame decals on the sides.

And I had the money to buy it, or at least I thought I did. I had been savin' my dollars bills and coins since I was nine years old. I mowed grass, delivered newspapers, washed cars, run errands, cut up and skinned deer, slaughtered hogs…you name it. Hell, I even run moonshine for Wilber Moss and his brother Henry. Anythin' I could do to make a little money at. I kep good track of it too…in a ledger book momma gimme. Last count I had $377.22.

I didn't have anythin' particular in mind I wanted to buy, I just wanted to feel like somebody. Knowin' I had a little money to my name gimme that feelin'.

Ya see, I had this aversion to evva bein' anythin' at all like my old man. He spent money faster that piss bein' poured outta a boot! Every penny I earned I stashed away in a White Owl cigar box that I hid behind the headboard of my bed. There warn't another soul in this whole world that knew it was there.

Now the day I finally decided to spend it and buy John Carpenter's motorcycle, I pulled my bed away from the wall and God damn it! If I didn't find that cigar box empty. I cannot even begin to tell you the things that run through my head. There was only one person who coulda took it. Momma was long gone…livin' with Henry Salter over in Bensonville. That left only my lyin', cheatin', stealin' bastard of a father.

Growing up, I was about ten or eleven years old when my daddy bought me a 12-guage shotgun to go out and hunt turkey for my mother. Up until then all I had was 410 gauge, a little single shot piece a crap! I learned to hunt squirrel with it but it warn't good for nothin' else really. The day I got that 12-guage, I put that little pea shooter of a 410 away in my closet for good.

As I told ya, my new gun was a twelve gauge, a Brownin' as a matter of fact, with an extra-long barrel and a modified choke out on the end of it. He come home with it one day when he had been in Nashville on business. From what I understand, he was a salesman. But I don't much recall what it was he sold. Mamma said he sold Bibles but I find that right impossible to believe. Holdin' a Bible in his hand woulda been like holy water to a damn vampire! I couldn't a give a shit back then what he did for a livin' but that gun he gimme, it had been my pride and joy ever since. It was a cryin' shame though the day Sheriff Colton saw fit to take it away from me after I used it for no good.

"I gotta take your Brownin' for evidence Willis Ray Junior," he said to me. "Don't make any guarantees ya'll gonna get it back either...just so you know."

I been called Junior most all my life. But whenever anybody called me Willis Ray Junior, my blood used ta run cold with contempt. The worst thing my momma evva done ta me was to name me after that son-of-a-no-good-God-damn-bastard father of mine. Pardon my language!

Now the day I found my money missin', the first thing I did was go for that shotgun and the box of shells I kep on top of my dresser. Once you took the plug out the Brownin', you could load five shells inta the magazine, pump one up inta the chamber and then push another one in to fill it up. That is exactly what I did that day...three times!

I took that shotgun outside with me and one by one I shot out every single window in our house. Then I waited for him to come home, sitting on the front porch with that 12-gauge layin' across my lap.

I had the time to think about a few things while I waited. Oddly enough, there was one particular story that crossed my mind. I still don't know why. It was a story my momma told me when I was not a whole lot older than ten, maybe eleven years old. It was the story of my birth and it went like this...

"When you was a'comin' out," she said, "Lord you had a big old head on ya! I wasn't ready for you yet and neither was the nurse.

She tried to push you back in. I tried my hardest to hold you in. But you wouldn't wait! I crapped myself...right there on the bed and when you come out, damn if you didn't land right in it."

Now if there ever was a way to sum up the story of my life, it would be the same as the story of my birth. I have been, one way or another, rushing head on into problems and trouble all my life and more often than not, fallin'inta the shit along the way.

When my father got home that day, he took one look at the windows and another look at the shotgun. Then he looked right at me. There is no doubt in my mind that he had no earthly idea what was coming next...

"We can make this real simple, daddy," I said. "Just gimme my money back. That's all I'm askin'."

"You the one busted out all my windows?" he asked.

"Not quite sure," I answered. "You the one stole my money?"

"I don't know what yer talkin' 'bout boy!" he answered. "You figurin' on usin' that shot gun on me?"

"Stronger 'n not possibility daddy," I answered. "Gimme me money back and I'll think 'bout puttin' her down."

"Somebody's gotta pay ta fix all these windows Junior," he said. "Now iff'n I had your money, which I am not sayin' I do, I would be a right foolish man ta not subtract the cost of these windows from your $377.22 life savin's account."

"So you knowed exactly how much was in that cigar box did ya?" I said

BOOM!

I pulled the trigger and blowed the windshield right out his car! Tiny pieces of glass exploded everywhere.

"Now ya kin take the costa that outta my savin's account too, daddy" I said as I pumped another shell into the chamber.

BOOM!

I peppered the front of his grill and just smiled like that Cheshire cat as I watched the antifreeze start puddlin' on the ground beneath the car. To my daddy's credit, he never even as much as flinched. And ta be honest with ya...that scared the hell right outta me!

"BOOM!

Click.

BOOM!

Two more shells, both his headlights gone.

"I know you stole my damn money," I said as I was replacin' the four shells I just spent on his Chevy. "I ain't got no expectations whatsoever of gittin' it back from ya either. You low-life piece a shit! Prob'ly spent it on your whores over in Chattanooga. But you're a dang fool iff'n you think I ain't gonna exact my revenge on your sorry ass. I got half a mind to blow your shit straight to hell without so much as another word."

"Now boy," he said to me. "Ya done got yourself backed inta a corner. You're either gonna have to use the Brownin' on me or I'm a gonna take it 'way from ya."

I honestly did not expect what he done next. He just lunged at me...scared me so quick I fell backwards in that chair. As I was tumblin' ova, he had a grip on the barrel of the Brownin', yanking the damn thing outta my hands. But my finga musta been on the trigga or somethin' 'cause that shotgun went off and tore right inta my daddy's chest.

Ya know how ya see in the movies when somebody takes a load a buckshot from a shot gun...how they go flying backwards...well God damn if that ain't exactly what my daddy done. One moment he was a comin' straight at me, the next he was flyin' backwards like somebody was pullin' him with a rope,

He landed on his back right in fronta his Chevy. He warn't dead but he was lookin' at me with the damndest looka confusion on his face...as if ta say, "God damn Junior...I can't believe ya done this ta me!"

And I gotta be honest as well. I couldn't believe I done it neither. It made me sick ta my stomach to the point where I doubled over and vomited.

"I reckon you betta call me an ambulance boy," he said with an eerie calmness about him. "Iff'n I leave this world on account a you shootin' me, your ass is in a worlda trouble. So go on...git in there and call me a damn ambulance."

It took damn near a half hour for the ambulance to git out ta where we lived. Daddy was holdin' on but barely. The ambulance pulled in first and Sheriff Colton was right behind 'em. The men from the ambulance went right to my father but the Sheriff was headin' directly toward me and that man had a look on his face of serious business...as if he already knew what gone on between my daddy and me.

I nevva did know what I'd done to make my daddy hate me so, but he left no doubt in my mind he was not at all proud of me as his son. So of course I'd been goin' over in my head what the hell I was gonna say when the authorities arrived.

"Yeah, Sheriff," I'da said. "I was angry...down-right pissed off as a matter of fact. The man stole all my money and spent it on whores and liquor. In one way or another he's been abusin' me all my life. If he warn't a cursin' at me or beatin' my behind with his leather belt, he'd ignore me for days at a time. This was just the last straw Sheriff. I can't even say I regret what I done."

That's what I planned on sayin but I nevva did get the chance ta. My daddy called for and motioned to Sheriff Colton that he had somethin' ta say...

"Sheriff," I heard him strugglin' to speak. "The boy didn't have nothin' ta do with this. I brought it all on myself. I come home in a foul mood and seen him sittin' on the front porch. He was cleanin' the Brownin' I bought him a few years back. As I said, I was in a foul mood and took the gun away from him, callin' him a lazy so and so.

Then I went crazy I guess...I shot out the windows in my house and boogered up my car right fierce. The boy tried to take his gun back from me after I threatened ta keep it. One thing led to another and the damn thing went off. Tore me up right badly. But this ain't the boys fault. He had nothin' ta do with it."

Then he started coughin' and up come blood and some pink bubbles outta his mouth. The ambulance men loaded daddy up into that ambulance and took him away. That just left me and Sheriff Colton standin' there lookin' at each other...

"Is that what happened Junior?" he asked me.

I did not know what to say at that very moment. My head was tellin' me to say, "Hell yes...that crazy bastard come right at me. I thought he was a gonna kill me!"

But my conscience was tellin' me to just tell the man the truth. "No Sheriff, he lied to you. I shot him. I shot out the windows. I shot up his Chevy. Then we struggled and I shot him."

That's what I shoulda said. My momma had taught me that the truth always prevails and the lies we tell will trip us up every time. I do not know what overtook me, but I pushed my momma's words right outa my thinkin'...

"What he said was pretty much the truth Sheriff," I said instead. "I was mindin' my own business...like he said, cleanin' my Brownin' when he come home and started squallin' and blowin' snot about somethin' or another. Before I knew what happened, the gun went off and he caught hisself a load a buckshot in the chest."

"You sure about this Junior?" he asked me. "Cause if you are, that's the way I'm a gonna write this up. But there will be an investigation and if you are lyin' you gonna be in a heap a trouble son. I don't see no gun cleanin' kit up there on the porch Junior! So do you wanna rethink your statement?"

I just looked at the man. My head was spinnin' with a thousand possibilities concernin' my future iff'n I told the real truth about what happened. I would no doubt be arrested right there on the spot. I'd go ta jail and stand trial and go ta prison afterwards, for how long I did not know. I couldn't do it.

"Yessir," I said. "I am sure about what happened. It was just like my daddy said it was."

"Alright then. I gotta take you in Willis Ray Junior," he said. "ta make a formal statement. And I gotta take your Brownin' for evidence," he said. "Don't make any guarantees ya'll gonna get it back either...just so you know."

From what they told me, my daddy died on the way to the hospital. There never was an investigation after that. Sheriff Colton closed the case but I nevva did get that Brownin' back. I know he kep it for hisself. That was just the kinda bastard he was.

I was officially alone now...an orphan from what the County woman told me. She wanted to know if I had any family I could go ta live with. There was my Uncle Gib and Aunt Darla but I had no intention a steppin' outta the fryin' pan and inta the fire. Uncle Gib was daddy's brother and a bad drinker. He was twice as ornery as daddy was and I had no desire to live with him. Besides that, I did not like my cousins neither.

So I said no...I ain't got no family. But I insisted I could take care of myself. The County woman insisted I could not! It was the law, she said...on account a me bein' a minor and all, that she had ta take me to a foster home until my eighteenth birthday...which ironically was comin' up in four months.

I let the woman do whatevva she wanted, 'cause I fully planned ta run away the very first day from wherevva she was gonna put me. And that's what I done.

I run away and come back to my house. Sheriff Colton got wind of it and I guess he figured I'd go back home and damn if he wasn't waitin' for me when I showed up. He stuck me in the back of his car and took me back to the foster home. I just run away again in a few days and went back home.

We had this routine it seemed...I'd run away and Sheriff Colton would take me back. But after the fourth or fifth time, he took me to a juvenile detention facility in Burkette instead which is where I stayed until my eighteenth birthday. I walked outta that place and went straight home and there was nothin' anybody could do about it.

But the electric had been shut off for non-payment and the well didn't pump no water on account a no electricity. All the food in the refrigerator had spoiled and stunk the house to high heaven. The roaches and mice had gotten inta the dry good and fouled all them beyond what could be eaten any more. The windows were still all blowed out but someone had come by and nailed plywood up over 'em. I was in a world a hurt. No food! No electricity! No money!

This is when I got my first lesson in the irony with which God treats his favorite creation...

"God damn it!" I said out loud though nobody was anywhere around ta hear me. "Will ya just look at that?"

I'd been snoopin' through daddy's room and come across a envelope in the top drawer of his dresser. When I opened it up I nearly swallowed my tongue. Right there before me was $377.22. He'd stole it from me sure 'nough, but he didn't spend it on whores and liquor like I blamed him a doin'.

Truth is I will nevva know why he took my money or why he chose ta hide it underneath his underwear like he did. I got myself another bout a guilty conscience as I stood there countin' out the bills for the third time. I done some bad things on account a believin' my money was gone. My daddy was dead and I was in a hell of a predicament. And just as I thought things could not get any worse I heard a car pullin' inta the front yard. Then there was a knock come ta the door.

It was Joe Driscoll, the mail man...

"I gotta certified letter for you Willis Ray," he said, pointin' to a green card stuck to the back of the envelope. "Ya gotta sign for it...right here."

"Who's it from?" I said, reluctant to even touch it.

"Says here it's from the Selective Service System," he said. "No doubt it is your draft notice. Looks like you gonna be a soldier Junior!"

"And it if I don't sign for it?" I asked.

"Then I'll just take it back and deliver it ta ya agin tomorrow," he answered. "And if ya don't sign fer it then, well I will return it to its sender."

"Then take it back," I said. "I want nothin' ta do with bein' a soldier."

"But ya gotta know something Junior," Mr. Driscoll told me. "Just 'cause you ain't signin' for a letter don't mean these people's just gonna go away. You piss these folks of Junior...they'll drag your ass straight to jail."

"I'm willin' ta take my chances," I answered. "Have a nice day now Mr. Driscoll."

He come back the next day just like he said but I did not answer the door. Things were quiet for the next week but it warn't meant ta stay that way.

"Willis Ray!" I heard a most familiar voice shoutin' while bangin' on my front door, wakin' me from a sound sleep. "Open up Junior! We got some important business ta talk about."

Damn if it warn't Sheriff Colton agin. And he was holdin' that envelope from the Selective Service System in his hand.

"Ya'll gonna sign this for me," he said, "or I'm a gonna take your ass to jail straight away. Do not doubt my intentions son. Sign the dang letter!"

I was wiping the crusty sleep outta my eyes and tryin' ta make sense of the threats he was makin' at me...

"I respectfully decline to sign for that letter," I said, "which is my legal right Sheriff. I done talked to the legal aid people in Burkette at the courthouse and they told me flat out I had no obligation ta sign for it."

"You got no obligation whatsoever," the Sheriff said ta me. "They are correct. But I want you to know I got me a legal obligation to turn you over to the Federal Marshal who will come ta take ya ta Nashville. You'll be charged with evadin' the draft and I sure as hell would not want ta be in your shoes once that happens. I ain't leavin' here without your signature or you hands in cuffs. Now what's it gonna be Junior?"

"Well," I answered. "Gimme a minute to brush my teeth and comb my hair Sheriff. Then ya'll kin put me in those cuffs and I'll submit myself to whatever my fate is a gonna be."

"I will give you five minutes Willis Ray," he said. "The clock is tickin' son!"

There was a small window in the bathroom that I was able ta climb outta. I come a crashin down onta the rain barrel that was underneath it. I picked myself up and ran off inta in the woods. My days of livin' in Drydon County had come to an end.

Truth is I didn't even make it outta Burkette before two of Sheriff Colton's deputies picked me up along Dubbs Creek Road. I was taken back to Sheriff Colten where he give me the choice one final time a signin' for the letter or goin' inta a holdin' cell where I would await the arrival of a Federal Marshal from Nashville. It was at this point my sensibilities musta finally caught up with me. I signed for the damn letter!

I will not bore you with the details of my illustrious military record but to say howevva, I did experience the paradise known as Vietnam. But I nevva did make it outta a supply depot in Cam Rahn Bay where I first marked the center of gravity of jeeps being lifted offa boats to be sent to the boys who was really fightin' that war. I done that for two months before I was assigned to a desk with the quartermaster where I spent the rest of my time in country processin' the paperwork to send the dead bodies of them boys who was done fightin' that war, back to the States. To quote one of my favorite country song writers... "I left to be all I could be but come home without a clue!"

I come home on one a those ships carryin' the dead bodies of boys whose paperwork I had previously processed. We came in to the Navy Yard at San Diego. I spent a little time kickin 'round Southern California afta they gimme my DD 214. But as I said the longin' my body felt for home eventually took ova and I made my way back to Tennessee.

I knew better than ta go back to Drydon County where I was not wanted nor needed and so I settled just outside of a little town called Whitwell Crossroads here in Collins County. I done odd jobs for a few years, tryin' to find my way in this life. I eventually took a civil service test and ended up gittin' me a job as a mailman at the ripe old age of 26! That was back in 1975 as I recall.

I worked quietly and peacefully for the next thirty nine years deliverin' all sorts a mail...junk mail, magazines, Christmas cards, utility bills...you name it. I always gotta sick and uneasy feelin' in my belly any time I had to deliver a certified letter and have ta ask someone for their signature. More of those ghosts I told ya 'bout.

I retired in 2015 and for some reason started right inta drinkin'...slowly at first but then I must admit, things did get a bit outta hand. I bought me a little red sports car for some reason...maybe a later than usual mid-life crisis...I dunno. It was a 1969 MG B convertible...biggest God-damn mistake I evva made. It was how I met old Buck Price though and we become pretty good friends.

Two days ago somethin' rose up inside a me and I felt a hankerin' to go see my daddy's grave over in the Collins County Cemetery. I must admit somethin' to you that is quite embarrassin' for me. It was the first time since he died that I went there. I went there not knowin' what to expect because had I been expectin' what happened ta me, I never woulda gone.

I used the fancy little computer at the visitor's center to find where he was buried in the cemetery. It spit out a map that I could follow over to Section 2 where I would be lookin' for grave numba 22 in row 4. Didn't take long at all to find it.

When I got to the end a row 4, I will admit I was reluctant to continue, but I did. I was expectin to find a grave stone...a headstone I guess is what I mean. Somethin' that would tell perfect strangers that here lies Willis Ray Newton, Sr...maybe a few words about bein' a lovin' husband and father. But as I was passin' by grave numba 19...Miss Wilma Barton's final restin' place...then grave numba 20 where Francis McGinnis, a Korean War vet'ran, was spending his eternity, I took notice to a gap in the headstones.

Standin' in fronta the graves of Glenn Collins and his wife Arthella right aside him, I looked at the space of flat ground to their left. A headstone was conspicuously missin'. All there was to mark my daddy's grave was a metal plaque in the ground, half grown ova with crabgrass and weeds. I just stared at it for what seemed like forevva.

The sum total of a man's existence...the man who was responsible for me bein' brought me inta this world, lay before me unnoticeable to anyone and forgotten by everyone. I felt the strangest sensation come ova me though...like a quiverin' in my chest and belly. Next thing I knew a tear was comin' from the corner of my eye. It disturbed me. It flat out frightened me. It was the strangest feeling I'd evva felt. I knew what it was but I refused to admit it to myself then and I damn sure will not say it out loud to you now.

Outta obligation and good manners, I knelt down and cleared away what was obstructin' my father's grave marker. While I was a kneelin' I done my best ta say a short prayer. There was his name...his date of birth and the date on which he died...exactly fifty years ago to this day! Not a damn thing else to tell anyone who or what he was.

There warn't no flowers aside his grave like any of the other graves. There was no tiny American flag to denote his service to the country in the Second World War. It was just a flat piece a metal in the ground...that's all it was.

I had the strangest experience then...what I was tryin' ta tell you a minute or so ago. Had I known I was gonna have it, I'd a steered clear of the cemetery completely. Right before my eyes I watched the name on that plaque turn to Willis Ray Newton, Jr. In a flash of sick'nin' realization, I understood that my fate would be no different than that of my daddy's.

I had no one to bury me. No one to mourn my passin'. I had spent my entire life avoidin' any kind of closeness or companionship. I'd nevva fallen in love. I'd nevva even as much as held a woman's hand to feel its warmth or softness, other than my mother's. I'd never known what it felt like to make a promise to someone and keep it in good times or bad...sickness or health. I was to end up no damn different than the man I killed.

And so this is the reason I got myself so damn drunk last night. I was tryin' to rid myself of the emotions I felt standin' at that man's grave. I'd spent my entire life believin' I hated him. Then alluva God-damn sudden my heart was racin' and my eyes was blurred with tears a love. I remembered how happy and proud I was the day he gimme that Brownin' 12 gauge shotgun. What was more, I remembered how proud he was ta give it ta me.

I had moments of other mem'ries comin' back ta me too...mem'ries I'd purposely blocked outta my mind. I remembered daddy and me fishin' for brook trout up by the old mine on Dubbs Creek. I remembered, of all things, playin' catch with him in the yard out back. I remembered sittin' on his lap in his Studebaker on Sunday mornin' as we drove through Burkette to get the Sunday paper and a carton of his Pall Mall cigarettes.

Where these mem'ries were comin' from, and a hundred more, I had no idea. Where the hell I stashed 'em for all these years remains a mystery too. How could anyone forget such happy mem'ries?

The choices we make when we are younger become layered and compressed ova time. They coalesce into sediment and then turn into the bricks and blocks with which we build the foundation of our lives. The poorest and worst decisions we make are those made outta ignorance and anger...like the day I decided to use the Brownin' for no good purpose other that hatred.

Everythin' is a choice. Every choice has a consequence...be it a good one or bad! We choose to choose every day even if we choose not to choose! John Carpenter didn't choose to go to Viet Nam...somebody else chose for him. I guess I did choose to go but no one can evva explain ta me why I come home and he didn't.

And it don't take a damn rocket scientist or a genius to know that not every one of our choices is gonna be good for us! They don't always end up as somethin' of value. I chose to shoot out my daddy's windows and look where in the hell that decision took me.

More often than not, the choices I made were poorly thought out. I have been forced to live with the consequences for a long time! Just take a look at my life iff'n ya don't believe that!

Most people are afraid of goin' down the wrong path in life...of ending up empty and unfulfilled. But please! If there is only one thing you take away from my sad story, let it be this...

This is your life. You get to decide the rules. You get to say what goes and what stays, what matters and what don't. But also know this. Iff'n you don't make the choices, somebody else is a gonna make 'em for you sure as hell!

Until the day that I myself die, I don't think I will evva understand why my daddy done for me what he done.

Vignette 11 ~ Dancing With A Limp

NOW THERE IS A BEFORE AND AN AFTER THE 13TH OF NOVEMBER. It is true...

Over the weekend I agreed to meet an old friend of mine...one I'd not seen in some time. The moment I saw her again I felt guilty...I hate it when I allow so much time to go by without checking in on the people who mean so much to me. Luciana and I decided to sit and take a coffee together at a small caffè here in Piazza Re Enzo in Bologna near where I live. The last time we'd seen each other was nearly two years before.

Europe has become the new ground zero for Muslim extremist terrorism. Italy has been spared so far but it is just a matter of time. Fear has been placed into our everyday lives and it is a difficult thing to get used to. It finds us everywhere we turn in these days. Our response is to show that we are stronger than it is. We do our best to get on with our lives. We go to the cinema, to the theatres and the concert halls. We go out to restaurants and we even sit at a quiet sidewalk caffè like the one I am sitting at as I tell this story.

In a way, what I am going to tell you about is this terrorism. I will spare the truly harsh details but please understand, some of this you must hear to be able to know what Luciana has gone through to better appreciate where she is now. Yes...it is about terrorism but I am afraid the real gist of my story is about the loss of innocence.

I'd met with Luciana in the weeks that followed the horrifying terrorist attack in Nice, France...the day a madman suddenly and violently drove a truck through a crowd of people, killing 84 of them...some of them innocent children. As my friend had watched the news of it unfolding on her television, it tore open a fresh wound that she believes will never, ever heal.

You see, it was a mere nine months before the attack in Nice that she had finished burying her own innocent child. A son, barely 20 years old, in his first year at the University here in Bologna. His name was Massimo but his friends and even his mother called him Max.

Max had the whole world still out before him when he died so unexpectedly. Anyone who knew him knew he was going to be someone and something special. But now he is gone...forever. And the world is going on without him.

Luciana had called me last week and told me she desperately needed to talk to someone and that it was my face that kept coming to her mind. Was I busy? Could I meet her in Centro later in the afternoon?

"For no more than an hour," she said. "I promise."

"Of course," I answered. "Where would you like to meet?"

"Piazza Re Enzo," she answered. "At the café. Can you be there at 5:00? Just for a short coffee."

"I told him that I didn't want him to go," she began, when we were finally sitting together. And just like that, the tears began to flow from her eyes and slowly streak down her face...

"I asked that he stay home instead, with me. But his friends from the University were all going to Paris for a long weekend. They were going to leave early Thursday morning and Max begged me to be able to go with them. The flight was cheap he said...with Ryan Air, and so I gave in and said yes."

Before I go any further, I want to tell you that Luciana's son and I had a bit of a history together. I had the pleasure of meeting him twice and the way I remembered him, was as really a fine young man.

He and Luciana had come out to the farm several Christmases ago. His father had abandoned the two of them the year before and they were barely coping. So Diana and I opened our home and our hearts to them.

They'd come earlier on Christmas afternoon than expected. I was still out in the barn, cleaning stalls and feeding animals if you can believe that. Max asked if he might help. I was anxious to get out of that barn, into the shower and start making our Christmas dinner, so of course I said yes...

"I'll fill it," I said, "and you will drive it." I was talking about the bed of the little three-wheeled utility truck I have here on the farm. When it was filled with the manure and old straw, I gave him the keys and got into the passengers side.

We drove up toward the vineyard and as he negotiated the steep and rutted lane I was able to get him to talk a little. To tell me a bit about himself...

"What I would really like to be is an astronaut," he said. "But I know that is only wishful thinking. But I want to have something to do with the Agenzia Spaziale Italiana...it is like your NASA, only much smaller. Someday I would like to go to the International Space Station."

"Such big plans," I thought to myself. But the more time I spent with Max and the more I got to know him, the more I believed I would someday read great things about him.

But then came a most fateful Friday...Friday the 13th. That terrible day when Max was on the Boulevard Voltaire in Paris...at the Bataclan to see a rock concert.

Max and two friends, Gianpiero and Matteo picked up a flight at the airport in Bologna and landed at Beauvais Tille airport 85 miles north of Paris a few hours later. They caught the train to the Gare du Nord station in Paris and then took a taxi to their hotel, three blocks from the Bataclan.

"Allahu Akbar," were no doubt the last words he ever heard. They were the last words many young people heard that day. Max and his friend Gianpiero were killed while they stood waiting for the Eagles of Death Metal to return to the stage. Three men who had emerged out of the shadows on the mezzanine above them opened fire. Max and his friend were undoubtedly among the first to be killed.

Matteo somehow survived and when she was finally ready, he told Max's mother what went on that night...

"That night was unimaginable," he began. "A war had come to Paris and Max, Gianni and I were in the middle of it. That's what it was you know...it was a war. Nobody could believe such a thing could happen in the center of Paris.

We were standing on the main dance floor waiting for the band to come back to the stage. For some strange reason the thought of where the entrance and the exit were came to my mind. They were both behind us...at the back of the hall. The band had just begun to sing "Kiss the Devil" when suddenly there was a sound from the back of the room. It almost sounded as if firecrackers were going off...like the ones we hear when the Bologna football team wins.

As soon as the band stopped playing, we knew immediately that the noise was not part of the band's act. Then all of a sudden there was this very loud, very distinctive sound coming from the back."

Matteo explained how the lights came on suddenly and for a few seconds they all were blinded and disorientated...

"I began looking around to see what was going on," Matteo continued. "That's when I first saw one of the terrorists. He was standing no more than five meters from me. He was holding a rifle...I guess it was an AK-47. It was the first time I'd ever seen a gun so I am not sure. And then all I could see was the flash of the light coming out of the end of the barrel. He was shooting everyone. He was walking through the bodies on the floor...he kicked them. If they showed any sign of life he shot them in the head. I remember being shocked to see how calmly he could take another's innocent life."

Matteo said that as the shooting became more intense, he'd become separated from Max and Gianni. People were scrambling and running over top of the bloodied bodies. They did what they could to hide...

"It was one of the most bizarre things I'd ever experienced," Matteo said. "I expected there to be screaming but instead there was only silence. I was lying on the floor with someone on top of me. My heart was beating so fast and I started feeling claustrophobic...not being able to move with this person on top of me.

I remember laying there for about 10 or 15 seconds...I guess it was when they suddenly stopped shooting and everything became quiet again."

We know now that the periods of quiet that took place that night were when the terrorists were reloading their rifles...

"They'd basically shot so many people," Matteo continued, "they needed to reload and all you could hear was the sound of the reloading echoing around the hall...a few whispers here or there. At that point, I took a chance and got onto my hands and knees. I looked toward the stage where I could see a door. I thought to myself, "I've got to get to that door if I want to survive. Forgive me...I beg of you. But all I could think about was getting out of there. I was not thinking of Gianni and Max."

Matteo explained that everywhere he looked, all he could see were bodies and bleeding people, screaming and crying out for help...

"There were a lot of bodies and people frozen with fear," he said. "Then they started shooting again and I just prayed I wouldn't get shot. It was like this weird rhythm of stop and start, stop and start. They were shooting all their bullets and then they reloaded their guns."

When Matteo finally made it to the door, he thought he'd managed to escape. But he found the door was locked...

"There was a security guard standing next to the door," he said. "I was shouting at him to open the door. Everyone behind was running toward us. But I remember he looked at me with a totally blank expression and then he looked back towards the men who were doing the shooting. He seemed frozen by fear. I realized at that point that it was every person for himself. So many people just kept coming. Somehow the door opened and dozens of people rushed to try and escape."

Matteo was pushed to the floor...

"I was knocked down and people were pushing me from behind. My legs got trapped under a couple of bodies. I was getting trampled on, literally people stomping on me in blind panic. I really thought I was going to get trampled to death. I desperately pulled my legs from under the weight of dead bodies by sliding myself along the floor. I lost my one shoe trying to pull my foot free. I don't know how but somehow I managed to get up."

Matteo said that after getting out of the hall, he ran up to the second floor where there was a group of people cowering against a wall, waiting in silence...

"When I asked them why they were not moving," he said, "they told me there was no exit. My heart sank. There was only one way in and out the hall and that was on the ground floor where the terrorists were. Suddenly, there was a really loud explosion from below us. It literally shook the whole building. Smoke appeared from below. At this point I'd given up...I could not see any way out. I was accepting that we would all die.

The explosion Matteo had heard earlier was the first of the terrorists to detonate the suicide vest he was wearing, blowing himself up...

"That's when I really started to panic," he said. "I was thinking, "How the hell are we going to get out of here?" I thought I was going to die for sure. I now know what a trapped animal must feel like."

A short while later, Matteo noticed that the ceiling of the stairwell had a sky window. Everyone started breaking off the bars so they could climb out...

"It was surreal," he said. "That is all I can say. It amazed me actually because people were suddenly very quiet and very calm. There we were...one-by-one queuing up, we were being so polite as we tried to escape the building."

Once they were all on the roof, Matteo noticed a man pulling survivors through a window of his apartment on the third floor. Immediately he ran towards him...

"We were in there for three hours," he said. "Maybe longer. I don't know. I had no idea what was happening down below us. We heard one loud explosion after another which made the room vibrate. Then there were many bursts of gunfire. It seemed as if it would never end. It was frightening, not knowing if the terrorists would find us at any moment."

It was at that point that Matteo remembered Gianni and Max...

"I wanted to call them and find out if they were ok and to tell them where I was," he said. "I wanted to tell them to come to where I was because it was safe. But I realized somewhere along the way I lost my phone. The man in the apartment who'd saved us gave me his phone but I did not remember Max's telephone number. The television was on in the apartment. It was the BBC. Seeing what was really going on made me sick. I could not believe how terrible it had become."

Matteo and the other survivors were eventually rescued by French Special Forces around 1:30 in the morning and whisked off to the police stations and interviewed for the rest of the night. Fortunately, Matteo only suffered minor injuries during the attack, but the whole ordeal had a significant mental impact on him.

"When I found out Max and Gianni were dead," he said. "I was overcome with a feeling of total and utter hopelessness of ever regaining any sort of normality in my life again. All I wanted was to be left alone. I did not want to see anyone. I did not want to speak to anyone. I wanted never to think about that night again."

When Luciana finished telling me the story Matteo had told her, I was dumfounded...

"When someone you love dies," Luciana said to me, "and you're not expecting it, you don't lose them all at once. You lose them in pieces...bit by bit...over time.

It is the way the mail stops coming for them. Or how their scent begins to fade from the pillows on their bed or from the clothes that still hang in the closet or lay folded in their drawers.

Gradually, you accumulate all these pieces...the ones that are gone. Just when the time comes when you think you can breathe and get through the day without tears, there's another particular missing piece you find...and it overwhelms you. You realize all over again that they are gone...forever."

I did not know what to say to her. Her quivering voice and tear-weary eyes...the obvious shell shock of what had just happened in Nice, had overwhelmed me too. Feebly, I was searching for any words that might provide her even the slightest comfort.

I had that feeling to say something philosophical and wise...to try my best to set her straight. But not this time! I couldn't do it. This time the words that came out of my mouth were not coming from my brain...they were flowing straight from my heart.

"I want to tell you something Luciana," I said. I reached across the table to hold her trembling hand. "I know this makes no sense to you now, but I promise that in time it will. I hope you will trust me when I say, I assure you that this crushing sadness you are living...this combination of searing pain and complete numbness, is a gift. It is a gift that will provide you in the days and months and years to come, a layer of compassion for other people who hurt...just as you do.

It will be an understanding that will come to you. One that you simply could not have gained without first walking through this valley of grief.

You will come to realize in time that you have lost someone that you *can* live without, though your heart will try over and over to convince you differently. You will come to know just how terribly broken is your heart...and you will have to accept the fact it will never completely heal. But this is not only bad news Luci...it is also something very, very good.

You see this way, Max will live forever in your heart. Your memories of him will fill in those cracks. It will become less painful over time.

It's like having a broken leg…one that never heals perfectly. The pain is always there…especially when the weather gets cold. But you must simply learn to dance with your new limp."

I had no idea from where my words were coming. All I could do is hope they were the right ones to be speaking to her. I wanted Luciana to believe me…but I don't think she did. I don't think she was ready.

We talked for a few more minutes and then she gathered her things and looked across the table to me…

"I must go now," she said. "I'd hoped this might have helped me today…I prayed that it would. I will think about what you have told me…honestly I will."

She leaned across the table and kissed me on the cheek…

"Such a kind soul you are," she said. "Such a sweet man. Max adored you. He often said he wished his father was more like you."

And then she left, walking across the piazza, turning down via Clavature and disappearing into a crowd of strangers.

Since that day I've been burdened with doubt and even a bit of guilt…asking myself if I did the right thing or spoke the right words? Did I comfort her? Or did I make it worse? What I told my dear friend was tough medicine to take, I know. Maybe I should have said something more before she left. I should have at least acknowledged her pain. I should have warned her that she will never be that person again she was before that horrid day in November.

If I could go back to that day with her in the piazza, I would say a few more things…

I would tell her grief is the price we pay for sharing our life with someone who is worth missing. It is the price we gladly pay for loving them. I would tell her that she must be gentle with that broken heart and she must be kind to herself. She needs to listen for the voice inside…the one that is telling her that she will survive…that this will pass and that the sun will shine on her again.

I would tell her not to listen to those who tell her to snap out of it, any more than she should listen to those who tell her to take her time. She is the only one who can survive her loss and the only one who can re-write her future.

This past Saturday afternoon as I was leaving the bakery on the via Emilia, I saw Luciana walking toward me beneath the portico. She'd already recognized me and was wearing that beautiful smile of hers. But I also noticed she was dragging her left leg behind her. At once I became terribly concerned…

"Luci!" I said, "Dear God, what has happened to you?"

"Nothing has happened to me my dear friend," she answered. "And yet everything has happened. After you and I spoke in the piazza that day, I came to realize something very important. I came to understand that grief wasn't just coming to visit me for a horrible, temporary holiday. No…it had its own plans of moving in with me.

It brought with it humility as a housewarming gift, though it did not care whether I wanted it or not. And when I am least prepared for it, I find another little missing piece and I add it to my collection.

This grief is an uninvited and unwanted guest. It has put down roots and I discovered it was only going to leave when I say enough is enough. And that is what I've done. I have taken your advice my dear friend. Basta! Enough!"

"But your leg?" I said again. "Have you injured it? What has happened to your leg?"

"There is nothing wrong with my leg. My little act was meant to make you smile," she said. "You don't remember what you told me to do, do you dear man? You see, I am learning to dance with a limp just as you told me I must!"

All of us will lose someone near and dear to us and all of us will be visited by that unwanted guest we call grief. I would hope when it is my turn, I can meet my adversary with the same courage and dignity as my dear friend Luciana.

The truth is that grief is a lifetime sentence. At the end of our days we will either be reunited in some glorious mystery with those who have gone before us, or we will simply have reached our last day of mourning their loss.

Vignette 12 ~ Strange Fruit

IT WAS IN THE LAST WEEK OF AUGUST IN 1964 when a black civil rights worker by the name of John Otis Trimball was standing in the Meridian Mississippi bus station waiting for the next bus to pull in. He had come to pick up a young man who would be arriving on that bus. The young man's name was John Chamberlain and he was a white college student from Wisconsin. Mr. Chamberlain had come all this ways to take part in a school desegregation event that would be a turning point for many of the people involved. Chamberlain came as a volunteer, recruited by Mr. Trimball's civil rights group that was known as Freedom Summer.

To be honest with you, in my opinion John Chamberlain really never should have come to Lauderdale County or ever come to Mississippi for that matter. This wasn't his concern...he had no dog in the fight as we say down here. Besides that, there were men in Mississippi waiting for the opportunity to kill outsiders like John Chamberlain...white men who did not want their white worlds changed in any way.

The 2:10 bus from Montgomery Alabama finally arrived and John Chamberlain stepped off of it. John Otis Trimball introduced himself quickly and then took Mr. Chamberlain's one bag of luggage and loaded it into the back of a 1955 cream-colored Ford Country Sedan station wagon.

Together they drove south toward Waynesboro, a small town of a few thousand people located at just about the very center of Wayne County and twenty some miles below Meridian. Just south of town, Trimball turned that station wagon left onto a dirt road pocked with puddles and pot holes. The road wound past a few clusters of cabins and shacks before narrowing into a densely wooded corridor. It seemed to John Chamberlain to be a road to nowhere, or at least nowhere he might want to go. A fork in the road revealed the Chickasawhay River, and a rusty bridge.

The steel-framed span loomed thirty feet above the muddy water of the Chickasawhay River. At the far end of the hundred-foot bridge, there was a forest that swallowed up a dirt road. That road used to lead to somewhere but with the barricades that had it blocked, something made John Chamberlain think it no longer did.

Years of cars and trucks rumbling across the bridge had worn parallel streaks of black rubber into the broad, wooden planks. Rusting, metal rails sagged in spots. Still, the reddish-brown truss beams on either side stood stiff and straight. The braces overhead cast shadows onto the rotting planks below. On that rusty bridge frame, between the lines of vertical rivets, someone had painted a skull and crossbones and scribbled the words "Danger. This Means YOU Nigger!"

"Why did you bring me here?" John Chamberlain asked, obviously made uncomfortable by the sign.

"This," John Otis dryly responded, "This is where they hang the Negroes."

The way he said it made it sound like it could have happened a hundred years ago, or last week. It made John Chamberlain very nervous.

"The bridge is closed to traffic now," he said. "But the Hanging Bridge remains. They refuse to tear it down. It's a landmark here in Wayne County. This is KKK country."

"What happened here?" John Chamberlain asked, completely unprepared for the answer he was about to receive.

"Back in 1938, just five days after Easter Sunday," Trimball began to explain, "a white mob dragged four young blacks here...two brothers and two sisters. The sisters were both pregnant. All four were lynched."

John Chamberlain took in a deep breath and pursed his lips, a grimace coming to his face...

"They hung those people from those rails there," Trimball said, pointing to the steel bars on the right hand side of the bridge.

"What were they accused of?" John Chamberlain asked. "Were they guilty of something?"

"Ya'll don't gots ta be guilty down here to be lynched Mr. Chamberlain," John Otis replied, mimicking the way the older blacks would talk. "All ya'll gots ta be is black!"

"What did they do?" John Chamberlain asked again.

"Their white boss turned up dead a few days before," John Otis said. "There was no need to get the Sheriff involved. The mob claimed the four confessed and a trial would have been a waste of money and time."

"Surely there was an investigation though?" John Chamberlain asked innocently enough.

"When the NAACP came down here from Washington, they demanded an investigation," John Otis answered, "Our Governor at the time, a Democrat by the name of Hugh White, told them all to go straight to hell."

"This is why I am here John Otis," Mr. Chamberlain said. "This is America. This cannot be allowed to take place here."

"Two years later, a mob of white vigilantes lynched two more back children right here," John Otis continued. "Ernest Brown and Jasper Lang. They were fourteen and fifteen years old. A white girl from Waynesboro accused them of trying to rape her. There was no evidence and there were no witnesses. The vigilantes did not wait for a trial in this case either."

"And again?" Mr. Chamberlain asked. "No investigations?"

"Newspapers across the country ran photographs of those two boys' bodies hanging from this same river bridge," John Otis explained. "The headline from the *Jackson Clarion-Ledger* read something like, "Waynesboro Bridge's toll stands at six lynch victims." The CHICAGO DEFENDER placed the figure at eight...counting the two unborn babies.

The DEFENDER *IMMEDIATELY* sent a black journalist down here to what they called America's new lynching capital. He came into Meridian just like you did John Chamberlain...looking for answers and wanting to help. When he asked a black taxi driver for a ride to Waynesboro, the driver refused...

"No sir," he replied. "I'd just as soon go to hell as to go Waynesboro."

"Why did you bring me all the way down here?" John Chamberlain asked.

"I just want you to know what you're getting involved with," John Otis answered. "This is deadly serious business down here Mr. Chamberlain. If you don't think you have the stomach for it, tell me now. I'll take you back to the station. I will think none the less of you."

"I know what I'm getting myself involved with Mr. Trimball," John Chamberlain answered. "My father was one of the liberators of the concentration camps during the War. The stories I've heard him tell are heart breaking. I simply cannot sit back and do nothing when the same thing is happening here in my country."

I am compelled to take a moment to tell you at this point in my story that my world, Mr. Chamberlain's world, John Otis Trimball's world and the world of an old woman from Czechoslovakia were about to collide...

"Unless we teach people to understand each other...to tolerate, accept and respect our differences, there really is no future for mankind. We will vanish from the face of the earth having destroyed ourselves with our own hatred."

These words were spoken by a most unlikely advocate by the name of Elinor Szabò-Taylor back in 1964...sixteen years after she'd come to America, leaving Europe and the Holocaust far behind her. She was truly a remarkable woman but if you don't recognize her name there is good reason...not many people know her story. But I do...I know her story. And you will know it too. By the time I finish, I promise you will not be able to help but admire her for what she accomplished.

Elinor Szabò-Taylor was no one special...just an immigrant. But then again she *was* special. Anyone who had endured and survived the Holocaust deserves to be thought of as special if not extraordinarily special. Blessed. Revered. Honored. These titles too should be rightfully attached. Having once seen evil in its most unadulterated form, she found she could not stand idly by when she saw it rearing its ugly head again.

Elinor had known very little if anything about America before she'd arrived in Mississippi, of all places, with her husband in 1947. But by the time the 1960's had come around, she knew more than she wanted to know. Many of her pre-conceived notions and ideas of the land of the free and the home of the brave had been destroyed...shattered by images reminiscent of the Europe of the late 1930's. The first time she saw a photograph of those four black children hanging from the steel girders of the Chickasawhay River Bridge, she came to understand that in America hatred and evil had simply replaced the Jew with the Negro.

Elinor had been an exceptionally intelligent person her entire life and as a grown woman she continued to read anything and everything she could get her hands on...and on a wide variety of interests and subjects. As a survivor of the Holocaust, she was drawn to the stories of discrimination, Jim Crow and segregation that were so ever-prevalent here in the South. She despised any kind of persecution of innocent and defenseless people, especially children as you will come to understand why as I tell you more about her.

She'd spent more than a year at Auschwitz and saw more babies, young children and terrified woman sent to their deaths in the gas chambers than she will ever be able to forget. After the war when she'd been liberated from the death camp and before she met the American who would become her husband, she worked as a translator in the war crimes tribunals in Berlin...doing her part to punish the demons who'd killed those babies, young children and terrified woman, and either buried their emaciated bodies in mass graves or incinerated them to get rid of any and all evidence of their existence. In today's world I guess Elinor Szabò-Taylor would be known as a social justice warrior.

In America, she'd taken issue with the way the black children were being treated in the southern public schools and the fact that the "separate but equal" laws that had been passed by white politicians and then abolished seven years before, had done nothing to stem the hate or violence that was terrorizing young black children whose only crime was wanting an education. Nothing had changed after these laws were abolished. But Elinor Szabò-Taylor would have something to say about that. She would become a force to reckon with in the years to come.

She spoke those words I'd previously mentioned to a group of angry men and women...white men and women, who had gathered at a protest outside an all-white high school in Meridian. It was their most earnest intent to keep young black children out of that school. Elinor was *not* one of the protestors...she was the one trying to tell those people that hatred and blatant discrimination just was not the answer. And believe me, Elinor Szabò-Taylor knew what she was talking about.

Let me tell you a little bit about my friend Elinor...

Born in 1926 in Bratislava, the capitol of what was once called Czechoslovakia, to a Slovak mother and a Hungarian father, Elinor had a first hand understanding of the power of hatred and the vast reach of the evil men who practiced it. While the blacks were being hung from trees and bridges here in America, young Jewish children were being gassed to death in concentration camps in Germany and Poland and their bodies cremated.

Elinor had an older sister whose name was Trude...born in 1924. As young children, they lived a quiet and peaceful life in Bratislava, but that was soon to change...war was coming to Europe and it would soon shatter young Elinor's little world and scatter her tiny family to the wind. It all began for Elinor on 24 August 1942.

Elinor's mother took a telephone call that day. The woman on the other end of the line, a friend of the family, was concerned if the authorities had come by to "fetch up" the girls yet. She was warning her that Jewish girls were being rounded up by the local police and being turned over to the Nazis. They would then be sent to the Eastern Front where they would be forced into prostituting themselves for the German soldiers. The dignity of those poor young women would be sacrificed for Hitler's war effort and to bolster the morale of his nearly defeated army.

After hanging up the telephone, Elinor's mother panicked. She knew she had to do something to protect her girls and that she must act quickly if she was to save them. She and her husband came up with a plan to dress the girls in peasant clothes and put them on a tram, sending them out of town to the small village where their grandparents lived. There they would hide for several days while arrangements could be made to get them to safety.

Safety meant getting them out of Czechoslovakia and across the border into Hungary. To leave one country and get to the other would mean having to crawl on their bellies in the middle of the night, under barbed wire and search lights, across a stretch of veritable no-man's land between the two borders.

It was too dangerous for the girls to stay with their grandparents so they were sent instead to the house of an aunt, their father's sister. But once they'd arrived there, the aunt refused to help them...too afraid of the repercussions should the Germans find out. It was the local priest that actually took them in, saving their lives by hiding them in the attic of the church...

"You must remain absolutely quiet and show yourselves to no one," he ordered. "No one must know you are here. Do you understand? You will place us all at great risk if you disobey and you are discovered."

Elinor was 16 years old at the time...Trude was 18. The priest secretly met with a man in town who would end up taking the girls away from the church. He was a respectable man...a Christian man and an attorney. And although his most earnest intentions were to help them, he would unintentionally end up doing more harm than good.

The man's name was Gábor Pázsitka. By day he was an attorney, but after hours he worked for the resistance, helping Allied airmen to escape the Nazi POW camps throughout Hungary. Elinor and Trude ran errands for him during the day, unknowingly carrying envelopes filled with the most dangerous documents. It was only a matter of time before they found themselves swept up in the attorney's resistance business.

One day, while they were trying to deliver just such an envelope to a client, they were stopped by the SS. The authorities had been watching their movements for quite some time and suspected them of being spies.

Taken to police headquarters, they were interrogated and when they could not prove who they were or explain why they were in Hungary, they were eventually arrested and sent to a local prison for the next three months. There, life became a nightmare for both of them. They were raped repeatedly...beaten and tortured. Elinor somehow survived...Trude did not.

On the day she was to be released, once outside the prison Elinor was immediately arrested again...this time for being an illegal immigrant. This time she was sent to a refugee camp in the north. It was there that it was discovered her mother was a Jew.

The German's eventually invaded Hungary as well...in 1944, and Elinor's situation became even more dire. She and dozens of other girls just like her were rounded up in the middle of the night and taken to a local brickyard where they were chained together and marched to a train station. There, they were loaded into cattle cars. Their destination...Auschwitz.

She spent the first six weeks in the death camp existing on starvation rations. Crammed into a cold, filthy barracks with a thousand other girls and women, she was forced to survive in the most inhumane of conditions by doing the most unspeakable of things.

One day there came a call in the barracks for volunteers...women to become nurses. Twenty five prisoners were to be taken from the camp and put on a slave transport train headed for the city of Ruhr in Germany. Those who volunteered and were chosen were promised to be fed and given better clothing.

Elinor volunteered immediately, though she knew nothing about nursing. Others in the barracks tried their best to warn her and dissuade her from going. She knew she was taking a risk and had no way of knowing if the train she hoped would be taking her to freedom would actually take her instead to the gas chambers. Although she was not killed, she did not become a nurse either. Instead she ended up working as one of those slaves in an armaments factory, assembling artillery shells for the German Army.

The war was going badly for Hitler and soon the Allies had pushed through the German defenses and were within two days of entering the city of Ruhr. Knowing the end was near, the German soldiers evacuated the camp, killing as many of the workers as they could as they fled. Some were spared and Elinor was again among those who survived. She began to believe that perhaps God favored her.

For nearly a week the surviving women assembled every morning at the front gate of the factory and there they waited to be liberated. The end of their nightmare came on the morning of Easter Sunday in 1945 when the first of the American tanks came into view. Cheers and tears of joys rose up into the gray skies.

After being freed, Elinor found herself having nowhere to go. Certainly her family had all been killed back in Czechoslovakia. She lived again in the cold, dank basement of a church. By luck, or perhaps by providence, she was offered a job as a translator for the American Military Governance Forces in Germany. It was there that she met Bert Taylor, a handsome young American Captain with the 21st Army Group.

They dated for a short while and soon fell desperately in love with each other. He proposed to her one day in a park by a lake with swans and geese. And she accepted. They were married in December of 1946, three days before Christmas. Shortly afterwards, he received orders that the war was over for him. He was being sent home. It took a massive amount of doing and many strings being pulled, but he was able to take Elinor back with him.

Back to the States for Bert Taylor meant back to Hattiesburg, Mississippi. They bought a small house in the suburb of Petal and this is where she has lived ever since. Bert died in 1992...of a heart attack. She never remarried.

A fifteen year-old boy by the name of Calvin Washington thought his new high school would allow him to become the best person he could be. He envisioned making friends, going to dances and maybe even singing in the chorus like he'd done in his all-black high school back in the Merrehope neighborhood where his family lived.

After the landmark legal battle that is known as Brown versus the Board of Education, segregation in public schools was made illegal. But old habits die hard and the deeper into the South you went the less that court decision meant. Desegregation would take a long, long time to come to Meridian Mississippi.

All Calvin had ever wanted to be in life was a doctor. When he made the decision to step off that school bus that morning he thought he was on his way! His father had told him about the mobs of angry white men and women who would be waiting for him at Central High School, but he and his family had prayed hard the night before and he was quite sure that God would protect him.

But, his hopes and dreams quickly vanished. As he and the four other black students who chose bravery over fear...to cross over the boundary of their black neighborhood in Merrehope and travel the length of 24th Avenue to attend Central High School in 1964, they were taunted, ridiculed and even physically battered. On his first day of school, Calvin faced the horror of the Mississippi National Guard blocking his entrance to the building. He suffered the terror of an angry, white mob encircling the school as they chased him and his four other brave friends down the street, far from the front door of that school.

Calvin Washington and the four other black students who had also just stepped off the bus, stopped for a moment to listen to a white woman who was speaking from the back of a pick up truck. She spoke with an accent the likes of which they'd never heard before...

"Please! I ask that you listen to me...allow me to speak," the woman pleaded. "The mistakes you will make here today will be seen the world over. Is this truly what you want your proud city of Meridian Mississippi to be known for?"

It was Elinor who was doing the speaking. She was talking to that group of men and women who had assembled outside the school, determined to keep it all white. She'd no sooner finished when the mob began to boo her...threats of violence rose into the air. Someone yelled, "Go back home Jew!" Another shouted, "We shoulda let Hitler finish the job!"

"Unless we teach people to understand each other," she continued, "to tolerate, accept and respect our differences, there really is no future for mankind. We will vanish from the face of the earth having destroyed ourselves with our own hatred."

Elinor's husband had always suggested she not talk much about her past. The people in Meridian were not all that tolerant and a lot of boys had not come home from fighting a war many of these people saw not so much as stopping Hitler, but trying to save a few Jews from the ovens.

During the 1960s, most of the Jews in Meridian feared being associated with the Civil Rights movement. Fear kept many of them silent...fear of losing their businesses and their hard-earned social acceptance. And they feared becoming the targets of Ku Klux Klan violence themselves.

But the vast majority of the Jews in Meridian were American Jews...ones that had been there since the end of the Civil War. None had experienced the Holocaust as had Elinor. She did not fear these mobs or the KKK. She'd stop fearing the evil men could do years before.

She was one of several Jewish community leaders who felt the need to speak out in support of the black Christian churches that had been bombed or burned. She said she was compelled by her conscience to speak out for the black children who knew nothing of racism and yearned only to learn and have better education.

As a result of her outspokenness, her own Temple Beth Israel was set fire to in the middle of the night and the education building bombed two weeks later. The home of prominent Jewish businessman Meyer Davidson was bombed and his two daughters were killed as they slept in their beds. Bert Taylor worried they'd be next but he would never think of silencing his wife.

Calvin Washington and those four other teenagers, none of whom were particularly political, and all of which were only looking for wider opportunities than their all black high schools could afford them, were thrust into the crucible of the burgeoning Civil Rights Movement.

There came a certain point that morning when Calvin didn't know if he'd be alive at the end of the day, let alone live to graduate from high school...

"I am looking at you children," Elinor said, speaking to the five of them. "I see you. We all see you. The world sees you too! Do not fear these cowardly people who want to keep you from bettering yourself. They want nothing more than to keep you right where you are...so they can continue to exploit you. Those men with guns standing at the door...be careful of them. They will prevent you from learning today. They have orders to keep you out of this school. But do not let this stop you from coming back tomorrow or the day after or the day after that...for however long it takes.

It was just about that time that John Otis Trimball and a group of thirteen other black men joined by three white men, John Chamberlain among them, came marching up the street, side by side, arms locked together at the elbow. They were perfectly quiet. I do not believe however for one moment they were perfectly calm. It must have been terrifying for each one of them.

The Meridian Police saw them coming and opened the back doors of their police cars, pulling on the leashes of German Shepherd police dogs.

That collision of worlds I'd told you about before...it was about to happen.

The mob that had been surrounding Elinor now turned and moved toward John Otis Trimball the other Freedom Summer workers. They were carrying bats and shovel handles. They came together in a horrible clash of fists and kicking boots. Trimball and the others did not fight back...they followed the non-violence that Dr. Martin Luther King Jr. had preached.

Without reason or provocation, the Meridian Police let loose their dogs. It was obvious they'd been trained to attack the Negroes because not a single one went after anyone who was white. The police allowed this to continue for more than five minutes. The dogs ferociously shredded the Freedom Summer worker's skin and clothing. They were all badly bitten and bloodied.

What made him do this no one is quite sure, but John Chamberlain picked up the handle of a shovel that someone in the mob had dropped. With one violent swing, he brought the handle down on the neck and head of one of the dogs who had been mauling John Otis Trimball. The dog yelped and rolled off. Chamberlain had not killed the dog but the reaction the police had in witnessing what he'd done would end up nearly killing him.

Two policemen rushed toward him with their black jack clubs at the ready. They were on him in an instant and they beat him mercilessly. He was covered in his own blood and unconscious by the time they stopped. He was dragged to a waiting police car and taken away.

The remaining Freedom Summer workers were left lying in the street, bleeding and crying. They were refused any medical attention once the police had rounded up their dogs.

In the meantime, Elinor and two other women rushed Calvin Washington and his four friends to their cars as the mob chased after them. They drove them to a safe place where their parents could be called.

Elinor and her two friends had convinced the parents to have the five children standing at the bus stop the next morning, explaining how critical is was for the future of other black children in Meridian and throughout all of Mississippi that they not back down.

Calvin Washington and the other four were ready to try again the next morning but much more worried than they'd been the day before. When they stepped off the bus on the second day, they encountered the same hateful resistance of angry white men and women. The soldiers of the Mississippi National Guard had again taken up their places in front of the doors to Central High.

They were unsuccessful on the second day as they would be on the third and the fourth. But on the fifth day the bus was met by eight US Marshals with a Court Order in hand signed by Robert F. Kennedy himself, demanding the Guard troops step aside and allow Calvin Washington, Horace Green, Emmet White, Mavis Davis and Beulah Taylor to freely walk into Central High School.

With a Federal Marshal on their left and right, each child walked into their future and made history that day. The sight of it brought Elinor Szabò-Taylor to tears.

Last year Elinor came to me complaining of a mild discomfort in her belly, believing that she had what might be a cyst on her ovary. But after I examined her I had to conclude that she had all the classic symptoms of something far more serious. I ordered all the standard and necessary tests and had a full blood bank pulled and workup done. The news was not good. Elinor was in the latter phases of Stage 4 ovarian cancer. It is what we call Stage 4b…

"The cancer has spread to the fluid that surrounds your lungs Elinor," I told her. "We are also seeing signs of it in your spleen and your lymph nodes."

"Well then" she said calmly. "I suppose I should be readying myself for whatever it is that comes after this life, if there is anything at all."

"You need not fear death Elinor," I said as my nurse was taking her blood pressure and writing a few notes in her file. "It is simply the next phase of your life you know."

We'd become somewhat good friends in the six months I had been treating her. I believed in being frank and honest with all my patients and she was appreciative of that. I was looking at her latest test results…I could see she was not getting better. She was getting worse and quickly…

"How soon will I die?" she asked me. "I am 91 years old now and have become rather impatient in my old age. I would like to get on with this."

I took this opportunity to wax philosophically with Elinor…

"We never die Elinor," I said. "We simply change form…just as we did in the moments when we were conceived."

"I wish I could have your confidence," she answered in her soft, broken English. She'd never lost her European accent...

"My greatest fear is that it is all just a void," she continued. "A black place where there is simply nothing. I fear I will be alone...and I don't do well on my own."

"I have spent a good part of my life around death," I answered. "In my business it is something we see every day. I have sat with people and I've held their hands while they've waited to pass. I have listened to them telling me what they were seeing in their final moments. I have studied theology as well...I am aware of what Scripture and the religions say about life and death. I have come to the conclusion that death is not something to be feared. When it is time for you to move on from this life Elinor, I suggest you do so joyfully and with the greatest anticipation of what awaits you."

"I used to think God had a plan for us," she said, "a rough plan I guess I should say...but a plan all the same. That was until I became 16 years old and the Nazis stole my innocence and my faith. After those terrible years, I changed the way I see things."

"You are not going to tell me you don't believe in God...are you Elinor?" I asked. "You of all people should have a faith as strong as Gibraltar!"

"I honestly don't know what I believe now," she answered. "I guess I believe there are a thousand ways this life can end. Every breath I've taken...every decision I've made...every thought I've had for 91 years have all influenced the original plan I came into this world with. It certainly has not remained the same.

It has expanded...shortened...twisted itself all around. It's always been changing. Those of us fortunate enough to make it through the multitude of diseases and horrors of this life...well, we simply grow old. We get tired. Eventually we close our eyes."

"And then?" I asked. "Where are you then?"

I knew it was a silly question to ask her...as if she could possibly know the answer. As if anyone could. But in fact she didn't hesitate for a moment to tell me her thoughts.

She took my hand and placed it on her own chest, in the place where she knew her heart to be. I could feel it beating...

"Here," is all she said. "We will reside in the hearts of those we have met along the way, at least for a short while."

I could not help but smile...

"At last!" I said. "At last someone who has told me the truth."

"You see doctor," Elinor continued, "when I die, it doesn't matter what I've believed. My religion does not matter nor what God I've worshiped. These are things of the world...not things of eternity. The simple fact is that none of us know what exists beyond this life. Is it immortality? Re-birth perhaps? Eternal life? Nothingness? You tell me."

I closed her file and listened to her speak her words of wisdom...

"But there is one thing I know for sure," she continued. "I know there is a silent wind that blows behind each and every one of us…it propels us through our lives. It begins at the moment of our birth and continues all the days of our lives.

We never see it, though we feel it always. We cannot command it, though often times we foolishly convince ourselves we can. We don't even know its purpose…not until it is much, much too late.

I would have liked to have stayed a bit longer...if Bert had lived that is. But now my wind is taking me away. I will not miss it here though I will miss all my friends. But I am content in knowing that the power that propels me does so with a knowledge far superior to mine and knows what is best for me."

Elinor stood from the examination table. She buttoned the sleeves of her blouse and pulled her jacket over her shoulders…

"My wish for you my dear man," she said with a soft voice, "my wish is that you live with a peaceful and loving heart and I pray that your own wind will guide you into safe harbors."

Little did either of us know that she had already helped guide my life. My name is Calvin Washington. She did not know from where

I'd come nor did I know who she was, but in 1964 I'd been one of the first of the black children admitted to that all-white high school.

I was too young to know enough to be thankful for what she done and she was now too old to remember. But I, like Elinor herself, had overcome hatred and blind anger in my life.

It was not until I read her obituary and the article in the newspaper that I realized who my patient had been. There was a photograph of Elinor, standing in the back of a pick up truck making that impassioned and emphatic plea to be heard in front of the Central High School on September 7th 1964. In the far corner of that photograph I saw five children. I recalled immediately who they were. I had to put the newspaper down and collect myself. There is indeed a power that propels us through this life...and with an intelligence and knowledge far superior to ours.

And so this is my message to anyone who will listen. Hatred and anger is still very much alive in the world today. It always shall be. In these days I see so much of it...I cannot fathom from where it all comes.

We all get angry. I am guilty of it...so are you. I try to see my anger as if it were flowing water however. There's nothing wrong with it as long as I let it flow out of me. But when it stops, then it becomes stagnant. Stagnant anger, like stagnant water, becomes dirty...poisonous and deadly. Stagnant anger easily turns into hatred which, without notice or warning, will evolve into violence.

It was the Reverend Martin Luther King Jr. who said, "Darkness cannot drive out darkness...only light can do that. Hate cannot drive out hate...only love can do that." There is only one person I've ever met who would know this better than Martin Luther King. That would be that woman who spoke in an accent the likes of which I'd never heard before.

I will, until my dying day, never forget her words...

"I am looking at you children. I see you. We all see you. The world sees you too!"

Vignette 13 ~ The Hiker

"I KNOW A MAN WHO DRIVES 300 YARDS TO WORK EVERYDAY," Frank said while we watched our little bonfire burning on the beach. "Can you believe that?"

Frank was a dear friend of mine. I'd met him years before when I owned the big boat in Florida. We were docked aside each other as a matter of fact, at a marina on Grand Bahama. We'd become quick and lasting friends. He was up from the Florida Keys when he heard I'd returned to the States from Italy. We were standing and talking amidst the hundreds of tiny sparks that were shooting up into the black night that had enveloped us. We were discussing the adventure we had just returned from and the changes we'd both experienced in our lives as a result.

We were also sipping on the last of the Indian Pale Ales he'd brought along from Islamorada and were eating what was left of the chicken and roasted potatoes I'd made in the coals of the fire. The beer was now warm and the potatoes were cold. The chicken was almost gone...but we could honestly not have cared less. It was just really good to be alive.

"I know a woman over on the barrier island," I said. "I guess I should say I knew her. We had a bit of a disagreement. She would actually get in her car to drive a quarter of a mile to her gym."

"I can believe that!" Frank said.

"She goes there to do nothing but walk on a treadmill mind you!" I continued. "You have no idea how many times I have heard her complain about not being able to find a parking space in the lot when she gets there. One day I asked her why she didn't just walk to the gym from home and do five minutes less on the treadmill. She looked at me as if I was a complete asshole or something...

"You certainly are an opinionated man!" she barked at me, rather snottily I might add. "I can't possibly see how what I do or don't do is any of your business. But if you really must know, it is because I have a very special program for the treadmill. It records my distance and my speed, and I can adjust it for degree of difficulty."

"It sounds like she was reading from the owner's manual!" Frank said.

"I couldn't hide my reaction to what she said," I continued, "I felt my eyes begin to roll in my head and a smirk come over my face.

"Don't tell me you said something else to her!" Frank wanted to know. "I am almost afraid to hear what you had to say."

"Unfortunately...as a matter of fact I did," I answered. "You know me. There's an old saying, 'I had the right to remain silent...unfortunately I did not have the ability? That was me...guilty as charged. And somehow I think my sarcasm was wasted on her."

"This ought to be good," Frank said. "Go ahead...tell me what little nugget of wisdom you left with her. I'm all ears."

"Oh yes, of course!" I said. "It hadn't occurred to me how thoughtlessly deficient nature can be in this regard."

"And her response?" Frank asked with a chuckle.

"Well...she did conjugate the "F" word in several different tenses to respond to me," I answered. "I don't know why, but I was compelled to correct her grammar in two of them. Oddly, I haven't seen her since!"

"And you wonder why you're single!" Frank concluded.

I had returned to America, here to the Outer Banks of North Carolina, having lived in Italy for more than two decades. In that beautiful and ancient country I found myself surrounded by constant sources of beauty and history and nature. I had forgotten that here in the States, beauty and nature had become something Americans drive to.

I find it odd that it seldom occurs to anyone here that people and nature can coexist to their mutual benefit. Sadly, I returned to find life had evolved into something I no longer recognized…smart phones, video games, gas-guzzling, exhaust-belching SUV's…a generation of young people oblivious to the peace and beauty of nature that surrounds them, opting instead for life in the cities.

My friend Frank, besides being a boater and fisherman, is also a hiker…an avid hiker! He can honestly claim to have walked every foot of the Appalachian Trail…from Mount Katahdin in Maine to Springer Mountain in Georgia…two thousand two hundred miles one way…not once, but twice!

Having retired from the business of charter fishing around the Keys and Caribbean, he'd sold his big boat and bought an old live-aboard trawler. He was a writer now. He writes mysteries…a genre that has never really appealed to me. But he is very good at was he does. Each of his books is set on a different island in the Caribbean.

He writes one book every two years…at his own pace. In between, he hikes. Hiking has now become his new passion. I personally would call it more of an obsession of his, but I always kept my opinion to myself because Frank is a friend of mine. All the time I was in Italy we managed to stay in touch.

Besides that, it was absolutely none of my business…not until this year that is…not until I let him talk me into going for what he assured me would "a short walk in the woods"…out near Montreat in the western part of the state.

But he was not being honest with me! Had I known what lay out before me I probably would have said no to his invitation. What he had in mind was anything but short and not something I would describe as a walk. I'd grown up in the woods of central Pennsylvania…I know what walking in the woods is like. But I must say, the mountains in Pennsylvania were mere hills compared to what we explored in Montreat.

We got back to my little house on the beach yesterday. That's when he announced, considering what we'd just experienced, that he would spend a few more days with me…

"If it's OK," he asked. "I'd like to spend a few days relaxing on your beach and drinking what's left of the Channel Marker beers before I head back to my grind in Islamorada."

You see, our experience was nothing short of a spiritual journey...one from which we both would return changed and different men.

"The concept of distance changes completely when you take the world on foot," he told me on the first day of our walk in the woods. We'd taken a short break before descending into a very deep ravine with a trout stream flowing the bottom...

"A mile becomes a long way," he continued. "Two is quite literally a considerable distance. Ten is almost inconceivable and fifty miles will take you to the very limits of yourself."

And he was right. This world of ours is incredibly enormous. And in a way that only a small group of serious hikers like Frank knows. I now know it too!

I was amazed to find out how life takes on such a neat simplicity out there. Time ceases to have any real meaning. When it is dark, you go to bed...when it is light you get up again! Everything in between is just in between. It's quite wonderful, really.

"It is such a strange contrast isn't it?" he asked. "When you're out here, the forest becomes your universe, it becomes infinite and entire. It is all you experience day after day. Eventually it becomes just about all you can imagine. You are aware, of course, that somewhere over the horizon there are mighty cities, busy factories, crowded freeways, people rushing here and there...but here in this part of the country, where woods drape the landscape for as far as the eye can see, it is the forest that rules."

One night, just after we had pitched our tent and gathered kindling for a fire, Frank told me an interesting little story that stuck with me. I have no idea whether it is true of not, and because there is no telling, I choose to believe it is. You see, I have come to believe most things Frank says. When he told me that he not only met Bob Marley but used to get high with him quite regularly...well, who was I to doubt his story?

Even the one he told me around the campfire seemed a bit far fetched, but as I said, I choose to believe...

"I remember reading once about a tribe of Stone Age Indians from the Brazilian rain forest," he began as our evening fire crackled. "They had no knowledge...no expectation whatsoever of a world beyond their jungle. One day they were taken to Sao Paulo, for whatever reason I don't know. When they saw that city and what was going on...the tall buildings, the cars that they'd never even known existed, zooming around them in all directions, the airplanes passing overhead...well, it was so thoroughly at odds with their own simple lives. The way I heard it, they collectively and in unison pissed themselves."

You can be the judge of whether Frank's story was true. All I knew was that I could relate to that. Though I've never been to the point of pissing myself, I believe I had some idea how they felt.

Henry David Thoreau thought nature was splendid, splendid indeed, so long as he could stroll to town for cakes and barley wine. But when he experienced real wilderness on a visit to Katahdin in 1846, he was unnerved to his very core!

He found a place that was no longer the tame world of overgrown orchards and sun-dappled paths that passed for wilderness in suburban Massachusetts, but an oppressive, primeval, primordial country that was in his words, "grim and wild...savage and dreary," fit only for "men nearer of kin to the rocks and wild animals than we."

The experience of Katahdin left him, in the words of one biographer, "nearly hysterical."

Once we were finally deep enough into the woods that even the faintest sounds and sights of civilization had disappeared, for the first time in longer than I could remember I had no engagements, no commitments, no obligations or duties other than to survive this journey to which I'd agreed to take. I existed in a sort of tranquil tedium that was serenely beyond the reach of exasperation. All that was required of me was to maintain a willingness to trudge on.

And there was no point in hurrying! We weren't really going anywhere. However far or long we walked, we were still in the same place…in the woods. It's where we were the day before and where we would be the day after.

I found the woods of western Carolina to be one big, boundless singularity. Every bend in the path seemed indistinguishable from every other. Every glimpse into the tree canopies gave me the same view of the same tangled mass of branches, leaves and vines. For all I knew, we were walking in circles. But honestly, in a way it hardly mattered.

At times, I was perfectly certain that we had crossed the same mountainside three days before. I was all but sure that I had crossed the same stream the day before…clambered over the same fallen trees at least twice in the same day already.

Frank explained things to me…

"There is no point in over-thinking where we are or what we're doing my friend," he said. "It is in fact, counterproductive to the very reason we are here."

I remember thinking to myself as I was being assailed by mosquitoes, "Sounds like bull crap to me!" But of course, again I kept my thoughts and opinions to myself.

"Try to find your Zen mode," he continued. "Get yourself to a place where you can let walking for hours and miles become as automatic, as unremarkable, as your simple breathing.

At the end of the day don't think all you did was walk sixteen miles. Think to yourself, "Hey, I took eight-thousand breaths today."

But try as I might to take on this attitude, I must admit I found it a bit difficult to do...impossible at times. I found myself holding my breath more often than not while clinging to an escarpment with a 500 foot drop!

"Woods are not like other spaces," he told me. "To begin with, they are cubic. Their trees surround you, they loom over you. They press in from all sides. The forest can choke off views and leave you muddled and without bearings. They make you feel inconsequential and confused and vulnerable...like a small child lost in a crowd of strange legs."

He was right. I'd know instances like that of which he spoke. I have stood at the ocean's edge and looked out across the sea. I have gazed out into the vastness of a prairie. I have contemplated the foolhardiness of driving out into a desert.

When you are in those places, you know you are in a big space. But standing in the woods surrounded by those great trees and you can only sense its immensity. It is a vast, featureless nowhere, but so very much alive.

As he flailed for anything to help slow his fall, his water bottle flew out the pocket of his rucksack. Neither one of us heard it hit bottom. This did not look good!

He looked over his right shoulder for anything he could grab onto that could stop his slide. All he saw was more cliff, more nothingness beneath him.

One thought sliced through the fast-motion blur that was unfolding in front of me...my friend *FRANK IS ABOUT TO DIE!*

Just a few hours earlier, we'd broken camp and set out to hike toward a magnificent waterfall he'd remembered existing in the middle of nowhere...

"I remember, it was on the second or maybe third day of my last hike through this part of the forest," he told me the night before. "It was a good ten years ago now that I think back at it. I could hear the strangest sound coming from somewhere out ahead of me...a low, guttural roar. It wasn't a growl because it was continuous. The more I walked, the louder it became. The forest up to that point had been incredibly quiet so to hear what sounded like a roar raised my curiosity and made me change my direction."

As Frank had continued walking that day, he soon found himself standing at the bottom of a waterfall...

"I was at the edge of the small pool it had dug into the rocks with incredible energy of its falling water," he said. "The water fell at least for a hundred feet...probably more. It was incredible. I spent nearly an hour exploring the pond and climbing up the steep cliff to get a view from the top."

We were headed for that waterfall that day. I was anxious to see it too. If it were only half as beautiful as Frank had described it, it was worth any kind of climb to see it.

On his first trip, he'd climbed over a huge tree that had fallen across the narrow trail he had been following. He marked the trail fifty yards on each side of the tree with a small pile of rocks so he would be able to find it if he ever returned. Once we'd found the pile of rocks and the huge tree, he told me we had about another hour of hiking and climbing to get up to the trailhead.

And it was every bit of an hour of climbing...just as he'd said. We hiked up the steepest cliffs and when the trail leveled out, we passed through dense stands of trees that blocked out the sun. We finally made it to the top. We both stood there at the very edge...at the point where the water began its cascade and free fall. The word Frank had used to describe the waterfall...magnificent, simply did not do it justice.

I had the immediate sensation that I was standing in a Holy place and on sacred ground. Don't ask me why I felt this way, but the sensation was undeniable. We both felt it.

We decided we'd make a temporary camp and have our lunch right there on the escarpment. I gathered the kindling while Frank gathered the rocks to make a small fire pit.

It was close to two o'clock when we'd finished eating and decided we'd make our way back down the steep trail. We broke camp and made sure our fire was out. We even put the rocks back pretty much where we'd found them. The agreement we'd made to each other was to leave the forest no different than we'd found it at any cost.

For no particular reason I was leading our descent. We came to a very narrow place along the trail where it was literally straight down on our right...a good 200 foot drop. Frank knew the way better than I so we agreed to switch places...he'd take the lead. I stepped aside to make room for him and that's when it happened...

I have no idea how it happened or even if I may have caused Frank to lose his balance, but one moment he was standing there beside me and the next he was gone...sliding down over the edge of the cliff...and fast.

He slid on his left side for about ten feet or so, looking over his right shoulder back at me. I can't describe the look that was on his face. It was a mixture of 'Oh shit!' and 'Help!'. He was reaching out for anything to help slow his fall. Just as he grabbed held of a root that was exposed from the ground, his water bottle flew out the open pocket of his rucksack and went tumbling out into the air, end over end. Neither of us heard it hit and that's when we knew he was really in trouble.

He rolled onto his stomach and started clawing at the cliff. After a few feet he lost his grip on the root and started to slide again. Somehow he managed to grab onto a very thin tree branch and stop himself. We both knew it wasn't going to hold his weight. I could tell he was getting scared.

His heart must have been beating nearly out of his chest but he didn't dare move for fear that he would start sliding again. I looked down at his face and it had become completely pale. He looked as if he was going to throw up. I was looking down at the sheer drop-off below him. I think he knew I was trying to find a way to pull him up and he shook his head as if to say...you better hurry!

After a ten-second eternity, the thin branch snapped and he started to slide again. He didn't scream or yell. He slid in complete silence. I knew Frank and he was trying his best to stay calm and not panic. It was going to be the only way he could save himself.

He clawed at the cliff again and was surprised when he found his hands stacked one on top of the other, clinging to a root no wider than the width of his thumb. His arms were stretched straight over his head. He found a place to brace his left knee. Kicking wildly, he was able to dig his toes into the dirt on the side of the cliff.

Once he'd finally realized that he was hanging from a root and his life depended on it, he slowly looked up at me...

"You need to help me!" he yelled at the top of his lungs. "I'm not going to be able to pull myself back up.

I swallowed hard, having no idea how I was going to what he'd asked of me. I saw nothing but small bushes on the cliff and the rock face descended straight down everywhere. I knew the bottom was a long way down. I could hear Frank's breathing and his breaths were growing shallow and short.

Frank would tell me later that was when he felt his thoughts turn completely negative...

"I knew I couldn't hold myself up much longer," he said. "I knew I was going to fall. My neck and arms began to ache from holding on and looking up, so I took to closing my eyes or staring straight at the cliff in front of me. The thought crossed my mind that you were going to be helpless and have to watch me die. I felt so damn guilty for my clumsiness."

It was a hot afternoon and his hands were starting to sweat. I was doing my best to give him words of encouragement while I looked for any place I could stand or get to where I might be able to throw one of my repelling ropes to him.

After another two or three minutes or so, I saw what I thought was a way to get just above him and a few feet to his left. I took the repelling rope from my backpack and climbed toward a place I'd hoped was safe for me. What an irony it would have been had I fallen first and let him hanging there. Talk about guilt!

As I got closer to him, I was loosening rocks and dirt that were falling down onto his head and shoulders. I heard him say, "Hurry up man...I'm just about spent!"

I knew I couldn't let him down. I knew that whatever would happen to me, I needed to try to save him. Somehow...from some place within me I do not know, I found both the courage and strength to climb out there on that narrow ledge. I took a deep breath and said a short prayer. Then I did it.

I made it. For a few seconds I held on for dear life. The part of the cliff I was standing was just wide enough and deep enough for my feet to fit. I knew that if I would lean too far forward I would fall. I had no doubt about that. I had no idea what to do next...

"Hold on to that small tree behind you," Frank said. "Better yet, tie yourself to it. That way you won't fall. But you gotta hurry man...I'm out of juice."

I did exactly as he told me and I felt a bit safer knowing that if I fell at least I would dangle, not tumble off into oblivion. I leaned out toward him far enough to be able to loop the rope around his waist. But I could only reach him with one hand. I would have to tie the knot with that hand and hope it would hold.

I tied the other end of the rope off to the same small tree I was attached too. If we both fell, it would never hold us. I pointed to a spot on the ledge next to me and told him that on the count of three I wanted him to step toward it without letting go of the root he was holding on to.

"I can see the ledge Frank," I said. "You can't. So you will have to trust me. I will tell you when your foot is in the right place. Then shift your weight. Don't let go of the root until I tell you. OK?"

"Whatever you say brother," he said calmly. "My life is in your hands."

God I wish he wouldn't have said that!

He was able to get his leg over, but the part of the ledge on which he stepped crumbled and fell away. He nearly went with it but regained his balance. My stomach jumped up into my throat.

"OK," I said. "Plan B. I am going to get below you and try to push you over to the ledge I'm on now. There's an outcropping of rock just below you. You can't see it, but again...I can, so trust me. If I can get to it, I can push. Don't go anywhere, OK?"

"I'll stay right here," he answered. "As long as I can hold on. But I'm telling you, it won't be much longer."

Once I was in place I could see it wasn't going to be as easy as I'd thought...

"I'm going to push you up," I said. "I have the rope tied off tightly. I need you to pull yourself over to the ledge I was on...pull the rope at the same time."

I pushed him up from below as he pulled on the rope just like I told him. All I can say is that God must have been with us because he made it.

"OK!" I said. "Good job. Take a few minutes and get your strength back. I need you to get back up to the trail with the rope and tie it off to a tree. You'll need to help pull me up. It's a hell of a lot easier coming down than getting back up."

I climbed up about 35 feet all together, with Frank pulling on the rope the whole time. I had one scare when a piece of the cliff I was standing on separated and crumbled into small pieces. I could hear the pieces bouncing off the rock face below me but I refused to look down.

"OK brother!" I said to Frank. "Now it's my life that's in your hands. Don't let me down. Get me the hell out of here, OK?"

When I got within arm's reach of the top that is exactly what he did. I had never felt so scared in all my entire life. I crawled onto the path for a few seconds getting as far away from the edge as I could. Frank helped me to me feet. That's when the tears finally started to come.

When I was a little boy, I spent a good amount of time up in the woods of the Allegheny Mountains. I would to play a game where I'd ride my bike up to the top of Sulfur Springs Road and then imagine I was in danger somehow...being followed by evil men who wanted nothing more than to capture and torture me! I have no idea from where such thoughts came...but they were very real in my very imaginary world of youth.

I would have to avoid the main road where my pursuers lurked and find my way back home...all ten miles, by riding on the trails and paths through the woods.

I always made it back safely and became so good at it that I believed I could do it blindfolded! I was relying on some mysterious instinct I found deep within myself that drew my heart back to where it belonged...back home.

We wander through this life, questioning so much along the way. We look outside ourselves for the answers, but too late we discover the answers have been waiting for us all along in our heart. Our identity, our purpose, the meaning of life and the face of God are all in there...inside each and every one of us.

Everything and everyone has a place to be. We each have our place in this world. And whether we choose to believe it or not, happiness awaits us there. It's just a matter of how we get there and when, that determines how long we have to enjoy that happiness and how much of it we can claim before we move on from this world.

I must tell you, I got an enormous amount of satisfaction from my two week-long experience in the mountains of Western Carolina with Frank. Once again, I'd gotten to pitch a tent and sleep beneath the stars...as I did when I was a young boy.

For a brief, proud period of time I felt young again...fit and healthy. My accumulated years meant nothing out there. I regained the profound respect my father had instilled in me...respect for the wilderness and nature and the benign power of the dark woods.

Once again I was able to appreciate the colossal scale of the wonderful world in which we live. I found courage and fortitude that I didn't know I had. I discovered my America again...one that millions of its own people scarcely know exists.

I spent good time with a dear friend. We saved each other's lives and I am not exaggerating an iota when I say this. I prayed prayers that day that I know were heard.

I've come home happy and confident and at peace with myself and the world. I am ready to begin living again, if life will consider having me.

Vignette 14 ~ My Brother's Secret

THERE ARE TIMES WHEN I HONESTLY BELIEVE I was the only one who ever really understood my brother. He was one of the most beautiful souls I have ever known...beautiful in so many ways, but oh so very, very troubled.

We had a lot in common, though he would never allow me to get very close to him. His name was Andrew...Andrew James Fallon. He was so much different than his brother Matthew. I only say this because they were identical twins and twins usually grow up being very much alike...able to finish each other's thought and sentences. But my two brothers grew apart and ended up being as different as night and day.

Just so you know, I am nine years younger than Andrew and Matthew. I don't know if that is important but maybe it was one of the reasons Andrew would never confide in me when we were young.

Andrew carried with him throughout most his life, at least the part of which I can remember, a lot of shame...a lot of guilt. He was always apologizing for himself for one reason or another and I never understood why. But in those rare times when he did let me get close...when he opened up to me, he told me that he felt vile and unclean inside...impure and unworthy. Had I only known the heavy secret he carried within himself...I may have been able to save him. But nobody knew. He never told anyone, at least not anyone in the family.

For the last ten or twelve years of his life, he became devoutly religious. Hardly ever would you see my brother anywhere around town when he wasn't carrying his Bible or reciting a rosary. He became nearly obsessed with God and having a pure heart...of being pure in his faith. He told me once that if I could become perfectly pure in my own heart and my own faith in this life, that I would most certainly get to see the face of God long before I need stand in judgment before Him.

Andrew's life, toward the end, became about nothing other than gaining heaven. It was if he was in the greatest hurry and almost couldn't wait to see the face of God. All I know now is that he is finally in his glory!

My name is Mary Margaret Fallon and I am the seventh of nine children born into an Irish Catholic family. We were much more Catholic than we were Irish though, as you may be able to tell by the names my parents gave us.

The boys were James, John, Mark, Andrew, Matthew and Thomas. That covers half of the Disciples! The girls were Rachel, Sarah and me...Mary Margaret. We all grew up in the small town of Ontario...the one in Upstate New York, not Canada...along the banks of Lake Canandaigua in the Finger Lakes.

My father was a very good and honest man...of the utmost integrity. He was a very good provider but with nine hungry children to feed, there was rarely any money left for the little luxuries other kids enjoyed. I always thought of our family as a middle-class family, even though we probably weren't. We knew enough not to ask for money to go to the movies or shopping...it wasn't there for such things. And if we did ask, it was never for more than a nickel here or a dime there...maybe a quarter if there was something we wanted really, really bad!

But I must say, we were content. We wanted for very little. We had everything we needed as far as food on the table and clothes on our back. To keep ourselves entertained, like most kids back then we relied on our imaginations. There were plenty of things to do in our little town...things that didn't cost any money.

We did most things together as a family. We always ate dinner together...every single night without fail. On weekends we would go to Kershaw Park in town and play football as a family...the six boys against my parents and we three girls. To make things more even, James played on our side from time to time.

Out in the street in front of our house, my brothers would play catch and we girls would run bases, from one manhole cover to another. They would tell us when to steal and we would take off running. They would throw the ball back and forth, trying to tag us out. Sometimes we'd win...sometimes they would. But no matter what, we always felt we were part of a very special family.

As I look back now, I remember my father having had many jobs, but the one I remember best and most was when he was a delivery man for Sunshine Bakery over in Rochester. I have the fondest memories of him from the time before I started kindergarten. He would drive up to the house and beep the horn out front...

"Mary Margaret!" he would shout. "Do you want to come along and finish my route with me today?"

Well he never had to ask twice. I had my sneakers on and was out the door before he'd even stopped talking. I would sit on a big metal box right beside him as he drove, shifting gears on the steering column and listening to WMBO AM on the radio. I asked him one really warm day why the box was so hot to sit on...

"The motor is under there Mary Margaret," he answered. "It keeps me nice and warm in the winter time. In the summer I just open all the doors and windows and let the breeze blow through."

I can still remember how that truck smelled, filled with aroma of fresh breads and cakes and pies. It was heaven.

As we all got older, Daddy knew that being a bread delivery driver was not going to earn him enough money for the things teenage boys and young girls were going to need. He was very good with his hands and he had a mechanically-minded brain. So he started his own business repairing lawnmowers and snow blowers right there in the garage behind our house. He worked a lot of long hours on his delivery route and then he'd come home and go right out to his shop. There were times we wouldn't see him until my mother had dinner ready and waiting on the table. He'd come in long enough to say the blessing and eat...then he went back out and work in the garage again. His business became known by a lot of people and they all knew and trusted him.

There is something important I want to say here, before I go any further. We didn't have a lot when I was growing up...not like the other kids. And my father worked very hard to give us the things we did. My parents believed that it was my mother's place to be in the home for her children and so that is what her life became...a home maker. After Sarah, the youngest of us all, finally went to school, my mother took a part-time job, working with my father in his business, keeping his books and ordering parts and things for him.

But if there was one thing that was never, ever in short supply in my family, it was love. When we were young and all together, you could feel how we all felt about each other. OK...I just needed for you to know this before you hear any more of my story.

I think I already told you we were Catholic...very Catholic. I cannot remember a single Sunday in my youth when I was not in the front row of St. Mary's Church promptly at 9:00 with my brothers and sisters and parents. We went to the 9:00 Mass because it was the High Mass. Father Mainardi said the special parts in Latin. We had no idea what he was saying and if we ever giggled, my mother could give us a look that made us stop instantly!

It could get terribly cold where I grew up and the winters seemed to be filled with snow. But no matter what, we never missed Mass.

"If God can give us another week of life," my father would say to us, "we can surely give up an hour of our time one day a week to honor and worship Him!"

As I said, there were nine of us children...six boys and three girls. We lived in a small house...tiny now that I come to think of it, much too small for eleven people. But we never felt it was too small...it was normal. It was all we ever knew.

There were four bedrooms with only one bathroom. I need not tell you how that made for chaos on school and church mornings. Besides the kitchen, dining room and pantry, there were two other rooms downstairs...one was a parlor I guess you could call it...where company sat when we had visitors. And the other is where we would gather as a family to watch TV.

So do the math if you will...eleven people and four bedrooms. Of course my parents shared a room alone. That left three bedrooms for nine children! So we slept three to a bed for as long as I can remember. Now my sisters and I, though not loving the arrangement, learned to live with it. We got along quite well. My older sister Rachel and I slept side by side. When Sarah came along, she was small enough to sleep at the bottom of the bed...at least for a while.

But I can't say that for the six boys who shared the other two bedrooms. That's because they were real boys...rowdy, rambunctious and loud.

Somewhere along the line my father got the idea to buy two sets of bunk beds for one of their rooms. Mark and John took the top bunks and James and Thomas the bottom. This left a room for the twins to share. And I guess this is where I want to start telling you about Andrew.

Andrew was born on October 22nd in 1951, the second born in a twin birth. Nine minutes after his brother Matthew was born so dramatically, crying and kicking for all he was worth, Andrew came into this world peacefully and quietly, almost as if he were an afterthought.

Andrew was a quiet boy when he was little, much quieter than Matthew, and as I said, it was very strange for twins to be so different. Matthew was bold and gregarious...always on the go, dragging Andrew along here and there. Andrew was very quiet, very private, content to stay home and play by himself. But I will say this about him...he always had a smile on his face.

He was fascinated with building things out of wood. For Christmas one year his one gift was a little wooden tool box. Inside were a hammer and a saw, screwdrivers and pliers and things like that. He took it right out to the garage and started cutting pieces of wood and nailing them together. By the time he was done he'd built a little two-wheeled scooter out of an old apple crate and the left over wheels from an old cart my grandfather had once used to use to collect the leaves he'd raked up in his yard.

As the years passed and Matthew and Andrew eventually turned twelve, it became time for them to follow in the boy's family tradition. Each of the older two boys, James and John had paper routes. They earned their spending money that way. James, being the oldest and having his driver's license already, found it time to give up his paper route. He had his eye on a certain girl in high school and that meant he'd have to look for a job where he could make a little more money.

And so he ended up offering his route to Andrew or Matthew. Matthew was not interested in the least but Andrew jumped at the chance...

"OK," James said to Andrew the first day he walked along to learn the route. "This is how you fold the paper. You fold this third of it like this, and then fold it over once again. You take this end and slide it into this end and give it a twist. That's all there is to it.

Some boys fold every paper at the pick-up spot and carry them like that. But I prefer to get going as quick as I can so I fold them as I walk. You do whatever you want...just don't miss any customers and make sure the paper lands on their porch or front stoop. Old Man Hanna wants his paper inside his storm door and Miss Bryant wants hers inside her milk box. Can you remember that?"

Andrew treated his paper route like it was a major business. He made up a special ledger for when he collected the money and made sure to use to use the punch on the customer's monthly card every time they paid him. He was so excited the first time he counted his money, setting aside what was needed to pay the newspaper and the rest was his. In his first month he made $16.60. You would have thought he was a millionaire!

But I remember the day Andrew came home in tears. He did his collecting on Saturday afternoons, wanting to make sure everyone was home. Something had happened this one particular Saturday and he was very, very upset. Rather than go to my mother or father, he went straight to James...

"I need to talk to you James," he said. "I think I did something wrong."

James could tell something wasn't right and so he took him out to the garage to be able to talk in private...

"Mr. Bodnar was drunk today," Andrew began. "He wanted me to come inside. But Daddy told me never go in anyone's house. Get your money while you are on the front porch he told me. So I said no to Mr. Bodnar, that I wasn't allowed to come in."

"What happened when you said that?" James asked.

"Then he grabbed me and pulled me inside James," Andrew answered. "He locked the door and wouldn't let me out."

"And what else?" James asked, sensing there was more. "Did he do anything to you?"

"He pulled down his zipper and asked me to touch him...in there," Andrew answered, pointing at James's crotch. "I didn't want to do it James. But he told me if I did, he'd let me go...as long as I promised not to tell anyone. So I did...I touched him...real quick. When he unlocked the door I ran like heck. I left my bag with the money and the punch there in his house, by his couch. What am I going to do now James?"

"You are not going to do anything Andrew," James answered. "I will take care of this. I will get your bag and your money back. You stay home. You stay right here."

James went to get his brothers John and Thomas. After grabbing their baseball bats from their rooms, they went to pay Mr. Bodnar a visit.

As soon as the man opened his door, Thomas and John rushed in and held him against the wall. James came in last. The man, taken by surprise, spilled his beer all over himself.

"If you ever touch my brother again," James threatened, "I won't think twice about using this bat and caving in your head. Ya got that?"

Mr. Bodnar was scared...very scared. At first he denied touching Andrew at all, saying all he did was offer him bottle of Pepsi out on the porch.

"My brother is not one to lie," James came back. "He said he left his bag and his punch in here...on the table beside the couch. And well, what do you know? There it is. Just like he said. I am going to tell you one last time...touch my brother again and you will regret it!"

Nothing was ever said about what happened to Andrew that day. My parent's never knew and either did my sisters or I. My brothers handled it all.

By the time Andrew had turned 14, James and John and Thomas had already moved out of the house. James was in the service and John and Thomas both got married and found good jobs up on McIntyre Road in the Industrial Park in Canandaigua. Mark was the youngest of the boys now. Andrew and Matthew had moved into the second bedroom and shared it with Mark. Rachel, being the oldest of the girls, got a room to herself while Sarah and I got twin beds and shared the other bedroom.

I don't know if I've already told you this, but I was born in 1960, so Matthew and Andrew were about nine years old when I came along. I don't remember much about them being small or what they were like but I do remember they didn't do things together or hang out like most twins.

Something must have happened to Andrew that year, something we didn't know. I say this because he changed. He stopped talking and smiling. He was always in the bathroom, taking a bath or washing his body. It became very strange and even caused an argument or two between my father and him.

"What are you doing in there all the time?" my father asked him one day. "You can only get a human body so clean Andy. This taking two and three baths a day has to stop. Our water bill is through the roof!"

Like I said, that was the year that Andrew changed so much. He became someone I no longer knew. In 1969 he and Matthew each turned 18. Rather than wait to be drafted and sent to Vietnam, my father recommended they both enlist...

"Your chances of staying Stateside or at least staying out of that war are much better if you sign up," my father told them at dinner one night. "If you wait for Uncle Sam to draft you...well, you know where you're going."

My brothers always took my father's advice and so later that week they went down to the Army recruiter and signed up. Within another month they were both in the Army.

Now I don't know how this happened or why, but Andrew was sent to North Dakota to do his service. Matthew got orders to go to Viet Nam. All I can say is, my mother's heart was broken. We worried non-stop about Matthew for an entire year. I guess that was only natural but in the process it seemed we all but forgot about Andrew.

Andrew was dealing with his own problems in North Dakota. We stopped getting letters from him after a few months. Believe it or not, my mother wrote a letter to the chaplain of the base he was on, telling him that her son had stopped writing and calling. She asked if he, as a man of God, could check in on Andrew from time to time and make sure he was OK.

From what I know, the chaplain wrote back to my mother...

"Andrew feels guilty that he is here in a safe place while his brother is fighting a war," the chaplain wrote. "It is only natural for brothers to feel this way and Andrew perhaps feels even worse because Matthew and he are twins. I check on him every week Mrs. Fallon. I make sure he is attending Mass on Sunday and I notice he reads the Bible regularly."

My mother was relieved to hear this, but before she would finish the chaplain's letter, her joy would turn to heartache...

"There seems to be something else that is haunting your son's conscience however Mrs. Fallon," the chaplain continued. "He does not wish to speak about it, and of course I cannot force him to. But nonetheless it is obvious he is terribly troubled by something. Might I inquire if something traumatic had happened to him before he joined the Army?"

My mother, knowing no differently, had to say there was nothing...nothing of which she knew. She herself wrote to Andrew, confessing it was she who had asked the chaplain to speak with him...

"Your chaplain is concerned about you son," she wrote. "So are your father and I We think there is something that lays heavy on your conscience. Is there something you need to talk about? Maybe there is a priest there that you can confess to. Whatever this is Andy, God loves you. God will forgive you. But you cannot keep it inside."

Andrew never answered that letter or called home again for the entire time he remained in North Dakota.

But Andrew finally did come home from the service. He asked my father if he might be able to stay there at the house until he could get a job and on his feet. And of course my father was happy to have him back.

Matthew had already come home the year before...back to town as the war hero. It did not take long for Andrew to fall into his shadow again. It took a few months but he eventually found a job...as a manager at the grocery store in town. He started as a trainee, making barely minimum wage, but learned the job quickly and was promoted. He worked many hours each week and sometimes it seemed as if he was always in that store. Andrew was hiding, but none of us knew why or from what.

He was finally making a little extra money but rather than finding an apartment of his own, he stayed living with my parents. He spent his money instead on a used white Mustang with wide, bright blue stripes and fat tires. He bought a saxophone as well, having taught himself to play while he was in North Dakota. He was really very good with it but this did not go over well with my father because Andrew had promised to pay rent for staying. Now most of his money went to make a car payment and a few other things.

He started to attend St. Mary's again and joined the choir. I never knew how much he loved to sing or how good he was until I heard him singing at Midnight Mass the first Christmas he was home.

He also joined the Irish American Social Club. I'd never heard of it before but my father said it was a club where people got together to eat and drink and sing Irish songs...mostly religious songs. He thought it might be good place for Andrew to meet new people. That was where he met Rebecca. For the first time in his life, it looked as if my brother was in love.

He surprised all of us by bringing Rebecca to Sunday dinner and announcing they were engaged to be married. They'd only known each other for a few months and this concerned my mother.

She took him aside after dinner and talked with him...

"How can you possibly be thinking about marriage Andrew James Fallon," she asked sternly. You don't have a home of your own and all your money goes into that car parked out at the curb. You're not ready. If you really love this woman you will wait...wait until you can provide for her. Have you learned nothing from your father?"

It was shortly after that conversation that Andrew sold the Mustang and bought a pick up truck with a cap on the back and a roof rack for ladders. No one knew why but since he no longer had a car payment, he could afford rent. But he also moved out of my parent's home immediately.

My sister Rachel had a few rental properties and she agreed to rent one to him. She gave him the two bedroom and one bath townhouse just off the Market Street in Canandaigua. Normally she could charge $400 a month plus utilities but she gave it to him for $200 and included his electric and water

Do you know something? Andrew stayed right there, living in that apartment until the year before he died which was last year...2017. That is nearly 41 years in the same place! I don't know about you but I find that incredible.

The following year Andrew made three more changes in his life. He abruptly ended his engagement to Rebecca, never explaining to her or any of us why. He also went into business with a friend and they installed concrete sidewalks, patios and driveways. He kept the books and it was actually a pretty good business, though they couldn't work in the winter. So throughout the cold months he tried his best to find indoor carpentry work. He was really trying to make something of himself. I was very impressed with him.

But perhaps the greatest or biggest change in his life was when he told us at the Sunday dinner table that he'd joined another church...not a Catholic church, and had accepted Jesus Christ as his Lord and Savior. He'd been baptized the Sunday before and now he wanted to lead us all in prayer. So we went into the sitting room.

I never heard anyone pray like Andrew did that afternoon. I could hear such pain in his voice. There was a crucifix on the wall and while Andrew prayed so fervently, he kept his eyes fixed on the body of Jesus Christ hanging on the cross. His eyes were filled with tears but he kept on praying. It was very emotional for me to watch. I got the feeling that Christ was talking to my brother that day...the two of them in a most holy and profound communion.

Andrew began carrying a Bible with him as well and attending Bible study classes at this new church of his. I think the average person would have thought he'd gone off the deep end. He lived and breathed his faith in God. He talked about little else.

He spent a lot of time at the homeless shelter in town, serving meals and ministering to the lost men who lived there. He evangelized whenever he could. He was developing a reputation as a Jesus Freak. That made me angry because they were insulting my brother. But Andrew took it all in stride...

"If Jesus could forgive the men who crucified him," he said to me one day, "surely I can forgive those who speak poorly of me."

But unbeknownst to us, Andrew was also living in another world, a world much darker than we understood. The constant bathing had never stopped. And he'd begun drinking at local bars...never to excess but everyone knew him as James and Maggie Fallon's son. He was becoming an embarrassment.

He wanted to have a relationship with his family again...the brothers and sisters he'd grown up with. But I must confess, my brothers and sisters had changed...they'd become people I hardly recognized anymore. They really wanted nothing to do with him because of his obsession with God, though they each called themselves good Christians. They had families and lives of their own and little if any time for him. I was beginning to see them for what they were...little better than hypocrites.

He would do carpentry work and odd jobs for the family but never charge for his labor...only what the material cost him...

"It is not about money for me," he explained. "You all are my family and I do it out of my love for you. That is really all there is to say."

There was nothing he could not build or repair. God had truly blessed that man with talent. But my family took advantage of his generosity and good intentions. Whenever he did anything for me I insisted on paying him. If he refused to accept it, I fed him instead...I baked him cakes or pies or homemade breads. I could never take advantage of such a tender and gentle man.

He would buy presents for all his nieces and nephews at Christmas and on their birthdays. His room was stacked high with gifts months in advance. But I don't remember many of them saying thank you to him or even as much as remembering his Christmas or birthday with a card.

Life went on for Andrew and for the most part it went on unchanged...or so we thought. He kept building his business and attending his church. He became the chorus instructor at the social club. His faith grew by leaps and bounds. But he was pulling away from his family. Try as I might to hold on to him, I could not.

He never had any children of his own and one day I asked him why. Why he'd never married or started a family...

"I can hardly take care of myself Mary Margaret," he said. "I'd be a terrible husband and father. I am pretty sure I was meant to be alone in this life. But it's OK...I have my friends at the club, I have mom and dad and I have you."

"Well what if mom and dad thought the way you do Andrew?" I asked. "What if they wouldn't have gotten married and had all us kids? Where would we be? We'd be nowhere. We wouldn't even exist. You might be keeping some really, truly great children from being born. Maybe children that will change the world some day!"

Before long Andrew even stopped coming to our Sunday dinners. We still all gathered like in the old days but it wasn't the same without him. Mom begged him to come. Dad even went to his apartment one day to insist he stop by more often. But over time he pulled away from us entirely. Whenever we did see him, at least I felt truly blessed to be in his company.

Andrew had the opportunity to fall in love again. But it was not meant to be. Several months after they'd begun dating, she confessed to him that she was still married. Only separated...

"But I swear Andy," she promised, "if this works out for you and me, I'll divorce him. I swear I will. But right now he supports me and I need the money."

This was a deal breaker for my brother. He broke up with her and they never spoke again. He went on living his single life, but depression was beginning to consume him. The last few years of his life he began traveling over to a casino in Seneca and gambling away his money. Several times he asked to use my car to go because his truck had broken down and he had no money to fix it.

I wanted to say no to him...I wanted to convince him to stay home and do something positive and constructive with his life again...like he did when he first came back from North Dakota. But I failed. He would not listen to me. I could not say no to him so I loaned my car, twice.

The last time I loaned to him, he promised to have it back to me by Sunday afternoon. When he wasn't back by Tuesday morning I called my oldest brother James...

"I am worried about Andrew," I said. "He was supposed to bring my car back on Sunday but I haven't heard from him."

"You're not worried about Andrew," James said. "You're worried about your car."

"How dare you say such a thing to me?" I said. "I am the only one who looks after him anymore. You could care less what goes on his life. Don't you dare preach to me about not caring!"

James drove over to Seneca and found my car. He also found Andrew, sleeping in it. It seems that he would sleep in my car at night and go back into the casino to gamble the next day. When the rest of my family found out about this, it was the last straw.

"Andrew has a gambling problem," my sister Sarah announced at the Sunday table one afternoon. "And a drinking problem. And an adultery problem. Andrew has a sin problem. He is a sinner."

"If this is what makes him happy," I said, "let him be. Listen to you in your glass houses! Are any of you without sin?"

My comments sadly brought an end to our meal. Everyone got up and left. It was only my mother and me left sitting at the table...

"There has been something wrong with your brother for a long time now Mary," she said to me. She stood up and went into her bedroom, returning with the letters she'd exchanged with the Army chaplain. "Something has been going on with Andrew since he was a teenager."

One Sunday my father went to his apartment and forced Andrew to come to Sunday dinner...

"We all have something we need to say to you son," he said lovingly. "Please come along with me...your mother is broken hearted."

And so Andrew came to dinner. One by one, we all told him how worried we were about him and wanted nothing more than for him to be a part of the family again.

And so Andrew agreed to return to the Catholic Church and to stop gambling and drinking. The priest at St. Mary's did not like Andrew for some reason and chose to refuse him Communion one day. But Andrew again took it all in stride. His faith was much deeper and much stronger than something any mortal man could break.

My sister Rachel had bought another rental property...a duplex here in Ontario. She had separated from her husband and moved into one side of it...the better side. The other side was a mess. Since she still wasn't done taking advantage of our brother, she made a deal with him. He could live there rent free if he remodeled the apartment. He moved in over the winter of 2016 and began living up to his part of the deal.

He remodeled the whole apartment, just as he said he would...walls, ceilings, bathroom, flooring...everything. He worked almost non stop at it, taking only a day here or there to do another small job that would pay him enough to buy food and a few personal things. The amount of time he spent there far outweighed the rent he should have paid but Rachel never offered to pay him. And once he was done, believe it or not, she started to charge him rent.

Andrew had grown tired over that winter...abnormally so. He had problems breathing and even complained to Rachel of pains in his arm and chest. She said nothing to any of us. Why, we will never know. In March of last year we had a very bad snowstorm. It dumped more than a foot of snow in town...more up toward Rochester I am sure.

Rachel's snow blower wasn't working so Andrew went out and started to clear the sidewalks with a shovel. After twenty minutes or so he started to have terrible chest pains. It was all he could do to get back into his apartment.

Rachel heard a loud crash from his apartment and rather than go next door to check on him, she pounded on the wall to get his attention. After a few minutes when he still had not pounded back, she went next door to check on him.

She found him collapsed on the floor in a puddle of water from the snow that melted off his clothes and boots. He was unresponsive. She tried to revive him by pressing on his chest. After a few hard pushes he opened his eyes...

"Oh thank God!" she said out loud. "Don't move. I've called 911."

"I have to go to the bathroom," he pleaded. "Really bad. Really bad! Can you help me get up?"

She did. She helped him into the bathroom. While he was in there the ambulance and two paramedics showed up. She told them where he was but when they found him, he was slumped over the toilet again.

They took his blood pressure and his pulse. They checked his breathing and scoped his eyes. They asked him a half dozen questions and then concluded he was OK...that he'd just overdone it outside in the snow. Maybe his sugar level dropped and he passed out. That is honestly what they said!

How in God's name professionals could render such a decision without any tests or blood work still infuriates me. Before they left, they told him not to shovel any more snow. Do you know what my sister said when she heard that?

"Oh great, now I will have to hire someone!"

Later in the evening he must have been having the same pains again but this time he called me. After telling me what happened earlier in the day, even I knew enough to say he'd had a heart attack...

"Listen to me Andrew," I said. "You have had a heart attack. You had all the classic symptoms. I am coming right over to get you and we're going to the hospital. Don't argue with me. I won't take no for an answer."

He didn't want me going out in that weather but he didn't said stop me either. I knew it was his way of asking for help. I got bundled up and went out to brave the icy streets.

Incredibly though, once I'd gotten there he'd changed his mind...

"I am OK," he said. "The paramedics were right. I just overdid it."

"No Andrew," I insisted. "You are not OK. You've had a heart attack and you need to be checked out. Please do this for me. I am begging you."

"Mary Margaret, please," he said. "I am OK. I told you not to come out in this weather."

I left. And boy was I angry at him. I gave him quite a piece of my mind too. I fumed all the way back to my own apartment.

And sure enough, the next morning the crushing chest pains were back. He actually drove himself to the hospital rather than to call an ambulance or ask Rachel to take him.

He went in through the ER and they took a look at him immediately. They drew blood and tested it. Within ten minutes they could see that his enzyme levels were very high. This meant what happened to him the day before did damage to the muscle tissue of his heart. They admitted him for observation.

The next day, St. Patrick's Day 2017, they released him and sent him home with three different medications. He did not tell any of us what had happened. Over the next weeks my conscience bothered me terribly for what I'd said to him and how I'd treated him, so I called to apologize and see how he was doing. He did not answer his phone. I called him four times over two hours...and each time there was no answer. So I decided to drive over and apologize in person.

He would not answer the door so I knocked on Rachel's and told her I was worried about Andrew. She found her key to his apartment and we went over. She knocked first and then rang the door bell...still no answer.

She used her key to unlock his door and we went in. It was pitch black in his apartment. All the blinds and drapes were pulled tight and no lights were on except for a sliver of light that was escaping from beneath his closed bedroom door. I was terrified at the thought of what I might find should I open that door.

There he was, lying across his bed, fully dressed, one foot on the floor and the other on the bed. His hands rested upon his chest as if either intentionally put there or having gotten there by grasping at the pain. Either way, he was dead.

We don't know if he died the night before when he was dressed or if he'd gotten up that morning, gotten dressed and was trying to get back to the hospital alone. We will never know the answer to that question.

I didn't tell you this before. Not because I was keeping anything from you. Rather, the subject just did not come up. Both of my parents had died several years before my brother's death.

I would find out later that before my father died, Andrew had gone to him. He had something he needed to tell him.

Back when Andrew was supposed to marry Rebecca, the woman he was engaged to after he came back from North Dakota, the two of them went to see a priest. Mark had been hiding a most terrible and heartbreaking secret from her and he could no longer hold it inside.

Mark spoke with the priest alone while Rebecca waited all by herself in another room. The priest came out after almost an hour. He looked at Rebecca and shaking his head, told her she was not getting married. Andrew had finally released the burden he'd carried since he was fourteen years old.

That same man, Carl Bodnar...the man on my brother's paper route who had locked him in his house that day and made him touch him, had never forgotten the way my brothers threatened him. He vowed to get even with them and he did.

The next time Andrew went to collect for the newspapers, the man met him at the door and apologized to him...profusely. So profusely as a matter of fact, as to somehow win Andrew's confidence again. For some reason that we will never know, Andrew went back into that man's house. He came out a forever-changed young boy.

The man had sexually attacked my brother and brutalized him. He threatened to kill him and his sisters should he ever breathe a word to anyone. And I guess Andrew believed him. He told Andrew that he himself and his brothers were to blame for all this. Had he not said anything about the first time, as he was told not to, none of this would have happened.

That was a lot for a fourteen year old boy to process. Andrew had lived between two tortured worlds ever since. One world was where his God lived...the other was where his fears and insecurities ravaged him and brutalized him over and over again...just as that most despicable man had done.

The only other person my brother ever told was my father. And my father promised to tell no one...to take it to his grave with him. And he did. He kept his promise.

We would find out about all this when we met his other family. The Andrew we thought we knew was no one like the Andrew who really existed. Everything we knew and thought about our brother was about to change.

The family gathered together back at James's home to discuss Andrew's funeral arrangements and what to do next. He'd had no savings, no life insurance, nothing. He lived very simply and loved every moment of it. But funerals and burials cost a lot of money and now it was up to us, his brothers and sisters, to pay for it.

Thomas suggested we sell his things...his tools, his furniture, the old truck...everything to offset the family costs. It seemed so cold to me at first but I understood. No one would have wanted my brother's possessions.

But when the Irish American Social Club offered to give us the hall and provide all the food free to our family and pay for the casket...well, to say the least we were dumbfounded. Why they would be so courteous and giving was soon to be revealed.

The night of his viewing at the funeral home, my eyes and my family's eyes were opened to all the lives my brother had touched with his. The line of people who came to pay their respects was literally out the door for hours. There must have been several hundred in all.

I remember my brother John saying, "What the hell is going on here? Who are these people?"

For the rest of the night I heard story after story of how Andrew had touched these people's lives with his music, with his talents, with his compassion and with his faith. These people absolutely loved him.

We had rarely seen Andrew in his last years as he mostly kept to himself. We saw him as a loner...as someone uncomfortable in his own skin...uncomfortable around his own family. We drew the worst conclusions. Sarah had called him a sinner. Rachel took such advantage of him. James and John and Mark and Thomas never reached out to him to go fishing or hunting or go to a high school football game. But perhaps worse than all that...Matthew, the other half of him, had abandoned him.

I tried my very best to remain loyal and loving to him but I will admit there were times I failed him. He was not an easy person to be around sometimes, no matter how easy going he was. But none of us knew the demons he lived with.

The entire Irish American Social Club Choir came into the funeral home and stood in front of Andrew's casket. They sang the most beautiful Irish song in Mark's honor. It was called Do Not Stand At My Grave and Weep. There literally was not a dry eye in the room when they'd finished.

But our education about our brother had one more thing to reveal to us...

"My name is Aaron," a young man said, stepping from the choir. "We all had different names for your brother but I knew Andrew as dad."

You could have knocked any one of us over with a feather. Did he just say what I thought he said? Dad?

Aaron walked over to the casket and placed his hand on Andrew's shoulder...

"My heart is broken," he began. "I will be lost without your guidance and love. I don't want to say good bye to you, so I won't. I'll just say that we will meet again soon my friend. I have known many blessings in this short life of mine...but to not only know you and be loved by you, but to know that you were my father makes me prouder than anything else."

Aaron turned and spoke to each of us...

"Your brother had an incredible and undying spirit of life and love within him. When he told any one of us that he loved us, we knew he truly meant it. You could feel his love deep, deep down in your soul. Many tears have been shed today and no doubt many more will come, but I do not cry today.

He and I have talked about this day. We both knew it was coming. Together we'd sit on my porch, just the two of us enjoying each other's company and he would tell me that I must not be saddened when this day comes, but to rejoice in the life he led and the wonderful time we got to spend together.

He touched so many of us...all of us, in more ways than we will ever know. But it will be his profound love that I will remember the most. Each night as we said good bye, he would tell me he loved me and I would say "Love you too Dad."

I just want to say it one more time now...OK? I love you dad. I can't wait to see you again, one day in all your glory."

Well I just could not stop crying...none of us could. It was too much to grasp. How did we miss all this? What were we thinking?

My brother touched so many hearts. He had a son and his true family were the people at the Irish American Social Club. Somehow, we had become outsiders.

At his funeral mass, it was Matthew who read the eulogy...

"Most people think Andrew's saxophone was his favorite possession in this life, but I am here to tell you that isn't true. His truest and best possession was his rosary. Andrew James Fallon was a man of prayer...a man dedicated to loving others as Christ would've loved us. The last I heard from him was when he texted me from the hospital. He said, "Hey brother. I love you. I am praying my rosary to the Queen of Heaven for you."

As I sat listening to Matthew talk, I realized I didn't need to know the details of what happened to Andrew, but now I understand why his life was like it was. I understand where the guilt and shame came from. I only wish I could've hugged him more and shared in his pain. Maybe I could have comforted him in some way.

My youngest sister Sarah had a Mass said for Andrew because she was worried he didn't gain heaven by dying.

"There were so man sins he did not atone for," she said, trying to justify such a horrible thing to do. "I am trying to release him from purgatory...that's all I am trying to do."

"Are you kidding me?" I said incredulously. "Really? Are you serious?"

There is no doubt in my mind that this humble man whom loved the Lord so much is now proudly sitting in heaven.

Vignette 15 ~ Heaven

WHAT I AM GOING TO TELL YOU NOW IS MY OWN TRUE STORY...there are no embellishments, no exaggerations. Just as good a recollection as I can muster. Many of you will not believe what I will tell you. But I will tell you anyway. For many others, you will know exactly of what I am speaking. I've come to learn that my experience, while rare and unique, has been experienced by others.

And I am not sharing this with you to impress you or to elevate myself in any way. I am sharing it because telling it makes me feel warm all over...from my head to my toes. For me, my experience was a game changer! It has forever eliminated any doubt I ever had about the presence of God in my life or the existence of a place called heaven. I have been there and let me tell you something...it is incredible!

My day began just as any other day did. I went through my morning routines of waking before sunrise, meditating in a quiet, dark place, praying, exercising and then making myself a good breakfast before I would shower and settle in behind my desk to do what I do...write. You could set your watch by my routines back then!

But on that particular day...this particular morning, for some reason I chose to vary my routine. I decided to delay writing for a bit longer after breakfast...just long enough to refill the animal feeders in my garden. My creatures depended on me so and I took my responsibility of feeding them throughout the winter quite seriously! I lived in Florida at the time and while the winters were not harsh, all things are relative and food for God's creatures becomes scarce there too.

I remember what happened to me that morning in crystal clear images, as if it was just yesterday though it has been more than a decade and a half ago now. Everything comes back to me in it fullest colors and sounds. Nothing has faded from my memory...nothing changes in my recollection. It has been branded onto my very soul and is there for my recall any time I choose. It has become the centerpiece of my faith.

I had just finished filling the bird feeders and putting the ears of corn on the spikes in a board I'd nailed to my oak tree beside my home to feed the squirrels when I began to feel an odd dizziness in my head. I heard a ringing sound in my ears, not harsh, rather pleasant as I recall. It was not a buzzing sound, but rather it sounded like actual bells, more like chimes I guess you could say. But it and the dizziness were noticeable enough to scare me and make me want to get out of the morning sun and back onto my lanai.

When I reached the terrace in front of the lanai it became more than just light-headedness I was feeling...I felt as if I were standing precariously at the very tip of a mountain peak, looking out into vast nothingness while the whole world spun around me at an ever-increasing speed. I felt an odd sense of being completely alone at that moment...as if I were the only person in the entire world. Then down I went!

I remember hitting the concrete...hard...really hard! My shoulder hit first and then my body bounced from the impact. As I lay there, though I felt no pain, only the dizziness getting more intense. I truly believed I was dying...there was no doubt in my mind. I tried to call out to someone, anyone, though I was alone. But I had no voice. I felt myself leaving my body...rising out of myself. I must tell you, it was the strangest sensation I've ever had.

Faster and faster the world around me was spinning, like a centrifuge. Everything was becoming a blur although I felt perfectly stationary and was completely aware of everything happening around me. I had the sensation of going somewhere though I felt no movement.

Never once did I lose control of my mind or the experience I was having. Though I had no pain or discomfort whatsoever, my body was becoming like dead weight. This may sound strange, but I existed in two places at the same time. As I hovered over the body that lay beneath me, I watched as that body crawled, literally clawing its way to the lanai door. I suddenly realized it was me and I felt such confusion...how could I be there and here at the same time?

Somehow a part of me remained in that body...the part that moved the arms and legs and everything else physical. But the 'me' I know...the part that thinks and feels emotion, was outside of it. It was if the part of me that was outside my body was directing with thoughts, the part of me that remained inside. I know that makes little sense, but that is exactly what I felt was happening.

The part of me that remained in that body managed to stand but everything around me was turning black...going dark. The bright light of the morning sun was dissipating quickly. More thoughts of dying were surging through my brain. But again, let me say, I had no fear. I was feeling more and more blissful with each passing moment

I spotted the chair the I'd left pulled away from the table at the far end of the lanai the night before and my only thought was that if I could get my body there...if I could just sit down, I could pull myself out of whatever it was that was happening to me.

Finally sitting, I realized what was happening to me was not going to stop. Then I felt my body sliding out of the chair...like water tumbling gently over a short waterfall, unable to hold myself back. I do not remember hitting the floor but I instantly became aware that I had passed from one world into another...a completely quiet and peaceful place. I was no longer attached to any part of that body. As a matter of fact I had no consciousness of a physical body whatsoever.

I was in the middle of a rolling meadow, completely surrounded by gently swaying tall grasses and an explosion of color everywhere I looked. Every thing was completely quiet. There was no sound at first, no sensation of temperature, no smells in the air, nothing...only the beauty that existed at that exact moment...and complete, total and utter peace. If I would have to describe what bliss feels like, it would be exactly what I was experiencing at that very moment.

I no longer had any conscious thought of death. All I was doing was reveling in everything I saw. What I did notice however is that the manner in which my senses sensed when I had a body, now had completely changed. This new world to which I'd passed was filled with the most beautiful flowers of every color, shape and size and I experienced their color as music...the most incredibly, glorious music you can imagine...symphonies, choirs, angels...all at once. Incredible music. A sensation of complete freedom and detachment overtook me...I was consumed by total peace.

I suddenly felt as if I was seeing something that had always been right there but had somehow been hidden from my eyes all my life. I am woefully lacking in my ability to put it into words that which I saw and heard and sensed. I know now it was because what I had experienced was beyond my senses...beyond my worldly experiences.

It is difficult to explain in words because there are no words to explain it. The sky became the most exquisite color of cobalt blue and it lulled me into total peace. The grass was almost fluorescent in its greenness and each blade quivered in harmony like the strings of a harp. And those flowers...oh dear God those beautiful flowers...how they were singing to me.

There was no one in this new world of mine...no one at all anywhere to be found. I felt and knew that I was completely alone. But oddly, my aloneness was incredibly satisfying. It was more than enough. This is difficult to explain and my attempt may sound cliché, but I felt as if I was one with everything I saw and heard and sensed. I was not separate from it and it was not separate from me. There was no physical sensation, as I said...only a sense of knowing.

I cannot tell you if I lay on that floor for five seconds, five minutes or five hours. All I know is that just as I'd experienced myself slipping into that world, I began feeling myself slip back out of it. My senses came back to me, returning to their original state and functioning. I felt the weight of my body again and the parts of it that hurt as a result of my falling.

I pushed myself up from the floor and sat quietly in the chair again. I thought about shouting out for help but something continued to hold me close...that understanding I'd experienced did not leave me. There was no reason to be afraid. As a matter of fact, to this very day it remains in a most special and peaceful place in my consciousness.

I discussed my experience with a few people afterwards, each of which had a perfectly reasonable, logical, medical or physical explanation...low blood sugar, heat stroke, reduced blood flow to my brain. But I was and remain a man very much in tune with my physical self. I know when something in my body is changing. I knew it was none of those things.

This is also what I knew. I'd been given a glimpse of what exists on the other side of this physical world, brief as it was. I have no idea why or who took me where I went. I am not so bold or egotistical to claim such knowledge. All I do know however is how real it was and that it really did happen to me.

And so for the last 15 years I have used that experience in every one of my prayers and every single meditation. It has influenced my thinking about life and death and God and heaven. It has influenced the way I think...the way I write and the way I live my life. I see it as the singular most important experience of my entire life...a real game changer.

Now flash forward to just a week ago...

One morning last week I chose to alter my routine a bit again somewhat. I am no longer living in Florida, but here with the love of my life in Italy. After my breakfast I walked up the hill to the edge of my vineyard. In the complete stillness and silence of my beautiful world, I still feel myself embraced by the understanding that came to me that morning so many years ago, 5000 miles from where I now live.

I climbed the hill that I've climbed so many times in these last years. The air was heavy with the sweet smell of autumn hay. I sat down to rest where I usually sit, on the small table and chairs that I've placed beneath the oak tree in the very middle of the vineyard for just such reason. I made it a point to take my Bible with me that morning too. I so enjoy reading the psalms.

I stood up from the chair and began walking back and forth across the small grassy area in the middle of the vineyard, beneath that beautiful spreading oak that has always seemed so out of place there. I held the book out in front of me and I recited out loud that which I was reading...

> *"Where can I go from your Spirit?*
> *Where can I escape from your presence?"*

Those words had no sooner left my lips than I could feel something inside me moving...something deep inside stirring, coming to life out there in the solitary silence of that Italian countryside. I had a sense that something extraordinary was about to happen to me again. I must admit, I was a bit frightened to be so far away from my home and my Diana should I have the same experience this time that I'd had so long ago.

Suddenly and without warning, I began to take notice of the very air that was surrounding me. While I could not see it or feel it or taste it or hear it of course, I had the distinct feeling of it being there...everywhere around me and in me.

As strange as this may sound, I realized that what I had up to that moment thought of only as air...was actually God! I was walking back and forth in God! Breathing God! And I became vividly aware that as I was walking back and forth in it, it was sustaining me, breath by breath. And this air that I was breathing and in which I was standing and walking about, knew me somehow, through and through, with a compassion greater than anything I'd ever experienced!

There was nowhere or no place for me to hide, nor did I feel I needed such a place. There was nowhere I could run, for everywhere I turned...there was God. Even if I tried to flee, God would be sustaining me, breath by breath. And in my flight from God, God would be waiting for me, sustaining my life, breath by breath, when I arrived at my planned place of escape!

I realized in some baffling, matter-of-fact way that since God is the infinity of the mystery of air, I have been living my entire life in God and have been held by God always. There were no feelings or sensations that came to me this time. No images. No sounds of beautiful music. No exploding colors. This was nothing like my other experience. I remained solidly within myself throughout the entire time.

There was nothing imaginary about what it was I was experiencing either. This realization that the air is God was as concretely real and immediate to me as was the smell of the hay in the air, the silence of the vineyard to my ears, the small book of psalms that I continued to hold in my hands.

I was simply amazed by it all. After a while I sat back down on the chair and I looked out through God at the vineyard and the woods just beyond. An occasional bee came buzzing by, to hover in the air beside me for a moment or two before ascending through God into the branches overhead. A pair of mourning doves that had been roosting on another branch suddenly took to the wing and glided out over the rows of grapes...gliding through God.

And I just kept sitting there, breathing God, for how long I do not know.

From somewhere far off I could hear my name being called. Diana was calling for me, wondering where I'd gotten to and telling me it was time for me to come home and get started with my writing. I walked back to the house breathing God. I ate lunch with my Diana on the terrace while breathing God. I fell asleep in a comfortable bed for an hour or so for an afternoon nap...breathing God.

I woke up later that afternoon still breathing God and in fact I walked around for several days in this state of mind. On this past Sunday morning before I was to leave for Mass, I decided to take a walk up into the chestnut grove behind the barn. From there I could follow, if I chose, a small, narrow and well worn path used by the deer and the wild boar that would take me to an old road that led to church.

I was walking along that dirt road that led up to a flat clearing where there was a large protrusion of gessi rock on which I would sit from time to time in the past. Many times I would sit there and read more of St. John of The Cross. I was walking along on this particular Sunday, breathing God, with that very book beneath my arm. Just at the point at which the road curved and headed up toward the church, I paused at a small tree that was hanging over the road.

Standing there, still very much breathing God, I reached up and touched one of the leaves on the hanging branches with one of my fingers. As I did this, I looked up into the sky. There was one cloud there above me.

I said, out loud, "Oh my God! It is one!"

The ground I was standing on, the leaf I was touching, the cloud in the sky, the air I was breathing, my very own self...everything was utterly, completely, undeniably one! It was that very same feeling of oneness...of belonging that I'd experienced in Florida.

I walked a short distance up onto the edges of the field just outside the church. There, I sat down in the tall grass. There was a gentle breeze blowing. I sat there all afternoon, missing Mass and half of the day.

I don't know the exact moment when I lost the awareness of breathing God. But at some point later that evening, it seemed to dissipate and dissolve. Diana said she noticed a change come over me. The air seemed to only be air again.

But, just as there was no denying the world I had passed into fifteen years before, there was no denying my experience of knowing what the air really was now. I was experiencing what I've come to learn is called unawareness. Soon, even that inner clarity began to fade as well.

I have come to realize that there is a long road ahead of me in this process of knowing God, but at least I know I am upon it! Whether I will ever learn to live habitually with the awareness of what I've learned I cannot say. All I can say is that I get closer and closer each and every day.

What has happened to me has most certainly left its mark. It has planted the seeds with which I question the purpose of life. Once I became aware that the main purpose of my physical experience here in this world is not to become famous or rich or powerful, but simply to know God, most of life's other problems have disappeared or fallen into place of their own accord...the fame and the abundance have come of their own accord.

As knowing God becomes more and more important to me, I tend to stop thinking about things that discourage me...people who persecute me...things I do not understand. My goal is to someday be able to live without worry or stress altogether.

The difficulties of life do not have to be unbearable for any of us. Living a life of peace and harmony is simply all in the way we look at it, either through faith or through unbelief. Nothing is right or wrong, as we've heard so many times, but our thinking makes it so. I suggest that we all occupy ourselves a bit more each day with the business of knowing God. The more we do, the more this world makes sense.

Most people will say, seeing is believing! I could not disagree more strongly. If God remains just a blurry, vague vision, one passed down from our parents or teachers...something we've contrived from a holy book, we may be kept intrigued for a season or two, but I assure you, our interest will fade and the world will take over again.

For me now, after experiencing what I have experienced, I know that believing is seeing! I am stunned by the joy I took away from my experiences and how beautiful life can be after the fog of my physical world cleared and I'd found myself precariously poised on the brink of that vast precipice.

Epilogue ~ Iris

Author's comments: I debated for some time whether to include an epilogue in a book such as this or to forego it in the wisdom of more conventional writing practice. I have learned one need establish a good, clear reason for using an epilogue, and trying to clear up loose ends the author has somehow missed in his or her main story is not a good, clear reason.

Since all of my stories lend themselves to loose ends, conclusions to be reached by my readers, I reasoned that perhaps I would use the epilogue to tell a final, different kind of story, one outside the mainstream understanding of what we've come to think of as God.

As I began telling you seventeen vignettes ago, for as long as our species has existed, man has looked to the heavens for answers to the myriad questions and problems that living on the earth presents him. It has only been in these more modern days that we tend to perceive God as an extra-terrestrial being, more in our own likeness than something from our science fiction imagination of course, but still, not mortal.

And as I began saying so many pages ago, God is what we perceive God to be. While there is indeed only one God...one Creator of All Things, we all perceive God in the light that our education, heritage and personal experiences permit. And you know...it was no different for our more primitive ancestors.

They perceived God in terms of their environment and that is what my final story is all about. And who knows...I might even be setting up a sequel!

WINTER HAD COME TO THE LAND just as it had each year for centuries before. But this year it came with a fury and ferocity like never before! This is a story told in a time before Man lived on earth and the animals of the forest lived without fear.

The coldest of winds blew in from the north! The streams froze and the sun did not seem to shine a single day. It snowed for weeks on end and when it would not stop the animals began to worry. They'd never known such cold or seen such deep snow. The littlest among them were buried beneath the tall drifts. The larger labored to walk through it…it was just too deep.

Along with winter, a great hunger had come to the woodlands and fields that year as well. The food that had once been in such plentiful supply was now covered over by the heavy white blankets and had become unreachable. The animals knew that if something did not happen and happen soon…if winter would not pass quickly and the sun return to the sky, they all would surely die.

There was a wise old owl that lived in the forest. Because he possessed such great wisdom and was known to be fair, he was chosen by the other animals to be their leader. On one of the coldest days of that winter they gathered before him as he sat roosting on a branch in a beech tree. They gathered at the bottom of the beech tree, standing in the deep snow, shivering from the cold…all so very hungry and frightened. They begged their leader to save them.

"I have been giving this a great deal of thought," Owl assured them. "I believe I may have found a solution to our suffering. We are but mere animals…it is impossible to keep the snow from falling. We cannot make the sun shine any brighter or warmer. We must send a message to The Great Creator of All Things and beg Him to stop the snow from falling and to return the sun back to the sky once again. This is our only hope."

All the animals looked at each other in confusion. They wanted to cheer what Owl had proposed, but to them it seemed impossible. They murmured and mumbled amongst themselves that none of them had ever seen The Great Creator of All Things, trusting instead to believe what their ancestors had handed down to them. None among them had ever spoken to The Great Creator of All Things before either. He lived in the heavens and was not like any of them.

But they also trusted Owl and believed in him. If any among them could speak with The Great Creator of All Things, it would be Owl. And while they understood the *why*, he had not yet spoken of a plan...of the *how* and *where* and *when* and *who*. They soon came to understand they had little other choice. Either Owl must fly to the heavens and beg The Great Creator of All Things to bring back the sun and stop the snow this day or surely they would all die...

"But I cannot be the one to go," Owl admitted. "I am myself too old and too tired."

"Then who will go?" they asked "Who amongst us is strong enough to ascend so high into the heavens and brave enough to stand before Him and ask for such a thing?"

They looked around at each other. There was the tiny hedgehog. He was steady and stable but he travelled much too slowly. It would take forever for him to get there.

There was the fearless squirrel that lived in the treetops, jumping from one branch to another with such ease and grace. But he was too easily distracted and he could not be trusted. Besides that...once he reached the tallest branches, no matter how hard he would try he could never jump to the heavens.

It was the same for the deer and the rabbit. They were both much too timid and hopelessly earthbound! And no one would ever consider sending the badger. He was always so very ill-tempered and quick to complain. Everyone feared he would anger the Creator of All Things and the winter would become worse.

And so they all looked back to Owl for the answer...

"You must choose which among us is strong enough and brave enough to go," they all agreed.

But Owl was as equally perplexed. As he brooded over the impossible decision, a flash of bright color crossed the sky. They all looked up to see a beautiful bird...one with feathers of the brightest colors...yellow and blue and red and white, flying across the sky toward them. It came to rest in the branches of the beech tree just above where Owl was roosted.

Owl had his answer. Finally he spoke…

"We will send Iris," he said, pointing to the beautiful bird whose feathers were those of nearly every color of the rainbow…

"You are strong and so very brave Iris," Owl spoke. "Your song is more beautiful than any music in the world. And you are humble enough to be able to speak with The Great Creator of All Things. You will go Iris…it will be you who will represent us. Our fate will be in your hands."

Iris was filled with the greatest pride…so honored to be chosen. She spread her glorious wings and ascended into the heavens, circling once and then again…dipping her wing to say goodbye. Then off she flew. All the animals waved and wished her Godspeed!

It would be an exhausting journey for Iris…three days of constant flight. She would fly past the tree tops…soar through the clouds…and travel beyond the moon and the sun and all the stars that hung in the night sky.

The winds tossed her about and there was no place to rest. But she carried on. She flew night and day until she came to that Holiest of All Places…that kingdom where everything is warm and beautiful and happiness abounds.

She alit upon the branches of a mimosa tree, bursting with yellow flowers and smelling like the sweetest of perfumes. There she rested for a few moments. But knowing her friends were suffering so, she began her search immediately for The Great Creator of All Things.

"Oh Great Creator," she cried out with her beautiful voice. "I am Iris. I have come to beg for your help and mercy!"

But there was no answer…only peaceful silence. And so she called out again…and again. But still she heard nothing.

"Perhaps The Great Creator of All Things is too busy to notice me," she thought to herself. "I know I am but a simple and insignificant bird. Who am I to bother The Great Creator? But I must do something. I must get His attention."

She remembered the words Owl had spoken to her before she left and she whispered them again to herself...

"You are strong and brave and your song is more beautiful than any music in the world."

It was then that Iris knew what she must do. She began to sing! The heavens became filled with her beautiful voice.

The Great Creator of All Things heard the beautiful song and was drawn away from His thoughts to look for who it might be that could sing so beautifully. Surrounded by the bright white light of pure love, He appeared before the beautiful bird. He listened and He smiled and He nodded his approval.

"You are one my finest and most lovely creations Iris," He said to her. "I am delighted that you have come to serenade me. What is it that brings you here? What can I give to you in return for your beautiful song?"

"I know that you are The Creator of All Things," Iris said humbly, "and that there are no mistakes in your kingdom. But the winter you have sent to us this year is much too harsh for us Lord. The winds are too cold and the snows are too deep. We are hungry...many of us are starving and becoming dreadfully weak. We will all surely perish if you do not make it stop. We have not seen the sun for weeks and we are dying! We feel as if you may have abandoned us."

"I have not abandoned you," The Great Creator said. "But what you ask of me I cannot do. For the wind and the snow and the ice of Winter have spirits and souls of their own. Just as I have given you and the other animals free will...so too have I given this gift to the Elements of The Seasons. You see, there is nothing in nature that is more important than anything else. Everything is One and the One is everything."

"Then I must return home," Iris said sadly. "I must tell everyone it is your will that we freeze with the winds and die beneath the deep snows."

"Don't be so foolish as to say such a thing little bird," The Great Creator said. "I wish for no such thing! I love each and every creature in my kingdom equally. And as I told you, not a single one of my creations is more or less important than any other. There is another answer however...

I shall send you back with a new and great gift that I want to give to the world. It is the gift of Fire! Trust in me little bird. Believe in my mercy and know you will not die nor will you vanish from the Earth. I will send this great gift back with you."

Then The Great Creator of All Things pulled a branch from a tree. He laid it against the face of the Sun until it burst into bright flames and gave off great warmth...

"This Iris," The Great Creator of All Things said, handing her the stick, "this is Fire. You must hurry back with it now...just as quickly as you can. Fly with all your might. But I warn you...do not allow the Fire to burn out completely."

The Great Creator of All Things gently laid his hands on Iris's head and blessed her. Once again she spread her beautiful wings and took flight. She began her long and exhausting journey back...flying as fast and as straight as she could.

It had taken her three days to reach Heaven and it would take her even longer to return home carrying the heavy burden of this new gift. The burning stick was heavy to carry and she worried the Fire would burn out before she could save her friends.

But it did not burn out. The Fire kept her warm as she soared back through the heavens, flying into the cold blackness of space where The Great Creator of All Things had chosen to hang the Stars and the Sun and the Moon. The closer she came to home, the hotter the Fire burned. It began to singe her beautiful feathers and the soot turned them as black as coal.

As she descended through the clouds and into the freezing skies over the open fields, the smoke from the Fire burned her throat and strangled her voice...turning her beautiful song into a horrid squawk!

Owl was first to see the Fire in the sky...but he had no idea what it could be. The closer it came, the more afraid he became. In the middle of the bright orange ball he could see a bird...a bird as black as night. And the shrieks it made brought every animal running to stand beside their leader's tree in fear and dread.

Cowering in fear, they watched as the burning orange fireball descended closer and closer to them. Suddenly the black bird spread its wings and landed in the field not far from where they were gathered. They hid their eyes from the brightest light they had ever seen. No one recognized the bird.

When she landed, incredibly the air became warm and the snow began to melt. The tiny animals...once trapped beneath the snow were set free. The larger ones who had taken shelter from the heavy snows beneath the boughs of the pine trees, slowly and cautiously came closer. But Iris warned them...

"Stand back, lest you too be burned and singed and transformed into something ugly and unrecognizable...such as what has happened to me!"

"Iris?" Owl asked in astonishment. "Is that you? What has become of you...and your beautiful feathers?"

"It is the will of The Great Creator of All Things," Iris answered. "I am heavy with grief. Why me Owl? Why did you have to choose me?"

The air turned wonderfully warm and the snow continued to melt. It was a time of great rejoicing in the forest and fields. The Great Creator of All Things had answered their prayers. All the animals sang and danced and celebrated...but not Iris.

She sat apart from them, saddened by what had become of her. Her feathers, once brighter than all the colors of the rainbow were now blackened and dull and ugly. Her voice, once more beautiful than any music in the world, was now shrill and struck fear into anyone who heard it.

Owl, the wisest creature in all the forest, made his way over to sit beside his dear friend, to do his best to comfort her...

"Do not be so sad Iris," he said. "All the animals honor you this day for the great sacrifice you have made for them. You will forever be a heroine in their eyes and believe me…you are a savior in their hearts.

While you were gone I had dreams…dreams I know The Great Creator of All Things planted in my sleep. In them I saw a new creature that will soon come to our world. He is called Man and although the Great Creator loves this new creature as he loves us all, my dreams tell me that Man is something to be feared.

The Great Creator of All Things has given him a very strong will…one that wants only to dominate and to take what is not his. Our world is about to change Iris. We will no longer be safe. We will be hunted for his sustenance and enslaved for his pleasure and commanded by him to do his work. But not you Iris…no, you will be protected from Man's hunger and his lust. He will not hunt for you."

"How can that be Owl?" Iris asked. "I am nothing now…look at what has become of me! The Creator of All Things has told me Himself that no creature in His kingdom is any more or any less important than any other. Why am I any different? Why should I be spared?"

"Because The Great Creator of All Things has taken favor with you," Owl answered. "He has chosen you to bring this gift of Fire to the world. You have become the anointed one Iris.

You may not see it as a blessing yet my dear friend, but He has made your flesh taste like smoke so that it will not be good to eat. Your ugly black feathers and your horrid voice will keep Man from placing you in a cage for his enjoyment. You will always be free."

Then Owl reached out to Iris and with a swipe of the tips of his wings, he brushed away the black soot from her chest and her back, revealing the purest of pure and the whitest of white feathers.

"This has been your baptism Iris," Owl exclaimed. "This will always be the badge of honor that you will wear proudly. Whenever anyone sees you or your descendents from this day on, they will know you have been a heroine…one who was a great servant to her fellow animals.

Everyone will always know your name and will forever speak of the sacrifice you made for us. You will forever be known as the Light of The World!"

The End…

My closing thoughts...

It was another one of my heroes, Mother Teresa, who said...

"Love is not patronizing and charity is not about pity. Charity is about love. Charity and love are the same. With charity you give love. You don't just give money but you reach out your hand as well."

I don't know about you, but I don't want to live in the kind of world where we don't look out for each other...and not just the people who are close to us. Every day we must reach out to every one and any one who needs a helping hand. There is nothing more beautiful than someone who goes out of their way to make life beautiful for others.

You see, it is not enough to simply have lived. We should be committed and determined to live for something bigger than just ourselves. Might I suggest it be creating joy for others? Sharing what we have for the betterment of our fellow man and woman and child? What could possibly be more noble or satisfying than bringing hope and comfort to the lost and fearful?

I have found that silence is what illuminates us as we stand before God...it is how we are able to see each other in the darkness. It is what unites us. In the beginning I had to force myself to be silent but it has been so worth the effort. It is from my silence that I've been drawn into an even deeper silence.

I would wish that each and every one of you could experience whatever it was that I've experienced....that which has compelled me to write this book.

I truly & sincerely wish for all of you, only the deepest love, the most immense peace, the purest happiness & the greatest of success.

Giacomino

Made in the USA
Middletown, DE
22 April 2020